PAREIDOLIA

DAMIR SALKOVIC

Editing: Kala Godin, Kelley York, Syd Tomac
Cover illustration: Jack Hill
Cover typography & layout: Kelley at Sleepy Fox Studio
Interior Formatting: Kelley at Sleepy Fox Studio

Digital 978-1-967547-73-9
Paperback (Trade) 978-1-967547-71-5
Paperback (KDP) 978-1-967547-70-8
Hardcover 978-1-967547-72-2

No part of this book has been created using Generative AI. Graveside Press and its authors do not consent for our works to be utilized in any form of machine learning training.

GRAVESIDE PRESS

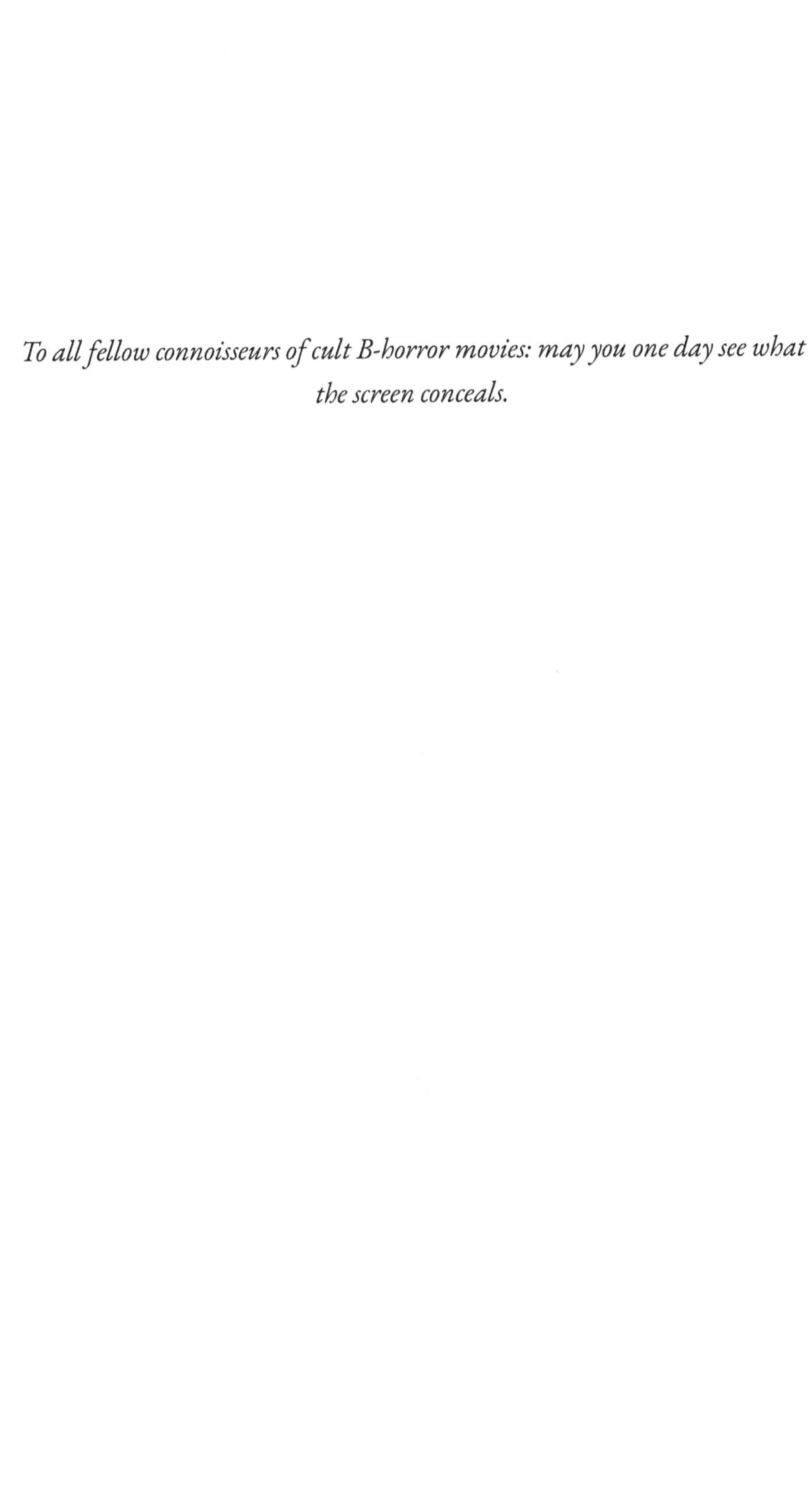

To all fellow connoisseurs of cult B-horror movies: may you one day see what the screen conceals.

Chapter 1

The man at the end of the bar was saying Don's name. Over and over, like a mantra, or a question that he couldn't get out of his head.

Don turned, the motion sending the bar into a controlled spin, stained wood and fake leather, diamonds of light gleaming off the rows of bottles on the shelves. The speaker had gotten up and was moving toward him unsteadily, wearing an expression between an apology and a smirk. A short, pudgy man in a bad suit, his eyes bloodshot, his scalp gleaming under a ragged comb-over.

"Hey. I know you, man. We met before." He belched, stuck out a pale hand reminiscent of a dead fish. "Jake Kebbler. Used to write for the Culture section of the Post. We were at the same party a few years ago. Dana Rolfe's place in New York? Yeah. I thought that was you."

The name sounded familiar, but the face didn't register. Don muttered something vaguely agreeable, half-convinced it was a mistake, that the man would realize it soon enough and they would part in mild mutual embarrassment. But his new companion seemed insistent, his mouth opening and closing with an expression of exaggerated friendliness. Don was barely hearing what Kebbler was saying: the last subway train had departed a while ago, the temperature outside had dropped into the low thirties, and his alcohol-muddled brain was working overtime, trying to tote up the taxi fare home and coming up short.

Any hope of a quick exit evaporated as Kebbler barked a sharp laugh, gesturing drunkenly. "I've read all your books, man. I'm a big fan. The one about the rocker dude, that was some great stuff. Pure genius."

His froggy features contorted into a solicitous look. Don knew that look well: he suspected lonely inveterate drunks all over the world acquired it in the small hours of the morning, right after most of the patrons had left but before the bartender kicked them out, just as they prepared to relay their life story to anyone within earshot. "Damn shame what happened. How they treated you. Just want you to know that I never thought it was right."

Was there a gloating note under the sympathy? Don was drunker than he had assumed. The dim interior of the bar swam around him in a sick, swooping circle. He tried to hold on to his thoughts, but they slipped through his grasp.

The bar was a hole-in-the-wall tucked in a maze of alleys east of Thirteenth Street, a permanently twilit nether-realm of smoke and shadows and piss-stained walls hidden among the cocktail lounges and trendy eateries of Midtown Village. A dive aspiring to loftier status, frequented by lonely deadbeats and cab drivers and the occasional alcoholic cop, infested by roaches and black mold. Don liked the place for its pleather seats and classic rock music and Thirsty Tuesday drink specials. Or maybe it was Thursday; lately he'd been having trouble keeping track of time. Daylight meant padding around his apartment, hungover more often than not, staring out of the window while pretending to work, waiting for the night to fall. Deadlines helped anchor him in this slow, bleak trickle of days, but those were coming fewer and farther between. This sparked a recollection. He had an article due tomorrow and should be getting on his way.

He didn't realize he had said something until the other man shook his head and put a hand on his shoulder.

"Been a while, man." Don found himself being steered into a corner booth, a proprietary move that would have aggravated him in a more sober state and with his dignity intact. Right now, his feet seemed to be working against him, obligingly following the stranger's instructions. Kebbler signaled to the indifferent bartender, sucked his paunch in to maneuver behind the table. "Look, I didn't mean to bring up the past. Bygones, and all that. What's your poison? It's on me."

"I was leaving," Don said. His words felt garbled, as if he didn't have complete control of his mouth. "I was *about* to leave."

"Just one drink." As if summoned by the proclamation, two heavy glasses were laid down on the sticky tabletop, ice clinking in amber. His interlocutor raised his drink and tipped it back. "For old times' sake. Just one, and you can go on your way."

Don glanced down the smoky bar, at the faces scattered around it, tired and faded by the bleak light of the place, drained of all semblance of humanity. The bartender perched on one end, a grim and doleful demon, lording over the pallid damned. He thought of his cheerless walkup apartment, the tiles flaking off the bathroom wall, the stink of damp and old cigarettes seeping out of the walls. Vision juddered like a broken film; he saw his hand wrap around the wet glass and raise it aloft, felt the whisky burn its way to his empty stomach and rebound up into his head. Exhaled the fumes in a long, shuddering plume.

"That's my man," said the pale, sweaty apparition across the table. It grinned, and for a mercifully brief moment Don could glimpse its skull, unclothed by rubbery flesh. He wanted to get up and run, but he had nowhere to go: not on this night, or any other night.

"Here's to old friends." Kebbler drained his glass with a grimace, signaled another round before Don could protest. "Don Ruby," he said wistfully, supporting his weight on his elbows. "Where have you been hiding all these years?"

Chapter 2

"Shitting you, I am not." Kebbler cast a morose stare into his glass, then looked up as if surprised by its near-emptiness. "No two weeks, no warning. No severance pay. One meeting, and I was out the door. They never let me explain my side of the story."

"Sorry to hear that." Don wasn't the slightest bit sorry. He had reached that elusive state known as the drunk's second wind. The bar's ugly atmosphere had mellowed into a pleasant glow, the glasses glittered like distant constellations, and his thoughts had a clarity he'd not known for a long time. Leaning back in his seat, he sipped his scotch, letting it play over his palate. Bottom-shelf stuff, but he was long past caring. Over the years, he'd gotten used to worse.

The bar had emptied out, save for a single veteran drunk slumped over in the corner, sleeping or sobbing or muttering to himself. Even the weary bartender had stopped casting poisonous looks in their direction and had resolved to ignore them. At some vague point in the past, Don had given up on checking his watch. Kebbler hadn't been kidding about paying for the drinks, and the only thing he demanded in return was a sympathetic ear to pour his frustration and resentment into. Of which there was a considerable amount.

The man seemed to keep a tally of injustices and wrongs, both real and perceived, to examine each one in meticulous detail. His litany had continued unabated over the time-span of five drinks, maybe six.

Don calculated he could cadge a couple more before Kebbler got either incoherent or belligerent, and leave the bar right before the subway opened for the day. It was still dark outside, but this corner of the alley stayed dark long after sunrise, as if reluctant to give up the shadows.

"Yeah." Kebbler leaned forward with a drunken leer, as if taking Don into his confidence. "You know the best part? Not even six months later, the magazine folded. Investors sold it to a French conglomerate. That bitch, she got fired. Last I heard, she's strutting her stuff on the street now." His tongue navigated the word with exaggerated care. "Serves 'em right. Motherfuckers."

In reality, Don found it very hard to feel any sympathy for Kebbler. The man was a sleaze, eager to gossip about members of the circle they had once shared—who had developed nasty drug habits, or gone through painful divorces, or died—with a gleeful fervor that seemed unbefitting even of a third-rate tabloid hack. Which was exactly what he had been a few scotches ago.

Don remembered how he knew this shifty-eyed, miserable scumbag, a self-proclaimed film and book critic who used to scuttle between Manhattan literary parties, sniffing out bits of rumors and scandal which he sold to the city's muckraking rags. It came to Don that he had almost punched Kebbler's lights out at a party thrown by a Doubleday editor over something the maggot had written about one of his earlier books. That had, of course, happened before the debacle of *Ashes Behind*, back when Don Ruby had been the darling of Fifth Avenue, lionized by both *The New Yorker* and the *Journal of American Literature*, wined and dined by Hollywood celebrities and their agents. All of whom hoped to be immortalized by the pen of the man *The Atlantic* had once dubbed the successor to Ellis Amburn, *"the next great pop biographer of our time"*.

Apparently, Kebbler had forgotten the incident or decided to ignore it. Don didn't care either way, as long as the drinks kept coming. "Anyway," Kebbler said, waving at the bartender, who was studying a beer glass with keen interest. "Enough about that. How about you? What's the great Don Ruby up to these days?"

"Trying to keep busy."

"Any new projects in the works?"

"A few," Don said. It could just be the drink, but he thought he heard a malicious sort of glee in Kebbler's tone, lurking just under the surface. "More than I expected. An article here, a feature there. You know how it goes."

His paid work right now consisted of a single article due before the close of business hours tomorrow, which was really today. It was a desperate last-minute pitch about religious themes in classical science fiction films to *Cinexotique*, a glorified blog run by a pair of hipsters whose combined age was under fifty and whose flippant attitude toward grammar and form made Don want to tear his hair out. Three thousand words tops, twenty-five hundred preferred; anything above that and you risked losing the reader's attention. *Cinexotique* boasted over two million unique visitors a day and employed a horde of underpaid freelancers to churn out a baffling mélange of cliches and clickbait under the guise of *trans-historical studies* and *countercultural film critique*. Rumors had been circulating about a major syndicate buyout in the works, but none of it affected Don. He wrote the articles, cashed the checks and swallowed his pride; by mutual agreement, his work was posted under an alias. *Cinexotique* steered clear of publishing anything controversial, the editors had explained, as if the name of Don Ruby alone was enough to offend the public.

"Tell me about it." Kebbler snorted, made a face. "It's all about the internet these days. Am I right? Some twelve-year-old posts a video from his bedroom, and before you know it, he's making millions. No one gives two shits about *real* journalism anymore." He sounded insulted, like he counted himself among this aggrieved category. Then his features brightened. "But not me. I might be packing it in. Not official yet, but I've got a book deal in the works. Gonna be a bigshot writer like you."

"Yeah?" Don feigned mild interest, wondering if Kebbler's largesse would extend to one last drink for the road. There wasn't a down-on-their-luck alcoholic journo in the nation, probably the world, who didn't have a *Grand Book Deal* in the works or was just about to sign a contract with a major publisher. He held out his glass hopefully. "Anyone I know?"

"It's a niche market," Kebbler said, staggering up to replenish their drinks. "A small press up in Michigan. They print horror chapbooks, limited editions, that sort of thing. Stuff for freaks who like to dress in black and hang out in graveyards. But the owner, he's ready to crack the big leagues. Offering the right kind of money, too. I made the pitch to him a few weeks ago, and he's interested."

"What's the book about?" In spite of his inebriation, Don felt a small twinge of jealousy. He was tainted goods, had not published anything under his own name in over six years.

"You're gonna love this." Kebbler stopped in his tracks, threw his arms out for dramatic effect. "Horror movies. *Slashers*. You know, the kind they made in the eighties and nineties." He sloshed the glasses on the table and mimed getting stabbed, eyes and mouth wide in a theatrical scream. "Tits and blood, screaming kids. But not just any kind. The real campy ones, with awful acting and special effects, corn syrup flying everywhere. Have you heard of Kirk Taylor?"

Don had to admit he had not.

"He was an icon of cheap horror movies," Kebbler said, smiling. His teeth shone wet with spittle. "*Night of the Blade. Don't Let the Devil Hear You Scream. Dead Shift.*" It took Don a moment to realize that Kebbler was enumerating movie titles. On second thought, he *had* heard of Taylor, had watched one or two of his movies in college, or thereabouts, when one of the cable channels ran a Fright Night marathon, usually around Halloween.

"Real gory stuff," Kebbler was saying. A neon sign behind the bar painted his face a sickly hue. "But that's what the kids want, right? The gorier the better."

Don had a sudden vision of a week-old corpse rising to the surface of a river, propelled by the gases of its own decomposition. He was trapped in here with a dead man and there was nothing beyond the bar's windows but the night, the void, utter emptiness. The thought was unhinged, but it came to him with absolute conviction. He saw how the skin hung on the bones like an ill-fitting suit, discoloration on the dead fingers from immersion in the water.

Sweat poured from his skin, a torrent of it, soaking him from head to toe. This was delirium, or alcohol poisoning. It had to be. The walls were alive with a squirming movement, worms, or insects, scuttling under the plaster. "Hey, you okay, man? You don't look that great."

"I gotta go," Don said. His word sounded hollow and distant, echoing off the sides of a tunnel he was suddenly descending, his destination unknown. He closed his eyes, waited for the vertigo to subside, but it didn't.

"Stay a while," Kebbler said, and this time Don caught a furtive look on the man's flabby face, something that he'd mistaken for gloating earlier but now seemed more like desperation. Kebbler had a secret, something he was compelled to share; with him, of all people.

Maybe he was overthinking things. Maybe they were both blind drunk, and that was all it was.

As Kebbler droned on, Don scanned the room, but the bartender was nowhere in sight. Signs and lights multiplied, danced before his eyes. In the big mirror behind the bar, a haggard phantom perched over a table, his eyes two black hollows in a long, unkempt face. Kebbler sat right next to him, a squat, balding troll. Don's mind labored through the haze of alcohol, trying to make sense of what he was seeing. Ribbons of dark, opaque stuff rose from Kebbler like oily smoke, eddied in the stale air of the bar.

Breath stopped in Don's throat. In the reflection, the smoke coalesced into a blurry, inconstant shape that vaguely resembled a human figure, coils threading from it into the unlit corners. This shadow, or phantom, stooped over his companion, as if to whisper into the man's ear. Kebbler gave no sign of noticing. Around them, the cloud grew luminescent, lit from some invisible source. A thick silvery cord trailed from Kebbler toward the ceiling, and beyond it, into the night sky.

Frozen, Don could only watch as the figure in the mirror turned in his direction. He didn't want to look at it; he knew he shouldn't look, but his neck muscles obeyed the dictum, his head turning against his will, and the unfinished face leaned closer to him, the mouth gaping open—

"...filmography," Kebbler said, staring at Don as if expecting a response. "That's what they want me to write. Or, as they put it, a contemporary analysis of horror movies as a reflection of the collective American psychosis. Social alienation, body issues, the erosion of the American dream through the lens of the auteur. Actors and filmmakers who made cult horror in the eighties and early nineties. But now they're completely obscure. Got a title for it already. *The Forgotten Frontiersmen of Fright*."

Don let out a long breath he didn't know he'd been holding. There was no dark shape hovering over Kebbler's head; there wouldn't be one if he looked back at the mirror. "Whose filmography?" he asked, but the conversation had somehow skipped ahead and Kebbler was talking fast, almost urgently, as if unburdening himself.

"Kirk Taylor. Victor Hudson. Some of these guys—you've never heard of them, but they made more movies than any Hollywood bigshot." Apparently, they were back on the topic of grade-B horror and its luminaries. "Four, five, six a year. That was my pitch. Many of these movies have never seen the light of day. Some died in Production Hell, others never made it past censors. But they're all products of our collective subconscious. Even the unmade ones. They deserve to be discovered, as do their creators."

"What do you mean by unmade?"

"The ones that simply disappeared," Kebbler said, his watery eyes fixing Don over the table. He no longer looked drunk. "Either they ran out of money, or the distributor dropped them, or the studio went bankrupt. Or the people who made them suppressed their release. Destroyed all copies, that sort of thing. If you believe the legends, several well-known names made movies that the world has never seen. Maybe they were really bad, or they pissed off the wrong people. You wouldn't think that's possible anymore, what with all the over-the-top trash they shot back in the day. But it happens."

"I wouldn't have thought people would want to read about lost movies."

"Isn't that what the adoring public always wants?" Kebbler's shoulders shook with silent laughter. "They enjoy seeing real anguish, real blood, even when they don't want any part of it. You ask me, that's where the real horror lies. In being left on the back shelf, or in a box in the basement. In some piece of you being forever trapped on a strip of dusty film. Unworshipped, forgotten."

He seemed to catch himself, looked away. "That's the book I wanted to write, anyway. But I got sidetracked. Ended up writing something else, or at least started to. You must know how it is."

"I don't know what you're talking about."

"Letting the story carry you away. Isn't that what happened with *Ashes*? The story got away from you. Took on a life of its own. It could no longer be constrained by reality."

Don was vaguely aware that he should defend himself against the implication but couldn't disentangle his thoughts in time to respond. The bartender set another pair of Scotches in front of them. Kebbler raised his, looked like he was about to say something. Then he shook his head, slammed his glass against Don's in an unsteady toast. "Last one. I better get going myself."

Chapter 3

An indefinable length of time later, dirty dawn coloring the patchwork sky, Don half-dragged, half-carried Kebbler out into the freezing wind. He'd taken the liberty of helping himself to the man's money clip, peeled off enough bills to placate the weary bartender. Thought about it for a moment, thrown another twenty on the counter. What the hell. The asshole had offered to buy the drinks.

Like a grotesque animal, an amalgam of ill-fitting body parts, they staggered along the empty sidewalk, Don trying to hail a taxi, Kebbler muttering incoherently, trash swirling around their feet. A cab appeared from the congealed darkness; the cabbie pulled to the curb, scowled when Don opened the door.

"I'm not taking him in my car. He'll stink the whole thing up."

Gasping, Don dumped the deadweight into the back seat, rifled through Kebbler's pockets for the clip again. Held out enough cash to forestall further protest. "Where is he going?" the driver asked.

Where indeed? The clip yielded a New York driver's license, a handful of credit cards. Don closed his eyes, waited for the cab to stop spinning. Something else was in there. A plastic rectangle in a worn-out paper sleeve with an address on it. The cabbie took one look, nodded. In a series of stop-motion cutouts, Don heard the slam of the door and watched the taillights flare around the corner before the car disappeared.

Wet neon cast a lattice of smeared light across the square. A sea of burning points danced around him, driving the dark away without improving his vision. He had no recollection of crossing the city, only a gradual cognizance of stumbling into his building and hauling himself up the dank stairway. Pushed his way into the dark, smelly apartment, scattering bills and takeout leaflets heaped on the piebald carpet by the door. He turned the kitchen light on and stood, swaying, waiting for his sense of balance to restore itself enough for him to pull a beer from the noisy, mostly empty fridge. Cracking the can open, he drank greedily, foam dripping down his chin, until an ache from the frosty liquid drove itself between his eyes like a nail.

But he couldn't sleep. An idea had wormed into his head, struggling through the fog of alcohol and fatigue, determined to assert itself.

Don sat down at his desk, fired up his laptop. Strained to focus on the letters and icons blurring on the screen: a language written by lunatics, an unintelligible mishmash of symbols that seemed to be poised on the brink of becoming something else.

It was no damn good. That much was clear to him, even in his current state. As much as he hated to admit it, Kebbler's book idea had potential. But the approach that the hideous little creep had sketched was all wrong. No one would buy yet another hundred-thousand-word treatise on film criticism, or the subconscious symbolism of horror as a genre. That was something for cinema geeks to fondle themselves over. These days they could do it on any number of online forums, free of charge. A good filmography or biography had to tell a compelling story, no different from any other critically acclaimed work, fiction or otherwise. Kebbler's concept was hackneyed, stale; at first glance, safer from a marketing point of view, but it would never sell.

Don smiled to himself as he let his fingers fly over the keys, the banked glow of the screen bathing his face. No harm in pretending that he was the one with the book deal. If he cleared his mind of all background noise, he could almost convince himself it was true. Much better to come up with the narrative of an era, the story not of a man, but of a movement. What had Kebbler said about a lost film, a movie made, but never released? Searching for it would be the perfect framing device for a book about horror B-movies. A real-world horror story—or a story that hinted at the uncanny—written about horror stories, suspenseful and dynamic and delightfully meta.

He laughed alone in the empty room, realizing that an outline was taking shape under his hands. In the pallid square of light, his own half-reflection laughed along with him. It had to be his own face regarding him from the screen, a vague white oval looming in the margins of his word processor window. That, or the alcohol distorting his perception of space, making the room quiver around him like the image on the display.

Maybe tomorrow he would find Kebbler, he thought as he stumbled across a floor as unsteady as the deck of a ship in rough seas. But he was a seasoned sailor; years of practice had given him his sea legs. Find Kebbler—he realized he couldn't remember the man's first name—and propose a collaboration. Rescue Kirk Taylor from decades of well-deserved obscurity.

He giggled and flopped down on the bed, burrowed into covers that smelled like wet towels left in a hamper. Not worth thinking about it, yet he felt reluctant to let it go. If only he could have one more chance. All those films, known and forgotten, all those miles upon miles of celluloid, would not compare to the story taking shape behind his eyes.

***

Don woke to smeary daylight creeping through the broken window blind. Faces crowded to peer in at him, scattered reluctantly before his bleary gaze. Turned into patterns of rain on the dirty glass. He groaned and rolled over, and felt the room roll with him. Head pounding and a sour feeling in his stomach, the remains of a dream he could no longer remember drained slowly from the base of his skull to be replaced by the early signs of a titanic hangover.

He flung off the damp covers, drained a glass of cloudy water that he couldn't remember pouring. Beyond his window, concrete blocks cut up a sky the color of dishwater into mosaic pieces. The clock on his cracked phone display showed a time much closer to noon than he'd expected, the numerals bleeding into each other, refracted along the shatter lines. Something about the passage of time stirred a dull anxiety in his belly, but he couldn't quite remember what it was.

He tottered into the dingy bathroom, urinated noisily, chewed a couple of Advil from a family-sized bottle, and washed it down with another glass of brackish tap water. Raided his fridge and came up with half a rotten head of lettuce, two cans of Pabst Blue Ribbon, and a plastic wrap containing a single slice of equally plastic cheese. Don dumped the lettuce in the overflowing garbage, opened one of the beers while waiting for the kettle to boil. The cheese could last another decade or two, possibly even survive a nuclear war.

The laptop was on. Moved by a vague foreboding, he ventured over to the desk. He must have been on a real bender last night. His efforts to remember brought up the blur of the screen in the darkness, thoughts swirling through his head like shoals of fish, too quick and slippery to be caught and examined.

At a touch of the pad, the screensaver dissolved, filling the screen with the layered blue of the desktop. Don sipped the beer, tasting more of the can than of its contents. It wasn't the first time that this sort of thing had happened. Yet examined in the cold light of day, his lack of recollection was disturbing. *Deadline.* Yesterday was meant to be an early night, a couple hours of writing the article for *Cinexotique*, which was due today. Flashes of sitting in the dark, staring into the computer's bright screen, fingers typing on autopilot. *Writing what?*

A rush of unreasoning panic took hold of him as he searched his files for a draft, found nothing. Had he drunk-emailed Krysten in the wee hours of the morning, maybe let her and the other editors know what he really thought of their online rag? He better not have; he needed the money, desperately more so than any other month.

Don logged into his email account, the beer sitting in his empty stomach like lead. Breathed a sigh of relief when he saw no new messages in his Sent folder. There was still time to finish the article and send it off. He was about to disconnect when a message in his Inbox caught his attention. At first glance, it seemed no different from the surrounding torrent of spam. He squinted at the sender's address, clicked it open.

Dear Don Ruby,

Let me begin, Sir, by expressing my utmost admiration for yr. work. I have read "Roads to Babylon" several times, and "Ashes Behind" ranks, in my humble opinion, among the best biographies written in the twenty-first century (I managed to snag one of the autographed copies before the publisher pulled it from the market, a coup of which I am singularly proud).

It should be no surprise, given this preamble, that your pitch has caused quite a stir among the members of our small but dedicated team. The outline seems most promising. Nothing could please us more than having you on board, as we have already communicated to your co-author, Mr. Kebbler.

On to more prosaic matters. Our esteemed associate has failed to forward us your banking details, and there is also the small formality of executing the agreement. You will find the necessary form and contract attached. Mr. Kebbler has already signed his consent. Is it too much to request both to be filed by the end of this week? We are eager to get the project underway, and process your advance before the books close for the month. Uncouth as it may be, an electronic signature is deemed acceptable.

Of course, should you not find the terms agreeable, do not hesitate to let us know so at your earliest convenience.

Might you be able to send us a revised synopsis, incorporating your changes? Mr. Kebbler sent us a two-pager some weeks ago but mentioned that you two brilliant minds will be subjecting the document to significant alterations. Our marketing team is champing at the bit to put out a teaser on our website for the public to salivate over. Always helpful for a few extra sales.

Should you wish to publish under a pseudonym, we can accommodate that request.

I remain, Sir, Your Most Humble Servant.

J. C. Latham
Chief Editor and Executive Officer, Occultation Press

Don held his breath as he skimmed through the message, over and over. The words raced past his eyes without imprinting on his consciousness; it took him several attempts to grasp their meaning. But it still made no sense. Kebbler could not have told the editor they were collaborating on the book. He hadn't even *seen* Don until last night and had certainly not mentioned working together. It had to be some sort of misunderstanding.

Or had Don simply blanked it out?

His hands trembled slightly as he navigated to his recent files, found the outline, checked the time and date stamps. Spent a few unreal moments searching for the outgoing email, realized he'd dragged it into his Submissions folder. He had no memory of having sent it out. Not all that surprising, given his condition last night. There was only one way to clear things up, and that was to write back to J. C. Latham and apologize for the confusion. Awkward, but less so than getting involved in whatever was happening between Kebbler and his publisher.

But was it a misunderstanding? Kebbler had wanted Don to join the project. The email left no doubt of that. Suppose that's what last night had been—an unorthodox business proposition? Don tried to think through the pounding headache, his brain working slowly, as if wading through molasses. All he could dredge up were scattered pieces. Kebbler laughing drunkenly, spittle shining on his teeth and chin; gloating over the fate of the magazine he'd been fired from; amber circling the glass, a micro-maelstrom in the dim lights of the bar.

A dark shape crouching over the man in the mirror, the trapped, terrified look in his eyes. Shadows rippling across the reflection, across the speaker's face, suggesting a transformation.

There was no harm in looking, he told himself as he opened the attachments. Jerked his hand back as he felt a faint shock in his fingertips that could only be nerves. The documents took forever to load, the spinning circle hovering before his eyes even after he looked away. Don's mouth ran dry as he scrolled through the contract, lingering on the advance payment terms. Ten thousand to each author, payable upon receipt of a detailed thousand-word outline. Hardly a fortune, but more cash than he'd seen in longer than he could remember. The throbbing in his head migrated into his throat. Another ten after the first draft was submitted. After production costs were recouped, profits to be shared equally between the authors and the publisher. That wasn't money he could afford to turn down, misunderstanding or not.

He ran a hand through his hair, stared at the words on the screen, trying to decide what to believe. Kebbler had talked about the book, so he must have brought up the collaboration. Don couldn't remember it, not right now, but the evidence was right before his eyes. It still might be an elaborate practical joke. But the opportunity beckoned, stronger than any available rationalizations. The advance would mean an end, however temporary, to anxious job-seeking, to being paid per-word for writing blog copy masquerading as film criticism. An opportunity to do some real writing again, to earn enough money to allow him to work on other projects. Maybe even clear his name of the stain of scandal a year or so down the line. It was probably too early to plan that far ahead, but a man could dream.

A search took him to the publisher's website and a list of related articles. Armed with a cup of instant coffee, Don scanned through them and liked what he saw. Never a fan of horror, he still appreciated good design and layout, an easy-to-use interface. J. C. Latham had forged a solid reputation in the independent publishing world, starting out with an online fan-zine that offered print-on-demand copies, building up a small but talented stable of contributors. Many of whom had gone on to become household names in the genre. A short story anthology put out by Occultation Press had received favorable reviews in literary magazines, thrusting its enigmatic editor into the limelight.

Writing for Latham could be the foothold Don needed for a comeback, the start of his long climb up from the lowest rung on the ladder. He knew he had it in him. His books, biographies of the wealthy and famous, had once been fought over by publishing leviathans: his last one, the one that had effectively killed his career, had been picked by Oprah's Book Club before being hastily pulled from the market. Three critically acclaimed titles and a National Book Award nomination to his name. But his name was poison in industry circles. His last self-financed attempt to break back into the market had left him with several maxed-out credit cards and depleted what goodwill remained among his few surviving friends. What work he'd been able to find wasn't even keeping him afloat, merely prolonging the agony. Soon, his money would run out, and the anticipation of that moment filled him with the kind of remote dread he'd read about in the accounts of car crash survivors: a sense of frozen drifting, a situation completely outside his control, disaster looming ahead.

Excitement and caution whirled inside Don in equal measure. Part of him was alarmed at the speed at which this was progressing, suspecting that the offer was too good to be true. Another part—the part that had sulked and railed against humiliation and obscurity—was already making plans, plotting improvements to the book. He couldn't waste this opportunity. It could be the last one to come his way.

Whatever the decision, J. C. Latham needed to know, probably before the end of the day. Don checked the clock on the screen. One in the afternoon, plenty of time to talk things through with Kebbler. As distasteful as he found the prospect of working with the man, penury was worse.

Which left the problem of contacting the creep. He went through his phone and the detritus in his pockets, found no number for Kebbler. Didn't know what name to search for online and didn't think it mattered. Don paced the room, rubbing his temples. *The address.* He remembered it from the keycard in Kebbler's pocket, was reasonably sure he'd heard the cabbie repeat it. After a couple of tries, he got it right and saved the directions on his phone, grinning. Time for a shower, then a courtesy visit to his co-author. Find out what all this was about. If Kebbler tried to renege on the offer, he had another thing coming.

Chapter 4

It took him a while to find the address, one in a row of ugly tenement blocks, past a corridor of boarded-up shop windows and overflowing dumpsters. Days-old garbage and the silty smell of the river in the air, the wintry sun sinking fast behind the dirty concrete, shadows already stretching out of the walls, from the narrow recesses between the buildings.

The entrance was locked and there were no numbers over the dark buzzer panel. He selected a button at random, kept going until he found one that worked. A woman's hoarse voice crackled out of the box, demanding to know who he was. Don said nothing, waited for the speaker to hang up, then pressed another button. On the third try, there was still no answer, but the door buzzed open. Don pushed it and went in, grateful to leave the darkening street behind him.

He didn't know Kebbler's unit number, and the identical doors held no names. Nor did mail slots set in a corner where the light didn't quite reach. Best to start at the top and work his way down.

The staircase stank of mildew and neglect. Dim lamps, shaped to look like candles, blinked at regular intervals along the hallway walls. Cockroaches, as long as his finger and entirely unafraid, scuttled away from the lit patches of stained carpet. A television blared behind a door; a man was talking on the phone, voice thick with banked violence. Somewhere above him, water dripped, a steady, rhythmic sound.

Not for the first time, Don had the uneasy feeling that he was being tested or playing a game according to rules he wasn't aware of. He chased the thought away. He could deal with Kebbler; he'd dealt with worse in the past. If only he could find the bastard. He ignored the shuffling noise that seemed to follow him through the walls, mimicking his footsteps. Wheezing from the climb, Don made it to the topmost landing. Here, the hallway was darker, quieter. He watched as a light at the far end winked and went out. Someone laughed on the other side of the wall, almost startling him out of his skin.

His foot squelched on the threadbare carpet. *Water.* The floor was soaked in it. Unseen pipes gurgled and gushed in the dark. Probably the source of the dripping he'd heard below. Someone must have left the faucet running, flooded the bathroom, or a kitchen sink.

Somewhere between the water and the door it was leaking under, his mind made an unpleasant connection and immediately veered away from it. Coming here no longer seemed like a good idea. Without knowing how, he understood that he had been *led* here. He was standing at a crossing. If he turned back now, if he didn't see what waited for him on the other side of the door, life could go on the way it had before. Unbearable as his old existence was, it was familiar; it made sense. By setting foot inside, he would set in motion events that he could neither control nor comprehend. But there was a need in him that transcended caution, a yearning more powerful than the fear that froze his hand above the doorknob, his socks soaking up water, his blood roaring like a tide in his ears.

With the inevitability of a dream, Don opened the door, hearing the click of the lock a moment before the knob turned, already knowing it was unlocked, that it was waiting for him.

The place was a hovel, cramped and dark, a few pieces of mismatched furniture strewn about an area that served as a kitchen and living room and bedroom at once. Takeaway boxes piled next to the couch, crusty dishes stacked in the sink, a heating unit that put out a clattering noise, but little heat. A bookcase packed with paperbacks and what looked like reference texts. The lights were off, a streak of sunlight angling in through the broken blind, struggling to cut through the gloom. A deep odor of old garbage and greasy food wafted from the kitchen alcove, joined by a sweet, almost cloying smell.

Every inch of the apartment bore evidence of continued neglect, of trash left to rot in forgotten corners, clothes turning musty in damp, dirty piles. Stale air and staler, hopeless ambitions putrefying in obscurity. Water rippled underfoot, already a couple of inches deep: he could hear it gushing in the bathroom, where a thin ribbon of light shimmered behind a closed door. He shouldn't be going any farther. His stomach had already guessed what awaited in the light, even if his brain refused to acknowledge it.

Turning the light on would only force him to confront the awful reality of it sooner. Instead, he waded behind the bookcase, where a table held a keyboard and an old desktop computer. This had to be where Kebbler kept his manuscript files. The wall behind the table was almost papered-over: Post-It notes, newspaper clippings, pages ripped from notepads and covered in scratchy scrawl. Don moved closer, trying to make sense of the notes, but it was either too dark or else the writing was gibberish.

It wouldn't be stealing. Not if Kebbler wanted them to write the book together. There was no harm in looking. Even as part of him realized what he was about to do, another part couldn't bring himself to switch on the computer, to disturb the dark blankness of the screen. His mind seemed to have fled to some distant corner of his skull, watching his actions with the dispassionate detachment of a neutral observer.

Behind the bathroom door, something splashed.

Don flinched, knocked a rustling object from the table to the floor. Picked up a thick hardcover notebook, scuffed and dog-eared. How would he explain himself to Kebbler if the man walked out of the bath to find Don in the middle of his living room? Rummaging through his papers like a thief?

"Hello?" His voice was strained, barely a whisper. There was no splashing, only the steady rill of water into the overfilled tub, onto the floor tiles. Could Kebbler be drunk, asleep, or unconscious in the bath? That didn't seem far-fetched. Maybe it was better to leave the bathroom door shut. Maybe it was better to go home and sleep off the headache and hangover, think about the whole thing in a more sober light.

"Your door was open," he said, a little louder now. Definitely loud enough to be heard over the running water. He sloshed over to the bathroom, cleared his throat. "Are you in there? It's Don Ruby. We spoke at the bar." Feeling stupid, because he hadn't asked to be in this situation, he placed his hand on the door. It wasn't closed all the way, not latched. "I want to talk about your book. *Our* book."

No response. Don's scalp prickled with anticipation. He hadn't done anything, he reminded himself, hadn't seen anything; there was still time to get the hell out of here and pretend none of this had happened. Even as the thought passed through his head, he was pushing the door open, stepping inside.

At first, all he could see was red. Angry slashes on the walls, blossoms spreading through the water, fading to a deep pink on the tiled floor. He barely registered the cracked mirror, the dirty sink clogged with hair. Then his brain caught up, and the bathroom tilted crazily, then righted itself.

Kebbler was lying in the overflowing tub, head thrown back, eyes wide open. Red swirled around him, leaked from him in thin filaments, matted his hair to his chest and belly. He looked wistful and at peace, as if contemplating the cracks in the ceiling, his mouth slack and open. A second mouth smiled dark and raw just below the first.

Gagging, Don tried to back away, lost his footing, crashed to his knees in the bloody water. The gash in Kebbler's neck was already pale around the edges, the last of his redness trailing off into the pink stream. One hand hung over the side of the tub like a bleached starfish; the other one was propped up on the edge, still half-curled around a vicious-looking straight razor. He'd slit both his wrists before opening his throat, sawing through with what had to have been heroic determination. Something white gleamed at the back of that ragged red smile: a hint of bone protruding through torn muscle and gristle, the cut wide enough to expose the darkness within. Don needed no second glance to tell that the man was dead, had been dead for some time.

Bile burned the back of Don's mouth, acid and coffee and the remains of last night's binge. He clenched his teeth and swallowed it back down, a voice in his head screaming that he must not be sick, that he couldn't leave any trace of his presence here. That he couldn't call for help for fear of being implicated in what happened. Holding onto the edge of the tub, he got to his feet. Lunged across the flooded floor to grab a dirty hand towel.

The dead man's eyes stared upward, unseeing, fixed on something beyond the world he had left.

In the mirror, Don's reflection was pale and dazed, an empty face like a bad mask. Shadows reared up behind him, rolled away to reveal a silhouette, long and thin and angular, floating in the middle of the main room like smoke.

He spun around, looked through the door. There was no one in the apartment with him. No one but the dead man in the bathtub, staining the water pink.

What had he touched on his way in? Where had he left his fingerprints? He scrubbed the towel viciously at the door, at the knob, trying not to think about the blood, *all that blood*, it was *someone's blood* swirling under his feet, soaking into his clothes. Dripping down the ceiling to the apartments below. Forensic investigators could find traces of it on his clothes, even the tiniest particles. Or was that only true on cop shows he'd seen on TV? There was no helping Kebbler, not even close. Even if he'd arrived here on time, he would not have known what to do. No one survived wounds like those.

He tried to take hold of his thoughts, to wrangle them into some semblance of reason. He had to get out of here. Once he was safe, once he was away from this carnage, he could start making sense of what he'd seen. But not now. All that mattered right now was putting as much distance as possible between himself and the corpse in the tub.

Halfway to the exit, he heard footsteps outside and froze. A fist pounded on the door, followed by a man's voice, a torrent of invective in which he could barely recognize Kebbler's name. There was nowhere for Don to run, nowhere to hide. The knob rattled and turned, but the door didn't open. The man on the other side cursed and gave it a hard kick, then stomped off down the hallway, the squish-squish of his footfalls fading.

Don crossed to the spyhole, saw only the blistered walls, the muted light of the lamps. He was almost out the door when he remembered the big notebook by Kebbler's computer. An insane thought to be having at a time like this, when the visitor could be back any minute, was probably already on his way. But he couldn't rid himself of it. As quickly as he could, he went to the desk, stuffed the notebook under his jacket, and fled down the hallway. No sooner had the stairway door swung shut behind him than he heard the heavy tread returning, accompanied by the jangle of keys. Don didn't stick around to see what happened next.

Out in the street, a thin drizzle had smudged sharp corners, wrapped the scarce lamps in smeary halos. Hunched against the damp, the notebook nestled next to his heart, Don Ruby strode away from the building without turning back.

Chapter 5

He woke at some indeterminate dark time, disoriented and afraid, without being able to recall the reason for his fear. A gnawing sensation had settled in his stomach. It felt like hunger but wasn't. He had no idea how much time had passed since he'd last eaten.

Through the window, the glow of the street intruded, the sky a dark, leaden lid above it. A glance at his phone told him the date and time. Almost four in the morning. Not the night descending, then, but the birth of a new day, its vast, oppressive weight rolling over the horizon to crush him. On the verge of consciousness, a shadow threatened, a sense of wrongness like the taste of a coming storm.

It wasn't the first time this had happened. He sat up in his rumpled bed, his head in his hands, and tried to put together the pieces of the last two days. Parts of the picture were missing, blank patches that his tired, abused brain kept skidding over. What he could remember failed to coalesce into a coherent whole.

The building lay quiet around him, but it didn't feel empty. Something was with him in the apartment, a presence unseen but felt, plucking at his nerve endings. Leaving him feeling naked and exposed.

Don edged off the bed, hobbled to the kitchen. Studied the remains of a stale loaf by his toaster. Even with the hollowness inside him, the very thought of eating, the tedious process of chewing and tearing, swallowing and digesting, was enough to deflate his stomach. He made coffee instead and let it cool untouched as he sprawled on the sofa, retracing his steps, trying to figure out what had brought him to this pass.

The notebook lay on his coffee table like an ill omen. Without knowing why, his mind recoiled from it. Yet he couldn't bring himself to touch it, to put it out of sight.

He was in trouble. A man had died, and Don had broken into his home, stolen his property. Discovered the body and failed to inform the police, which made him look guilty. Maybe even a suspect, because how could he be sure it had been a suicide? He imagined explaining his relationship with the deceased, the purpose of yesterday's visit. With each repetition, the story sounded less plausible, even to himself.

Don's chest felt tight, and he found it hard to breathe. He could no longer fool himself about getting away unobserved. A security camera had caught him somewhere, or the cops had picked up a trace he'd left at the scene of death. Witnesses had to have seen him enter or leave the building. They'd question him about his movements, search his apartment, find the notebook. Why had he taken the damn thing in the first place?

Kebbler had written in the notebook, filled its pages with his sickness. Nonsensical as it was, the thought lodged in Don's mind, started to repeat itself. The man was crazy—manic-obsessive, if the evidence from his apartment was anything to go by. At least suicidal with depression. Could his madness be contagious?

Don had a vision of Kebbler bent over the table, scribbling into the notebook, surrounded by moldering takeout boxes and old newspaper clippings. Chasing a revelation that eluded him, deeper down the rabbit hole of his obsession until he'd had some kind of psychotic break. Until he'd ended up in a tub full of water, a razor in his hand, the hole swallowing him up, taking him into the dark landscape beneath his flesh.

Another chilling realization followed the first. The book deal was off. Kebbler could no longer deliver his side of the proposal and had clearly not been of sound mind when he'd brought it up. Unless the whole thing had been a prank, a tasteless practical joke played on Don for some unfathomable reason. Or something more sinister.

What if he was being set up for murder?

At least he could find out what was in the notebook. Kebbler wouldn't need it anytime soon.

He picked it up, opened it at random. Few of the names he deciphered from the scrawl meant anything to him; the accompanying notes, written in a violent hand, were likewise incomprehensible. Movies were Kebbler's bailiwick. He probably only had to read a name to conjure up the star's entire career, hence the brevity. Still, the contents were troubling, like a chronicle of someone else's crumbling psyche. The handwriting grew erratic, strayed above and below the lines, as if the author were alternating between high agitation and confused lassitude. Several of the pages were covered in elaborate doodles, others in angry scratches of the pen, hard enough to tear through the paper. Don was just starting to discern some meaning from it when the phone rang, snapping him out of his engrossment.

Don glanced at the caller's number and grimaced. "Krysten," he said. "I was just about to call you."

"Yesterday." The voice on the other end of the line was upset and trying not to show it. "We said yesterday? The article deadline? I haven't seen anything yet?"

Cinexotique. Don almost groaned aloud. He'd forgotten all about the article he had been supposed to deliver yesterday. No, that wasn't quite true. He had thought about the article, had even intended to write it, honest to God he had, but the day had slipped away from him. Time in general tended to do that.

"I'm working on it as we speak," he lied brightly, knowing he was fooling no one. "It's...uh, I need an extension. Say, one o'clock? I'll have it for you by then. Would that work?"

"No, Don." Krysten lifted the ends of her sentences, making everything she said sound like a question. "No, it won't work. Because *Scope and Mirrors*, okay? Like, the one movie blog that everyone reads? That got, like, a *million* unique page hits last week. They tweeted about the same movie, and they're totally posting a review today. *Today*. Their post goes live at noon? Which means, like, no one will read ours?"

Don rummaged through the clothes for a pack of cigarettes. Remembered that he'd quit almost a month ago. Sat down at his laptop and brought up the draft article. It didn't look anywhere near ready. In fact, it didn't look like he'd gotten past the title. "I got this. I can deliver. Noon today, not a problem. I'm on it."

"We can't post it at *noon*," Krysten said, enunciating each word carefully, as one does when addressing children, or the very old and senile. A pent-up breath was released noisily into the receiver. A calming technique, most likely one promoted by the latest YouTube wellness guru or influencer. "Because at noon, it's garbage. I mean, even more so than your articles usually are." The affected accent was gone, a touch of New Jersey showing through. "Because we have to run your review no later than eleven. Jayde and Beckett need to tweet about it half an hour before we post. Spread the buzz on the social networks. *Eleven*. Is that getting through to you?"

"Eleven is fine."

"It has to be ten, Don." She sounded exasperated now, but there was something else in her voice too. Something that sounded like disgust. "Ten-thirty at the latest. It still has to go through editorial."

Don nodded furiously, but not in agreement. For an instant, he could see himself through the editor's eyes: a middle-aged alcoholic, a failure even by the standards of the online journalism community, scribbling garbage opinion pieces for next to nothing. Don Ruby, the once-darling of Fifth Avenue, a bestselling writer, National Book Award nominee. Now, an itinerant drunk who inspired only pity and revulsion. All this he heard in her voice and felt a rise of anger in response.

His free hand roamed the desk, found a loose page from a steno pad, squeezed around it. Worked it into a ball, tighter and tighter. "That's an awfully tight deadline."

"It's the best we can do. You have two hours, or I swear this is the last piece you'll ever write for us. Because I'm done with this. You're not indispensable."

Cradling the phone between shoulder and jaw, Don summoned his online banking application, keyed in his login and password. Waited for the screen to load. Tapped his foot. "We had an agreement, Krysten. Nothing legally binding, but still a handshake agreement. A mutual responsibility."

"My responsibility is to my staff first, and my readers second. *Cinexotique* is on the brink of something important, Don. In this business, you either get ahead, or you disappear. You're a liability. We can't afford those at this stage."

"You can't just cut me like that." The man on the screen grinned. It wasn't a happy grin. It looked like the expression of an animal cornered and terrified, baring its teeth in preparation for a fight to the death.

"Watch me," Krysten said. "You're a decent writer. No doubt about that. But for a guy who writes on demand and gets paid by the hundred words, you have an inflated sense of importance. I've got at least three others who can do it for less money, and probably better than you."

Her voice droned on, but Don was no longer listening. He was staring at the screen, at the balance in his bank account. Up until now, he hadn't allowed himself to believe that his fortune had changed, that J. C. Latham really intended to go through with his side of the deal. But the numbers didn't lie. The deposit had been credited to his account mere hours ago. Occultation Press must have liked his outline.

The only outline, he reminded himself with an inward shudder.

A sense of intrusion trickled into his awareness, a high-pitched, angry voice whining in his ear like a mosquito. He cleared his throat, waited for a lull in the monologue. "Krysten?"

"Yes?"

Don closed his eyes, savoring the moment. "I've given it some thought. You can take this job, or whatever it is, and shove it where the sun doesn't shine. Might be just the thing you've been missing. Guaranteed to improve your already sunny disposition."

He hung up, set his phone on silent, placed it next to him on the couch. From time to time, he glanced over, expecting it to ring. It didn't.

Everything would be different if he could get a drink. His head felt swollen, a balloon filling with blood. Not exactly a headache, but a constriction of his thoughts, as of a vise tightening around his temples. He had expected some satisfaction from hanging up on Krysten. But it felt like an abdication, a final severing of the ties that kept him tethered to the world.

Rather than dwell on it, or help himself to the crisp, icy vodka in the freezer, he reached for the notebook. Skimmed through the material, marking off sections that merited closer reading. Here and there, a name stood out; he wrote these down on a separate sheet, making a mental note to follow up on them later. He would have to do his own research.

At first glance, the notes were a filmography of B-movie horror, with annotations added under each title in Kebbler's uneven hand: summaries, scores, lists of crew and cast. Some of the lines had been crossed out and written over, making the original entry impossible to discern. Half-finished sentences proliferated in the margins and between lines. Other parts looked like fragmentary chapters, entire paragraphs taken down in a kind of incomprehensible shorthand, buried in cross-references that led nowhere. Layers of writing, one atop the other, pursued to obsessive lengths, a palimpsest of the author's madness. Unsure of what he expected to find, Don read on.

He was four pages in before an entry rang a bell in his head. *The Unveiling*, directed by Victor Hudson and starring Kirk Taylor in one of his final roles. It was the last movie the actor-director team had made together, following a series of cheap but successful exploitation flicks. Kebbler had been fixated on a lost movie, a big-budget production that the studio had pulled the plug on.

Not lost, *unmade*. That was the word he had used. Don's eyes widened as he read the production budget estimates. Even if Kebbler was way off the mark, it made no sense for the studio, a California outfit called Last Rite Productions, to sink that much money into a film that would never be released.

On impulse, he ran a search for the title. Neither Wikipedia nor IMDb had any matching records of *The Unveiling* in Taylor's or Hudson's entries. Not surprising, given that the film had never seen the light of day. Both careers had ended shortly thereafter. Victor Hudson's tragically when his yacht disappeared off the Greek coast, weeks before he was supposed to start shooting a new project for Columbia Pictures. Kirk Taylor had found himself cast in increasingly smaller roles in increasingly obscure horror movies. His last credit had been a supporting part in the straight-to-video slasher *Dread Derby* in 1994. By the end of the nineties, he seemed to have fallen off the face of the earth. His biographical listing was short on personal information, and the few external links were defunct. Wikipedia fared no better—a stub article lacking independent sources, already marked for deletion, saved from digital oblivion only through the intervention of squabbling editors.

An hour or so later, he was ready to give up. Search engines had given no hits on *The Unveiling*, nor had the slasher fan forums and pages resurrected through the Internet Archive's Wayback Machine. It didn't seem likely, but it was possible. Especially if the film had never been released, if neither the studio nor the producers wanted anything to do with it.

Don went back to the notebook, trying to discern more names from the scrawl. Kebbler hadn't had much more luck in tracking down the rest of the cast and crew of *The Unveiling*. Only the cameraman was listed, a Robert Callaway who had worked with Victor Hudson on two other films. He typed the name, waited for the search results to fill the laptop screen. According to his IMDb profile, Callaway had been a moderately renowned cinematographer, sought after by some stalwarts of the horror genre. Further trawling yielded a handful of YouTube clips, a few posts on the Bloody-Disgusting forums, a reference in a book about camera technique titled *Shot to Pieces*. With no credits after 2001, his last known work was a found-footage screamer too inferior to even merit an audience rating.

A face, or the contour of one, rose up to the surface of the screen. Don realized he was leaning forward in his chair, caught himself, and relaxed back. Three filmmakers whose lives had taken turns for the worse at roughly the same time. Hudson's death had been an accident, but there was a connection here that went beyond the unreleased movie they had worked on together. Was this what Kebbler had set out to uncover? It seemed like more than a coincidence, but the notebook offered no further clues.

Almost twenty years had passed since Rob Callaway had last worked in film. If he were still alive, maybe he'd have become an insurance salesman, or driven for Uber. But he too had dropped off the radar or else had found a way to render himself invisible to search engines. Even in this age of instant connectivity, a person could remain relatively anonymous if they chose to. Over time, the false hits and optimized keywords, the drifts and dunes of digital detritus, offered in themselves a kind of protection. Don fed Callaway's name to PeopleFinders, wrote down a dozen or so possible results. It was looking like he'd have to do this the old way, calling the numbers one-by-one.

The screen flickered and the room seemed to follow suit, a huge movement spreading through the walls and ceiling. Don closed his eyes, rubbed his face with his hands. He was still tired, still disturbed by what he'd seen the night before. That was all.

The thought of last night prompted an uneasy association he hadn't been aware of suppressing. He scanned the local news sites for some mention of the suicide, found none. Surely someone would have found Kebbler by now. He turned on the television, watched until the morning news gave way to the weather forecast. *Nothing*.

The blankness of the television set after he'd switched it off seemed to settle behind his eyes. Frozen frames shimmered on his laptop screen, a glitch or some sort of overload. Maybe suicides didn't make it into the news or would be mentioned in the evening segment. He couldn't have imagined it all. Rather than allow his mind to dwell on it, Don turned his back to the desk, picked up his phone, and started dialing.

***

Some time later, he'd left the last of the messages and was exhausted by the experience. Did anyone bother answering their phones anymore? No wonder that even telemarketers had moved on to email. One of the calls had been to Cedarstone Productions, the company that had last hired Robert Callaway, where a bored-sounding receptionist cut him off and hung up as soon as he'd stated his business.

He felt both tired and restless, the last week weighing on him, long nights coupled with excessive drinking. No more of that. He had a book to write, which meant setting some ground rules for himself. Like writing a thousand words a day before allowing himself a drink. Maybe five hundred. He mused on this as he crossed to the freezer, pulled out the bottle of vodka from behind the icemaker. Held the frosty glass up to the light. About a third was left, perfect for the job. His foray into sobriety could start tomorrow. Right now, he had some research to do.

He poured a generous slug into a pint glass, gave it a critical squint, added another inch. Topped it off with a can of seltzer water from the fridge and tossed in a desiccated lemon wedge for added nutrition. Breakfast of champions, or at least the closest he could come to thinking about eating. Stirring the drink with his finger, he settled down on the sofa and logged into his VisioBox account. He was behind on his monthly payments, but his subscription was still active, and the system accepted his credentials without protest.

By the time the streaming menu had loaded, the glass was half empty and Don was feeling pleasantly mellow. Maybe he could expense the subscription to his publisher as a research cost. He laughed, and didn't like the sound of his own laughter in the empty apartment; it seemed to reverberate through a much larger space, to chase its echo down an infinite hallway. The response he heard had to be coming from the TV set, on which patches of primary colors were taking too long to assemble into the VisioBox opening logo, a cube overlain by a stylized film frame.

Don clicked through the grid of movie thumbnails, fortifying himself with sips from the glass. The vodka drove a spike of frozen numbness between his eyes, smoothed over the jagged edges of the morning. Icons and letters ran like wet paint, threatening to dissolve into a cloud of pixels. He opened the search function in the sidebar, ran through the list in the notebook, painstakingly spelled out Kirk Taylor's last name.

His luck was up. VisioBox had several of Taylor's early movies available at no extra charge, including his debut, *Camp Carnage. You have to start somewhere*, he thought as he tapped on the poster icon, got up to fix himself another drink.

The circling symbol in the middle of the screen wound round and round, the background alternating between shades of darkness—an Ouroboros swallowing its own tail. Don started to put the bottle back into the freezer, thought better of it, and carried it to the sofa just in time for the opening credits.

Camp Carnage was a predictable slasher in which a bunch of attractive teenagers snuck into an abandoned summer camp, only to be dispatched by a deranged serial killer in increasingly gory and improbable ways. One in a smattering of cheap, forgettable clones trying to cash in on the popularity of *Halloween* and *Friday the Thirteenth*, it had been Kirk Taylor's first credited movie appearance. Don tried to follow along with Kebbler's notes for a while, then gave up and settled back to watch the action.

Somewhere between a decapitation with a hedge clipper and an impaling on a bicycle frame, amid poorly rendered scenes of terror and flight, every available surface dripping red, he came to an unexpected realization: Kirk Taylor could *act*. Youthful and handsome, he had an undeniable on-screen presence, an intangible something that separated him from the other protagonists and helped him dominate even the most ludicrous scenes. Even in his final act, a murky, shaky shot in which the scalpel-wielding psychopath chased him through a barn and cut his throat, he owned the screen. His square, outthrust jaw, his pale blue eyes glazing over as the blade bit into his throat, made his death look real, evoked a visceral reaction in the viewer. Real agony, real horror, despite the bad acting and unconvincing plot, in spite of the torrent of bright red corn syrup gushing from an obvious wax dummy. Even the tawdry scenery seemed to take on a sinister life of its own, as if feeding on the blood leaving the character's body: a cruel moment captured forever on film.

Don swallowed loudly, watched the tiny squares scroll from right to left as he replayed the death scene. Kirk Taylor dashed for the open door, tripped and fell, screamed. Silver flashed in the shadows. The actor's face filled the screen, expanded to fill Don's entire field of vision: eyes open wide, staring as if hypnotized, small muscles in his face straining and slackening, neck stretching out to meet the slashing blade. The blood also seemed more real now, the wound no longer fake—or was it just Don's booze-fueled imagination? Whatever the reason, he decided against playing it back a second time.

He tried to focus his attention back on the movie, but it was no longer possible to follow the plot. Bodies fleeing down shadowy corridors, a thin silhouette stalking them on long legs. Screams and scarlet slashes trailed down walls. Ritual sacrifice, a precise sequence of steps, leading to some indefinable terminus. There was a sensation of gliding along greased rails, rolling into a dark tunnel framed by the TV set, whose sides had extended backward, almost to infinity. He hadn't slept in a long time, not properly, and he struggled to keep his eyes open, to register the images rushing at him or assemble them in a coherent whole.

A heavy hand knocked against an empty glass, sending it falling to the floor a thousand miles away. There was no fighting back sleep, or the dream that followed it, as fragmented and disturbing as the movie playing silently on the screen.

***

I know who you are.

Don knew he was dreaming but couldn't quite break free from its clutches. A thin ripple passed through the surface of the screen as he was propelled forward into the darkness of the tunnel. Somewhere far away, he was aware of a Don Ruby who lay on his sofa, drunk and drooling slightly, an open notebook under one splayed hand. The whole scene was taking place in his head; all he had to do was wake himself up. But he couldn't reach that sleeping self, could not do anything to arrest his progress down the passage, its walls and ceiling flickering like ruined film.

A shape stood at the end of the tunnel, stark black against a white background. It resolved gradually, a simple squiggle at first, followed by a rough, hasty sketch, then the detailed rendering of a man. Tall and slim, dressed in black. A tuxedo, or a suit that looked like it had been cut from the night itself.

Was the figure approaching, or had the tunnel carried him closer? A sense of impending doom built up inside Don, of being poised on some terrible precipice. Yet his feet bore him onward, caught in the inexorable current of the dream.

The man was close enough to touch now. His suit was of an old-fashioned cut, but expensive-looking, and his hair glistened with oil. An actor from the black-and-white era, perhaps, or all of them at once: a touch of Clark Gable, a shade of Gary Cooper, some Tony Curtis thrown in for good measure. There were no walls or a floor around them, only featureless whiteness that hurt Don's eyes. The man turned and smiled at Don, flicked the butt of the cigarette he'd been smoking, ground it out under a perfectly polished heel. It was a friendly smile, but something about it turned Don's bowels to water.

Just in time for the final act.

Before Don could be sure whether he'd heard the words, or just seen the mouth shape them, the dream shifted, as if a backdrop had unfolded before him. They were standing on a stage in a huge, dimly lit theater, packed to the rafters with a silent crowd. The man in the suit bowed theatrically, produced a length of golden rope with the flourish of a stage magician. Mimicked a tugging motion and handed the rope to Don. He pivoted on his heels, pointed at the heavy brocade curtain hiding the rest of the stage.

Don's gaze followed the rope to where it vanished into the darkness of the ceiling. With the unreal logic of the dream, he understood that his life depended on not doing what the magician wanted him to do, that whatever lay behind the curtain had to remain locked out there. Desperate, he turned to the audience with a pleading look, but the stage lights blinded him. All he could distinguish were hints of bodies—an arm here, a pair of crossed legs there—and blank faces like pale ovals. Yet he could feel the tense anticipation wafting off the gathering, their hot, hungry stares rolling over him like a wave.

The magician cocked a mock-quizzical eyebrow. Facing the crowd, he raised his hands in an exaggerated shrug. Placed an elegant finger against his lips, deep in thought, then mimed an epiphany. He waved his hand at Don, a sort of abracadabra motion, and spoke a phrase under his breath. Don took an instinctive step backward, shielding the rope with his body. Or tried to, because he was no longer in control of it. Without warning, he was hovering above the stage, up by the lights, watching the scene unfolding below.

It was only a dream. The words repeated in his mind as he fought to return to his body, suddenly convinced that his terror was only causing him to drift further, toward some point of no return. Below, the magician made another melodramatic gesture. Don saw his arms move, saw the rope grow taut. His mind was collapsing, falling down an infinite black hole.

The curtain fell away. An eye peered into the theater, as big as the wall, bloodshot and rolling in fear. Galaxies roiled in its enormous pupil, exploded and trailed incandescent dust. The audience was on their feet, applauding, their clamor muffled and distant. The man in the black suit bowed, clapped his hands, once, twice, and the shadows swirled around him, a doorway of darkness that swallowed him like a mouth.

Don thrashed awake on the sofa, saw that the wall in front of him was gone. The space it had occupied was filled with the television set: a vague gray nothingness stretched behind it. Cold sucked at him, the absolute life-negating cold of the void. Into that void he went, flailing, powerless to halt his plummet, the screams of dying stars rising in his ears, a sound as wide as the sky.

Chapter 6

He woke a second time, sat up blinking.

The sound was his ringtone, chiming from under his sofa pillow. Pain hammered at his temples, wound tight, hot coils inside his skull. His mouth felt as dry as the Sahara.

Perhaps it was the residue of the dream that made the familiar lines of his apartment slow in reasserting themselves. He groped for the offending phone, almost tripped over the empty vodka bottle rolling underfoot. No sooner was the receiver by his ear than a man's harsh voice demanded, "Is this Ruby? John Ruby?"

"Yeah." Don didn't feel like correcting the caller. Every attempt to think seemed to require tremendous effort. He reached for a pen and paper, knocking over his glass. "Speaking. Who is this?"

"Callaway." It took Don a couple of moments to realize that the name was important, to recall the context. "You said you're looking for information about a movie. *The Unveiling*. What do you want to know?"

"It's for a book I'm writing. A book about, uh, the horror movement of the seventies and eighties. The Golden Age of the slasher film."

"*The horror movement*," Callaway said, voice dripping with sarcasm. He gave a wheezing chuckle. "Jesus. Is that what they call it these days? Talk about rose-tinted glasses. Bunch of no-talent bastards taking a shit on celluloid to get their rocks off, more like it."

"You're the only one I know of who worked on *The Unveiling*," Don said. *Only one still alive*, he almost added. "I'd like to hear more about it. I can pay for your time. Credit you in my book."

"A book." Callaway sounded suspicious. "Well, better get down to it, sport. I don't have time to waste or to turn away cash. It's getting harder and harder for a guy like me to earn a living these days. The fuckers digitized everything, and don't even get me started on amateur video. Any snot-nosed kid can shoot a movie on his phone camera, put it up on the internet for free, and get two million views just like *that*. Views from other zombies just like him, but who gives a shit anymore?" He paused, breathing hard. "Anyway. How much are we talking about?"

Don thought quickly of the expenses clause in his contract. "You name your price."

There was a moment of deliberation. Callaway was probably wondering whether to aim low and lose money or go high and price himself out of the deal. "Three hundred," he finally said; apparently Don's voice didn't exactly inspire confidence. "That's for a couple of hours. Maybe three. Cash only, no receipt. What Uncle Sam doesn't know about can't hurt him."

"I can cover that."

Another silence on the line. "Why are you digging up that stuff from the past? Why would anyone?"

"My book is about lost and forgotten horror movies. *The Unveiling* could have become a classic. It had a prominent director, a famous cast, enough production money to go around. You worked on it. Don't you think it should be saved from obscurity?"

A harsh bray of surprised laughter made Don flinch from the receiver. He couldn't be sure, but he thought he detected a touch of fear around its edges. "A classic. Saved from *obscurity*. Boy, you're really laying it on thick, aren't you? You don't have a fucking clue what you're getting yourself into. Either that, or it's some kind of prank. Who put you up to this?"

"I don't see why—"

"Tell you what, I'm probably better off not knowing." Callaway snorted, hawked, and spat. "Here you are, offering me money for my time, and I'm flapping my gums, giving away freebies. You want to talk, you come up here. Got something to write with?"

Don wrote down the address the cameraman dictated to him. It was in New Jersey, just across the state border. "I've got some time on Thursday, around three in the afternoon. Don't be late. I've got a gig in the evening, and I can't afford to miss out on it."

Perhaps this was a transparent play for more money. Don took it as a cue. "You still in the business? Making movies, I mean?"

This time, the laughter was genuine. "Sure. I'm beating off offers with a stick. That's why I moved to the film Mecca of Shitkick, New Jersey. Because I wanted to keep making movies. See you the day after tomorrow. Don't forget your wallet."

"You wouldn't happen to have a copy of it, would you?" It was a long shot, but Don saw no harm in trying. "Of the movie, that is? Or at least a rough cut?"

"What the hell would I want that for?"

"I could pay you more. A lot more." Don hurried to fill the crackling silence on the other end of the line. Not for the first time, he felt that the conversation was slipping away from him, that he wasn't getting the point. "If you're willing to part with it, of course. No one's ever found a copy."

"You've only got Victor Hudson to blame for that. He's the one who made it, then got cold feet."

"I don't think I understand."

There was a longer pause this time, as if Callaway were mulling over what to say. "Day after tomorrow. This is all you get without forking over some legal tender."

The line filled with a busy signal. Don ended the call, typed the address into MapView. A couple of hours on local busses. Maybe J. C. Latham would be willing to spring for a rental car.

He yawned, thought about the former cameraman's parting words. Robert Callaway was either an eccentric given to digression or deliberately coy, hinting at secrets to drive a harder bargain. Probably just pissed off that he hadn't asked for more money. No use worrying about it now. He'd find out soon enough.

To take his mind off the conversation, he pulled up his book outline, compared it to the chapter sketches in Kebbler's notebook. They weren't all that different, he realized with a slight shock. Kebbler had also wanted to use the lost film as a framing device to keep the reader invested, eager to turn the pages. The search for *The Unveiling* would form the story's central mystery, a rumor about a lost film that had somehow derailed the careers of both its key men. It would be a study in contrast: on one hand, Victor Hudson's trajectory, an *auteur* director forced by straitened circumstances into making cinematic trash. On the other, Kirk Taylor's commercial, hyper-masculine appeal, his meteoric rise and equally rapid descent into obscurity. All set in the context of the slasher-movie boom, a genre that gleefully thumbed its nose at the boundaries of good taste and public morality, cheered on by a voracious, insatiable audience. There were instances in which his vision and Kebbler's diverged. The latter had planned to bring in *The Unveiling* early on in the text, to devote several chapters to a tiresome psychoanalysis of horror film audiences. But the similarity was undeniable.

In fact, had he not known better, Don would have sworn that they were the same outline.

Frowning, he tried to log into his email, but the browser kept returning a 404 error. The website had to be down. It didn't matter. The file he'd sent to the publisher was the same one he'd just opened. Any similarities had to be accidental. He had not copied Kebbler's notes—that was downright unthinkable.

Wasn't it?

The possibilities didn't bear thinking about, not in his half-awake state, so Don chose not to think about them. Instead, he opened a fresh document and stared at the white expanse of the screen. Pushed away an unwelcome memory of that same dazzling whiteness, a dark-suited man who looked like he'd just stepped out of a forties noir movie standing in its center, smiling at him. There was a way to bury the vision, and that was to cover the page with words. They came tentatively at first, in short bursts, then faster, his fingers warming up, his mind running through the gears. By the time he got to the end of the opening chapter, night had fallen outside, but he took no notice. He'd found the conduit in the story. *His* story. The story that no one would take away. He typed on, oblivious to the world around him, the monitor bathing him in its unnatural radiance, lighting his way through the dark.

Chapter 7

Barren grass lots flicked along the highway, here and there giving way to buildings of grimy red brick, to chain-link fences guarding the ruins of abandoned factories, to shuttered shops and strip malls in various stages of decay. A featureless sky hovered over the landscape like a lead dome over the world in which the shrunken, distant sun struggled to break through. Across the river, pale daylight smeared across the suburbs, leaching color from the roofs and trees.

The bus passed under a railway bridge, its interior dimming to near darkness. When it emerged back into the light, the houses were smaller and further apart, the lawns patchy and yellowing, the vehicles parked beside them older and more rundown. It was mid-afternoon, but the streets were empty; many of the windows were already lit up. The cookie-cutter pattern repeated itself as far as the eye could see, a series of identical horizons opening up one after another, former suburbia eventually dwindling to country roads and sparse farms.

Don shifted in his seat, barely able to keep his eyes open. The juddering of the bus was putting him to sleep. The dreary, unchanging vista contributed to a creeping sense of dislocation. Above the stained backrests, heads bobbed with the motion of the vehicle, the last few passengers riding to the end of the line. Scrolling bars and rectangles of shadow made it impossible for Don to make out their faces. There was no reason for him to imagine that the heads were unattached to bodies, not heads at all, but egg-shaped sacs, their contents squirming and rippling under the mottled skin.

He couldn't give in to his weariness because his stop was coming up; a sign and a bus shelter on the far side of an intersection, almost swallowed by overgrown hedges. As he got off, he avoided looking at the faces of the other passengers, kept his gaze fixed on his phone until he heard the bus hiss and rumble away.

Robert Callaway's address was a ten-minute walk from the stop, but the repeating houses made navigation difficult, with nothing to distinguish one street from another. In a few blocks, Don was lost, trying in vain to make sense of the signs, to match the names on them to the blurred, scrambled words on his navigation app. Under the sound of the wind and the distant whoosh of scant traffic, he could hear someone walking right behind him, the sharp, smart rap of dress shoes on the pavement. But when he cast an uneasy glance over his shoulder, the street was empty; the only movement was the flutter of trash in the gutters.

It had to be the wind, carrying to him the flapping of a broken shopfront awning against the window, evoking phantom footsteps. Still, Don pulled his coat closer and hurried along the sidewalk, toward the lights of a convenience store at the end of the block. Easier and quicker to ask for directions or use the store as a landmark on his malfunctioning phone map.

Earlier that day, he had awakened hours before dawn and had not been able to fall back asleep. He'd tried to write, but the words wouldn't come, the cursor blinking at him gleefully from the emptiness of the screen. Even yesterday's efforts seemed curiously different on re-reading, as if the text had mutated overnight in some subtle but crucial way. The introduction felt vague and rambling; the story refused to progress in any coherent direction. A few of the references read like fabrications: he highlighted these for editing, wondering how he'd come upon them. Better not to make the same mistake again.

He had to find out more about the lost movie, use it as the backbone of the narrative structure. Without it, the book would remain unfocused, a mere regurgitation of online factoids and outlandish speculation. Confusing, like this maze of interchangeable streets, the furtive movement in the blank windows, light seeping away like a shadow had fallen across the sky. At least he could warm himself in the store, buy a cup of coffee, give his muddled mind a chance to collect itself. Feeling like a swimmer caught in a riptide, Don hurried across the pavement and reached for the door.

Suddenly he stopped, as if doused with cold water. Someone was standing in a window further down the sidewalk, staring at him. A man, dressed smartly in black and white, his face inches away from the flyblown glass. Chin thrust out, as if preparing for a confrontation. Don couldn't see the man's eyes, but had the impression of intense scrutiny, of the gaze pinning him like a moth under glass.

The headlights of a passing car dispelled the illusion. Not a man, but a mannequin in a dusty tailor's window, dressed in a faded old suit, surrounded by an arrangement of plastic body parts collecting cobwebs. Don breathed easier, forced a laugh. His peculiar disorientation lifted; his destination was just around the block, behind the building that hosted the store. Yet the feeling of being watched stayed with him, eager footsteps mirroring his every move, shadows fluttering inside darkened doorways, dead leaves rustling in cold gusts of wind. As if the watcher knew where he was headed and was following him there, determined but unhurried.

***

Robert Callaway lived in a small, shabby house in a row of similar-looking structures, fronted by a junk-littered yard. At the end of the driveway, a beat-up Toyota with Uber and Lyft stickers in the windows was parked next to a shed. Somewhere behind the fence, a dog was snuffling, rooting through the piled leaves.

Don looked around for a hint of life, but the houses flanking Callaway's were dark, one of them boarded up with a rusty FOR SALE sign leaning on its lawn. When he knocked on the door, the former cameraman threw it open immediately, as if he'd been waiting behind it.

"Did you stop by earlier?" he said, eschewing introductions. "Or call my phone? Leave a message?"

Don shook his head. "It took me a minute to find your place. I took the bus, figured I'd walk."

"Uh-huh." Callaway scanned the empty street feverishly, peered into the gloom. He appeared not to register the response. Hustling his visitor inside, he shut the door and jerked the curtain across the adjoining window with such force Don half-expected the fabric to tear. "Got the message about half an hour ago. That's why I thought it was you. Doesn't matter now."

He was a tall, round-shouldered man, with a bulge in his midsection and a broad face whose small features seemed to perpetually hover between a scowl and a cringe. Fidgeting in place, he looked embarrassed by the house's seamy interior, the worn furniture and boxes piled up everywhere, the unaired smell. "It's temporary," he said, scratching behind one ear. "This place, I mean. I'm just staying here until I work a few things out. Haven't bothered unpacking yet."

Embarrassed or not, he accepted the cash Don handed over without acknowledging the transaction. "Have a seat, if you can find one in this mess. I can't offer you much, but the coffee should be ready any minute."

"Coffee sounds great." Don found a place on the dingy sofa and carefully sat down. Callaway ducked through a doorway, returned with a steaming mug and handed it to him. For a moment he seemed lost for words, uncertain what to do next, so he stood in the middle of the room as if he were the stranger here. Then he folded himself into a frayed lounger, avoiding Don's eyes. "So, what's this article you're writing? I didn't think anyone knew about that movie anymore. It was never released or even advertised. Is that why you're interested in it?"

"Only tangentially," Don said. "I'm writing a book on eighties horror and some of the forgotten filmmakers. My publisher thought, and I agree, that a chapter or two on *The Unveiling* would give the story focus. A touch of the mysterious." He tried to keep his tone light without coming off as mocking, watching Callaway's twitchy face for signs of evasion. But the man didn't seem to be listening to him. He was staring over Don's shoulder, through the living room window, which gave onto what had to be the backyard, overgrown and dark.

"Mysterious. Sure." With apparent effort, the former cameraman dragged his attention back to the conversation. "It's been a while since I've thought about it, to be honest. I've been out of the business for almost twenty years. That sort of work gets under your skin." His long fingers played with a coaster. "Especially *that* film. Everything about it was a nightmare. There was some speculation that Victor destroyed the final cut himself. God knows I hoped he'd do exactly that. So did the others."

"That's a strange way to feel about something you worked on."

"By the end of the shoot, I wanted nothing to do with it. Or with the guy who made it." Callaway made a quick self-deprecating gesture. "Don't get me wrong. I needed the money, and I worshipped Victor. He was a genius, a visionary. Not ahead of his time, as the cliché goes, but outside it altogether. If he'd chosen another genre, he'd have been greater than Fincher and Cronenberg, better known than Aronofsky. Have you seen *Three Sequences of a Dream*? It's a collage of shorts he made while he was still in college, over in England." As Don tried to figure out a response, Callaway waved his own question away. "A copy sells for close to a thousand dollars on eBay. Even more on private auction sites, when it sells at all."

"That's not what he'll be remembered for."

"No. He chose to waste his talent. To make trash. Schlock. That was what the critics said."

"You don't agree with it."

"Victor knew it was the audience that mattered," Callaway said, a spark kindling in his eyes. His hands knitted and unknitted in his lap, two pale, restless spiders. Already the coaster had been reduced to a pile of shreds, but he didn't seem to notice. "The audience, and nothing else. It has power. Have you written anything I may have heard about?"

"A couple of books. They sold okay."

"Then you know it too." Stained teeth appeared in a grim smile of half-amusement, half-fear. "The letters on the page, the images on the screen, are only symbols and movement and colors. Real art happens in the mind. It catches like fire. It needs eyes to set itself loose. Victor knew it, and he had a knack for finding the right kindling. All the greats have it. Actors, directors, painters. Even cameramen. There's a certain energy in what we do, a strictly defined ritual. Do you see what I'm getting at?"

Don stared at him for a moment. "No," he said. "Quite frankly, I don't. Another thing I don't see is what this pseudo-mystical nonsense has to do with my book."

The smile curved down into a grimace. "Then you're like all the others. Thinking you have it all figured out."

"Right now, all I'm thinking is that I wasted my time and money coming here." Don made as if to rise, caught a flare of panic in the other man's face.

"Wait." Callaway's gaze darted to the door, to the window, like a trapped bird. A breath later, Don became aware of the sound. A scraping, grating vibration somewhere deep in the walls. Pipes, or heavy objects being dragged across the floor. Pure horror contorted Callaway's features, immediately replaced by a desperate slyness. "It's hard for me to talk about it. About the movie. You weren't there. You can't understand. Victor may have been a genius, but the film was a bitch to make. Things happened. Very *strange* things."

"What kind of strange things?"

"A lot of the problems were of Victor's own making." Callaway's tone was hushed, almost worshipful. "The sets, for one. He kept having them built overnight, then taken apart after the day's shoot was done. The workers were complaining about the long hours, about what they saw as an exercise in futility. Victor wouldn't have any of it. He was like a man possessed, a fanatic. He'd fire them on the spot, bring in a new crew. Brody, the set designer, would get into these screaming matches with him. He got fired too."

"Sounds like a thrilling guy to work for."

"That wasn't all of it. Someone kept breaking in at night, moving the props around. Or they would just be gone the next day. Whole sets would vanish, just like that. Nothing but empty floors, no footsteps in the dust, no trace of anything being moved or dragged around. But Victor didn't seem to care."

"Must have cost a bundle." Don decided he'd just about had it with Callaway's ominous asides. Still, if he left now, he'd have nothing to show for his effort. "Why do you think he did it? Changed the sets like that?"

"How would I know? Yeah, the cost had to be astronomical, but Victor could afford it. There were rumors he had a group of shadow backers behind him. That the studio was nothing but a front. Even that he was funding the movie himself. People talk a lot of bullshit. There was money coming in, and that's all I knew. Lots of it. At first, I thought he was doing it to scare the rest of us. Get the cast in the right mood, build up an atmosphere. Hitchcock did it, so did Polanski. But it went too far. Some of the sets were taken down without me ever setting foot in them. Some after we'd shot a single scene."

"He never told you why? You were his lead cameraman."

"Nothing was normal about it." Callaway paused, wiping the sweat beading on his brow. Clutching at his knees didn't quite conceal the trembling of his hands. "There were three cameramen. Me and two others. We shot the scenes out of sequence. None of us knew what the other two were doing. Half the time, I had no idea how my own stuff fit into the shooting board. There was an outline, a general idea of what we should be making, but Victor abandoned it by the end of the second week. Whatever we were doing came straight from his head. Like he had pictures in there. Sometimes I'd get a memo the night before, two sentences about what we'd be doing tomorrow. Other times I got no warning."

"But you stuck with it."

"What was I supposed to do? He paid me to be his camera monkey. Not to question his artistic vision." Callaway looked evasive. "But it wasn't just that. I was having a bit of trouble of my own at the time. A nasty habit I'd picked up over the years, one that was getting harder and harder to ditch. Word got round, and work was drying up. Victor understood. He never refused me a favor when I needed one. A few bucks upfront, a little pick-me-up here and there." A sorrowful smile danced on his lips. "Showbiz isn't exactly the endless debauched orgy that it's cracked up to be, but there's never a shortage of special supplies either, if you catch my drift. Especially on set."

Don took a moment to digest this. "You never asked him about it? About what was going on?"

"I couldn't be sure what was going on. What was actually happening, and what were just flashbacks and my own delusions. Let's face it, I was stoned a lot of the time. Even after my stint ended, I didn't really know what to think about it. Nor did I try too hard to remember. Took me years to figure out what was real and what wasn't. There are still blank spots in my memory today, like my mind refuses to go back to that time." He raised his moist gaze and spoke with such assurance that Don immediately knew a lie was coming. "But I'm clean now. I've been clean for years. Although, I'm not sure that it's made me a happier person. Whoever said ignorance is bliss wasn't half wrong."

"Did you stay until the end of the shoot?"

Callaway snorted, wiped his nose with his sleeve. "I don't think there *was* an end. I left during the last week, after the atmosphere became unbearable. By this point, even Victor was having doubts. Things had gotten to him or were starting to get to him."

"Like what?"

"He became paranoid. Doubled the security, banned all visitors on the set. Like he was afraid of being attacked, or something happening to the crew. He would leave the set for days at a time, stalling the shoot when we were already behind. A guy disappeared, one of the set design people. Their foreman confronted Victor. Said he'd go to the police, turn the whole place upside down. The studio made it go away—I suppose they paid everybody off. But they had words with Victor, and he didn't take kindly to that."

"They threatened to pull the funding?"

"Either that, or they weren't going to back the release. Victor was beyond reason at this point." Callaway paused, listened to another bout of scraping in the walls. "It was starting to get to the crew, too. Actors are a superstitious crowd, more so than baseball players. Some of them got pretty nervous. Gossip started about figures moving around the set, people who weren't supposed to be there, couldn't be accounted for. Animals getting into the props, tearing them apart. One of the grips said that he'd seen a door open into a hidden room, a corridor that went on for miles, but that it was gone the next time he checked. Karen Lombard, the leading lady, had some kind of breakdown and quit. Others saw faces in mirrors, staircases that went nowhere. All nonsense, but once it started spreading, there was no containing it."

He stopped abruptly, glanced around, as if fearful he'd said too much. "I wasn't sorry to hear that the movie was buried. Towards the end, I think Victor was glad for it too. He would never admit it, but he was shaken by the whole experience, and he wasn't someone who scared easily."

"What do you think about his death?"

"He drowned, like the papers said. A yachting accident. But it was just that—an accident. Maybe there were drugs involved. Victor never did more than dabble, but failure can change a man. Maybe it was intentional. By the time of his death, he had lapsed back into complete obscurity." The wan smile resurfaced. "To a burned-out, bitter loser like myself, it looked almost like a conspiracy of the studios. No one wanted to work with Victor, or *for* Victor, and his last few films were of no use to them. Too surreal to be *Real Horror*, too bloody to be considered *Real Art*. Had Victor been a pure stylist, like Bava or Argento, fans and critics alike would have fawned over him. Alas, he was something much more. Someone they couldn't categorize, therefore someone they couldn't understand. So, they discarded him. *The Unveiling* was the beginning of the end for him."

"Not just for him," Don said. "For others who worked on the film. Like Kirk Taylor."

"That sleazy bastard." Genuine anger lit up Callaway's face. "Victor made him up from scratch. Took a cornfed hick from nowhere Kentucky and turned him into a movie star. Then he abandoned Victor when he was needed the most."

"You didn't think much of him, then?"

"Still don't. A handsome face and a few muscles, but no real talent to speak of. Back in the day, you could cruise Ventura Boulevard for half an hour and pick up a dozen just like Kirk Taylor. Pretty, hungry, and vapid. Boys and girls both."

"I'm not sure Victor Hudson would agree. He cast Kirk in several of his films."

The former cameraman sneered. "Victor saw something in Kirk that the rest of us couldn't. Maybe something that wasn't really there. His genius shone so brightly it reflected on us all. Elevated us. *The Unveiling* was supposed to be the triumph of their collaboration. Instead, Kirk pulled out."

"You mean he didn't follow the script?"

"I mean he walked off the set," Callaway said. "Didn't even have the guts to do it face to face. He had his agent call Victor and tell him he wasn't coming back. Good riddance, if you ask me. There were far better actors making slashers back then—Brad Dourif, Tony Todd, Johnny Depp. Brad Pitt was in *Cutting Class*, for Heaven's sake. But when it came to Kirk Taylor, Victor had a blind spot the size of Texas."

"What do you think happened to Taylor? He seems to have fallen off the face of the earth."

"Whatever happens to untalented pretty boys when they get old, I suppose." Callaway didn't try to keep the malice out of his tone.

"They make commercials, or work the convention circuit, sign photos for fans. Anything to scrape together a living. Bruce Campbell made a full comeback after *Evil Dead* and is now more popular than ever. Or they open car dealerships, or stock shelves in a supermarket. Or they simply disappear. It's the price of fame, and everyone in the business knows it."

Don contemplated this. The former cameraman clearly had an axe to grind, but he didn't seem to be lying, or he was a far better liar than Don gave him credit for. "What do you make of it all? The missing rooms, the mysterious intruders. Do you believe some of it defies rational explanation?"

"Don't put words in my mouth." But Callaway's startled reaction belied his statement. "I just didn't like how nervous everyone got. Or what Victor turned into toward the end. The vision he had of himself as the *auteur*, the rebel, the one who would redefine how movies were made. The father of a new visual aesthetic, the artist-philosopher of a new age. He ranted a lot at the time, mostly to those who were part of his inner circle. His cabal. People like Kirk Taylor, who would have done anything to further their careers. Victor conceived of film as an extension of reality; the screen was another door to be opened. Interlocking spaces, rooms without doors, or hallways that ran in circles. It was total nonsense, all of it. I was glad his later movies had none of it, that he was making normal stuff again. Well, if you could call *Entrails* and *Entrails II* normal. But you get the picture."

"Were you ever in touch with Last Rites Productions directly?"

But the former cameraman had stopped talking. His eyes danced around the room, his mouth open in an expression that was part horror, part surprise. Now Don heard it too, the clamor in the walls getting louder. It had to be the acoustics creating the impression of something getting closer, scratching eagerly at the barrier that separated them. Either that, or rats.

"I think I've said enough," Callaway said, his voice small, like that of a child. "It was a long time ago, and my memory isn't what it used to be. You should leave now."

"At least give me some names. Someone else I can talk to about the movie."

"Forget about the movie." The other man rose from his chair. A fixed smile hovered on his face like a mask, hiding something darker, almost pained. "All copies were destroyed. The studio went bankrupt right around the same time, and there was a big fire at their warehouse some years later. Everything burned down. You won't find what you're looking for, no matter how hard you look."

"I have a book to write," Don said as he was herded to the door, as Callaway thrust the roll of bills at him. "Keep the cash. There's more where that came from if you're willing to help me out."

"Write about something else." A desperate fear surfaced in the cameraman's eyes. He was no longer seeing Don but some inner vision. "Don't you see? This is what Victor wanted. To live in the minds of the public forever. To catch in their imagination like fire. You can't let him do that. You can't let them win, or they'll never leave."

Before Don could make any sense of this, he was out on the stoop, the door closing behind him, the money fluttering around his feet like dead leaves.

Chapter 8

There was an email waiting for him when he got back to his apartment, an eBay seller offering a *rare and unedited copy of the 1980s horror film, The Unveiling*. Don's heart gave a little leap, even as he cautioned himself not to harbor unrealistic hopes. Two earlier offers had turned out to be nothing but spliced-together cut scenes from Victor Hudson's earlier slashers, sold by a user from China who specialized in fake antiques and curios. A YouTube search result linked in response to one of his forum queries had similarly turned out to be a mishmash of clips from Hudson films he'd already seen. Don deliberated over the eBay item, entered a bid, and crossed his fingers.

His interview with Robert Callaway had left him with more questions than answers. The former cameraman had taken his split with Hudson personally, almost like a jilted paramour: someone who'd held the director in great esteem, only to be discarded, or disappointed in some way that went beyond words. His disdain for Kirk Taylor, the vehemence of his hatred for the actor, had to be personal. Perhaps it had been a lovers' spat, a triangle of lust and unrequited emotions. It would hardly be out of the ordinary for a public figure to harbor a past indiscretion or three: even in the freewheeling world of seventies Hollywood, same-sex dalliances would have been kept strictly undercover. Especially considering Kirk Taylor's masculine image and its ramifications on the studios' profit margins.

But that didn't feel quite right, nor did it explain Callaway's odd behavior. There was something else nagging at him, some crucial detail he'd overlooked. Maybe it had to do with Hudson's film school project, the one that had revealed his genius. *Not ahead of his time, but outside it altogether.* He opened a new browser tab, typed in *three sequences of a dream Victor Hudson.*

Robert Callaway hadn't been exaggerating about the film. Amazon listed a single VHS copy, available in used but good condition, from an international seller, priced well in excess of ten thousand dollars. That wasn't an expense Don could justify to his publisher. Restless, he set up a saved eBay search, clicked out, and went back to his manuscript.

Except the manuscript had changed.

Don gaped at the screen, feeling ice creep up his spine. The chapter he'd struggled with, the lines he had written and rewritten, pored over word by word, were different. Surely, he would remember penning the introductory paragraphs, outlining the social changes that enabled the sudden rise in horror movie popularity—the emergence of cable television and home video, the shifting mores of an aging Free Love generation, now themselves facing parenthood. Surely, he couldn't have found the material for his next chapter, introducing Victor Hudson, in Kebbler's notebook, or in his own meager research. Feverish, he read the offending sentences.

> The Master's Daughter, *a movie that masterfully straddles the line between the Universal horror classics of the thirties and the low-budget exploitation films of the sixties, was the first full-length feature from prolific director Victor Hudson, who had previously made a name for himself in European surrealist cinema. An enigma to both critics and the public, an aesthete with an infallible instinct for shock, Hudson remained*

in the business for nearly thirty years, directing cult titles such as Occupancy Twenty-Seven, Night of the Stalker, Déjà Death, *and the infamous* With Open Eyes, *which in equal measures delighted and scandalized even the most ardent of his devotees. Born in a small town in Devon, the son of a local industrial magnate, young Victor studied filmmaking in Bristol, where in two short years he succeeded in appalling his teachers and incensing the British Board of Film Censors. Unfazed, Hudson moved to France, then spent several years traveling the continent, reputedly rubbing elbows with the likes of Dalí and Buñuel, before landing in Hollywood as a director. Some of these influences are evident in* The Master's Daughter, *a grindhouse feature in scenography and storyline, an arthouse experiment in form and style.*

Don flipped through the notebook to the blank pages at the back. One of them was no longer blank; the damp-damaged was paper covered in spidery handwriting, different from the rest of the notes. He read it, unbelieving, his mouth dry, his stomach in knots.

Victor Hudson debuted behind the camera in 1963 with The Master's Daughter, *a movie that critics still struggle to define and interpret. Schlock or arthouse? This dilemma will forever haunt the thirty-plus-year legacy of Hudson, a prolific aesthete with an instinct for horror, the director behind such cult titles as* Occupancy Twenty-Seven, Night of the Stalker, Déjà Death, *and* With Open Eyes. *This latter film earned him the animosity of movie regulators, the rancor of various self-appointed guardians of public morality, even confounded*

> *many among his stalwart fans. If Hudson stooped enough to notice, he gave no sign of it: Hudson was no stranger to antagonizing the prudish and hypocritical. Born in Devon, the son of a local industrial magnate, young Victor left home to study filmmaking in Bristol.*

It was all there, if not exactly word for word, written in his own hand. Yet he couldn't remember writing any of it. He went back to the beginning of the notebook, read through it slowly, at the same time scrolling down the file. Either he'd been too tired to make sense of Kebbler's chaotic scrawl earlier, or the loops and whorls had rearranged themselves on the page. There was an underlying order to the entries, a complex system of references and cross-references: sentences and entire paragraphs surfaced from the raveled lines, stood out in his perception like neon signs. He had no problem following them from section to section or tracing them back to the laptop's blinking screen.

> *Were these movies toxic trash, as critics bemoaned, cheap entertainment devised to thrill and titillate by appealing to the audience's basest instincts—for voyeurism, nudity, for senseless carnage? Or canny commentary on an era of technological change and social upheaval, on hidden desires and fears, packaged in a shiny, if bloody, wrapping accessible to the masses? The emergence of feminism and the patriarchal recasting of women as an object of horror; the indictment of suburban teen promiscuity as part of the reactionary backlash of the Reagan era, trying to reverse the aspirations and attitudes of the free-spirited sixties.*

Arguably, there were those in the genre who elevated horror—and its red-headed stepchild, the slasher—to the level of what could arbitrarily be termed 'art'. Filmmakers eager to challenge the ossified notions of what a horror film could or could not be about. Thus, we have the layering of stark docudrama and mystical surrealism in the works of Roger Corman; the insidious erosion of trust and character in the nineties films of David Fincher; the political nuances behind the cheery, subtly self-referential splatter of Carpenter and Craven. Herschel Gordon Lewis gave us dazzling, extravagant gore, as did the exuberantly over-the-top gialli *of Argento and Bava. Among these masters of horror, the name of Victor Hudson has become all but forgotten.*

Regardless of artistic merit, some horror movies will remain firmly lodged in the public's subconscious, like the icepick through the brain of the screaming blonde teenager killed off at the end of the first act.

Could he have unconsciously subsumed what he'd read in the notes, replicating the same structure in his own writing? No; he was sure about this. The passage he'd just read had not existed before today, either on paper or in his manuscript file. It wasn't possible, but the evidence before him could not be dismissed. Moving the cursor past the end of the chapter brought an irrational fear of what the next page would reveal. Had his thoughts shaped the text, or were the letters on the screen reaching inside his mind somehow, changing what he perceived?

It was absurd, of course. Don let out a pent-up breath of relief. There was the chapter heading he'd agonized over, *The Surrealist*

Phantasmagorias of Victor Hudson, followed by familiar sentences. Still, the uncomfortable feeling persisted, a peculiar dissociation from the material, as if the manuscript had mutated somewhere between being conceived and written, as if someone else had reworked it while he slept. The broad strokes were there, but the finished product was more concise and succinct, the arguments bolstered by additional research.

This was his work. *His* idea. He repeated this silent mantra as he turned away from the laptop. No one would know that he wasn't the author of those lines. He may not be their original author, but he'd be the one to set them free into the world, release them into the mind of the reader. The thought restored some of his confidence, even if the transmuted chapters didn't quite fit into any explanation he was capable of providing.

Briefly, Don toyed with the idea of phoning Occultation Press, making it sound like a casual inquiry about his writing collaborator. Then he realized how crazy that would be. Instead, he picked up his phone and entered Jess's New York number. Hesitated with his finger on the call button, decided against it.

You're being a coward, he chided himself, already running through the usual excuses. Her number was probably out of use. She wouldn't want anything to do with him. For all he knew, there was a restraining order out against him. He'd do the same if he were in her shoes.

But he needed someone—needed *her*, now more than ever before. Not as a lover, or even a friend. That ship had sailed years ago; that particular bridge had been burned beyond repair. But Jessica the agent, the sharp, incisive editor, the opinionated First Reader. Without her, this book would never live up to its full potential. The publisher wanted an homage to horror films and fandom, but Don Ruby had his sights set on something far bigger. Absolution. In a way, he could identify with Hudson the rejected filmmaker, Hudson the unappreciated genius, whose propensity for self-sabotage had condemned him to obscurity. Don had been given a second chance and would not make the same mistake again.

His reflection smiled as he went back to the screen, notebook in hand. The feel of the coarse paper under his fingers, the secret knowledge contained within, filled him with a sense of excited elation. All the work he had done before had been nothing but preparation, the first drafts of the story he was about to reveal to the world.

Chapter 9

A notion of being surrounded by dim figures, afloat on a sea of whispering voices, gradually flowed into his awareness.

The contours of his apartment—his bed, his television set, his kitchen nook—slowly swam out of the darkness surrounding him. He was on the sofa; he must have fallen asleep drinking again. But the familiar space seemed changed, depthless, alive with shadows that shifted on the fringes. The very air in the small apartment felt altered by the presence of something unseen. A visitation that he couldn't conceive of, but that was aware of him, eager with anticipation.

A door closed, or he had the impression of one closing. Bluish light seeped from under the laptop lid as though a fire smoldered inside the machine. Through the disorientation that followed his waking, a noise intruded, emanating from the walls: floorboards being laid down, panels sliding in runners, heavy objects dragged across protesting floors. It was the same commotion, his befuddled mind realized, that he had heard in Robert Callaway's living room. The clamor of the world being rearranged, of the hidden clockwork of the universe reversing or grinding to a halt.

The band of light from the laptop grew brighter, wider, like the lid was being raised from beneath. Don had a brief but terrifying vision of a vague head, composed of fluttering pieces of darkness, rearing in the air of the room, turning and twitching blindly as if trying to sniff him out. He knew he should get up and turn the computer off, but his body, sluggish and thrumming with fear, refused to respond.

Now the disturbance in the walls was loud enough for him to discern individual sounds. Voices shouted at one another, muffled by distance or barriers, incomprehensible. The light edged around the furniture, revealed the planes and angles of the room, guidelines that connected him to the waking world.

Don struggled up against the weight of a great invisible hand squeezing his throat. A man was standing at the end of the sofa, facing away from him toward the window. Narrow-shouldered and of medium height, a sparse bristle of sandy hair covering his round head. His outline was fuzzy, distorted, like a TV signal fading in and out through static. Don couldn't see the unwelcome visitor's face, but he knew, with that strange certainty bestowed by dreams, that the figure was that of the man whose lost work he was searching for. Victor Hudson had somehow found his way back into the world, into Don's apartment.

Paralyzed by panic, he could neither speak nor move. Time stretched like taffy. The intruder perched on the side of the sofa, unmoving. Terrifying as the apparition was, there was no aura of menace around it: only a flood of abject sadness, the shoulders slumped, the head bowed forward. Unaware of Don's presence, or unwilling to acknowledge it, the man kept staring at the window, as in expectation of someone—or something—coming through.

The whispers multiplied in Don's head, fluttering around like bats and crowding out all rational thought. This couldn't be real; yet it didn't feel like a dream either. Perhaps there was no reality, only a series of hallucinations nested inside one another like interlocking rooms. Could he ever wake up from them—*did he want to*?

Don started awake, his cry dying to a whimper.

There was no figure on the end of the sofa. Watery sunlight shone through the cracks in the window blinds and outlined the pile of clothes carelessly thrown over the back of his chair.

He rose on stiff, unsteady legs, and turned on every light in the apartment, restoring the space to its normal dimensions, chasing the last remnants of shadow from the corners. Feeling foolish, he grabbed the biggest knife from his kitchen drawer and knelt down to check under the sofa, then the bed. Nothing but an ancient takeout box down there, a single sock of indeterminate color gathering clumps of dust. The door was locked, the windows closed and latched. Not that anyone would seriously consider scaling five floors up the sheer face of an apartment building.

There was no way he was going back to bed.

He contemplated the vodka in the freezer and decided to check his email instead. His sixth sense, or whatever it was, had not come up short. Buried in the deluge of junk mail, somewhere between a gutter cleaning ad and a promo for erectile dysfunction pills, was a message from J. C. Latham.

Greetings Don Ruby!

I must express my profound gratitude, Sir, for the sample chapters you submitted earlier. Excellent work—but then again, I expected nothing less. The Editor assigned to your project is in full concurrence. He did make a note of some of the metaphors you used. I believe he used the term "campy". But his preferences are a trifle old-fashioned, and your style fits the overall tone of the book, so we're keeping them in, camp be damned.

Such trifling quibbles aside, we are in complete agreement about the quality of your work. It is the best we have seen so far, and we feel affirmed in our choice. Attached please find a handful of gentle suggestions, yours to accept or discard as you see fit.

On a related note, rumors have surfaced that a copy of your Lost Film—I shudder to use its full name—is being sold on one of those ghastly auction websites. Albeit far from our usual bailiwick, we understand that such rumors have been falsely circulated in the past, with the sole purpose of fleecing the credulous. However, should you find a credible lead on this enlightening artefact, please take all the necessary measures to secure it for your research. The coffers of Occultation Press, modest as they are, shall be placed at your disposal without reserve.

Yours. truly,
J. C. Latham

Unreality crept over him again, as if the message was a continuation of his earlier dream. He was torn between the desire to open the attached file, to check his account for the email he had no recollection of sending, and the equally compelling urge to flee his apartment, wander the streets like a madman until the world made some sense again.

There could be no other explanation. He had to have sent the chapters to Latham and then forgotten about it. But what if there was another answer, both more prosaic and more sinister?

Don's eyes traveled around the room, searching for a detail out of place, for any trace of disturbance. It wouldn't take much to break into the apartment. The building was a dump with no security to speak of, the front door lock so flimsy it would give with the least amount of force. Why go through the trouble? Nothing here was worth stealing, and if someone wanted to play games with him, there were easier ways.

Could they be after the notebook? It was in his desk drawer, right where he'd left it. Don took several deep breaths until he felt more in control. Crazy thoughts. He was thinking crazy thoughts. There was a way to prove his sanity was intact, to ground himself in reality. He found his manuscript and opened the copy edits. If he had to compare the two files line-by-line to make sure they were the same, he would do it.

At least, he intended to, until the text began to blur. The letters swam before his eyes, inducing a mild nausea, like reading in a moving car. He blinked, but they refused to stay still. They squirmed and changed, became incomprehensible but not without meaning, symbols in a language never spoken by humans.

Don looked away from the screen and rubbed his eyes. When he returned to it, the words had resumed their orderly march down the page. Yet the text felt different, changed in some fundamental but indefinable way. Paranoid or not, he couldn't shake the impression that the stillness of the letters was a ruse, an illusion carefully crafted for his benefit.

It dawned on him that he had overlooked the most obvious explanation. What if there was no break-in, no trick being played on him, but some sort of virus—a piece of code scrambling and changing his sentences? Sending them from the page into his head, erasing and rewriting his memories as it rewrote the manuscript, over and over?

He had no idea why he'd thought that last part, but there was a way to find out if he was right about the virus. Bad experience had taught him to back up his work on a thumb drive. Everything he'd written earlier would be saved and time-stamped.

Trying to still the shaking of his hands, he fumbled through the drawer, found the drive and inserted it into its port. Finally, he would have evidence of the manipulation, but was he ready for what he was about to discover? Of course he was; it was crazy to think otherwise, crazy to let his thoughts stray in that direction.

Never before had a document taken so long to open. No wonder, when he'd clicked on an expired shortcut. Don's jaw ached from grinding his teeth as the program ran through its shutdown sequence and stalled halfway, the window fading into the background. The icons seemed to chase one another across the screen; the names echoed in his head, alien and meaningless. He stared at them so hard his eyes began to burn. Were they conspiring to confound him?

No, for there was the file he'd saved the day before, using his usual naming convention. Title-date-version number. The window opened, expanded. He was halfway through the first paragraph, comparing it to the edited chapter, when the writing dissolved into black and white pixels. The screen flashed blue, then went black. His reflection stared back at him from the dead blankness, framed by the rectangle of the window—the expression of a trapped, terrified ape, his teeth bared, a frustrated howl building behind them like steam.

Chapter 10

When Don glanced down the street, he saw the man still there, standing on the sidewalk in front of a coffee shop. Tall, stooped, dressed in a motley assortment of rags. Just another footman in the city's ever-swelling army of homeless, ignored by pedestrians and skirted by the early morning traffic. His face was a dark smudge further obscured by a hood or hat of some sort jammed low on his head. Even though he was too far to tell which way the man's eyes were looking, Don felt a jolt of intense, unpleasant scrutiny. A cold comprehension wormed from the back of his mind; he'd seen the figure before. Perhaps he hadn't registered it consciously but on a more visceral level, a repeating motif in the pattern of dirty wet streets, following him around.

They faced off across the distance, surrounded by movement and noise but also isolated from it. The din of traffic faded into the background as Don contemplated his options, a sinking feeling in the pit of his stomach.

***

After his laptop had crashed, he'd wasted no time taking it to a repair outlet near Temple University. Desperately running through his options, trying to figure out how much of the book could be recovered. The chapters he'd emailed to his publisher were safe, but there were several pages of Victor

Hudson notes on the infected thumb drive. It didn't look hopeful, and his heart sank further when the bearded, indifferent shop attendant brought the defunct machine out of the back room, setting it down on the counter with a crack that made Don wince.

"Looks like a virus," the nerd said, sounding almost gleeful. "Fried your central processing unit and the fan couldn't handle it. It's an old computer. Pretty sure the fan was already on its last legs." His face was alight with malicious mirth, implying he'd seen it all before; the middle-aged perv surfing illicit porn sites, too cheap to fork out the cash for a half-decent antivirus program. "Did you open any weird email attachments? Visit some funny sites? Customers bring 'em in like this all the time. They click a link, download a file, and that's all she wrote. Can't do much after the fact."

"Can you recover the files?"

The attendant shook his head emphatically. "Sorry. Store policy. We don't want to get sued if your, uh, private documents are leaked online later. But it wouldn't be possible anyway," he hurried to add, seeing Don's expression. "Not in your case. The motherboard's burned out. As in, literally. Not a figure of speech. I haven't seen anything like it in a long time."

***

Don was still digesting that piece of news when he noticed his pursuer. Again, he experienced the odd displacement, as if a void had opened up beneath the known world. Blood sang in his ears, the noise of traffic softening to a distant hum. The bum hadn't moved from his position on the corner. Maybe he wasn't really there, just another phantom like the one Don had dreamed up in his apartment. But no. Passersby diverted their steps to avoid the figure, either instinctively or out of disgust. Still the man stood there, rendered invisible, nonexistent, by his difference from the crowd. A solitary pillar in the rush of movement and vitality around him.

A bright burst of anger cleared Don's mind, burned off the haze of indecision. At least this was a tangible problem, one that didn't feel like the product of alcohol and lack of sleep and a mind veering further and further out of its tracks. The events of the past few days, the bizarre interview with Robert Callaway, had shaken his confidence in reality, made him suspect there could be something unearthly, or supernatural, about the manifestations and strange dreams haunting his nights. Perhaps he was getting too close to the subject matter, he thought with bitter humor. Just like he'd gotten a little too close to the rockstar lifestyle, to the booze and the drugs, writing that fateful earlier book. But this was something he could get his hands on. Useless laptop gripped under one arm, he headed toward the figure, eager for a confrontation.

It was hard to keep his gaze on his target, the bum's slouched frame and vague face appearing and disappearing between the pedestrians. Even so, he had the impression the watcher had guessed his intent and raised his chin as if squaring off for a fight. Don's step falter at the prospect of violence. What if the man was armed, or insane, or worse yet, if he had followed him to provoke a scuffle? But it was broad daylight; the street was full of people, and the crowd gave Don fresh confidence. Mistaken or not, he was anxious to dispel the tingle at the base of his spine, the lurking suspicion that he was out of his element here, that reason alone couldn't account for the recent occurrences. Buoyed by his anger, he pushed through the swarm on the sidewalk, closer and closer to the figure on the corner. Its dark outline, crooked and stooped over, marked his thoughts like a stain.

A cyclist weaved through the throng, eliciting shouts and curses, a middle finger raised in response. A car honked at a bag lady pushing an overloaded shopping cart across the street. Distracted, Don looked away for a moment. The sidewalk seemed to retreat from him, to move under his feet like a treadmill. When he sought the watcher's face, someone's elbow clipped him and a gruff voice warned him to watch where he was going. A sweep of vertigo made him reach out for the wall to steady himself. The air in his lungs felt thin and he was suddenly struggling to hold himself upright.

Something turned in the depths of the glass, like a carp breaching the surface, something quick and composed of tattered darkness. Slipped beyond the edge of the café window, leaving behind the faces of the patrons on the other side, watching Don with expressions of mixed revulsion and fear. Like a man in a dream, he shook his head, raised his eyes to the street corner.

His watcher had disappeared.

Don craned his neck over the shuffling bodies, over the vehicles clogging the street, looking in both directions. The man was nowhere to be seen. Either he'd gone around the corner or stepped into the crowd.

Chapter 11

Crouched over the library computer, a stack of books by his elbow, Don chewed a pencil stub and tried to concentrate on his reading.

Victor Hudson's terse Wikipedia article had been edited since he'd last visited the page. So, there were others. Hudson's fans or collectors who would not let the director be forgotten. One of the footnotes led to a 1988 interview, which in turn linked to a longer entry on Hermeneutics and the occult societies that flourished in the last few centuries. The Process Church, the Temple of the Golden Dawn, the Fraternity of the Hidden Light. Hudson had nurtured an interest in the esoteric, hardly unusual among those of an artistic bent. Jimmy Page had once owned Boleskine House, where Aleister Crowley, the Great Beast, used to conduct rituals.

Don followed the breadcrumb trail of blog posts and forum comments to a chatroom called *Antipodes of the Mind*, long disused but archived on the Wayback Machine. Victor Hudson's name and references to his movies appeared in connection to a society for astral research calling itself the Order of Astral Enlightenment. There was some disagreement on whether Hudson was a sympathizer of the Order, one of the founders, or had simply used some of the society's teachings as inspiration for his own work. When the thread deteriorated into insults and name-calling, Don tried his luck with this new line of inquiry but hit a blank. The Order of Astral Enlightenment seemed to have ceased to exist by the end of the century, although some of the comments from alleged members were dated almost a decade later.

A loose association of spiritualists with no discernible central teaching, the Order had attracted a well-heeled crowd and steered clear of any major scandal. Online newspaper archives turned up nothing in the way of useful information. He tried the library's occultism and parapsychology sections but fared no better. Unlike other celebrity-backed cults, the Order seemed to have kept a low profile, its members careful to guard their secrets.

He stretched his arms overhead and yawned. Callaway had spoken about the shadow financiers who had backed *The Unveiling*. Did the Order of Astral Enlightenment fund the movie, only to fall out with Hudson at the very end and pull it from distribution? There was also the fire in the studio warehouse, which Callaway had hinted may not have been entirely accidental. Or was Don reading too much into it?

He pushed himself away from the computer, the wooden legs making a scraping noise on the floor loud in the silence, drawing a mumbled rebuke from the man seated in the adjacent cubicle. At least the silhouette looked like a man, bulging shoulders and a head barely visible above the partition, sinking lower the more Don tried to discern its features. The sunlight blazing through the tall library window failed to bring the face into sharper focus. Don picked up his pen and notebook and hurried over to the counter, where an elderly librarian accepted the reference books with a moue of distaste she didn't bother to conceal.

"Find everything you need for your research?" she asked, her pronunciation of the last word leaving no doubt what she thought about Don's interests.

"I thought there would be more in here."

The librarian tilted her face up instinctively, then let her professionally helpful look slip away as her eyes returned to the stack of books. Arthur

Goldwag's *Cults, Conspiracies, and Secret Societies* might not have raised an eyebrow, but *Ego Dismembered*, a study on the psychology of slashers, and *Through Inverted Eyes*, purporting to be the definitive guide to found-footage film, were a different proposition. "Perhaps this isn't the right place for a scholar of your, eh, sensibilities. The internet may be a better source. There's something for everyone's taste online. If taste is the appropriate term."

"Very true." Don angled himself to get a better look at the mumbler in the cubicle, but from the counter it looked empty. Could its occupant have left so stealthily? "Fortunately, it's a broad enough field to allow for different perspectives. No self-appointed gatekeepers to please, if you see what I mean."

The woman bared her dentures. Don's last remark had drawn blood. "There are those of us who believe that gates exist for a reason. Much easier to keep the trash out with the door closed."

"Not a fan of horror, I take it."

"On the contrary. Done well, it's just as much literature as anything else." She took her time stacking the books on her trolley, thin shoulders working up and down under a threadbare sweater. Don thought he caught a flicker of movement in the darkness between the shelves, but it was just the sunlight faltering as a shadow, probably a cloud crossing the sky outside. "M. R. James, or Le Fanu, to start with. Shirley Jackson is peerless, and Stephen King's early works are masterpieces. I'm partial to Gerald Chambers myself. But most of what came later should never have seen the light of day. Especially the movies." She waved a dismissive hand at the DVD section. "We have whole shelves of them in there. Why anyone would waste time and money making such trash, let alone watching it, is beyond me."

"Anything by Victor Hudson? The director?"

"Doesn't ring a bell." The librarian sighed, tapped the keys of an ancient computer terminal. Her demeanor had changed. All of a sudden Don was an ally, someone dependent on her expertise. "Can't help you there. His name is referenced in some of our books, but you seem to have gone through those already."

"How about the Order of Astral Enlightenment?"

Perhaps it was the light again, but a sly look seemed to creep into the librarian's crinkled eyes. "Oh, that's another matter. Another matter entirely. We have a robust section on occultism." A liver-spotted hand pointed at the rows of shelves. "You should be able to find a good deal of information on the Order. Parapsychology is a popular topic these days. Especially with college students." Her tone indicated that college students ranked only slightly above horror fans, in her opinion.

"I looked already. There wasn't much."

"Perhaps they're checked out." The librarian's face darkened. "Or destroyed. There was an incident a couple of weeks ago. I came in to find one whole shelf on the floor. Covers damaged, pages torn out. Like wild animals had been at them." She peered through her thick bifocals, not at Don, but at something over his shoulder. "Come to think of it, all the books were from that section. Occultism and history."

"Any idea who might have done it?"

"Students on a dare, or maybe the homeless. The library is a refuge for the destitute, especially once the weather starts getting colder. It's warm during the day, and the bathrooms are open to everyone." She wrinkled her nose. "The city should do something about them, if you ask me. There are more and more of them by the day, it seems."

Don felt a weakness in his legs, a numb sensation that spread up into his stomach. "Did they break in?"

The librarian shook her head. "All the doors were locked. I checked them myself. But that won't keep anyone out. We can barely afford to pay the bills here, what with the budget cuts and all." She scoffed, her voice rife with indignation. "The police said it was probably rats. Rats! Can you imagine? It's a shame what's happening to this city. In my day, you didn't worry about people vandalizing libraries or about getting murdered in the street."

Her keen expression faltered, seemed to subside into itself. "Let me know if there's anything specific you're looking for," she said. "If we don't have it, I can get it for you through interlibrary loan. It takes a few days but doesn't cost much."

Don thanked her and made his way over to the Occultism section; less out of hope he'd find something he had overlooked than to escape a barrage of glares from the seated readers. One of them, a skinny girl dressed in all black, watched him with open hostility until the shelves hid her from view.

Shadows enfolded him, the daylight failing to reach between the rows, the weak bulbs overhead offering scant illumination. Shelves, walls, a cart stacked with returns. They created an impression of movement without moving, as if the room was subtly rearranging itself, sealing him off in a new, hidden dimension. The smell of dust and old books rose into his nostrils as he navigated between the rows, plucking titles by the spine, skimming through indices and tables of content. But his mind wasn't really in it. Words passed before his eyes without registering, a narrative beyond comprehension. His time would be better spent writing or trying to track down a copy of *The Unveiling*. He felt his control over the story slipping, the lost movie taking over the narrative against his intentions. No one person, save for Hudson himself, had seen the film in its entirety, only pieces that hinted at the whole without giving it away. What secrets had the director hidden within? Or had he been afraid of what the frames would reveal?

Slowly, almost against his will, Don became aware that he wasn't alone in the section. Someone was standing on the other side of the shelves, farther down the aisle; movement glimpsed between the books, the old floor creaking faintly as weight was shifted from one foot to the other. Only the silence had made it possible for him to notice it. He held his breath and waited. The sound did not repeat itself, but the impression of occupancy became stronger.

It had to be the goth kids in the reading area, messing with him. All Don had to do was to remove a volume or two from the bookcase and he would turn the tables on them, but he felt reluctant to do so, suddenly uneasy at the thought of coming face-to-face with the culprit. Maybe he would move the books and see another space there, a corridor receding into an impossible distance or a room that hadn't been there moments ago, inviting him to look in. Or, worse yet, a puddle of a face with black holes for eyes, studying him with interest; his midnight visitor coming to introduce himself, to show Don what awaited in the beyond.

"Who's there?" he said, more to affirm his hold on reality than out of any desire to know. His voice came out warped, as if he were speaking underwater. Either one of the readers uttered a rebuke, or the librarian had requested silence. Surely, he couldn't have heard a word spoken in a tone so dim and garbled it could barely be called a response. And yet... *Here*, it seemed to say, or *you*.

Ignoring the protests of the other patrons, Don rushed to the end of the aisle, peering around the shelf. A shadow, or the hint of a ragged figure, was stepping behind a corner at the far end. Whoever it was, they wouldn't escape him now. He doubled back quickly, colliding painfully with the cart, scattering books everywhere.

There was no one on the far side of the row when he reached it. He searched the wall for a door, or even an open window. They couldn't have gotten past him, not without making a sound or vanishing into thin air.

He jumped as the voice whispered in his ear, saw no one when he turned round. Sharp footsteps echoed across the floor, heading his way. Don raced to meet them and almost knocked over the old librarian, who flinched away from him, banging her elbow on a shelf.

"This is unacceptable!" Her small, wrinkled face was red with anger. She straightened her skirt, squared all five feet of herself against Don. "Our patrons are complaining. If you can't stop making noise, I'm going to have to ask you to leave."

With great effort, Don managed to string together a few sentences about someone muttering behind the shelves. "You had to have seen him run out," he said, realizing how desperate he sounded. "Talk about making a racket. He tramped right into the reading area."

Her expression was at once malicious and condescending. "No one came into this section after you. Not that I've seen. There's nowhere for anyone to hide." She stared up at him, as though daring him to speak and make an even bigger fool of himself.

Rather than give her the satisfaction, Don walked past her, down the steps while glancing back over his shoulder. He hoped that he was mistaken, that his nerves had gotten the best of him. That he wouldn't catch a glimpse of the watcher's face, following him from dark corners.

A gray, freezing drizzle filtered down, the gutters and sidewalks agleam with mirrors. Ghost shapes passed by and disappeared into the blur. Soaked and cold, Don shielded his eyes and looked up and down the street, unsure what he was expecting to see. Almost as an afterthought, he noticed he was shaky and tired, as if he'd run sprints up and down the library steps.

A derelict faced him from a dry nook across the street, shouting and grimacing, his voice lost in the noise of rain and the hiss of wet tires on asphalt. Not his watcher. This one was portly and wheelchair-bound, legs wrapped in layers of filthy blankets. Head turned up in defiance of the gods and the elements, hurling voiceless imprecations at an indifferent heaven. Two teenage girls in plastic slickers glanced up at Don, broke off mid-giggle, and hurried past him, their black shoes slapping a quick rhythm against the pavement.

Don stood in the street for a while, shivering and wet, waiting for the world to return to him, trying to understand where it had disappeared to.

Chapter 12

They wouldn't find him if he stayed quiet, if he could command his traitorous heart to silence, his gasping lungs not to struggle for breath. He could hear them out there, scuttling across the boards, long nails scratching at the walls. Looking for *him*. As long as he didn't leave this comforting darkness, snug in his hiding hole, he would be safe. No foul miasmic breath would fall upon him, no merciless hands would seize him by the soft meat of his neck and drag him out kicking and screaming onto the dusty floor of the stage, into the glare of burning lights to join the others. The lost ones above. Those who staggered under the curtains and mumbled snatches of half-remembered dialogue, enacting fragments of lives long forgotten, trapped in a nightmare of their own making.

They wouldn't find him if he stayed quiet.

But what if the walls kept moving away; gliding on unseen casters, conspiring to expose him, to draw the attention of the quick, hunched thing rooting around in the shadows, that was now rising on its haunches, unfurling its ragged form?

Don woke up in his bed, a breathless whimper on his lips.

He had wept in his sleep, dried tears cracking in the stubble of his cheeks. Thoughts rattled like dice in the vacant hollow of his skull.

A sound had insinuated itself into the void between dream and wakefulness, soft but insistent. He recognized the ringtone of his phone, muffled and distant. Slowly, he stood up and waited for the room to steady itself around him, to cease its sickening lurch.

Memory returned to him with the sight of the empty vodka bottle by the desk, a cereal bowl overflowing with cigarette butts. His throat and lungs felt raw, as if he'd been screaming. Probably just the smoke. Scrawled pages lay scattered on his desk, around the rental laptop. He'd been writing again last night, another frenzied, booze-fueled session. But he couldn't quite remember what he'd written. Something to do with surrealism in low-budget horror, a tie-in between Victor Hudson's early efforts and his better-known work. Beyond that lay a featureless blank.

By the time he found the phone, buried under a heap of clothing, it had gone silent. A restricted number, most likely a telemarketer with an automated string of voice samples offering payday loans or car insurance. Don leafed through the handwritten pages, trying to find the thread of last night's story as he tore open an instant coffee packet and chewed on the contents.

The apartment stank: stale cigarette smoke, unwashed clothes, his own body odor—rank and animalistic. A mostly full carton of fried noodles moldered away in the sink. He vaguely recalled ordering it days ago and giving up after a few bites. Could it have been that long since he'd eaten? It didn't seem like enough to keep him alive, and he'd definitely lost weight, but he was feeling pretty good. Better than he'd felt in years. Under the haze of hangover, his mind was clear and focused, his body thrumming with energy like a live wire.

Maybe the Beatniks had it right all along. Maybe alcohol and cigarettes were ambrosia for the creative spirit. The book he'd set out to write was more or less writing itself. Just wait till he got his hands on some acid or Benzedrine. Don laughed and his laughter sounded strong, healthy. How long had he gone without feeling confident about anything, without seeing a way out? This was different. He fired up the computer and started going over the manuscript.

It was all there, intact. Don washed down the instant coffee with a swig of water from a dirty mug, heartened by last night's efforts. Concise, compelling, vivid on the page; like the movies he was writing about, but without the over-the-top parts. In the reasonable light of the morning, sunlight pushing its way into the tomblike reaches of his apartment, the dread and confusion of the past several days seemed laughable, chimeras of a delusive imagination.

He cast a guilty eye at the empty bottle and the makeshift ashtray. Some of his less pleasant habits would have to go, he supposed, and those that had made an unexpected comeback would have to be curbed once again. A new leaf, a new project, a new man. He wasn't even forty-five yet; there was plenty of time to reinvent himself. Nothing appealed to the American public more than a redemption story, the deceiver somber and repentant, determined to make a fresh start. Don sighed over the clutter on his desk. Better put things in order before he got booked on Oprah.

A buzzing at his elbow brought him back to full wakefulness. It was only his phone, announcing a new summons. Another restricted number. Probably the same tele-stalker, hellbent on chasing down that elusive commission. So clear was the picture in his head that he spoke a moment before he'd brought the phone up to his ear. "Whatever it is you're selling, I'm not buying."

A woman's laugh, startled, slightly embarrassed. "Ouch. So much for my irresistible charms. The least you could do is let a girl down easy."

Don gaped at the phone, stunned. It wasn't a restricted number, merely an unfamiliar one with a Chicago area code. As he struggled for something to say, Jessica chuckled. "Bad time? Sorry, I should've texted first. Call me when you get out of bed."

"No." Don tried to regain a sense of balance. "I mean, yes. I mean, I'm up already. Not a bad time." How long had it been since they'd last talked? Not since the truth about *Ashes* had come to light. The fallout from that fiasco had dealt a blow to her budding career. One that she seemed to have recovered from—her name was a fixture in articles and writers' yearbooks, not that Don was stalking her—but probably not enough to want to reconnect. Had four years really passed? "It's just a bit of a surprise, that's all. It's been a while."

A sound somewhere between a groan and a sigh. He could picture Jess rolling her eyes in that half-amused, half-exasperated way she had. "Vintage Don Ruby. As evasive as ever. Never commit to anything, never give it away. Am I going to have to pull the big news out of you?"

"Didn't realize there were any."

"Neither did I until someone called me at two in the morning. Left that cryptic message on my voicemail. Remember?" She still sounded jovial, but a faint edge had come into her voice. "You haven't changed your mind about telling me, have you?"

Don racked his brain frantically. Where the memory should have been was only static. "I wasn't sure you wanted to hear from me," he said, a desperate bid for time. With sudden, overpowering intensity, he needed her voice, *needed* to keep talking to her. He was terrified of her hanging up and leaving him stranded with nothing but his uncertain thoughts for company. "I felt that I might have gotten carried away. Not about telling you. Never that. But that I'd gone too far. Overstepped my bounds."

"What do you mean?"

"You know what I mean." He closed his eyes, took a deep breath. In the past, he would have tried to steer the conversation away from the shoals of unpleasant topics. He'd gotten quite good at it: keep smiling, distract with a witty remark, effortlessly change course. But he was no longer than man, and the mask felt out of place now, a false persona he didn't want to be associated with. "The way things ended between us. Or rather, how I ended things. I wasn't exactly your favorite person for a while. I wouldn't blame you if you never spoke to me again."

Jess let the silence stretch out until it was almost unbearable. "I thought you sounded strange," she finally said. "Like someone else speaking in your voice. I'm not going to lie to you, Ruby. What you did to me, it hurt. Both emotionally and financially. I stuck by you because I refused to believe you'd do such a thing. Then I hated you. I hated you for a long time."

"You had every right to."

"Let me finish." Her image appeared in his mind as if she were standing before him. The firm set of her jaw and eyes, what he had more than once called her angry teacher face, disapproving but kind. At that moment he felt a rush of emotion for her. Not love exactly, and not lust, just the desire to pour his heart out to her, to hear her tell him what to do. "It's cost me a lot of effort, and not an insubstantial amount in therapist fees. But I'm getting over it. At least, I'd like to think I am. Coming to terms with my past. That's what my therapist says, and she's paid way too much to be wrong."

Don smiled, in spite of himself. "Wouldn't want to do that. Think of how traumatic it would be for her."

"Good." She shifted her tone from guarded to reserved friendliness. "Now that that's out of the way, can we get to the point and talk about this book deal you've got in the works?"

He told her about the book, leaving out the details. No mention of the blackout episodes or of the strange sightings in the streets. "There could be more to come," he said, rinsing his cup in the sink. "The editor wants a whole series of retrospectives. Artists who remained largely unknown but developed a cult following." He stopped himself, realizing that he was repeating Kebbler's exact words. *It could be a way back. For me, for both of us.* Whatever link had been reestablished between them, it was too tenuous to hold a statement of such weight.

"Hopefully you've run the contract past your agent."

"Sure. My agent and my tax accountant, as well as my personal trainer and private chef."

"*Don.*"

"Jess. I'm not exactly what you'd call a hot commodity right now. Most months I'm stacking shelves at Safeway to make rent." He heard an intake of breath, hurried to cut her off. "I'm not trying to make you feel sorry for me, but I've got to take what's on the table. This is all I've got going right now."

"Are you drinking again?"

Don paused, the lip of a fresh bottle poised over the rim of his cup. He swore inwardly, cradled the phone between his face and shoulder to screw the cap back on. Hoped she hadn't heard the telltale clink. "Nope. Dry as a bone. Dusty like the Sahara. I'm a changed man."

"Is that what this call is about?"

"No." *I don't know*, he wanted to say. It made no sense at all to call Jess. It made all the sense in the world. "I guess—I dunno, I just wanted to share the news with someone. See what they make of it."

"What's the publisher's name again?" She was all business now, no time for reminiscing. He dictated the name to her, heard the clicking of keys. "Can't say that I've heard of them, but horror isn't really my thing. I'll call up a few people, check the press and the editor. I've got contacts."

"Business picking up?"

"I'm doing well enough." Her tone took on a colder inflection. "Ruby, I need to think this through. Okay? This is all very sudden. Don't expect things between us to go back to how they were in the old days. *Definitely* not to how they were in the old-old days. But I'll do my best. Am I making sense?"

"Perfect sense. This is already more than I deserve."

"Cool it with the self-recriminations, Ruby." He heard the faint tapping of a pen against teeth, a sign that she was intrigued. "Give me a couple of days. Oh, and send me the contract for a quick once-over. The outline, too. I'll give you honest advice; take it or leave it. That sound all right?"

"Sounds great," Don said, which had to be the understatement of the year. "We haven't discussed commission, but fifteen percent would not be out of the question."

"Just as I was thinking that I might consider liking you again. You can send the stuff to my old email address. Talk to you soon."

He held the phone for a few moments after the line had gone dead. Allowed himself to think about what might have been and what couldn't be. Yet, the memory of the dream kept intruding, jabbing painfully into his mind, a splinter under a fingernail. To prevent it from working itself deeper, he picked up last night's notes and went back to work.

Karen Lombard. The name appeared at the top of the last page, thickly underlined. Callaway had mentioned her; the leading lady in *The Unveiling* who had suffered a nervous breakdown on set. As with Hudson and Taylor, her career had stalled in the mid-nineties. Unlike the other two, Lombard had seen the writing on the wall, gotten out of the movie business, and married an insurance executive. Online sleuthing didn't reveal an address, but her phone number was listed—although under Noreen Schlegel, her pre-Hollywood name. The area code suggested Monterey or Santa Cruz.

Don considered this. California would be sunny this time of year, or any time of year. Even if Karen Lombard didn't give him the time of day, he could spend a couple of days on the beach, working on both his book and his tan. If the airline gods smiled upon him, he'd be there and back before the end of the week. An expense account made all the difference; J. C. Latham would be happy to cover the cost.

Everything was starting to come together. He didn't have the whole story yet, but he could glimpse how the pieces were connected and could follow the leads to the end. It was about more than just turning in the manuscript for publication, he realized. More than seeing his name in print again. Typing the first draft, straightening out wayward sentences; he had crossed the threshold that separated the author from the reader, becoming absorbed by the work.

The story had him now, and he needed to know how it ended. All other concerns—the contract, the money, the opportunity to work—had taken a back seat. What mattered was immersing himself in the tale unfolding around him, becoming a protagonist, a living part of it. Letting the story write itself from the inside out.

Chapter 13

"I don't entertain much." Karen Lombard ushered Don into a wide, shadowy foyer. She made a loose gesture, trailing cigarette smoke. "I suppose that's obvious. Pretty big house for little ole me, and I had to let go of the help. You'll forgive the mess?"

"It's a beautiful house, Mrs. Lombard." Jetlagged and exhausted, Don allowed himself to be led into the big Victorian home, which squatted like a grim and abandoned temple in the foothills above Santa Cruz. It wasn't completely untrue. Taken on its own, each of the house's features was well-designed, a memento of better times. It was only when the eye took them in all together that the neglect and decay became apparent, the dingy furnishings and watermarked walls adding up to an atmosphere of gradual but irreversible decline. Dwindling light seemed more to obscure than illuminate the interior. With its scuffed floors and banisters and patches of off-white plaster under a murky ceiling, the place seemed to aspire to faded grandeur without quite pulling it off.

Karen Lombard—Noreen Schlegel—chuckled. Over the red coal of her cigarette, crinkled eyes watched Don with an almost preternatural sharpness. "Might as well cut the crap, Mr. Ruby. May I call you Don? You're paying me to talk to you, so let's dispense with the pleasantries. This place is a dump, but it's a roof over my head."

After an exhausting two-stop red-eye flight into San Jose International, Don had rented a car and driven down to the address the former actress had dictated to him. "Road's a little hard to follow," she'd told him over the phone, her instructions supplementing a terminally befuddled navigation app. "Phones get confused up here. You'd think it's the Bermuda Triangle. Just keep the ocean to your right and head uphill. Can't miss it."

She'd asked him what paper he worked for and seemed miffed when he told her about his book. "All that was a lifetime ago. My career is deader than any of the snotty bitches I used to play in the movies. But you're welcome to spend your money how you see fit. Early afternoon works best for me. It's easy to get lost up here after dark."

Don could see what she meant. The house lay at the end of a narrow road that skimmed the edge of a ravine, isolated amid scrub and dead yellow grass. Once the sun sank over the ridges, it would be in shadow long before the night arrived with no lights to guide the way down and no guardrails between the blacktop and fifty feet of empty air. The property had been given to Karen by her third husband, a moderately successful real estate developer. Judging by the state of the place, the alimony had dried up a while ago. Rundown but not to the point of looking lived-in; the house turned Don's spirits downwards, made him feel like an intruder in someone else's squalid, lonely life.

Whatever deterioration had taken hold of the house seemed to have stamped itself on its sole resident. In the nineteen-eighties, Karen Lombard had strutted onto the screen and become an instant sex symbol, a sultry, dewy-eyed scream queen. With a heart-shaped, finely structured face, long reddish-brown hair—except for one appearance in *Sorority Slayings*, where it had been dyed an unconvincing blonde—and a body that was somehow both slender and generous of curve in all the right places, she had inflamed the fantasies of an entire generation of slasher fans. Her iconic shower scene from *Taken By Night* was still ranked in the top ten most erotic moments in horror cinema.

The woman scowling at Don from across the entryway was barely recognizable as the hard-bodied, blood-drenched goddess whom Fangoria had once dubbed the Diva of Darkness: thin and shrunken inside a shapeless blouse and pants, overly tanned skin sagging from the exquisite bones of her face like a badly fitted mask. Lips that had once been moistened by a pink tongue and parted in screams had collapsed into the deep grooves around her mouth. Even her eyes, at first glance untouched, shone with cunning and alertness and a calculating malice. Their searing gaze made Don feel diffident and out of place, studied for some unknowable purpose.

He'd found little about Lombard's life after *The Unveiling* and no mention of her collapse during the shoot. For a while, her exploits had taken up the front pages of the gossip tabloids, lurid accounts of wild parties and substance abuse as her star waned, soon relegated to the back shelves. Another casualty in the war of attrition between time and beauty, unlamented and quickly forgotten.

She caught his look and seemed to read the thoughts behind it. A wry smile twisted her mouth, and her eyes grew bright with something akin to alarm. "Did you see anyone on your way up from town?"

"I haven't seen another car in at least half an hour." He had the impression that he'd misinterpreted the question. She looked like she was about to say more but changed her mind.

"Make yourself comfortable," she said, leading the way into a vast and sparsely furnished sitting room. It smelled of dust and disuse and cats, although there were none in evidence. Uncomfortable silence pressed down on the roof and the walls. Karen raised a half-empty glass from the kitchen counter, twirling it until the melting ice clinked. "Get you one of these?"

Don's tongue thickened; the need for a drink was a physical compulsion, an unbearable thirst. He managed to shake his head. "Thank you. I'd better not."

Her look told him she wasn't fooled for a second. She shrugged and refreshed her glass. "Got coffee in the pot, if you'd prefer. Fresh made."

He couldn't smell coffee and didn't want to set foot in the kitchen, which looked at once dingy and sterile with not a dish or cup in sight. "I'm all right, thanks."

"Suit yourself." Karen motioned him to a long sofa abutting an end table. From the elusive birth dates circulating online, Don had estimated her to be in her late fifties. But her slow, careful gait and the stiff clumsiness with which she sat into a faded armchair belonged to a woman twenty years older. It was the hopelessness in her face and eyes, in her stooped carriage; a woman broken and re-broken by loneliness and disappointment and misery until she could no longer remember her original self. There was something else at work as well, sly and fearful at the same time, hollowing her out from within. Maybe this was the reason for the shaded windows and dimmed lights in her desolate home.

But her hands were steady as she lit another cigarette, chased the smoke down with a ladylike sip. "This isn't easy for me," she said, as if the notion had just occurred to her. "I don't get many visitors, and I haven't thought about Victor or that damned movie in a while. I've been trying not to think about it."

"It was a long time ago."

"Not nearly long enough." A harsh, rasping laugh. "I was happy to be done with it, and with the likes of Victor Hudson. It cost me dearly."

"Are you talking about anything specific?"

"Let's not get into that." She favored him with another sharp look. "You said you're writing a book? What is it about?"

Don straightened up, repeated his spiel about low-budget slashers and forgotten artists.

Karen Lombard's face twisted into a sneer. "You mean washouts and losers and has-beens. Like me. Another muckraking piece of garbage about the not-quite-famous."

"It's more than that. There's a revived interest in the industry. In those who made it what it is today."

"Smut." Karen took another drink, gave an angry shake of her head. "Exploitative trash. People like to turn it into a metaphor, give it some meaning it was never intended to have. Social commentary, the suppressed fears of the nation. It's all nonsense. Horror is about seeing people scream and bleed in vivid color. About seeing them destroyed. Blood and guts and testing the limits of what the audience can handle."

"What are the limits?"

"There aren't any." She set her glass on the table and crossed her legs. "All those ghouls and freaks want to see is the beautiful being ruined. They get off on seeing us afraid and slobbering, pleading for our lives. Before we're flayed, beheaded, disemboweled. Then after we're no longer on the screen, they get to see it all over again. Our struggles and failures, our despair. Our second death in the real world. Like a sacrificial ritual. They get to kill us themselves, slowly, one more time."

She squinted at him, her mouth hardening. "Is that what you're after? There isn't much to write about, you know. No lurid piece about drugs and decadence and the long plummet from fame."

"Maybe I'm looking for what happened in the background. For your side of the story."

"There are no sides. I was still in my teens, naive, blinded by the stage lights. I'd taken my clothes off in front of the camera a few times and thought I was the next Jamie Lee Curtis. It went to my head, but I was hardly the only one. Just another young, dumb thing in a town where they grew on trees." She raised her glass in a toast. "Like not-quite-virgins, sacrificed on the altar to propitiate the dark gods of public adoration."

"Wasn't that the plot of one of your movies? The hitchhikers who become involved in a pagan ritual?"

Karen Lombard snorted, almost choking on her drink. "*Where the Summer Ends*. What an abominable piece of dreck that was. Tits and screams and blood, more tits when things got boring. New Line really dropped a deuce there, but the director had an ironclad contract, so they let him run with it."

"It did all right at the box office."

"Made no difference to me." Karen leaned into her seat and let out a booze-tinged sigh. "After that fiasco with Victor, I was done. The studios wouldn't hire him, and anyone who'd worked with him was tainted by association. No more Final Girl roles for me. Twenty-seven and already over the hill." She had been in her mid-thirties, but Don didn't feel like arguing the point. "My agent did his best, but my fifteen minutes of marginal fame were history. Rumors spread quickly, and there were plenty of other nubile young things to take my place."

"Was it because of Victor's film? Because of what happened on set?"

A mask seemed to clamp down over her features. "It wasn't any *one* thing. But the movie sure didn't help. I was going through some personal trouble too. Who told you about the set?"

"Robert Callaway." When the name prompted no reaction, Don flipped through his notes to hide his confusion. "He was, uh, the lead cameraman."

"Doesn't ring a bell. But we had a different cameraman every day." The luster in her eyes, Don could see, was simple drunkenness. Whatever else lived there had retreated, at least for the time being. "Now that you mention it, there was a guy who showed up more often than the others. Some junkie who worshipped Victor. Everyone did back then. He was a mystery, unlike anyone else in the business. Those who understood his work were fanatically loyal." The last two words gave her some difficulty. She flicked her tongue across her lips. "His followers, his little cabal, thought he was a genius. Victor ate it up. He was a vain man, for all the fake sophistication and put-upon accent, the European mystique he hid behind. A weak and self-centered man, perpetually afraid."

"Afraid of what?"

"Of what had followed him here from the old country. What he spent his entire career hiding from. Surrounding himself with illusions, building his grand palace of dreams..." Karen seemed to realize what she'd just said and cast a nervous gaze around. "He infected us with his obsession. His madness. I suppose that's what all cult leaders do. They have a gift for seeing inside your head. Finding that little something that makes you vulnerable, latching onto it, and never letting go. I've spent over twenty years looking over my shoulder because of that man."

"What sort of cult?"

She focused her blurry gaze at him. "You really have no idea what you're after, do you? What Victor's movie was about?"

"I'm hoping you might change that."

She took a huge gulp, winced in discomfort as it went down. "No one among us wanted to be there. Not after the first week and definitely not by the end. Victor really pulled out all the stops. People got upset. Saw things they didn't want to see."

She had to mean the set design, the erratic schedule. Callaway had talked about it obsessively. "I heard there was some sort of trouble."

When Karen Lombard opened her eyes, fear had erased a decade off her face. "We couldn't be sure whether something was happening, or if it was just another one of Victor's tricks. He delighted in them. Called them his illusions of the flesh. 'It's like fire,' he used to say. Feeding the images on screen, retelling ancient stories, making them stronger. Stoking them until they take a life of their own. A worship older than time. Then again, Victor was so full of shit he squeaked. By the time I left, there were precious few to endure his whims. He, himself, had changed. Started having second thoughts."

Don had heard all this already and didn't need to go over it again. He decided to change tracks. "Why did you stay?"

Karen shuddered, finished her drink. "I hated every minute of it. We all did. One of the sets Victor had built for us was just a bunch of connected pipes. Narrow, low ceiling, claustrophobic. He'd have us shoot in there for hours. It felt like days. Crawling around until we were exhausted, recreating some nightmare from Victor's mind. Transcendence. Leaving the physical body behind. Not a day passed without someone breaking down in tears. But at that point, we were all committed. It was to be our big break. None of us had done an art movie before, and Victor had serious money behind him."

Could the room have gotten darker as she spoke? Don looked out the tall window. The sun hadn't moved in the sky, not that he could notice, but the bar of sunlight had retreated across the floor. *It's easy to get lost up here after dark.* His host was speaking again; with some effort, he focused his attention on her words.

"The church was the worst. Black towers, black windows, a door twice the normal size. It was only a shell, of course. But the way Victor shot it, you couldn't really tell. Even when you walked inside and saw the guts of it, the wires and beams, the missing walls, you still felt it around you. Standing in front of it was worse. Shadows moving behind the glass, footsteps walking across nonexistent floors. Sam Brody was the set designer, and he knew his stuff. Used to work in England, for the studio that made those old Dracula movies. He killed himself shortly after filming ended."

"It must have been hard for you," Don said.

"I dealt with it the only way I knew. Took too many pills, all of them different colors. You could practically get them over the counter, and if you couldn't, there were helpful doctors who'd write you a prescription for a nominal fee. Halfway through the shoot, I got a little careless. Had a few too many pills, chased them down with a touch too much liquor. They made it sound like a suicide attempt. Snuck me out to a miracle clinic and covered all the costs. 'Nervous strain,' they said. Overwork. I never saw a need to challenge that version of events. Everybody used back then. It was just how you got through the day."

"Who paid for your stay at the clinic? The studio?"

Karen frowned at him. "There was no studio. No backers. Only those freaks from the cult." She clearly enjoyed his reaction; a nasty yellow smile spread across her face. "I suppose you don't know as much as you think you do. Last Rite Productions was a false front. That's what some of us found out later when we tried to sue for payment. It existed on paper only, plus in a storage unit near Burbank. Just like the money men, the fake execs Victor paraded on set."

"A front for what?"

"Some sort of religious thing. More like a cult, although Victor didn't advertise the fact. They weren't preachy, but they gave me the creeps."

"Can you remember what this organization was called?"

"The order of something or other. Or the brotherhood." A deep divot creased her forehead. She cast her gaze toward the ceiling, from which came a faint scratching, like squirrels in the attic. To Don, she looked like she'd sobered up in an instant. "We never really got to talk to them. Their name wasn't on the movie, or any of the material." Fear flared in her eyes.

When she pretended to focus her attention on Don, he knew that her mind was somewhere else. "Maybe I'm remembering it wrong. I was young, impressionable, easily freaked out. I'll tell you one thing, though. Whoever has the power to make movies disappear, they can do the same with people. I'd stay away from them. If you keep looking, you might end up wishing you hadn't."

"Others must have felt the same way. Kirk Taylor, for one?"

She hid her agitation behind another cigarette. Through the smoke, he felt her suspicious stare linger on him. "Pretty, pretty Kirk Taylor. We had a brief fling on set. Met at a party a few months earlier, made eyes at each other across the room." She pointed her cigarette at Don. "Wasn't really my type, but with someone that good looking, it doesn't matter. It was expected of us, you see. The press would be all over it. Free publicity for the movie."

Like a sacrificial ritual. "Did you see each other after the shoot?"

"It was over after a week or so. Kirk started acting strange. Morose and withdrawn, quite unlike himself. He spent a lot of time with Victor, who worked him mercilessly. On set and off."

Don busied himself with his pad, trying to phrase his next question. "Do you think that Victor—"

"Did I fuck him too? He never seemed interested." She gaped at him then burst into unpleasant laughter. "You mean Kirk and Victor? I wouldn't put it past Kirk, you know. There were always rumors about how he got some of his bigger roles. But sex wasn't Victor's thing. No booze either, and drugs only on rare occasions. Something to do with keeping himself pure. It was a spiritual matter with him, part of his weird mysticism."

"Was he a member of the cult?"

"It was hard to tell with Victor. He wasn't the follower type. Had too high an opinion of himself. But there was a connection." She hesitated, then shrugged her shoulders. "Victor had big plans for Kirk. He introduced him to all his creepy pals. They wanted to make him a star." Smoke swirled around her derisive laugh. "Kirk couldn't get two lines right if his life depended on it. But boy did he look good."

"It didn't work out. They never made another movie together."

"Kirk got cold feet. That was just how he was. Always after the bright, shiny new thing until something brighter and shinier and newer came along. Victor wanted a protégé. Someone loyal, reliable." She glanced at the window and stubbed out her half-smoked cigarette. "This has been wonderful and all, but I think you'd best be going now. Whatever happened with the movie is no business of mine. I've earned the right to live out the rest of my days in peace. Or at least, unbothered."

Don handed her the money, feeling no closer to the truth, with every step he took only opening other, darker avenues. His mind swarmed with a hundred questions, but he only managed to get one out. "The set designer. Brody. You said he killed himself, but not how."

"Family kept it out of the papers." Karen weaved to her feet woozily. When Don reached out to steady her, the hand that grasped his bare elbow was clammy. "He starved to death."

"I don't understand."

"It's better if you don't try to." She walked him to the door. The glassy look was back in its place, a mask shielding her from the world. "He got lost. That's what it was. Please drive carefully. There aren't many lights up here, and the road isn't very good. It's easy to get lost if you don't know where you're headed."

Chapter 14

On a rational level, he knew he was dreaming. That fatigue and confusion had taken their toll—aided by the two Lorazepam he'd washed down with a double bourbon—and transformed the cabin of the 777 into a long corridor suffused by uncertain blue light. Yet, that knowledge made it no easier to break out of his stupor or disperse the feeling that what he was seeing was real. He whimpered and shifted, struggling up from the depths, but the dream held him fast, trapped beneath its surface, incapable of breaking through.

When the voice reached him, he thought it had come from his own mouth. None of the sounds it made could be called words: a garbled jabber, a travesty of human speech. It traveled along the thick stone that had replaced the bulkheads and floor of the plane, accompanied by the tread of wet footsteps. Not a single voice, but a chorus of them. Crying, pleading, wailing that sobbed away into indeterminate laughter.

He turned his head away, as if that would help drown out the voices or keep him from seeing what trudged past his seat, dragging its feet across the slimy stone. Naked and gaunt, pale from their endless trek through this dreadful, abandoned place. Mottled skin and loose flesh on old bones, threadbare heads whose eyes stared unseeing into the light. They waded past him without noticing him or each other; a long column of the damned, each locked tightly inside their own pocket of misery, bent by sorrow and suffering.

Yet something else had taken notice of them. A shape like the shadow of a huge insect scuttled down from the murky ceiling, raised a head hung from an overlong neck. It was agitated, or excited, as if it had sensed something. As if it had sensed *him*.

Torn between the urge to flee and the hope that stillness would render him invisible, Don dug his fingers into the armrests, pressed himself into his uncomfortable seat. Far away, he could hear the creak of plastic, the rumbling of the engine. Echoes of the real world ticking outside this hopeless passage, beyond the regard of its inhabitants and their shadowy tormentor.

Suddenly he was hurled out of the tunnel into a juddering space lit by muted lights. He was being shaken awake, pulled out of the dark fathoms of the dream. Don opened his eyes, heard a pre-recorded voice exhort the passengers to make sure their seatbelts were on.

Never before had he been grateful for turbulence. The plane was high up over the flatlands of the Midwest, screaming across a deep blue sky. It had to be the thrum of the jet engines and the murmuring of the passengers that had invaded his doze, his imagination turning them into the laments of the damned. He couldn't remember the cabin being so unoccupied. His entire row was vacant; only a few slumped forms, brought low by weariness or in-flight alcohol, could be glimpsed further down the aisle, faces indiscernible in the dimness of the cabin.

Don peered over the headrest in front of him. Saw heads crowning the seats, shaking with the motion of the plane. Past the windows, the heavens were shading into purple dusk, the bleary overheads failing to disperse the velvety darkness that crawled along the cabin, swallowing the rows one by one.

Was that a different movement diagonally across the aisle, a shape composed of smoky shadows unfurling segment by prehensile segment?

He was afraid to look, afraid to have his nascent suspicion confirmed. If the occupants of the other seats turned to look at him, what faces would they have?

He breathed through his panic, recounted the events at boarding to stave off another slip into a nightmare, another intrusion into his consciousness. The passenger next to him had been a nondescript, middle-aged man in a bad business suit. They had exchanged a superficial nod, smiles that discouraged further pleasantries, but otherwise Don couldn't bring to mind the man's exact features: the shape of his head, or even the exact color of the suit. Gray or light blue? Now the seat adjacent to his was empty, as were those across the aisle, at least one of which had been occupied by a pretty young girl in a very short skirt.

Had everyone moved seats while he was asleep? But where would they go, shut in a pressurized tube of plastic and steel thirty thousand feet above the ground? On closer inspection, the dim shapes in the cabin merely suggested human form. They writhed and mewled as though in troubled sleep, huddled together and cowering like anxious children. Beyond the windows, utter blackness reigned, absorbing the reflections in the glass.

Don craned his neck forward and squinted into the gloom. His body felt oddly disconnected, his movements not of his own will. When he let go of the armrest, his hand was damp and smelled of unaired fabric. He must not have been paying attention earlier; now he saw the seats were dirty and torn, the headrest covers stained yellow and some spotted with mold. He levered himself upright, casting a look around. The cabin was old, plastic fittings and bulkheads cracked and grimy, and lights dimmed not by design but by age. Even the roar of the engines sounded more like a death rattle, as if something was chewing the machinery from within. He was on a dead plane, filled with corpses, shrieking across sunless skies. Until the last vestige of power left the motors, and it began its terminal plummet down to a hopeless, abandoned earth.

The back of Don's shirt stuck to his body like a wet sail. Instead of escaping the tunnel, he had opened the wrong door and ventured deeper into the nightmare. There was no logic behind this notion, but it didn't need any to root itself into his mind, to spawn like a parasite. When the nearest of the wretched figures whined and made as if to raise its head at him, he lurched down the aisle toward the galley at the end of the cabin.

Another pocket of rough air jolted the plane. Don careened like a drunk, grabbing at the cold, slimy seats for balance, the stench of age and rot enveloping him like a musty blanket before he pushed on. A reek of spoiled food assailed him in the empty galley. The locker doors hung askew, and the few still intact were rusted shut. His feet stuck to the gummy floor. There was movement up ahead in the first-class section. Mouth open, he allowed himself a small breath of relief. Everything would be different in first-class; the airline couldn't get away with treating them like mere mortals in coach. Several passengers had stood up and were stretching between the seats or reaching for the luggage bins. Had the plane landed, or was it about to? It didn't matter, as long as he would soon be safe on the ground.

He had cleared his throat and was about to ask where the flight attendants had gone when the darkness shifted, giving him a better view of the figures standing in the passage. *Specters* was the closest his benumbed mind could come up with, silvery and insubstantial. He could see right through their bodies, he realized, all the way to the red sign above the cockpit door. The motion that the plane was imparting to them resembled terror or extreme distress. They raised their thin arms toward the ceiling, as if groping for some lifeline that was quickly receding from their grasp, their struggles more desperate by the moment, more eerie for the utter absence of sound accompanying them. Ghost imprints on celluloid, lit from within by a pale, flickering blue radiance.

They had sensed an intruder in their midst even though it didn't seem like they could pinpoint his location. Featureless heads turned his way, skeletal hands reaching in his direction as he tried to shrink himself against the bulkhead. If they touched him, he would go insane.

Water gurgled behind him, gushed under the closed door of the lavatory, followed by the stink of raw sewage.

Don turned to retreat but found that his legs had turned to lead. The magician from his dream was advancing down the aisle, slow and unhurried. He wore the same wide-lapel suit, and his slicked-back hair glistened under the overheads. His feet didn't so much touch the sodden carpet as glide across the surface. Smiling, the man held his hand out to Don, beckoning playfully. Around him, the murky interior shuddered with palsied movement in the seats.

Where the light fell on the magician, however, the carefully knitted disguise failed and revealed him to be a flickering outline, a negative image; his suit and hair dazzling white, his hands and face inky black. Whatever humanity he had once contained was gone forever, leached out by the black void he'd crawled out of. In that rudimentary face, Don read only a terrible intent, a relentless desire to do harm, a bestial determination.

I can close my eyes. When I open them, he'll be gone. But he couldn't bring himself to do it; it was too much to take on faith.

Don staggered back, clawing behind him for the lavatory door. The EXIT sign above him cracked, dripping a black, viscous liquid down the sides of the cabin. He felt the wall give, folded himself into the tiny space and flipped the latch with trembling hands.

If he locked himself in, was he cutting off his only way out? There was no time to think about anything other than putting another obstacle between him and the grinning thing in the aisle, buying himself a few precious seconds. He threw himself against the closed door, pushing with all the strength he could muster.

The lavatory shook and tilted, turbulence hitting the plane from all sides. Don knelt in black water that spilled from the faucets and sloshed over the rim of the toilet bowl in a steady tide. He leaned his shoulders against the door, braced his feet against the opposing wall. His last glimpse of the magician's face repeated over and over behind his eyes, something that his mind could only process by couching it in terms it was familiar with.

Fists hammered on the thin partition, the last few budging it out of its frame and offering flashes of what awaited on the other side.

But there was something worse in here, with him. Bubbling and frothing under the outpouring of sewage, filling the air with a stench of cold ashes and wet, burned carpet.

It broke the oily surface in a burst of bubbles, trailing long, viscous ropes, its misshapen head carefully probing this new medium. A tangled knot of burnt film, melted and fused together into a monstrous anatomy, as tall and wide as a man's torso. Somewhere inside the horror, a single eye opened, the color of molten gold; uneven jaws hinged wide to haul in an eager, shuddering breath.

White noise filled Don's head. He hugged himself into a ball and sank into the reeking water.

A blow cracked the door from outside, and an arm in a black tuxedo came through the opening. It swiped at the latch, its shape changing from a manicured hand to a long, gnarled claw, to a smoky phantasm dissolving at the edges, soot flaking from its charred, bubbling fingers. The thing in the water paid it no heed. It was out to its waist now, leaning over him, crackling as its melted reels hardened and cooled.

Which one would get to him first?

Don had the time to ask himself this one last question as the vast face of the celluloid god pressed up against his, its touch intimate like a lover's; as its mouth began to whisper in his ear, a stream of gibberish that burned his brain like blast of arctic wind, and he was swirling down the drain with the water, eddying into pitch blackness.

***

The hand had him by the shoulder and was shaking him roughly. Don whimpered and squeezed his eyes tighter. Felt the seat under him, heard the voice from above. A human voice, calm but concerned.

He opened his eyes. A man in a blue uniform was leaning over him, face only a few inches above Don's own. One of the flight attendants. Asking him if he was all right, if he needed help. There was a hint of anxiety under his polished, professional smile as he tried to decide what to do with the deranged passenger. Don sat up, tried to speak. His throat felt raw.

Heads craned over the seats, gawkers taking in the spectacle. Their derision and resentment hit him like a physical force. The sight of their disembodied faces evoked an unpleasant memory of what Don had seen in his dream. If it had been a dream; it hadn't felt like one at all.

At the front of the cabin, the map graphic showed forty-three minutes to landing in Philadelphia. As he watched, the screen shuddered, distorted into pixels that suggested a lurking shape, faded to a blank blue.

Chapter 15

The growling of his stomach reminded Don to look away from his laptop.

If he'd eaten at all that day—or since his return from California—he couldn't remember when or what. Even the alcohol in his fridge had gone untouched; his sole sustenance had been endless cups of black, bitter coffee. Morning and afternoon had merged seamlessly without him so much as lifting his head from his material. When he finally got up from the uncomfortable chair, his back and neck aching and cramped, he wasn't all that surprised to see it was dark outside.

Another day had slipped by without him noticing. Lately, he'd fallen into a pattern of working himself to exhaustion, catching a few hours of uneasy sleep, then writing again until he could no longer keep his eyes open. Without the punctuation provided by meals, reduced to infrequent basic bodily functions, he had lost all concept of time. He supposed he could track it using a calendar... That felt meaningless to him, something he'd once thought important but had turned out to be insignificant. Finishing the book was the only thing that mattered now, and toward this end he bent all his mental powers.

Coming back from California, the manuscript had been the last thing on his mind. Something was happening to him. The terrifying dreams felt like a prequel to something far more sinister, something he had no way of explaining to himself or of putting up rational barriers against. He was being pursued, targeted by some game or process to which he had unknowingly consented. It sounded insane, the delusions of a paranoid mind, but it was true. The blackouts, the nightmares, the way time that seemed to pass by him all pointed to it.

Even the progress of his work was starting to frighten him. Paragraphs and entire chapters seemed to leap into his head fully formed or appear on the page without passing through his fingers. He'd read about automatic writing; a hackneyed staple of ghost stories where supernatural forces moved the writer's pen, spelling out messages from the other side. But that was absurd. Or was he cracking up, churning out reams of nonsense, like Jack Nicholson's character in *The Shining*, deluding himself into seeing an underlying logic to it? Either possibility made him sick to his stomach.

But there was one explanation that fit the facts. Like Sherlock Holmes, if he eliminated the impossible, he would be left with the improbable. That explanation, improbable but not impossible, involved Jake Kebbler.

Kebbler, who had just happened to run into Don in a bar and proceeded to ply him with drinks. No questions asked as long as he kept them coming. Could a drug have been slipped into one of those drinks? Something that brought on paranoid delusions, a sense of hostile pursuit, visual and olfactory hallucinations, perhaps? The more Don thought about that night and the sleazy-looking type tending the bar, the less implausible this theory sounded. Frat boys did it all the time in clubs and at parties. Don's own drinking habits and the vulnerable state of his mind could have prolonged the effect. Possibly causing a permanent dissociation.

It was only in the context of Kebbler's subsequent suicide that the theory started to come apart. But could Don be sure about what he'd seen? Panicked by the gruesome discovery, he hadn't paused to check the dead man's pulse or gone anywhere near the corpse. All in all, he'd probably spent less than five seconds in the gory bathroom. Kebbler could have staged the scene, confident that his mark would be too shocked to pay attention to details. These days, you could get elaborate Halloween costumes online, available from Amazon with next-day delivery. Corn syrup blood and a couple of stick-on wound patches would have done the trick. No local newspaper had reported the suicide, and search results only showed various articles Kebbler had written for online publications.

Which begged the question of motive. Don thought he had an answer. Professional jealousy spun out of control, the perception that the opportunity that had launched Don's career had somehow derailed Kebbler's own. They had moved in the same circles, had come from similar backgrounds. It wasn't true, but Kebbler could have construed it this way; his resentment festering over the years, transforming into an irrational hatred, a fixation on destroying the man responsible for his lack of success. The confrontation at the Doubleday party could have been the final straw. The maverick outsider ostracized by elitist gatekeepers, the industry insiders closing ranks against him. Don had heard enough rants from unsuccessful authors, drunk or otherwise, to know that facts and logic rarely made a dent in their fervid persecution fantasies.

Maybe Kebbler was playing this game with no end in sight, content to torture his nemesis into madness, to make Don question everything he held familiar in the world. Maybe he had accomplices, hackers who gained access to Don's computer and were changing his words overnight. Or he'd saved some monstrous revenge for last, some foul move yet to be announced.

None of that explained Karen Lombard's insistence on Hudson's shadow backers, the Order of Astral Enlightenment financing a movie, or the extraordinary bad luck that had trailed the project. These were the missing pieces of the puzzle that would allow everything else to fall into place, that would put the whole situation into perspective. There was a story inside the story, he realized, deeper and much more complex than the mere search for a lost film or an account of the strange misfortune that had befallen its crew. A tale of minor Hollywood players indulging in obscure depravity; two deaths, a suicide, a disappearance, all linked by an unfinished movie. A cult-like organization hovering over it all like a curse. Why had the Order poured money into *The Unveiling*, indulging Hudson's every caprice, only to suppress its release? Did the whole story somehow tie back to Kebbler's personal vendetta?

Whatever the answer, he would not find it online. Search engines failed to come up with a connection between Hudson and the Order. He'd found a handful of citations on the latter, most of them secondary references in articles about other, better-known organizations in the sixties and seventies. No articles or copies of pamphlets, no holy writ setting out their beliefs, no tell-all books by former members. For a group that had appeared to wield both money and influence, the Order had left few traces of itself. He spent several fruitless hours browsing secondhand book websites, looking for the publications that had been stolen or destroyed in the library vandalism case. All long out-of-print and unavailable, either jealously guarded in private collections or remaindered in a warehouse somewhere.

Defeated, he had gone back to Kebbler's notebook. But he felt uneasy doing so, in a way he couldn't entirely attribute to guilt. On his first night perusing the notes, he had seen the cramped handwriting change before his eyes. He could chalk it up to drugs, or his own conscience, but he was sure it had happened. *Almost sure.* For whenever he tried to think about the notebook and its meandering declarations, his thoughts likewise lost coherence and direction, and he would disappear between its pages. Going from phrase to phrase, stitching together broken sentences until connections started to take shape, patterns repeating between the letters, spinning off the paper and into his mind. Eventually he would look up and find himself hunched over his keyboard, several pages further into his manuscript, unaware that he'd been writing or for how long.

Quitting would only make things worse. For all the blackouts and lost chunks of time, his writing kept the hallucinations at bay. There had been no nightmares, no spectral visitations after dark. An undefined fear had taken hold of him that the notebook contained revelations he wasn't ready for, that the words were just a code obscuring some other, more meaningful message. Or a trap he was slipping deeper and deeper into. There was nothing to do but see it through to the end.

Don rubbed his unshaven cheek and decided it was time for a drink. Revelations or messages, he didn't have to face them sober. He was already in the kitchen when he heard a faint sound, claws scraping on bare tiles just outside his front door.

Now that he was aware of it, he realized that the scratching had been there all along. Like most background noises, it was only its momentary absence that had rendered it conspicuous. Long claws dragged across stone, yellow bones rubbed together inside moldy rags, dry scales slithered against bark. It was as if every rustle conveyed its own image, dredging it from some place deep within his head.

He stilled his breathing and listened. Someone was probably walking a dog up and down the hallway. As if in agreement, another sound came from behind the door, a throaty emanation that was neither a growl nor a whine.

Did anyone in the building keep a dog? The management company maintained a strict no-pets policy on paper but never bothered to check and enforce it. Dog or not, the animal was clawing at his door now, paws scrabbling on the wood as if seeking purchase or access inside.

He ought to open the door, see what was happening. But he felt cold, unwilling to make a move as the scratching intensified. Oddly, the noise seemed to replicate inside his walls, a frenetic scrabbling back and forth. Perhaps the dog had smelled a rat, or a whole nest of them; it snuffled and whined, redoubled its clawing, the door rattling against its frame.

Was the animal's owner encouraging this behavior or was the dog a stray? Hungry and desperate to get out of the cold. The thought of confronting feral eyes and mangy fur, sharp teeth displayed in rage, kept Don rooted to the floor of the kitchen. He glanced around for a weapon, could think of nothing but his shoes and a tattered umbrella. Before he could make up his mind, he realized that both sounds had stopped.

Carefully, he opened the door, tensing to slam it shut if the dog proved to be aggressive. There was no dog on the other side, no one at all. The stale smell of rancid sweat lingered in the air. He ventured into the hallway, but the shadows betrayed no movement, no beat of retreating feet.

Yet someone had been there because the door was defaced. Something was carved into the wood, right above the lintel. Don narrowed his eyes, ran a finger along the edges. Probably teenage delinquents on a dare, scrawling profanities. The last character in the sequence was larger than the others, a rough circle inscribed with a five-pointed star. Crude but recognizable, etched in with what looked like a key. But it was the message that preceded it that made Don cast an apprehensive look over his shoulder and hurry back into the dubious safety of his apartment.

THEY SEE YOU.

Don double-locked the door and put the chain on, hurried to the window and stared at the empty street. Anyone could be hiding in the night, watching him. He pulled the blind down, turned off the kitchen lights, and reached into the fridge for the bottle. Took a long, greedy gulp, welcoming the spreading warmth; the low, calming hum in his nerve endings.

Was the pronouncement a warning or a threat? His eyes went to the notebook he'd left on the counter. It was probably just projection, but it felt alive somehow, a lurking, shifty thing, imbued with hideous intent. The very thought of opening it again made him physically ill. He didn't need it anymore. He had his own notes now, his own leads to pursue. Even picking it up by one corner sent a surge of irrational loathing through him. He tossed it into the trash and slammed the lid down with more force than was needed. *Let's see them get in now*, he thought, then wondered what had prompted him to think that.

When he fell asleep some time later, the bottle cradled in one arm, the pages of the notebook rustled open inside his mind's eye, and the scratching of the animal's claws returned to follow him into his dream.

Chapter 16

"There you are," said the man holding open the double doors. "Welcome. We've been waiting for you. Everyone's eager to start."

Don followed him into light and warmth and murmur, hearing the doors close softly behind him. "Start what?" he said, struggling to make sense of the scene around him or remember how he'd ended up here.

A dog. He'd been pursued by a rabid dog, fleeing down winding corridors and bewildering junctions, up and down staircases that seemed to spiral into infinity. Then he was at the door, knocking. He turned to try to get his bearings and saw only a narrowing shaft of darkness as the doors clicked shut. Outside was dark. Inside was light. He looked at his host, who gave him a genial smile and steered him in by the elbow.

"You'll see," he said. They were walking across a vast, brilliantly lit room, decorated in *fin de siècle* style; heavy dark oak and mahogany and velvet-draped furniture with crystal chandeliers clinking overhead. His scuffed sneakers squeaked across a lacquered floor that caught and threw back the light. The double glare hid the far ends of the room and made his eyes water.

It was a costume party of some sort, the revelers sharply dressed and wearing masks. Here, a fox in a slinky, beaded flapper dress; there, a badger, stout and self-important in a bespoke tan suit. Light sparkled and bounced off cocktail and champagne glasses, obscuring all but the nearest faces. To Don, their postures suggested a feigned nonchalance, as if everyone was trying too hard not to notice him. He couldn't rid himself of the impression that they'd stopped speaking just before he entered the room.

Embarrassed by his own shabby attire, he started to apologize. The host—who on second glance looked vaguely familiar—waved it away. "You're here. That's all that matters in the end." He gestured across the room at nothing in particular. "Now, if you will, we'd like to start."

Don wanted to ask the question again, but he found himself unable to speak. His legs were carrying him across the polished floor with no conscious input from his brain. The man who'd met him at the door was leading him by the arm, feet barely touching the ground. Sensations mingled and swirled, a kaleidoscope of stimuli too quick to discern: blinding light, the exuberant chatter of an invisible crowd, ice tinkling against glass, high heels clicking on the floor. Either the room had expanded or he'd been wrong about its dimensions. Figures moved against the overbright background, vanished over the rim of this featureless space.

A whirring, snicking sound grew closer, the rapid switching of huge, oiled gears. "Where are we going?" Don asked, raising his eyes to his host. He knew the handsome face with the widow's peak, the glossy hair that shimmered under the chandeliers. Any moment he'd remember who it belonged to.

"You don't want to miss the opening," the host said. Don couldn't tell if the man's lips had moved or if the words had traveled from the other's head into his. The grip on his arm was as hard as steel and burned like ice. "A masterpiece. Superb. The maestro has really outdone himself with this one. Glad to have you at the premiere. The others didn't believe you'd make it, but I had every confidence."

He smiled, the grin of a shark gliding through the depths. Light flashed and sizzled around him and the face was erased. In its place was an oval with two dark holes, like burnt-out lightbulbs. Realization set in with a small lurch. "I'm dreaming," Don said to himself, although the words failed to relieve his terror. "I can wake up."

"We're all dreaming," the magician said. He helped Don into a plush seat, sidled up to him. "We exist in the imaginations of others, or of beings beyond our understanding. But here in this palace of dreams, we are all one, if only for an ephemeral moment." Gently, almost lovingly, he adjusted Don's head, which had begun to loll on a neck that felt like taffy. Rows of seats stretched as far as Don could see. An amphitheater, fronted by an enormous cinematic screen on which colors and shapes danced in the beam of a projector.

"I know who you are," Don said, his voice oddly slurred. He'd never drooled in a dream, but now he could feel saliva coating his chin, dribbling onto his chest. "Your name is Victor Hudson."

The magician smiled and shook his head. "Close, but no cigar. Merely a humble showman, setting off the talent of others. Victor's indisposed, as they say. Pity he couldn't make it to his own show, but there's always another time."

"I want to wake up."

"I gather that you're writing his memoir." The magician tutted and dabbed at the corner of Don's mouth with a silken handkerchief. "There are a few corrections I'd like to add. A few clarifications. But it hardly merits mentioning. Once you've had your eyes opened, so to speak, you'll have no trouble seeing the truth. You'll be seeing it forever."

"What do you want from me?" The false patina of opulence had fallen away from Don's surroundings. Everything appeared much older now, the walls bulging and peeling with damp, the seats torn and speckled with mold, the draperies fading and frayed, nails sticking out of uneven floorboards. A place uninhabited for decades, every flat surface coated in dust and grit, the few surviving windows and light fixtures festooned with cobwebs.

The celebrants had changed too. Thin and frail, sagging inside their oversized, moth-eaten finery. In their whispers, Don could hear no coherence, only the jabber of madness. Crones and wizened ancients wearing rags and ratty old masks, doddering after their terrible host, scrambled into the seats like rats, their glass eyes aglitter.

It was the dream from the airplane again; somehow he'd slipped back into it and become engulfed in its insalubrious light. But if Don was dreaming, why couldn't he wake up? If he was already awake, why was he unable to impel his will upon his body; to arrest his progress toward the flickering screen on which an image was taking shape, as if in response to his arrival?

"Let me go," he pleaded now, frantic. His words seemed to stir fresh movement among the pitiful crowd, which murmured and clambered closer to him, enveloping him in the smell of their bodies and old clothes, of formalin and poorly cured hides. "I want to leave."

"Leave? My boy, we can't let you do that." The host's voice was also changing, shedding all pretense of humanity. "You'll have to let the show roll, I'm afraid. That's the price we pay for art. You've probably noticed that there are no doors here, no way out. But worry not. There's nothing here that would harm you. It's all entertainment, you see—only shadows and colorful lights. Nothing more."

Don wanted to tear himself free, to lash out, but an irresistible lassitude had clamped down on his muscles, his senses. Hands were holding him down, small and clawlike, the fingers bare bones draped in liver-spotted skin. For every one he succeeded in shrugging off, three others took its place. By some phenomenon akin to motion, he was carried to the front row, firmly ensconced into a seat directly in front of the screen.

Clapping and cheering, the celebrants settled in around him. The magician ascended a small podium under the screen and bowed with a flourish. His mouth opened and closed, but whatever he said was lost in a cascade of roaring noise.

"Look up," the magician was shouting down at him, the entreaty taken up by dozens of deformed mouths. Don had no intention of complying but wasn't given any choice in the matter. Dry, bony hands gripped his chin, his brow, pried his eyelids open, sharp digits digging painfully into the corners of his sockets. He couldn't struggle for fear of the mob clawing out his eyes in their unwholesome zeal, couldn't turn his head to the side or avert his gaze.

Captive, helpless, he could only watch what was unfolding on the screen.

At first, it seemed that the projector was broken or casting a rectangle of carbon black. Then bright spots of gold appeared in the depths, twinned and separated: streetlights reflected in wet pavement, lamps burning behind the windows of a huge, forbidding brick edifice. The setting, or what it hinted at, rang in Don's skull with awful familiarity. Any hope that he was wrong evaporated at the sight of the protagonist, who walked—or rather stumbled—along the sidewalk.. He paused in front of the building's entrance, his stance and posture stamped with hesitation. At long last, the door opened and the man went in.

It was a dramatization of his visit to Kebbler with the set and décor reduced to props. Don whimpered, tried to lift his head up and felt it immediately forced down.

The scene cut to a fast closeup of the gangly frame and disheveled head without revealing the protagonist's face. Yet his discomfort and anxiety were unmistakable, accentuated by the camera angle, the tremor of the accompanying score.

Another shot tracked the protagonist through a dark space, climbing stairs, looking up numbers in a long passage lined with doors. Black water swirled around his feet, dripped from the ceiling, but the man didn't seem to notice it. The camera panned past him, focused on a door at the end of the passage. Now there was no music; the only sound was the sloshing of feet through water. Silvery light shone through the gap between the frame and the wall, pulsed under the water.

The man entered the camera frame, paused before the glowing door, apparently gathering the nerve to proceed. A cutaway to the inside showed him entering, the camera switching to a first-person angle representing the protagonist's point of view. The seedy apartment was more or less the way Don remembered it, with minor changes as if to remind him that what he was seeing wasn't really a movie, but his own memory feeding into the dream. Still, his heels drummed against the floor in a futile attempt to halt the progress of the figure on the screen. He didn't want to see what lay behind the half-open door to the bathroom, behind which water gushed and a red-tinted glow filled the scene. The camera rushed forward, shaking as if held by unsteady hands, and the door swung open. Don felt a scream gathering in his throat as the frame became a closeup of the dead face in the bathtub.

His face. Not Kebbler's. Eyes wide open, deep gouges in his forearms, soft pink billowing into the water, spinning off the strands of deeper vermillion. As Don watched, helpless, the face began to blacken, the flesh started to sag and fall away in wet clumps, revealing the bone beneath. The horror of it redoubled his struggles, but the rest of the dreadful gathering was already upon him, swarming over the seats to join those holding him down, iron-hard nails raking his skin and peeling it off in long strips. By the time the first small claw reached into his mouth and ripped out his tongue, he found that he still had the voice to scream.

Chapter 17

The waiting line snaked out of the rain-soaked alley into the parking area. Droplets formed colorful halos over the battered but bright neon signs. Dark smells of the city mingled in the night air: wet pavement and exhaust and bodies huddled together—their collective exhalations hovering above them like mist—the faint undercurrent of garbage piled in the nearby dumpster. The club was a repurposed warehouse in Fishtown, corroded iron and steel girders artfully arranged to suggest urban decay, industrial posters lining the grimy brick walls. Heavy bass and hardcore electric guitars clashed from within, a machine tearing itself to pieces.

"I saw them in Columbus last year." The girl standing in front of Don, angular and pierced and elaborately tattooed, raised herself on her toes to shout in her companion's ear. "At this club. Maskfall are, like, totally different. Some of them danced for Taylor Swift and Demi. But this isn't anything like that." Her companion, a tall, androgynous figure in denim and studded leather with green spiky hair defying the drizzle, bobbed their head up and down, either in acknowledgment or along with the music.

Don shut his eyes and tried to concentrate on the thumping of the beat. He swallowed against a sudden upsurge of claustrophobia that had reared its head as soon as he'd seen the open door. The awful residue of the nightmare he'd found himself in, that he'd been unable to break out of, had left him wrecked for days and glued to his computer screen. It had to have been a drug-induced dream. He refused to consider the alternative, to allow the worm of doubt in his sanity inside his head.

Maskfall, he'd come across by accident on a website dedicated to art inspired by the slasher craze. It happened as he had been taking a break from his writing, dedicating some time to organizing his notes. His recent visions were the result of overwork, of self-medication with alcohol and his growing obsession with Victor Hudson's lost movie. If only he could distance himself from his search, recharge his mental batteries, then everything would go back to normal. That was what he'd convinced himself of. It had almost worked. A week had passed without another vivid nightmare; proof that the drug was leaving his system, that the theater and its wretched denizens had merely been the last flashback. The world was returning to normal, pieces falling back into place.

He had continued along this train of thought and managed to keep it together until he found a reference to Maskfall in Kebbler's notebook.

The notebook that he'd thrown into the trash over a week ago only to find it under a pile of printouts, a little worse for wear but very much intact. A discovery that had shattered whatever fragile peace of mind he'd salvaged from the relative calm of the intervening days. Not the deliverance he'd hoped for, but a reprieve over barely after it had begun. The confluence of names could be a coincidence, but Don doubted it. He was being warned not to let his work in progress lie idle.

Afraid to fall asleep, he fueled his marathon writing sessions with near-lethal combinations of vodka and caffeine pills, getting up only to attend to his body's most basic needs. Time stuttered past in blinks and stretches, the manuscript expanding as his own consciousness seemed to recede into its shadow, an occultation he was powerless to prevent.

He had a relatively clear memory of consigning Kebbler's scribblings to the trash can, hauling the liner to the building's malodorous garbage chute, and the hinged door slamming shut over it. Yet there it was, staring him in the face. Some of the pages had gotten wet and the ink had bled through the paper, but the pages were still legible. Some of the text flirted with coherence, although Don couldn't tell how much of it was the product of research and how much sheer conjecture on Kebbler's part. Step by step, these snippets had brought Don to the club in Fishtown and to Alan Wagner, the principal choreographer of Maskfall, a dance company billed online as "a performance art project from beyond the five senses".

According to the notes, Wagner had been the original choice for art director of *The Unveiling* but had parted ways with Hudson over creative differences before filming began. There were hints of a closer association, but nothing concrete. Wagner had enjoyed relative success over the years; a smattering of Broadway credits, international tours with Maskfall, recognition from the critics. Online articles mentioned his work in film and television, but Don's attempts to cross-reference the name with Victor Hudson were met with failure. All he could find was a string of notifications about items erased via the search engine's public removals tool. Someone had gone through a great deal of trouble to expunge any link between Wagner and Hudson from the Internet, including its archives.

This absence of clues screamed louder at Don than any ghastly revelation would. Maybe Alan Wagner had experienced similar tribulations and had removed the links to protect himself. Maybe he could shed some light on the events that had cast a shadow over Don's life, a shadow growing more sinister with every passing day.

As he stepped past the doormen, the noise blasted him like a tidal wave. The cathedral ceiling and iron girders picked up the cacophony and poured it back down amplified a thousandfold. Disoriented by the darkness, he staggered forward while buffeted by jostling bodies. The auditorium was almost full, the stage backlit by powerful floodlights that scattered elongated shadows across the seating area. Dim commotion suggested that the warmup act was leaving or settling in.

Don inched to the closed backstage door, where a stage manager in a yellow frilled shirt and tight jeans barred his way and informed him that the choreographer had not arrived yet. On the possibility of an interview, the man was noncommittal.

"Up to you and him," he said, watching the crowd filter through the entrance. "As long as it doesn't interfere with their set. Gotta warn you, though, Alan isn't big on interviews. He's had some unpleasant things written about him in the past." He refused to be pressed for details and shrugged off Don's feeble attempt at a fake backstory.

None of this came as a surprise. One couldn't fault Alan Wagner for severing all links with the lost movie and its doomed director. *Tainted by association,* Don mused as he settled into a corner table and the lights dimmed, the music dropping to a low, slow beat that nevertheless conveyed urgency, a deep reverberation that he felt in his chest and temples.

Lower and lower, slowing down to match his heartbeat. Ghostly figures appeared onstage, taut bodies crisscrossed with strips of black, white paint reducing their faces to blank circles. From the front of the crowd came a titter of nervous laughter as the frontmost of the dancers descended into the audience, moving between the darkened tables like wraiths. Legs and muscular arms twined with the steel cables covering the center of the stage, drapes parting to reveal a section of pipe about seven feet tall, fashioned into a portal or the mouth of a tunnel. An invisible voice intoned a mournful, wordless litany beneath the dying lights.

Don downed the vodka-seltzer he'd been nursing, a familiar twist of nausea kindling in his guts. The music grew louder, piping and shrill. Bucking figures chanted and stomped their feet in time with the score, leapt and twisted into the tunnel, their motions at once rendered both jerky and sinuous by the strobing light. It had to be a trick of stagecraft, but no matter how hard Don strained his eyes, he couldn't see anyone emerge from the other end as if the pipe swallowed them all.

A torrent of black water spurted from the portal—or so Don thought until he realized it was a clever lighting effect. The score became harsher, more discordant. In the dim light, the faces at the neighboring tables looked frozen and dead, glassy eyes and fixed grins affixed to them for perpetuity. Before he could puzzle out the bizarre perspective created by the stage elements, the overheads flashed red then faded to black.

When they came back on, the opening was gone, the scene set up in a new configuration. A sinister figure had taken center stage, unnaturally tall and clad in a long black robe, wearing a face that was all sharp bones and oversized nose and hellfire eyes. From its fingers dangled long threads of reflected light, which glimmered as it moved its hands up and down like a monstrous puppeteer conducting a show. The dancers followed its commands, bending and contorting themselves like marionettes around the giant's feet, a frenzy of shadowy motion further obscured by a fog of dry-ice smoke that drifted from curtain to curtain. Bare heads and painted faces, symbols inked in the skin of their chests and shoulders. Then there were no longer dancers, but fish belly white things that crawled down an endless corridor, seeking a way out but finding none.

Light receded to a pinpoint in the sea of darkness.

Don could no longer discern individual bodies in the mass that pulsed and writhed onstage, pouring toward the audience like a black wave. Above it all, the figure, which had to be a performer on stilts, capered and cavorted, waving its long arms. Ashes and filth rained down from a gray, churning sky.

Despite the roar and thump of music, Don could hear them whispering, an endlessly repeated, sibilant cadence that seemed to originate deep within his own skull. Indecipherable still, but it touched something deep inside him, some long-dormant center that awakened to the summons: a vague near-understanding, an atavistic truth. An intense yearning filled him, the promise of dark joy. Swallowing hard, he got up and lumbered in the direction of the stage, across a dark expanse rapidly losing its boundaries, melding with the greater void beyond.

Shouts went up from the tables. Hands and shoulders checked him, pushed him back. He kept his eyes fixed on the stage and shoved forward, peering past the flashing limbs and torsos. Through the smoke and the crowd, he could barely make out the towering puppeteer whose robes had come apart, rags whirling in a demented dance. Nothing beneath the fluttering fabric, only more darkness.

Was it also a construct, a shell moved by unseen hands? Only moments ago, it had seemed alive, full of awful purpose. Don glanced up into the wings and saw a man standing there, short and stocky, clapping in time with the beat of the music. When he leaned forward, his round pink face shone like a halo. Don recognized Alan Wagner, but couldn't see a way through the melee, nor would his voice carry all the way to the art director. He was backtracking to the tables when he saw Wagner's head jerk up, posture rigid with terror.

Disoriented, Don tried to follow the man's gaze. Someone pushed him from behind and he lost his balance, grabbing a thin arm in a denim jacket and hearing a girl scream. A table tipped over with a crash of glass. He toppled forward, got up to his feet, fought his way to the far corner of the stage, concussed by the music, blinded by a sudden flare of lights.

Eyes smarting, he looked past the angry patrons and frightened dancers just in time to see Alan Wagner dash from the wings and toward the glowing red rectangle of an exit. The door swung open onto an empty street, and backstage was empty.

Or not quite empty. For a vanishing second, Don thought—no, he was sure that he'd seen someone standing in the hallway just past the stage. A tall figure in a long overcoat, appearing like a darker stain against the night, there and gone in less than a blink.

He was almost at the backstage door when a heavy hand dropped on his shoulder. He turned to confront the stage manager, florid-faced and glowering. Behind the manager, a shaven-headed bouncer filled most of the corridor.

"I didn't say you could wreck the show," the manager said, throwing his arms up. "Who the hell are you, anyway? Let's see your press credentials."

"It wasn't me." Don tried to peer over the manager's shoulder, but the bulk of the thug in the back obscured all view. "I didn't do anything. Didn't even get to speak to Wagner."

"You must have done *something*." The manager huffed, mopping his brow. Costumed dancers filed past them, hurrying toward the changing rooms. "I never got to speak to him before the show started. He couldn't have known you're here." Beneath his fury, the man seemed flustered, as if he'd seen something he couldn't quite reconcile. "What was all that ruckus in front of the stage? *That* was you, wasn't it?"

"Sorry about that." Don almost recoiled as a tall man in a leotard emerged from the shadows in the wings, a pair of stilts slung over one shoulder, a voluminous pile of black fabric under the other arm. Just another dancer, he realized with embarrassed dismay. "Look, I can set this straight. Let me talk to Wagner now. All I need to do is ask him a few questions."

The manager and the bouncer exchanged troubled looks. "I'm afraid that's not possible," the manager said, suddenly formal. "Not possible right now. You need to leave."

As if to emphasize his words, the bouncer flexed his stump-like neck, rolled his shoulders.

Don started toward the exit sign, suppressing an irrational urge to look back into the wings to the spot where he'd seen the ragged figure. "Take your friend with you too," the stage manager said, a malicious tone in his voice. "The other one. Just between the two of us, but you may want to tell him to take a shower every now and then. He wouldn't have to sneak in if he did."

The door slammed shut before Don could make sense of this parting remark. There was no one with him. He'd come to the club alone. But a nasty premonition had seized him, and he remembered the figure he'd encountered earlier on the crowded street. The watcher pacing him through the city, the ominous figure lurking in the corner of his eye. Wagner had shared the same vision, and the sight had sent him into a blind panic.

An ambulance siren wailed in the distance, getting closer with strobing blue light scattering across the sidewalk. Don lit a cigarette and watched as the vehicle pulled up in front of the club, as the paramedics rolled a gurney through the doors, then out the same way. A crumpled form lay on it, unrecognizable under a blanket and oxygen mask. That effectively ended that line of investigation: trying to get hold of Alan Wagner again would be a waste of time. When the ambulance took off, Don made his way through the drunks and stragglers, trying to hail a cab.

His gaze passed over the tall, gaunt shape standing in the shadows on the other side of the street just outside the bright circle of a streetlamp. Immediately he knew who it was: the same vagrant who had followed him before. Had he stalked Don in the club? The stage manager's spiteful words made sense now. *Your friend. The other one.*

Don's shock only lasted for a moment. Whoever the watcher was, he wouldn't escape him again. Almost without volition, his hands squeezed into fists and he stepped off the curb.

A sudden blaze of brightness blinded him, erasing the world.

Tires shrieked and a hurtling mass rushed past him, missing him by no more than a foot, the driver's face a grimace of surprise and horror as the car fishtailed down the street, swerved, braked to a halt. A few heads turned Don's way then quickly dismissed him for the more dramatic spectacle unfolding in front of the club. Petrified, he stared after the departing car, then at the spot where the figure had appeared. There was no one there now, only the grimy wall of the alley, the light dwindling around it, the night pouring in.

Chapter 18

Don went over the prompts he'd jotted down on his notepad for what felt like the tenth time that morning. None of it helped. Again and again, he found himself unable to type so much as a coherent sentence. The blank word processor page shone back at him, a pristine, unbroken barrenness whose sterile reflection seemed to cloud his brain, to slow down his thoughts to a trickle of rudimentary consciousness. Last night's episode had disturbed him deeply and filled his head with a buzz of frantic activity from which he was unable to extract a single rational note.

Alan Wagner was dead. Don had discovered this when he'd turned his computer on. His browser had remembered the most recent search terms he'd used and filled his feed with morbid headlines from local-interest blogs and celebrity news websites. A massive cardiac event was the generally accepted explanation, although the more sensationalist sources speculated about its cause: an overdose or alcohol-fueled orgy. Flame wars already smoldered on a dozen online forums, peppered with amateur videos of Maskfall's latest performance. Don zoomed in on the shaky, blurred footage, uncertain of what he expected to find. Nothing looked the way he remembered it. Only gyrating bodies and flashing lights, the music a white-noise roar broken up by cheering and hooting.

There was probably a sensible explanation for all of this, one that tied all the incomprehensible pieces together, but in the end it all came down to one blunt, terrible fact: Alan Wagner had been pursued by something that could kill simply by manifesting itself. Something that Don had brought with him or invited into the club. Something the art director had known about and had taken great pains to avoid.

There was also the matter of the other apparition, the watcher from the shadows. Don didn't understand any of it, but he was sure about one thing. That man was real, neither a phantom nor the product of a mind disturbed by drugs, but a creature of flesh and blood. A denizen of back alleys and subway stations. Just another homeless madman muttering and shuffling through the crowds, invisible through ubiquity. Or something altogether different. His presence alongside that other manifestation was no coincidence. If Don was to have any hope of regaining control of the situation, his mysterious stalker would be the key.

Other more practical concerns intruded. Over the past days, unwilling to leave the confines of his home, Don had lost track of his work and was contemplating giving up altogether. A bout of steady drinking had dulled the razor edge of his terror, relegated his nightmares to vague disturbances in stretches of unsettled sleep, his mind mercifully failing to retain any specific details. But deadlines loomed, and J. C. Latham would be expecting the first draft in a little over four weeks. This was still achievable—in his trancelike writing sessions, he churned out page after page effortlessly—but for it to happen, he'd have to open himself up to that invisible intrusion once more. Another piece of him would be gone, and then another, until there was nothing left of Donald James Ruby but his miserable body. With its bad right knee and weak lungs and something else looking out through his eyes.

But there was no choice. He didn't dare think what would happen if he failed to turn the manuscript in on time.

The notebook sat open on the coffee table, seeming to mock him.

Don closed his laptop and pulled on his jacket and shoes. A walk would help him clear his thoughts, and he would be safe in daylight. Outside the apartment, he paused to survey the repairs to his door. The janitor had grudgingly fixed the damage, which involved sticking two lengths of duct tape over the symbols. No doubt that the landlord would have kept ignoring Don's calls had he not been lured with the promise of collecting the back rent. The strips of tape made the flimsy door and the apartment behind it look like less of a shelter than Don had deluded himself they were. Fighting a sudden attack of nerves, he tromped off down the gloomy hallway and stairs, letting himself out into the street.

Thin sunlight struggled through gray corrugations of clouds. Bathed in its feeble rays, the street looked even uglier than usual; the buildings grimy and hopeless, the bare trees in the dog shit filled patch of park like skeletal hands clawing upward. Concrete and grimy brick buildings; tattoo parlors with dirty windows and secondhand clothing stores. The occasional restaurant braved the decay behind security bars. Men huddled on front stoops in warm clothes, smoking and talking in low voices. There were times when the place felt to Don like a rung above homelessness, an unwelcome preview of the fate he was sliding toward with every bounced check, every unpaid bill.

He zipped his jacket and shivered in a fetid gust that rolled trash along the sidewalks, walking without purpose or direction. Sleep deprivation left him lightheaded, and lately he had been subsisting on nothing but alcohol. It occurred to him that he hadn't seen the city in daylight for longer than he could remember. Hadn't really taken in all its essential ugliness; its indifference and casual cruelty, the despondency and despair of those who plied its streets. Perhaps his recent escapades had warped his perspective, leading him to see only the worst in his surroundings. Every trail he'd followed in his quest for Victor Hudson's lost work had led him straight to the irreparably broken, the destitute, and the deranged. Perhaps all he needed was a diversion, the simple pleasure of walking, of muscles flexing and stretching, each step taking him outside his own head.

He'd barely gone down the block when he noticed he was being followed. A figure was matching his movements—its presence sensed more than seen—keeping its distance but not letting him out of its sight. Under different circumstances, Don's mind would have dismissed it as just another of the city's homeless, as much a part of the backdrop as the sidewalks and the grim building entrances. But now he knew better. His heart skipped a beat as he resisted the impulse to turn around and face his pursuer. Instead, he walked on, pretending to peer into the still-glassed shop windows. It took him a few attempts to get a good look at the figure. Tall but stooped, shoulders slumped as if in despair. No doubt about it; it was the same man from the night at the club.

Around the corner was a small deli, its front window facing the park. Caught between panic and the desire to do violence, Don slowed his walk to allow his tail to catch up, then pushed the deli door open with a sweaty palm.

After the blustery street, the warmth and smells of the shop were stifling. Don nodded to the elderly proprietor, stepped past the two customers waiting in line, to the other side of the counter. He half-expected the owner to protest, but the man looked away and said nothing. The neighborhood had seen better days. Crack dealers sold their vials alongside food trucks, gunfire broke out in the middle of the day, and those who had chosen to stay—or had nowhere else to go—knew better than to ask unnecessary questions. Don's wild, disheveled appearance probably helped. He caught sight of himself on his way to the back of the shop and wished he hadn't looked.

A claustrophobic corridor led him past a tiny kitchen and a bathroom the size of a closet. He went out the back door and emerged onto a trash-strewn lot. After crouching by the dumpster to make sure the coast was clear, he hurried around a corner that led back to the street, trying to make as little noise as possible. Adrenaline coursed through him, cutting through the fog of bewilderment and fear. This was the best chance he would get. Still, he felt out of his depth, thrust in the middle of a situation he had neither asked to be part of, nor knew how to handle.

The vagrant stood some thirty paces down the sidewalk, half-hidden by a vandalized phone booth, watching the deli. His back was turned, attention on the door through which his mark had disappeared.

An empty bottle clinked against Don's foot and rolled into the gutter. The hobo heard it and turned. Gray eyes blazed at Don from twin nests of wrinkles, fixing him with their stare, robbing him of the element of surprise.

Don drew breath to speak, but the heat of his anger had fled. All he felt now was a weary resignation. The man before him was old, or aged by rough living, but his shoulders were broad, and his frame, hunched as it was, towered at least four inches above Don's own six-one. Dirty and unkempt, the cuffs of a filthy sweater protruded through the arms of a coat at least a size too small. Features were lost in a matted beard gone completely white. Only the eyes remained distinct, smoldering with demented fire. All this ran through Don's head as the stranger stepped closer to him, engulfing him in the smell of unwashed clothing and flesh. Don took an involuntary step back, as much to get away from the stench as to avoid danger.

"What do you want?" He heard himself croak and hated the weakness in his voice. He was no fighter, hadn't been in a physical altercation since a playground scuffle in middle school. Surely the bum wanted something from him. Money would be a good guess. His mind, as if to torment him, played a series of newspaper headlines. *Homeless man stabs failed writer. Body found on train tracks.*

A hand with huge bony fingers closed around Don's elbow. He snorted to clear his throat of the smell strong enough to turn his stomach. But it was the man who backed away now, letting go of Don's arm as if singed, his eyes widening.

"They've put their mark on you," he said. His gaze blundered somewhere past Don, down the street. "But it's not too late," he added vehemently, as if arguing with himself. "There's still hope."

Something about the old man's voice jogged Don's memory but not quite enough for recognition. He'd have to proceed with care; the vagrant was unstable and looked more than capable of aggression.

"I've seen you following me," he began, stalling for time. "Watching me. Who are you?"

Then he knew and felt the world swim out from under him. Bedraggled and underfed, hardened and bent by inebriation and poverty, the man had changed, but the voice had not. Nor had the stare in those flintlike eyes. It unlocked the cipher of the vagrant's face, the years sloughing off like a mask. The same face Don had seen on the screen, the same voice delivering those trite, implausible lines. Even after everything that had befallen him, the man's presence had barely dimmed.

"We need to find a safe place to talk," Kirk Taylor said, glancing around, his eyes focused now and afraid. "Not your place. It's not safe anymore. It has been spoiled by their gift." He smiled, revealing a row of yellowed teeth. Distaste, or pity, or both rippled across his lined features. "You can never go back. You mustn't. Because it's close, and you gotta keep moving or it catches up with you. *They* catch up with you, and they don't believe in letting go. You can take my word for it."

Chapter 19

Kirk Taylor ate like he had not had a decent meal in months, which may very well have been the case. Two cheesesteak sandwiches disappeared with astonishing speed into the former actor's whiskery mouth, chased with long gulps of root beer. When he was done eating, he wiped his hands on his already greasy coat and stared off into space.

They sat on a bench in Washington Square, warmed by the tentative rays of the sun, neither of them ready to speak. Walkers passed them by—office workers on their lunch break and families with strollers—giving the strange pair a wide berth. A bum and a haggard drunk sitting next to each other without talking. Don tried, and mostly succeeded, in suppressing the insidious suspicion that he was being herded into a trap, that the entire city had become one. A place within a place from which there would be no escape, because it was inside his head. Only a few days ago, his decision to engage his pursuer in conversation, to hear what the vagrant had to say, would have seemed absurd. But that mindset was long gone, his precarious mental balance tipped over into paranoia.

Taylor had refused to accompany Don to his apartment. "They've been there," he said, in the exasperated tone of the man repeating a self-evident truth. "They know where to find you now. I'm not setting foot in that place."

"It's my home," Don said, trying to hide how much the remark had unsettled him. "I have nowhere else to go."

Kirk Taylor's weathered, begrimed face turned toward him. His eyes burned with the same spark Don remembered from the screen, now fanned into an all-consuming blaze—terror, desperation, or plain old insanity. "Did you hear anything I just said? *There's no going back.* Not today. Not ever. Your only hope is to hide your trail."

Maybe it was only the man's delivery, but the words chilled Don to the bone. "Who are *they*? What do you know about me?"

"I know enough. I've seen enough." Taylor scanned the park fearfully. Some distance away, a small child was chasing a big red ball, cheered on by a pair of beaming parents. "They are the trapped ones. The corrupt ones. Who got left behind. Neither living nor dead. He's sent them after you just like he did to me. Once they catch your scent, they won't rest until they have you. Until they drag you back with them. To the lightless place. The unclean place."

He finished his root beer and let out a long belch, but there was no relaxation in his posture, no softening in his stricken face. "They hate us for what we are. Maybe because we're alive while they simply endure. Because they crave the light, but it's forbidden to them. I don't know. But I know this. You have to run. Stay ahead of them as long as you can."

Pity and horror swarmed through Don as he took in the awful import of the man's words. He looked into the leathery face, the dark hollows around those haunted eyes. Thought about the years spent on the street, decades of moving from place-to-place, plagued with delusions and trying to outrun the phantoms inside one's own head. "Is this why—is that what you're doing? Someone's following you, and you're trying to escape them?"

Kirk Taylor shook his head so vigorously that oily gray ringlets danced around his brow. "There's no escape. Don't you see? Space means nothing to them. They can't be kept out by doors and walls. Nowhere is safe. All you can do is run. Like I'm doing. Run, and hope that they grow tired of you. Or find someone else, another target."

"Did Hudson put them up to it? Victor Hudson? He's the reason they're after you now." Don would have asked more questions, but the umbra that passed over the old man's face stopped the words in his throat. Never before had he seen such despondency, such a mix of sorrow and hatred.

"Victor wanted to negotiate with them. Reason with them, learn their secrets. Elevate himself to the exalted realms, as he used to say. He thought them glorious, divine. They're nothing of the sort." Another shake of the head. "All that fuels them is wrath. Wrath and hatred, a darkness without end. They have been trapped in the lightless place for so long that it has changed them. If they were ever human to begin with, it has stripped every last trace." A hand clamped down on Don's forearm with ferocious strength. Reflexively, he tried to pull it back, but Taylor held him in place like a vise. "They have come after you, but their hold isn't strong yet. I can sense that. Victor taught me things. But they're not done trying. Patient and sly. They can afford to wait because they're beyond time."

"What do they want from me?"

The hand retreated to a filthy lap. "That's between you and them. I just know what I've seen. What I've sensed. I can smell them around you. On you. If you let them get closer, close enough to show you their real faces, you'll wish you'd never been born. Once the slippage starts, it can't be undone."

He couldn't be referring to the ghastly masked party from Don's dream. To push this thought aside, Don tried to come up with another question. "Was it the movie? I spoke to some of the people involved with *The Unveiling*. Karen Lombard, and a cameraman named Robert Callaway. Are these—the people who are following you also trying to find it?"

"They saw nothing." Taylor closed his eyes tightly. "They know nothing. Even if they did, it would make no difference. There's no movie, and there never was."

Don thought to the fire at the studio, wondering if Taylor had somehow been involved. "Allegedly, a few copies survived. I found them online. Don't you think it should be released, after all these years? I'm sure you could use the royalties in your, uh, present circumstances."

Kirk Taylor gaped at him for a moment, then threw his head back and brayed with laughter, shrill and unpleasant. Without making eye contact, the couple closest to the bench picked up their toddler and ball, moving on in a hurry.

"You're just not listening, are you? There is no copy, no movie, other than the one you're living in now. It only *looked* like a film, but it's something completely different. Something waiting to be found and fed. To be worshipped. Victor took too long to realize what he was playing with, and it cost him everything. It cost all of us. Like a curse he put on us forever." Don was about to ask what the outburst meant when the former actor silenced him with a gesture. "Forget about the movie," he said. "Forget you'd ever heard about it, or about Victor. Or any of us. Many very important people spent a great deal of money and effort trying to erase it from the public eye, and with good reason. Move on and move often. That's all I have to tell you."

"I don't think I can do that."

"Then stay and be damned," Taylor said matter-of-factly. "You'll have plenty of time to regret it. All the time in the world and much more. They're agitated. More than ever before. So is the man in the suit. He's been waiting for a long time, and he doesn't give up. It's not his style."

"Whose style? Victor's?"

"The magician. The one who lost the way back. The prophet who wanders the gray wastelands. Victor warned me about him." Suddenly fearful, the old man pressed his lips into a thin line, as if trying to prevent further divulgences from spilling out. "It's the first time I've seen him in decades. You've seen him too. He has plans for you, but I don't know what they are. Trust me, you'd be better off dead."

Even if he wished to deny it, Don knew who Taylor meant. The sinister, suited figure he'd seen in his home, on the plane, in his dreams. Kirk Taylor was probably unstable, his sanity eroded by whatever cultish beliefs Hudson had foisted on him. But was it possible that he and Don would share the same hallucination? Or that the old man knew about the eerie nighttime visits?

Nowhere is safe.

The uncanny coincidence between his visions and what the vagrant was describing made Don's head swim, like he was being disconnected from reality.

Kirk Taylor must have read Don's expression. His bearded face softened with sympathy. "Victor's friend," he said quietly. "He and his living representatives. They had a plan for us too, you know? That's what the movie was all about. Not a movie, but a ritual. Something to focus its attention, its power."

"Representatives?" It took Don a moment to sift through the flurry of words. "You mean the cult? The Order of Astral Enlightenment?"

The former actor nodded. "They still had money back then and influence. Their California chapter did, at least. Victor told me of another group out east, in New York. There had been a third chapter somewhere in the desert. Arizona or New Mexico. In the fifties. But something had happened to them. Something terrible. Victor said that we had to be careful. Give them what they asked for and get everything we wanted in return."

"Everything you wanted?"

Taylor shrugged his shoulders. "It's different for everyone," he said. "For me, it was fame. I was young and had a few leading roles under my belt, but my big breakthrough never materialized. Typecast, I suppose you'd call it." He rolled the greasy sandwich paper into a ball, playing with it absently. "The going was good, but I could see the writing on the wall. In two years, I'd still be making low-budget movies. In ten or fifteen years, I'd be doing the same. Only I wouldn't be the lead anymore, but the sidekick. Or the dad. Or the hapless bystander who gets killed off within the first twenty minutes. Until I couldn't get hired at all anymore. Back then, you couldn't take out the trash without tripping over another aspiring movie hunk. Younger, better looking, hungrier. Sharper."

He sighed, making a vague gesture. "It's impossible to resist, you know. Everyone has a crack in their soul, a secret desire we hide from everyone else. That we hide from ourselves, except in the dead of the night. Sooner or later, that hunger must be appeased. Now, for Victor, it was never about fame. Or money. Knowledge was his secret desire. To see past the veil, into the hidden machinery of the universe. To know the truth, whatever it may be."

Or to redeem oneself, Don thought with a pang. Living on the screen, dying once the lights came on and the audience walked out of the theater. Until the reel came to its end one last time and they were forgotten. No wonder so many had been drawn to Hudson's promise of a better place, an existence without sorrow.

"So, the Order funded Victor's film. But at some point, he changed his mind and went against them."

"Victor was a dreamer." The eyes that had once graced the covers of *Fangoria* and *Blood Orgy* had gone wistful. "He had gotten involved with the occult in his youth, and later, when he traveled Europe. Astral projection, planes of existence that occupy the same physical space, but are not in contact with each other. Spiritualist trances in which a clairvoyant, or medium, could pass across their borders. Nothing that hasn't been described before. Frauds and charlatans of all stripes have been peddling the same ideas for centuries. Promising secret knowledge, an end to pain and loss, a path to the higher spheres. Preying on the desperate and the gullible. But these days, you have serious scientists talking about other dimensions and parallel universes. So maybe it's not as crazy as everyone seems to think.

"Victor thought there was something to these theories. Except he wanted to make these celestial planes accessible to everyone. Teach them to access their astral doubles, their other, truer selves. It was a skill like any other, and many had mastered it through the centuries. Saints and shamans, clairvoyants. But Victor wanted to open it up to the masses. He'd been given a special talent, and he believed he'd found the ideal medium for putting it to use."

"Movies," Don said. "Dreams made real, projected on the big screen. Given life, even if only briefly, and in two dimensions."

"Projection." Taylor gave him an almost beatific smile, decades of misfortune sloughing off his grimy face in an instant. "A story—any story—is a kind of controlled mass hallucination. To Victor, movies were a way to visualize the alternatives, expand the consciousness to perceive these higher realms. The storyteller was a sort of guide, the one who would lead you through to the other side of the screen into a different reality that intersects our own. They would banish the boundaries of time and space, the limitations of the flesh. Our spirit essences, free from suffering.

Only he planned to liberate hundreds of thousands at a time, even millions. Esoteric revelations for the mass-production age."

"What did you make of all this?"

Taylor chuckled self-consciously. "I thought he was full of shit, of course. Just like you think I am now. A degenerate Brit, an old fruitcake, feeding me some nonsense about astral bodies as a segue to getting his grubby little hands on mine." At the sight of Don's surprise, the chuckle became a laugh. "Hey, it happened far more often than you'd think. Besides, you haven't seen me after I've cleaned up. I could name quite a few big names who caught their break with their pants around their ankles. Men and women alike."

"You don't think that was part of it?"

"No. Word around town was that Victor was queer. On some level, it may have been true, only not in the way people meant it. He certainly never acted on it and definitely didn't pursue trysts or harass actors, as so many did quite openly. I don't think he had sexual preferences at all. To Victor, the body and all its desires were unclean. A prison for the mind, the source of all the negative emotions that plagued the true self. Driven by base need and hunger and the demands of sleep, constantly running down, an imperfect machine. Dying even as it came into the world. Once you understood that, once you've beheld the pure, beautiful essence inside this meager shell, the flesh became meaningless, a hindrance. All material things did."

"Sounds like a great opening line for a cult pamphlet," Don said. "*We can relieve you of the misery of the material, so hand over your cash.* Not a particularly innovative approach."

"I told you it was never about money for Victor. The Order of Astral Enlightenment was something else. Secretive, rich, with influence at every level of society. Not a commune for social misfits and drug burnouts, nor a fraud scheme designed to bilk naïve and lonely heiresses. Although many gave money willingly. No member of theirs ever broke silence. Their principals weren't narcissistic sociopaths craving sex and adulation. They didn't organize publicity stunts or install thetan-auditing booths at pseudoscientific conferences."

"Then why the secrecy? Was the Order involved in something illegal?"

"It's possible, but I doubt it. Victor wouldn't have been involved in anything criminal. He had a code he lived by. Like a holy man, a monk."

"You really admired him," Don said, incredulous. Even after everything that happened, Victor Hudson's former associates still thought the man walked on water.

"He recognized something in me," Taylor said. "Ever since I was a boy, I knew I saw things differently from other people. Patterns where there seemed to be chaos, a grand design weaving through everyday existence. If only I could put it all together, see the whole picture at once, everything would fall into place. But my mind was too small to accommodate this revelation, and I didn't know how to expand it. My parents went to church, but they weren't religious. Dogma never appealed to me anyway. Greedy hypocrites ranting about fire and brimstone, or preaching hatred, or selling salvation in easy installments. Victor showed me things I'd never imagined possible. That I'd never *imagined*, period."

"You were someone he could trust."

Kirk Taylor nodded. The long confession was tiring him out; sweat gathered on his forehead, his breath whistling through his beard. "I'd heard about these experiences from others in Victor's inner circle. Big names. Actors, directors, producers. But I'd never taken them for anything other than the effects of coke and booze and Victor's theories on addled and impressionable minds. None of them stuck around for very long." His voice dipped low, as if admitting something embarrassing. "What happened was I came close to dying. I'd taken some stuff at a party; from a dealer I didn't know. Passed out in this empty room. Nothing in it except this big mirror. The next thing I knew, I was standing up, looking down at a dead body on the floor. *My* body. Its eyes were open, but I was no longer inside it. I was inside the mirror, looking out at the room. Only it had changed. It was bathed in this pale blue light that came out of the empty husk on the floor.

"Then Victor was in there with me. In the mirror. Talking into my ear, telling me not to be afraid. To let the light inside myself and embrace it. I saw the room, the world, as they were really meant to be. Beautiful. For the first time in my life, I was free—free from sadness, free from misery, free to explore this new vision in any way I wanted. That other world, the one with my body on the floor, was only a cheap illusion."

The old man's eyes had taken on that feverish glow again. "When I came to," he said, "Victor was leaning over me together with some of the others. But while they were worried, he was smiling. Because he knew what I'd seen. Somehow, he'd followed me, although his physical self never left the room, had kept moving around, laughing, bantering. That smile told me everything I needed to know." His gesture took in the park, the hurrying strollers, the barren trees. "*This* was the lie. That other place was where the truth resided, the beauty and joy. I had glimpsed something wondrous, something that changed my life in an instant. And I'd spend the rest of my days looking for it."

"Victor showed you how to find it again," Don said, feeling a cold certainty form in the very center of him. Taylor had used projection to follow him around. To appear in the street, or the club, and vanish without a trace. The old man had done it to deliver a warning, but the idea of being watched without knowing it, of having his inner sanctum breached with no regard for locks or walls, went beyond horror. What else had followed

Taylor through the lightless places, picking up Don's trail, tracking him like an animal by his spoor while he lay asleep and defenseless? "He taught you how to expand your awareness."

"With enough time, I would have gotten better at it. That's what Victor said. I wasn't the only one, but none of the others learned as quickly as I did. He encouraged me to practice on my own, to let go of the inhibition."

The truth was that Victor Hudson had sensed a weakness in the actor and found a way to exploit it. A spiritual addiction to replace the chemical ones, to turn the younger man into someone he could control, someone who would remain loyal no matter what happened. But Don kept his thoughts to himself. "He was preparing you for what was to come," he contented himself with saying.

"We were both learning," Taylor said. "The movies we made together were trial runs for Victor's big project. For him, the screen and the space within it were elements of the story. The horizon, the trees and buildings, interiors and exteriors; all these are lines waiting to be discovered. Framed correctly. All the artist does—and I saw *all*, but really this is the crucial point—is fill in the missing parts. People as symbols, bodies as letters. Did you know that every letter, every symbol that humans have ever used, was once a shape from nature?" Without waiting for a response, he continued, his voice climbing higher. "When you put people in the empty spaces, when every symbol is in its correct place, you've written a code. A language older than words that can unlock secret rooms inside the mind. Patterns known and hidden in the unconscious, and Victor was mastering them. I don't suppose you've seen *With Open Eyes*?"

Don said that he had.

"They made him cut out a segment near the end," Taylor said, almost triumphant. "No one could tell why, but a focus group left the screening disturbed. Later the studio destroyed the uncut version. Victor didn't care.

He already knew he was onto something and this confirmed it. All that was left was to find backers who would help him realize his potential."

"*The Unveiling*," Don said. "He was going to show it all over the country." His mind shrank away from the implications. Could the Order of Astral Enlightenment have planned some sort of mass attack on movie theaters? Pumping hallucinogens into the air supply, or slipping them into soda dispensers, all the better to further one man's deranged vision? "But it didn't last." He felt he had to reassure himself. "Something changed Hudson's mind."

Kirk Taylor's face seemed to confirm Don's thoughts. The haunted look was back, the jerky, almost manic glances to the side.

Could it have gotten dark so quickly? The square and the paths were empty, the shadows under the trees longer than he'd realized. Don had the impression of movement in the distance, over by the monument, too dim to discern.

"He wouldn't go through with it." Taylor was leaning into him now; Don drew back from the stench emanating from the man. "Victor was careless with his gift. He left the door open too long, and the others saw him. They hunger, and they never forget."

"Who are these *others*?" The conversation was going in circles, and Don had had enough of it. He wanted to seize this grubby apparition by the shoulders, to shake it until he knocked some sense loose from it, but the very idea of laying his hands on the filthy rags, of inhaling the rancid smell, held him back. That, and the vague sense that he was on thin ice here, an impression of the world thrumming like glass in a window behind a passing truck, on the brink of shattering and letting something through, some comprehension that his dazed brain couldn't accommodate. "What were you and Victor involved in, and where do I come into this?"

"Listen." Taylor was whispering, as if there was anyone around to hear him. "I spent a lot of time at Victor's place. He had these old books there that he'd brought over from England. Creepy books and even older manuscripts. He said he'd made some mistakes in the past, and that he was trying to put them behind him. I may be a high-school dropout, but I'm not stupid. I know what it's like to get in way over your head and have your mistakes follow you around. That's what happened to Victor. Something followed him across the ocean. Some sort of scandal that he never talked about." He wiped his mouth and then flinched as if struck. "Back then, you could bury your skeletons. Make them go away. Especially if you had money and power."

"What was the scandal?"

"I don't know. But I'd never met a man so haunted by the past, so eager to make amends. America, Hollywood—that was going to be his second chance. Redemption on both fronts. As a filmmaker and as a student of the paranormal."

"Paranormal? As in seances? Talking to ghosts?"

"Victor was what the Brits call a toff," Taylor said. "His father had money, sent him to the best private schools. The rich move in their own circles, make their own rules. One thing that hasn't changed over the years. He fell in with the wrong crowd."

He cast a pleading look at the unopened bottle of water in Don's hands. Took it when proffered and drank gratefully before continuing. "They called themselves the Brotherhood of Lament. Magic practitioners, for the most part, leftovers from a much bigger Victorian-era secret society. Satanism, ritual magic, ancient Egyptian spiritualism, psychic research. Rubbed shoulders with Aleister Crowley and the like. I never went for any of that stuff myself. Frauds, mostly, or rich degenerates looking for a thrill."

"Sounds familiar. Like the Order of Astral Enlightenment." Don didn't know what to make of this new piece of information. "Do you think some of his old associates followed him to Hollywood? Or that Victor sought out a new magic society?"

"He spoke about an old debt about to be collected. But after they showed up at the shoot, he became a different person. Frightened, unfocused, always looking over his shoulder. It was like the film was feeding on him. On all of us. Filling our heads with dreams." Taylor put his large hands over his face, pressing the heels of his palms against his eyes. "I knew they weren't dreams. It was the slippage. Except I had no control over it anymore. Now I could see other things in there. I saw the dwellers in their unclean lair and the magician. Victor's old friend."

"Who is he?"

"*What is he*, is the question you should be asking. Except there's no answer. He's the one who comes to you when you're vulnerable. Afraid and all broken up inside, ready to do anything to be whole again. The one who offers his hand to take you out of the void into the light. Only there's no light. Just more goddamn darkness."

The former actor was getting lost in his panic, becoming incoherent. Don fumbled for a way to get him back on track. "Are you saying the Order was behind what happened on set? The disappearance, the designer who died? They had something to do with it?"

Kirk Taylor seemed to be on the verge of tears. "It wasn't meant for us," he said. "All that beauty, all that joy. It used to be, but mankind had cut itself off from it. Corrupted what was once pure. There were other things in the passage. Other *presences*. No one called them down. No one needed to. They take the fear from your head, the images from your nightmares, and wear them like skin. That's how they get through.

"It starts with a token, you see. A gift from the other side, taken of your own free will. Little by little, until they can come in without an invitation. Victor realized what the Order was after. He refused to go through with it. But he'd gone too far, and they're not the sort of people to take no for an answer."

"Not the sort." Don tried to corral the thoughts ricocheting inside his skull. "So, the Order got rid of Victor Hudson. They killed him. It was no accident."

"They didn't kill him," Taylor said. "He may have wished for death. Begged for it, even. He might still be wishing for it."

Suddenly his body went rigid, as if galvanized by an electric current. Don followed his dull gaze past the square, past the thin silhouettes of trees, past a lone walker with a dog. A motionless figure was standing over by the monument, facing them. Not a figure, but a shadow, a black hole cut into the world, a negative of a human being. Its existence ached inside the mind, a malevolent psychic touch reaching across the distance.

"Something has stirred them up," the old man was saying. "I think it has to do with you. But I'm not sticking around to find out. I'm staying at a shelter in Glenwood, but tomorrow I'll be off. You should leave too. It doesn't matter where, as long as you don't let them catch up." He paused. His eyes shone with tears. "Sorry I couldn't help you. I can't even help myself. They'll destroy me if I try to get the word out."

"Are they after me now?" Don heard himself say through the blood rushing in his ears. His surroundings were fading into the background, sinking into unnatural darkness. "Are Victor's companions out to harm me? How do I stop it from happening?"

Kirk Taylor got to his feet stiffly, moving away with a painful but determined slowness. "You can't," he tossed over his shoulder. "There's no stopping what's coming. All you can do is quit doing whatever is attracting their attention. Quit trying to bring what's dead back to life."

Don glanced back at the monument, trying to locate the lone watcher. The figure had disappeared from sight, but he retained a vague, unpleasant notion that it had done so by stepping behind a tree, that it was coming closer.

Just as abruptly, the dark pall lifted from the heavens.

Sun and warmth returned to his senses, the noises of birds in the trees, the honking of cars on Sixth Street. But they returned slowly, almost reluctantly, as if each time he went away—

—*with each* slippage—

—it became a little harder to come back, like a swimmer who had drifted a little too far from the shore.

He looked up. Kirk Taylor was a hunched, ragged comma on the other side of the park, soon lost in the crowd. Don was alone on the bench, unwilling to move, shivering in the November cold, utterly isolated from the world.

Chapter 20

This time there were no walls, no floor, and no oppressive confines from his previous dreams. Only a notion of space, undefined by borders and suffused by a soft blue lambency, and of bodies moving past him. Swarming him on all sides. Above him and beneath, suspended and drifting along in the emptiness.

He struggled to get away from their cold, greasy touch, but his efforts failed to change the direction he was floating in. Or was being pulled toward: a thin, blue line flaring wider across the black gulf, shimmering in the inconceivably large distance.

His companions in this strange, directionless expanse seemed to pay him no heed. Shriveled and weak, heads twitching on scrawny necks hung with loose skin, they mewled and made feeble pedaling motions, each trapped in some dismal nightmare of their own. Don could only see those directly around him with any clarity but knew there were more in the darkness. A great many more drifting toward the light. Weeping and uttering broken phrases, their complaints echoed as if in a vast stairway.

Whatever process had brought him here had wrought the same transformation upon him. What he could see of himself left no room for doubt. A thing: pale, skeletal and hunched over, squirming like a worm, piebald skin stretched tight over long, frail bones. He felt more than heard a moan loosen from his throat, merging with the endless litany of sorrow and torment rising from the mass of the damned as they were dragged onward.

Only there's no light. Just more goddamn darkness.

Fear rose in him. He could still feel it even in this reduced state: he was afraid of the light and of what lay behind it. Surrounded by the damned, he whined and clawed at the void, succeeding only in propelling himself faster toward the gaping brightness. Close enough to see the things that waited on the other side of it, wet teeth inside rotted animal masks, dead eyes glittering. To see the naked, miserable throng surge past him, clawing one another in unwholesome eagerness.

Even after he'd woken, sheets soaked and foul with sweat, the sense of being surrounded hung around him like a miasma. An impression of being in two places at once, both here in the room with the neon glow leaking in through the toothless shutters, and falling through the outer darkness, a drowning man caught in an undertow. How much longer before he failed to haul himself back to the shore altogether, before he was separated from his other self and carried on unfathomable currents?

Don reached for his cigarettes, looking around his apartment. More light intruded under the front door. He could not remember the lamps in the hallway outside burning so brightly. Yet his hand hovered over the bedside switch, unwilling to turn on the lamp. Some of the numbing terror from his nightmare—

—his slippage—

—lingered, a sensation of foreboding. He was afraid that direct light would reveal something uninvited and unpleasant, something crouching in the darkness of the apartment, savoring his apprehension. The fine hairs at the back of his neck stood up as if electrified. When he finally dared to breathe, to take a labored gasp at his cigarette, the air itself seemed changed. As if the unseen presence had somehow rendered it poisonous.

Could he smell something besides the usual mold and cigarette smoke, the pileup of dirty laundry on the other side of the bed? Wet fur and ashes, the acrid odor of burning plastic. No, not plastic. Celluloid. Like the charred monstrosity that had found him on the plane.

Don wanted to move, to obey the instinct that told him to get out, away from whatever had crawled into his living space or followed him back from the dream. But what would he see when he opened the door or if he tried the window?

Space means nothing to them. Nor can they be kept out by doors and walls.

Maybe by turning all the lights on he would stop the intrusion, prevent the hideous luminescence from entering the apartment. But no sooner had his bare feet touched the floor than he became aware of the sound. A labored, spasmodic scratching that originated in the walls, matched by a bumping, shuffling noise out in the hallway. The scrabble of claws on brick and drywall could be a rat, but it sounded much larger; there was a pattern to it that suggested intelligence, a determined purpose.

It took Don's foggy brain several attempts at the switch to recognize the lights were not coming on.

As if spurred by his actions, the noise in the walls intensified. Now he could tell it was coming from the bathroom. Something heavy flopped onto the floor, rustled on the tile, nails clicking as they sought purchase on the floor. Its efforts evoked in Don's mind the image of a bulky, lumpy shape trying to push itself upright.

Air whistled in blackened lungs followed by a snuffling grunt.

Don scrambled for his phone, turned on the screen while toppling the bedside lamp and a handful of small objects onto the floor. He found the flashlight application, shone the shivering beam around the room as if trying to fix its layout in his mind, to stop the transformation he could sense taking place all around him. *The slippage.*

Twice he drew breath past a swiftly constricting throat before he could force the words out. "Who's there? What do you want?"

Long shadows twitched through the half-open bathroom door. The occupant inside had propped itself up, arms and legs thrashing about, its wasted body struggling beneath the ungainly weight of an oversized torso and head. Huffing either in frustration or fervor, it swiped a long, clawed limb through the air, toiletries crashing into the shower stall.

Not daring to move the beam from the door, Don moved as far from the bathroom as he could, slapping his hand along the wall until he found the main light switch. Nothing happened when he turned it on. The overhead fixtures were just as dead as his bedside lamp.

Somewhere deep inside him, in some forgotten center that remained untouched by paralyzing terror, he was grateful that the faint beam of his phone couldn't reach far enough into the bathroom to give him a good look at what thrashed and grunted there. Grateful that it revealed only faltering glimpses of a mottled body barely able to stand, a collection of mismatched body parts; a huge head—or a shape where the head should be—flopping obscenely on an elongated neck. A wounded beast, or a marionette with twisted strings, tottering and bumping as it tried to find its center of gravity. With each passing second, its movements grew more confident, its desiccated lungs hauling eagerly at the unfamiliar air. Bony legs shivered, locked, held. An enormous hand, fingers tipped with long yellow nails, grasped the doorframe.

If they were ever human to begin with, it has stripped every last trace. The magician, Victor's friend, and the things that served him in the lightless passage. *If you let them get closer, close enough to show you their real faces, you'll wish you'd never been born.*

Without a cautionary flicker, the phone went dead, plunging Don into blindness.

There was a wet, triumphant explosion of breath as the intruder launched itself at its quarry. Then the hollow sound of bone striking a solid surface, the shower curtain ripping, claws tangling inside it. Something heavy struck the floor, ripping the plastic in a frenzy, followed by a howl of such rage and frustration that Don's paralysis vanished.

He threw himself at the front door, praying that he'd forgotten to lock it, hearing the bathroom door snap off its hinges and slam against the wall, the rush of clawed feet across the cheap carpet.

His luck was in. The door swung open and Don burst through it, feeling—or imagining that he'd felt—the thing's foul breath on the back of his neck along with the swishing through the air of those lethal talons. As he fled down the stairs, almost tripping over his feet to navigate the landings, he imagined that he could see his attacker out of the corner of his eye, a shape at once humanoid and insect, flowing down the wall like a stain. Its shriek filled his mind without bypassing his ears.

He made it down to the ground floor, threw his full weight against the fire exit door. Sudden disorientation as the sky opened up above him, the orange glow of the streetlamps the most welcome sight he'd ever seen. Lights were going out inside the building, extinguished in the wake of the intruder's passage. Rough pavement, wet and cold, scraped the soles of his bare feet. But he didn't stop, *couldn't stop*, until he reached the other side of the pavement.

A single thump shivered the door in its frame, the slam of an immense fist. But it couldn't come outside, no matter how hard it tried. A guttural roar bellowed from behind. Then silence. Don waited a few breathless moments, but the intruder was gone. He could *feel* it had gone.

He sat on the curb, watching the lights reappear in the black squares of the windows, shivering in his T-shirt and underwear. Waiting for the first weak sunlight of dawn. Too afraid to ask for help, too afraid to contemplate what had just happened.

They hunger, and they never forget.

Chapter 21

Sunrise the following day found him in a hotel room across the river, huddled under a blanket on the sofa, falling in and out of a fitful doze. Every light inside the room burned bright, along with a couple of lamps he'd salvaged from his apartment. He'd kept them on throughout the previous night; not that he needed any help staying awake. The disjointed chaos in his head made sleep an impossibility. Exhaustion finally did the trick, aided by what looked like the entire contents of the hotel minibar: an hour or two of troubled slumber into which nameless—and fortunately unremembered—horrors intruded.

After running out of his apartment, he'd spent several hours in a freezing back alley, huddled behind a reeking dumpster, teeth chattering with the cold. Jumping at the slightest noise, waiting for the first daylight to chase away the creeping shadows. Even then, it had taken all the reserve courage he could summon to enter the building and go up the stairs and into his home of the past three years, now irrevocably tainted by the presence of those *others* Kirk Taylor had warned him about.

At the door, he hesitated, thinking of the clawing in the walls that signaled the creature's arrival. He imagined it lurking just beyond the threshold, a long hand reaching for him, dragging him to some unimaginable fate. It took him no longer than a second or two to realize how misplaced his anxiety was. There were no windows in the bathroom, no apertures through which the intruder could have come in. But it *had*.

Doors wouldn't be of any use against what had visited him in the night, nor would any sort of conventional weapon. *They* could get him anytime, anywhere.

For the same reason, his reluctance to enter the apartment made no sense. But it was still with trepidation that he turned the doorknob and pulled the door open. Braced himself for the burst of movement, the fervent scratching of lethal claws.

When it didn't come, he stepped inside and tried the light. It didn't come on, but there was enough daylight from the window to see by.

The apartment was in disarray, but no more so than usual. A faint, indefinable burning smell lingered in the air. It could just as easily have drifted in from an adjacent unit through the shared vents. His bedsheets lay in a tangled heap where he'd tossed them, and the lamp was on its side on the floor, surrounded by his keys and coins. Otherwise, the place looked just like it always did; cramped and dingy, cheap furniture over cheaper flooring, the square of linoleum in the small kitchen discolored with age. The tears and snags in the carpet and scuff marks on the bathroom door could have been there before. Almost as if the whole episode had taken place in his imagination.

Don had dressed quickly, piled some clean clothes into an overnight bag and shoved his laptop and notes alongside them. The place was empty, but it no longer felt *safe*. He was being driven out of here by something he was powerless to fight. Kirk Taylor, who had evaded *them* for decades, had finally taken to the streets in the hope of escaping the worst. Don could not stay here, waiting for his inhuman pursuer to return.

Only survival mattered now. In the wake of last night's experience, all Don's skepticism had been burned right out of him like morning mist in the sun. It no longer mattered what was real and what wasn't. *Stay ahead of them. Survive.* Awful as it was, the clarity was something he could hold on to, a beacon he could follow out of the darkness.

His brief visit to the bathroom to collect his few belongings reinforced his determination to leave. It wasn't the sight of the shower curtain that lay in the stall ripped to shreds, or of the snapped metal rod that disturbed him. At first glance, nothing else seemed different. The bulb over the sink came on, albeit reluctantly, revealing the same cracked tile, the same huge, moist stain in the corner that the landlord kept assuring him wasn't black mold. It was the afterimage he saw when the bulb fizzed and went out that lasted no longer than a fraction of a second, but long enough to imprint itself on his mind, repeating in maddening cadence.

Not a stain, but the negative image of a body, misshapen limbs folded in irrational directions, like the legs of a spider. Thin torso reduced to a collection of ribs and long bones. A huge domed skull with deep-set eye sockets above a nose like paired slits, a cavernous jaw lined with small, sharp teeth, too many to count. Caught in a roar, or a shriek of pain. The film imprints a nightmare crossing over into the waking world. Gone almost before his brain caught up with it, but enough to drive him back out into the street, clutching at his bag and muttering to himself like a madman.

A taxi had taken him across the city and into a nondescript hotel, where he'd turned on every light in the room, checked the closet and under the bed, and proceeded to drink himself into a stupor. The light wouldn't keep *them* out, but he hoped it would let him spot the early signs of intrusion, giving him time to get out. Occasionally he got up to shine his phone into the corners, searching the walls for strange writing, obsessing over every crack that looked like a symbol, peering at every stain, unblinking, until his vision blurred.

Now, a day later, he felt no closer to salvation or resolution. The pounding of his hangover was the only real thing he could focus on, a familiar sensation in a world grown bizarre and incomprehensible. A night had passed without disruption or visitation, but he suspected the truce, if that was what it was, wouldn't last. *They* had his scent now. It was only a matter of time before the hunt resumed.

There was nothing else ahead of him but flight, snatches of broken sleep, and paranoid glances over his shoulder. Until *they* caught up with him and carried him off into the lightless place. Or until he opened a door, any ordinary door, a door he'd walked through countless times before, and became lost in the space that appeared beyond it. Like Brody, the unfortunate set designer. Like Victor Hudson himself, if Taylor's rambling was to be believed. An existence of fear and misery that would do no more than delay the inevitable. The wretchedness of his situation, the despair it engendered, were almost tangible, billions of tons of water pinning him to the bottom of the ocean, destroying his will to live.

He had to try to find a way out of his plight. Impose a semblance of control over his life, as much as such a feat was still possible. One thing he was certain of was that his book project was at the root of the problem. Whatever was happening to him, his writing, his research, were only making it worse. He had to send a warning to J. C. Latham and anyone else involved with the book. Jake Kebbler had taken his life with good reason, probably unwilling to cope with the presence of the *others*. Those dwellers in the lightless space whose attention had been drawn to Don and his writing. Anyone looking for information on Victor Hudson and *The Unveiling* was likely to meet the same end.

Even if the situation existed only in his head, his work on the manuscript had only made it worse, evoking demons from his deepest subconscious. He was done with the dreams, done with the trancelike writing sessions, done with the obsession that had reduced Hudson's old associates to human ruins. Done with feeling like the story was writing *him*, inexplicable as that sounded; that he was being replaced in the world, piece-by-piece. That the mysterious figure he was pursuing through the pages was becoming more corporeal with every passage, while Don Ruby, the specter dutifully hitting the keys, was fading into the background. Until that other someone took his place entirely and he was relegated to that passage neither of this world nor the other, stripped of his humanity, his thoughts and memories leached by the encroaching dark. He refused to accept this fate.

Maybe he should forget about movie critique and try his hand at a horror novel. After all, what could be more metafictional than a crazy writer writing a story about a writer driven crazy by the story he was writing? The bubble of dark laughter in his throat was cut short by the harsh, intrusive ringing of the room phone.

Don felt his resolve crumble further with every repetition of the sound. He crossed over to the table and stared at the offending piece of plastic but couldn't make himself pick it up. His hand refused to obey the instructions of his brain. No one knew where he was. He was sure he hadn't told anyone where he was going. No one could have tracked him here. *They* didn't announce their arrival over the phone.

The ringing stopped for the space of two heartbeats. Started up with renewed vigor almost making him jump out of his skin.

He snatched up the receiver, said something into the mouthpiece but wasn't sure what. The voice on the other end of the line repeated a phrase with professional patience. Don had to hear it several times before the words clicked. It was the front desk clerk, informing him that he had a visitor.

"I don't. I'm not expecting anyone." His mind couldn't even summon up the name of the hotel. Briefly he imagined Kirk Taylor standing in the lobby, dirty and ragged, loudly demanding to be allowed upstairs. Or was this another one of the dream-magician's tricks, another ploy to torment his target?

The clerk's response was erased by a burst of static on the line. "Don't let them up," Don said, but the man could no longer hear him. Muffled voices, the sound of footsteps echoing in a wide, hollow space, the scrape of the receiver being lifted to someone's ear.

"Don? Is that you?"

Confusion robbed him of a response. He stared at the phone, trying to think of what to say. When he finally managed to get the words out, he was barely aware of them. The speaker on the other end of the line didn't seem to be bothered by his incoherence.

"Why don't you get dressed and come down," Jess said, speaking slowly, as if to a frightened child. "I'm in the lobby. Take all the time you need. I'll be waiting."

***

"I got worried," she told him over fried eggs and toast at a nearby diner, her voice straining over the commotion. She had suggested a quiet place to have breakfast and catch up and was surprised when Don picked the busiest greasy spoon in the neighborhood, choosing the table closest to the big, brightly lit window. In typical Jess fashion, she had given Don ample opportunity to break the silence first, but he'd said nothing, his thoughts a million miles away. "You didn't respond to any of my emails. Then I tried to call your cell. It kept going to voicemail, which I know Don Ruby never listens to or answers. Then I started calling hospitals."

"How did you find me in the end?"

"I have my methods." She smiled, but her eyes were tired. "You've pulled this disappearing act before, Ruby. It didn't end well. So, I decided it would be best to check on you in person."

"Yeah." To avoid meeting her eye, Don stared at the pile of congealing cholesterol on his plate. "Thing is, I haven't been myself lately. There's a lot going on. A lot on my mind." He tried to articulate a way to tell Jess about what he was going through. Maybe leave out the unbelievable parts. At least for now. "It's got to do with the book I'm working on. It's taking a lot out of me."

"As it should. It's only the best thing you've ever written." Jess speared a chunk of vegan sausage and swirled it in runny yolk. "That's what got me worried in the first place. Your chapters came in like clockwork at first. A couple every week, sometimes three, then nothing." There was concern in her gaze, a gleam of indefinable wariness. "Is it writer's block? If it is, I can talk to the publisher. Get an extension sorted out. I'm sure he won't mind. He's champing at the bit to get this book out on the shelves just like you are. I sent over a few of the polished chapters as a teaser, and he had nothing but praise for them."

Don gazed at her across the table. *Good old Jess.* Time had been a lot kinder to her than it had to him: she'd cut her hair shorter and lost some weight, but the changes looked good on her. Maybe the fine lines around her eyes hadn't been there before, or the sharp bones on her face used to be a touch less prominent. But the spark that lit her up from the inside was still there. She'd slipped back into her former role of agent and advisor effortlessly, the past and present merging without a seam, as if they'd never been apart. Warmth kindled inside his chest, a great shapeless loosening.

"I'm done with it," he said. "The book. I'm not doing it anymore. I'll pay back the advance. Don't want you involved with it either. Or anyone else."

Jess sat back, as if waiting for the punchline, then frowned when she realized none was coming. "You really mean it," she said, reaching for her coffee. "Are you sure you want to pull the plug? This guy Latham is committed. I talked to him over Skype. A peculiar man, but lovely." Her eyes narrowed. "What's going on? You don't look too good."

"You, on the other hand, are as lovely as ever."

"I'm serious, Don." Her voice grew softer. "You call me out of the blue, after God knows how many years, to talk about a book you're writing. You send me the first few chapters, and I'm hooked immediately. Then you ghost me, utterly and completely. No emails, no messages. Nothing. Until yesterday, when I get another weird fucking call from you."

"Call? I never called you." But even as he said it, Don couldn't be sure what had happened. His phone was dead. In his hurry to get out of his apartment, he'd left the charger behind. Unless someone had gotten to it while he was shivering in the street outside. "Wait. What did I say?"

Jess set her cup down and shook her head. "Forget about it. I'm in no mood for weird, Ruby. I've had enough weird to last me a couple lifetimes." *Thanks to you*, her tone seemed to imply. "We've done this dance already, remember?"

"It's not like that." Don rubbed the side of his head. "Not this time. You have to believe me. It's just... Things started to happen as I was writing the book. The people I spoke to." He cut off abruptly, unsure whether to continue or retreat from the concern in her eyes. What if the knowledge put her in more danger? He tried to say something dismissive but couldn't get it past the lump in his throat. The breath he held came out as a sob.

"Hey." Jess reached across the table, took his hand. "Hey. I'm worried about you, Don. Just like I was last time. You weren't yourself back then. Not just because of the drinking and the drugs. You made a bad place inside your head, and there was no getting you out of it." When he tried to reply, she squeezed his hand gently. "It was awful being around you. Trying to drag you out of that dark hole as you kept digging in deeper. Do you remember?"

He nodded, aware that they were starting to draw glances. "But that's not what's happening now. I'm in real danger, or my sanity is. So are you. It's not good to be around me." Desperately he searched for the right words, but they eluded him in the crowded din of the diner. "Things are happening. Things that I can't explain. I think they have to do with what I'm writing. I have to stop."

"You're not in the right place to figure out what's going on," Jess said, doing her best to smile. "But it might help if you shared it with someone. Tell me what you think is happening."

Don told her everything, not sparing her the details of his nightmares, all up to his encounter with Kirk Taylor in Washington Square and the visit that followed. The story poured out of him in an uncontrollable torrent, leaving him drained but exhilarated, a vast and invisible weight lifting off his shoulders. When he was done, the diner was all but empty, the morning patrons having moved on with their day, the elderly waitress at the counter sending irate looks their way. He drank his cold, oily coffee and searched Jess's face for traces of skepticism or pity. If she gave up on him, if she made an excuse to leave and stopped returning his calls, he'd understand.

But she sat there, silent and inscrutable. When she was sure he was done, she tapped on her phone for a few minutes then turned the screen toward him.

It was an article from the online edition of the *Metro*. Don read the headline several times before the meaning sank in. At the top of the page was a photo of Kirk Taylor from his slasher heartthrob days, shirt unbuttoned over a muscular torso, grinning at the camera. A still from *The Chain Gang*, one of his pre-Hudson features, in which he'd played a rare bad guy role. It had taken the police some time to identify the body found in a local homeless shelter, the article explained, going on to describe the actor's short-lived career. Don's shaking finger navigated down the page. Taylor had died in his sleep, most likely from natural causes; foul play was not suspected.

Don looked from the phone to Jess, uncomprehending. "That's him," he said. "That's the guy. He told me he was staying at a shelter." He pinched the bridge of his nose, sucked in a hissing breath. "He said they were after him. That they had woken up. The others in the lightless place. That they wanted him silenced."

Jess started to speak, hesitated. Nodded, as if indulging a particularly slow child. Took his hand again. "Or you read this same article last night. In whatever state of mind you happened to be. Thinking that the book you're writing is changing reality somehow. That you're being pursued by some kind of—I don't know—malevolent supernatural force." She held her hand up when Don tried to speak. "Just hear me out. It's a hell of a coincidence, I'll give you that. You're writing a book about a lost movie. The lead actor shows up dead in a homeless shelter in Philly. No one has seen him in years. No one knows what he's been up to or why. I can see how this sort of thing can play havoc on your nerves. Especially if there's alcohol involved."

Don jerked his hand back as if singed. "You think I made it all up. Hallucinated seeing Taylor."

"I think you could be mistaken," Jess said, annunciating each word carefully. "It's clear that you've been under a lot of pressure over the past few weeks. Working yourself into the ground. Trying to make up for lost time." She paused, then spoke faster, like someone ripping off a Band-Aid. "I just want you to consider the possibility—only the possibility—that you may have taken the news of Taylor's death unusually hard in your present condition." The allusion to his alcoholism made Don squirm in his seat, but he couldn't muster the self-righteousness to deny it. "Your mind could have provided the rest. It wouldn't have taken much."

"Didn't realize you're also a psychiatrist on the side."

"All I'm asking you to do is consider it." She picked up the check that the waitress had deposited and waved away Don's protest. "You said these others, or whoever they are, got inside your apartment. Broke in. That's against the law. Did you call the police?"

"No." She wasn't getting the point. But she would. He just had to find a way to describe it without sounding crazy. His mind grasped at the memory of that terrible night, trying to preserve it even as it crumbled away into blankness. "No. I had to get out of there. The police can't help anyway. The only thing that helps is staying on the move. Where they can't find you."

"We should go back together, then. Figure out if anything was stolen."

"They didn't take anything," Don said, realization dawning. *A gift from the other side, taken of your own free will.* Like the notebook he thought he'd stolen from Jake Kebbler, the one *they* kept bringing back. "They don't take things. They leave them for you to find."

"Okay." Jess glanced at him warily. She took a long moment to compose herself before speaking again. "Okay. You're in that bad place again, Don. That's my opinion. I think finishing your book is the only thing that can get you out of it. Exorcise those demons onto the page. It's a cliché, but it might be just what you need."

"That's the last thing I want to do."

"Hear me out." She raised her hands in a placating gesture. "You have to clean up your act first. Take some time to get your head straight. No drinking or any of the other stuff. No more running around the country interviewing people. Kooks with nothing better to do than relive their old exploits, feed you lies hoping to squeeze a couple bucks out of the situation. We'll find a place where you can be alone. Undisturbed. Shut yourself in and see this thing through to the end. We'll work on it together."

She spoke the last sentence casually, with a slight pause to let the import set in. "When it's ready, we'll send it over to your publisher. I haven't brought it up with him, but he'll be willing to wait. As long as it takes to make sure your book is as thorough and complete as possible."

Don heard what she was saying but could barely understand her. *We.* His entire being concentrated upon the word, shivered with the jolt that it had sent through him. Jess *understood*: she may not believe a word of his story, but she was determined to stand by his side until he could find his feet again. If he could never have her back, this felt like the next best thing.

When she reached for his hand again, he squeezed first. The crooked smile that warmed her face made him think of happier, simpler times. There was no fixing the past, only the hope of living the future the best way that he could. "You really think I'm onto something with this one," he said.

"I'll tell you what I think. It's not just the best thing you've ever written, it could be the biggest." She was warming to her topic now, voice deepening. "Sure, it's a small press, and the first run will be limited. Five hundred, maybe a thousand copies. But Latham has plans to expand, and I'll be going over your contract very carefully to make sure you haven't signed your rights away forever." Her eyes were bright, but distant, as she tipped the waitress and gathered her purse. "I think this book will change everything. For you, but also for others. All those eager fans."

Don strove to keep his tone offhand but was betrayed by a slight tremor in it. "Do you think you'll stick around a while? Or is it back to Chicago on the next flight?"

"Are you kidding? I'm not leaving without another chapter." She stabbed a slender finger in his direction. "You owe me at least twenty pages, Ruby. Latham may be ready to cut you all the slack you want, but his acquisitions department is getting antsy, and there has been some hand-wringing over the advance. So, we feed the sharks more chum to keep them circling. Play your cards right, and I might even parlay them into covering your hotel. Anything to keep those creative juices flowing."

He held the door open for her and followed her out onto the rainy street. Walkers passed by, cowled and wrapped in swathes of dark, shapeless apparitions flitting down the sidewalks. Commuters venturing up from a subway station put him in mind of miners at the end of a shift. Everyday banality that he now yearned for but that he had been banished from forever. Wet gray had engulfed the sky; he felt it invade his head, smothering his thoughts beneath a blanket of nothingness. Dark heavens and rain-streaked glass made the street look like the negative of a summer day.

"What happens after I deliver the chapter?"

"That's a surprise." He couldn't see Jess's face clearly from her jacket hood, but he heard the smile in her voice. "I'm not allowed to tell you any more about it. But I think you'll like it."

"Whose surprise?"

"You don't want to miss it." She flagged a cab and ducked into the back seat. Grinned a secretive grin up at him. "Don't disappoint me, Ruby. There's a whole lot riding on you. I'll be expecting that chapter by the end of the week."

He watched the cab merge with the blur, then started back toward the hotel. Already the meeting with Jess felt like it had all taken place in his mind. The conversation had helped, but he was unsure of his grasp on the world, of what he would have to face once he was alone with his thoughts. What might have followed him to his new abode.

Chapter 22

If The Master's Daughter *introduced Hudson's work to the American audience, it was the success of* Last Church *that cemented his place in the ever-expanding pantheon of schlock-horror filmmakers. Less of an oddity in directorial style and cinematography than its famous—or infamous—predecessor,* Last Church *still balks at convention, stubbornly refusing to follow the hackneyed formula which by that time had become entrenched in the minds of slasher fans. In a manner that unconsciously augurs the tongue-in-cheek* Scream *metaslasher serial of the early aughts, Hudson toys with the viewer's expectations, subverting cast-in-stone genre tropes, parodying nascent conventions while maintaining an implacable poker face. These days all but forgotten,* Church *is a chainsaw's cut above any other horror film made on a similar budget, the auteur director's magic backed by stellar performances from a young, ambitious cast, most of whom will fail to replicate this early success over the rest of their acting careers.*

Heather Chance was not Hudson's first choice for Maggie: the master's vision initially called for someone less all-American, less-girl-next-door, but darker and more reticent. Yet, it was Chance's irresistible mix of everyday good looks and wide-eyed innocence that delivered most of the snap and sizzle on screen—and I'm not just talking about that grisly pool electrocution scene. Her chemistry with her male lead is undeniable from the start.

Vince Castle, playing the conflicted Tony, brings a brooding, slightly sinister patina to the production. The audience wants to buy into both aspects of his character, and this is the pivotal crux about which Hudson masterfully turns his story. Is Tony a haunted man, doing his best to save his friends and the woman he loves from the menace looming over them, or is he a deranged killer, the menace itself, hunting his victims one-by-one, dispatching them in the most gruesome ways conceivable?

Hudson never lets up the tension, never lets the viewer be certain. Nothing is the way it appears to be, a characteristic that will come to define, to a greater or lesser degree, the director's entire opus. The frames and sight lines are a clever trap, a pit for the audience to navigate around or to fall into. In the eye of Hudson's camera, lines and corners trail off to nowhere and inanimate objects take on a menacing life of their own. By the time the killer's blade appears from the shadows, its gleam is almost welcome, a giddy release from the unendurable buildup of simmering tension. A flight from the darkness that has gathered around you, unobserved, leaving you with no way out.

Just when the audiences accepted this innovative style, just as they thought they had the British import all figured out, Victor Hudson turned their expectations upside down with his next feature, Occupancy Twenty-Seven, *which assails the senses with all the subtlety of a ten-megaton nuclear explosion. Limbs are sent flying, blood spews from severed necks in almost gleeful arcs, black in the flickering lights of the abandoned motel. Gory walls show the way deeper into Hell for the movie's hopeless and hapless protagonists, into madness and torture and cannibalism and worse. Was Hudson still finding his feet, experimenting with archetype and audience appetites, or simply giving free rein to different facets of his creative persona? Facets that his tragic, untimely death prevented from fully expressing themselves? It is rare that a director's work expresses any sort of consistency regarding his personality. His touch is refracted, reflected through the prism of the other participants in the process; the camera crew, the script writers and producers, most obviously the actors. The end product is something outside the conscious control of any one of its makers.*

This was the point that Hudson would spend the rest of his career trying to convey. Not a single sight line in any of his films is off, without that distortion itself serving a purpose. Each frame, every remorseless slaying seeing through his voyeur's camera lens, contributes to the narrative. But he goes further than that. Hudson anticipates the reaction of the audience, the echo of the received idea in the viewer's subconscious, weaving the experience of those on the other side of the fourth wall into his grand design. The creator and his creation, along with those purporting to be mere observers, all become part of the event. At the mercy of what lies beneath the placid dark waters of the conscious, contributors to the great unveiling taking place before and behind their eyes.

A passenger riding inside their minds, unacknowledged and unnoticed, drawing power from their focus. A god, or a demon, or a thousand things undreamed, donning their flesh as a costume. In this interpretation, the screen is both gateway and mirror, separating the stories unfolding on either side of it, yet connecting them through conduits unseen by the naked eye. Passages through the gray wasteland that abuts our world, into the realms of enlightenment, forever sealed off from our reach.

Or are they?

Hudson certainly entertains a different belief; his surrealism is disturbing but purposeful. Familiar things and locations made strange, coated with the patina of that gray place that beckons—maddeningly—from beyond the veil. The creator is transformed; the watcher observed. Blood is the secret that opens the conduit, but death is only the means to an end. Something latches onto the eyes of the audience, growing stronger with every mind it touches.

A sacrifice...

Don looked up from the keyboard, stared at the block of text he'd just written. Erased the stub of the last sentence, then the preceding paragraph.

Struggled to force some sort of order on his thoughts on the sentences that seemed to rise unbidden from the blankness of the page.

It was just a draft, a rough draft. He would have ample time to clean it up, to populate it with the ideas that felt as though they were crowding him out of his head. His fingers flew over the keys for a few more minutes, but the words that were forming in his mind didn't seem capable of making it onto the screen. His hands, his traitor digits, were no longer a tool, but an obstruction.

He rolled his stiff shoulders, willed his body to rise from the uncomfortable hotel chair. Jess had worked her magic again; his room was paid for through the end of the week, courtesy of some line she had fed to the publisher about Don's apartment being temporarily uninhabitable due to infestation. Which was close enough to the truth to make Don want to laugh and scream at the same time.

He was now in the second week of his self-imposed confinement and starting to feel a cautious optimism about both the work and the absence of visitations. Although it would be some time before he went to bed without the lights on, without carefully checking the lintels and corners for marks left by exploring *others*. Vigilance hadn't helped Kirk Taylor, for *they* had gotten to him in the end, hauled him screaming from the pitiful pile of skin and bones and rags, into the endless wasteland beyond. But the ritual comforted him, gave him some sort of peace of mind.

Sleep was coming back to him, albeit reluctantly, aided by pills. No more nightmares, even though every noise in the walls, every footstep in the hotel's busy corridors, still jerked him awake and set his heart racing. A shadow had fallen over his life, invisible but large enough to blot out the sun, to deny him all but a fleeting glimpse of hope. But he thought he saw a way out of it now, a path to follow out of its darkness.

Jess had wrought this change within him. His only friend who had never given up on him, despite the hurt he had caused her. He had lived an absurd existence, foolish and destructive, fueled by self-pity and anger. In many ways, those bad days had been worse than what he was going through now, the meaningless horror to which he had reduced his existence just as dangerous as the presences stalking him from beyond the wall of sleep.

Staying sober was helping, and catching up on his sleep had given him the clarity of mind to think about Jess's advice in a calm and rational manner, to consider all angles. More and more, he was becoming convinced that his attempt to frame his experience in rational terms was, in itself, irrational. Perhaps what was happening to him could not be explained in mundane ways; it didn't necessarily follow that it was malevolent or that he had placed himself in peril. He couldn't fathom exactly *what* it meant, only knew that recent events had eroded his ability to think in logical sequences. His thoughts floated like a thin mist, dissolving when he tried to examine them closely.

One certainty prevailed: he could not stop writing now, couldn't give up on his research either, regardless of what he'd promised to Jess. The book was his connection to the lightless place, to what he felt scrabbling toward him from the other side. If he broke off that connection, if he defied *them*, any chance to regain a degree of normalcy in his life would be forfeited.

There was no walking away, not anymore. Wherever he fled, however long he kept running, he would be found. For as long as he lived—as long as *they* let him live—he would carry *their* taint upon him. Until he grew tired or until the hunt closed in. Then the gray wraiths would claim him, and he would roam and gibber with the rest of the damned, vainly searching for the light. All his life Don had refused to confront problems, had cleaved to the path of least resistance, the easy way out. That wasn't an option now.

If he wanted out, if he wished to rejoin the world of order and sanity, he had to trace the mystery back to its source.

Seeing Hudson's early movies, the ones Robert Callaway had raved about, would be a start. If nothing else, it would mean more material for his book. But he felt there might be more to it than that, that those first efforts would reveal some vital clue. Something about the Brotherhood of Lament, or the magician who tormented Don's dreams.

Knowing better than to look online for an answer, Don had resorted to the dog-eared notebook, which he had brought to the hotel against his better instincts. If he couldn't get rid of the magician's gift, maybe he could turn it against him and find a hint buried in the maddening scrawl that charted Jake Kebbler's descent into madness. Within a few pages, he came across a section on Hudson's early life as if it had been waiting for him.

Victor Hudson had studied at Bournemouth Film School in the sixties. Callaway had referred to the director's short films, the ones he'd *made while he was still in college, over in England*. Perhaps the school or a local library would still have the originals. An email to the head of the school, whose name had been prefaced by a confusing and obscure British title, such as *Vice-Chancellor* or *Proctor*, had confirmed this assumption. Victor Hudson's short movies were kept in the University's archives and could be made available to authorized researchers with the Vice-Chancellor's, or Proctor's, permission. Don had forwarded a copy of his contract and a link to Occultation Press' website, featuring an announcement for his book. He had booked his tickets as soon as the school responded in the affirmative. Baltimore International to London Heathrow on Friday morning, then back, through a trick of changing time zones, to Baltimore on Sunday afternoon. With any luck, he would make the round trip with no one the wiser. That 'no one' being Jess.

Don felt guilty about lying to her—although did an omission technically count as a lie? She had been worried about him, insisting that he needed rest and seclusion to focus on the book. Surely that was only out of concern for the manuscript deadline, her anxiety over distractions that could sideline the project. He could explain it later, show her how the trip to Bournemouth had actually helped him finish the book faster.

If he emailed her the new chapter before he left, there was a possibility that she wouldn't read it before Monday when he was safely back at the hotel. On the other hand, for all he knew, she could still be in town and might turn up at any time to check on him. He couldn't remember what she'd said about her itinerary or even if she had one. It was a risk he would have to take.

To distract himself from his guilt, he went to his publisher's site, clicked the *upcoming releases* link. A banner soaked in pixelated blood announced the *Grandmasters of Grue*, a *rediscovery of forgotten masters of cinematic horror by Don Ruby, biographer to the stars*. Below it, a series of stills captured the most iconic moments from Hudson's slashers, alongside a rare black-and-white image of the director himself, standing next to a camera and staring off to the left of the photo.

Don leaned forward and zoomed in. Someone was standing behind Hudson in the photo, a man-shaped shadow, crouching slightly, as if to sneak up on the oblivious director. No; it was bending its head to whisper in his ear, a movement both sinister and intimate at the same time. One shadow-arm curled around Hudson's shoulder, as if to restrain him.

Then the image was gone, the zoom too close to keep it in focus. Cursing, Don scrolled back, restoring the page to its normal dimensions. There was no one in the photo but Hudson. But he knew he wasn't mistaken. His mind seemed to lurch, to fall into the page, a giddy sensation that was becoming familiar, like a conditioned reflex.

He hurried to the comments section, desperate to avoid the collage of photos, all of which seemed to be on the verge of becoming something else. Several horror fan sites had linked back to the announcement. The responses were enthusiastic, inquiring about preorders and signed copies. Don hovered the cursor over the pingback links and clicked one that caught his attention. It was a page on a free blogging platform, advertising something called the Macabre Marquee Society, *howlings from the ether for the aficionados of atrocity, the celebrants of camp, the purveyors of the psychotronic.*

Intrigued, Don read on. The blog post paid homage to *The Unveiling*, calling it *one of the great lost films of an unforgettable era*, making obscure references to the *peculiar fate that had befallen its cast and crew. An abandoned project by one of the genre's geniuses*, opined the author, an improbably named Thaddeus D. Headstone, Esq. This tied in with Don's Occultation Press book enough to capture his attention.

For an amateur website, the content was well laid out with the black-and-red background complementing the text frame. The Macabre Marquee Society featured reviews of low-budget horror films, occult publications and Gothic graphic novels, along with a semi-regular column titled *Fresh Blood*, which covered more or less anything that attracted the attention of the Society's owner, chairperson, and sole contributor. Based in New York, the Society also arranged screenings of old horror movies at a club in Brooklyn. Some of the titles were familiar to Don from his research, but the majority he'd never heard of. *Driller Killer, Silent Scream, When a Stranger Calls*; a mini-festival, or five screenings, dedicated to the work of Dario Argento, with a scheduled *lively debate* dedicated to the recent remake of the Italian filmmaker's magnum opus, *Suspiria*. Victor Hudson's *Last Church* and *Occupancy Twenty-Seven* were featured on the list and linked to a column entry in which Thaddeus D. Headstone, Esq., lamented the demise of the small independent film studios.

> *Like the characters in the movies they produced,* the article proclaimed, *many of these indie outfits were bled to death by diminishing returns and unrealistic expectations of financiers, faced the bloodied chainsaw of critical opinion, or were swallowed whole by the leviathans moving into the market. Some, like the eerily vanished Last Rite Productions, went up in flames—not the flames of public opinion, lit by the self-appointed moral majority, but an actual fire that consumed the company's studio in Burbank, California. Priceless pearls of the psychotronic were lost forever; every now and then, a rumor surfaces of a copy of one or another dark treasure being rescued and found. But Yours Truly has yet to encounter them in the morbid and malodorous back alleys of the World Wide Web, through which he scuttles tirelessly like a spider.*

> *But that's what public forums (or is that fora?) are for. If you have one of these gruesome gems, or know someone who does, drop me a line in the comments. Together we can make their cries from the crypt, their echoes from the ether, heard in the vast all-engulfing void that is cyberspace. I would love to know that they still exist somewhere on this celestial plane.*

The entry linking back to Occultation Press was recent: someone was checking the page, at least occasionally. After a moment's hesitation, Don tried the Contact page, which turned out to be a dead end. He thought about this some more, then left a comment under the latest entry, introducing himself and cautiously mentioning his interest in Victor Hudson's lost film. If Thaddeus D. Headstone had any leads worth following, a trip up to New York was in order. More likely, he'd turn out to be a crank who would pester Don with collaboration offers or demand credit in the book.

Don shut down his laptop and paced the room, unwilling to acknowledge the source of his agitation. For the first time in weeks, everything seemed to be on track.

But it wasn't...

The sight of Kebbler's notebook, its very existence, seemed to mock him. A reminder of the power *they* still exerted over him, of eyes following him through the walls. Ugly and with a cracked cover, it intruded into his mind like a thorn and filled him with loathing.

Daring him to touch it. Daring him to destroy it, to try to get rid of it again.

Revulsed, he picked it up by one corner and flung it into the narrow closet. There was no reason for him to open it again. Even after he slid the door shut on it, he remained acutely aware of its presence, as if locking it in the darkness somehow made it more real. Helped it gain a foothold in the world.

Chapter 23

"Your message was a bit of a surprise," Thomas Priestley said, ushering Don out of his office into a glassed-in passage brimming with light. "Almost no one outside the faculty knows of Victor Hudson's association with our school, and precious few inside do. I admit to having to browse the archive ledgers to refresh my memory, but I believe I found what you're looking for."

Don's eyes smarted in the light, sleeplessness compounding his jet lag. He'd fought to stay awake on the entire flight from Baltimore to London, horrified by the thought of another slippage during the long haul across the nighttime expanse of the Atlantic. Even on the train ride from London to Bournemouth, the rhythm of the tracks lulling him to sleep, or at least a dreamlike stupor, he'd dosed himself with strong coffee to stay awake, mistrustful of the shapes protruding over the headrests, of shadows congealing in the corners of the near-empty carriage.

"I'm just glad you could accommodate my request on such short notice," he said, following the Dean of Media and Performance across a neatly trimmed lawn. On the way over, he'd imagined his destination to be a crumbling, windswept place with vaulted ceilings and dark halls lined with oil portraits of forbidding, long-gone schoolmasters and medieval weaponry hung on the walls. Not these airy, modern structures with simple, clean lines, among which he felt out of place and embarrassed by what he was about to ask. Students sat at sunlit outdoor tables, working and laughing and chattering. A world he was utterly cut off from, a normalcy he might never regain.

"No bother at all." Priestley produced a card, letting them into a narrow reception area that smelled of old books and warm dust, part of an older red-brick building on the other side of the common. "It's not often that we get queries about Hudson, and it must be decades since anyone has seen his short films. Certainly not in my time here. We're usually quite good at keeping track of our famous alumni. Helps draft the promotional material, if I can be perfectly honest. But Victor Hudson seems to have fallen by the wayside."

He peered at Don over a pair of glasses stylish enough to be an affectation. "Hopefully the book you're writing rescues him from obscurity," he said, swiping the card again. "By all accounts, he was considered a great talent in his days here. Also, before my time, I should say, but one hears all sorts of stories."

He held a door open for Don and nodded to a smiling young librarian.

"That's my hope too." Don glanced around the gloomy archive. Rows of shelves on all sides, piled high with dusty boxes stacked two or three deep. "It's hard to find out much about Hudson. But there is renewed interest in his work." He laughed nervously, moving closer to the center of the room into the light cast by the overheads. "At least my publisher hopes so."

Priestley returned a distracted smile. "It might take a minute to get through all this bumf. New coursework is all digitized, of course, but we haven't gotten round to the old films yet. Our archivist would be of far more use to you, but he's not in on weekends. So, you'll have to make do with me, I'm afraid."

He disappeared among the shelves. Don heard the scraping of wooden legs on the floor, saw a metal stack tremble as the professor clambered up to retrieve a box. "Didn't get that," he said in response to a muffled phrase.

When it wasn't repeated, he wrapped his arms around himself, shuddering as if with a chill.

The boundary of the light seemed to shrink around him, darkness pushing in. An ancient projector in one corner of the room, too old to serve as anything but a prop, stared at him through a single dull, cracked eye.

"Bit of a horror buff, are you?" The voice from the stacks chuckled apologetically. "Lots of critics slag it off as rubbish. Not high-brow enough for their tastes, apparently. Too common, as if that's a bad thing." A grunt of effort was followed by a low thump. "I don't see the appeal myself, but that's no reason to dismiss it. Just human expression, just like any other sort of film. Like any art form."

"Have you seen any of Hudson's movies? The slashers?"

"Afraid not." Priestley emerged from behind the shelves, toting a box and dabbing at his forehead. "Only the experimental work from his Continental period. Many of Hudson's horrors were banned here in Britain. The Board of Film found them too gruesome for our refined sensibilities. So, Hudson never developed a following. Some of his titles would have appeared later on illegal videotapes. Today I imagine they're all available online. I never really went in for that sort of thing, but I might after this. He seems to have been a fascinating man."

He set the box on a table and pushed his glasses higher up the bridge of his nose. Gray streaks of dust marked his sleeves. "Here's two of his early ones. Nineteen-seventy-one, from what we have on record, but that's just the date they were inventoried. It's a miracle any survived. The archive is for graduate work only, so these must have been added long after he was gone."

"His graduate movies weren't stored with the rest?"

"Victor Hudson never graduated," Priestley said. "Not from the Arts University, in any case. Left in his third year, never came back." He cleared his throat uneasily. "I tried to dig his file out for you but couldn't find one. Bit silly, I have to say, but there seems to be an unspoken agreement among the faculty. No one talks about Victor Hudson. Not that there's anyone left who knew him back then, of course."

"Do you know what prompted him to leave?"

"That's where things get interesting." In spite of the silver in his hair and goatee, the Dean's eyes glinted mischievously; he looked like a boy delighted by the discovery of a secret. "Apparently, he caused quite a stir. Several professors wrote directly to the Chancellor, demanding that Hudson be expelled. Mind you, there were no stuffed shirts teaching here. Artists, visionaries, bohemians, just as the countercultural sixties were getting into full swing. Some of them dabbled in the, er, esoteric. Or at least cultivated the rumors that they did. Whatever young Hudson did to scandalize them, it must have been dire." He patted the box, rubbed his hands on his trousers. "Shall we have a look?"

Don was suddenly reluctant to open the box; sweat pooled under his arms and in the small of his back. "You said these are the two that survived. Were there more?"

"Oh, certainly. At least a dozen, if the records are accurate. Maybe more."

"What happened to the rest?"

Priestley shrugged. "As I said, we usually only keep records of graduation films. All entries are tracked, but fifty years ago our system was not as robust as it is today. Hard to tell exactly, but some of the Hudson reels disappeared when the archive was moved in the nineties. Several of the films were acquired by a production company in Canada." He opened the box, removing a document from a thin cardboard folder.

"You mean they purchased the rights?" Don asked, jotting down the logo on the stationery. *Revelation Films*, based in Ontario, Canada. He doubted the company would live up to its name; it was probably just another dead end.

"They must have had the necessary paperwork," the Dean continued. "Or the blessing of the then-Chancellor Some of the staff were very keen to see the films go. Then, of course, others were stolen."

"Stolen?"

"It happens," Priestley said, looking resigned. "We keep the archive under lock-and-key. But it isn't all that difficult to get in, and there's always someone eager to try. Students, horror film fans, delusional people looking for messages hidden in the frames. Even ghouls looking for mementos after Hudson died. We've had our share of those over the years. Films are returned damaged or not returned at all. Or a snippet is cut out for keepsakes, ruining the whole reel. Things get dodgy around intellectual property, so it's not worth it to the school to pursue legal action. Shameful, really. But there's no accounting for people's obsessions."

"So, Hudson was a pariah," Don said. "Yet someone on the faculty saved his movies. All of them. Even the early ones."

"His work was supposed to be very good. Later, when he achieved fame—or notoriety, depending on whom you ask—his experimental films became part of his legacy, and, by extension, the school's." Priestley hesitated, seemed to be searching for words. "But I suspect there may have been another reason for keeping the films here."

"Like what?"

"Perhaps the school board wanted to keep them locked up. Out of sight." The Dean waved a hand as if to dismiss his own words. An uncomfortable silence ruled for a moment. "Anyway, this is all that's left."

Don reached into the box and took out the two canisters. Yellowing labels identified them as *Untitled One* and *Experiment Seven* in neat, almost mechanical handwriting. "What did you think of them?"

"Can't say I ever watched them." Priestley seemed unwilling to elaborate on the reason. "The faculty kept a copy of the Canadian videotape, until that too grew legs. From what I was able to track down, Hudson's approach was rather avant garde. Experimenting with light and framing, splicing in bits of old black-and-white film to suggest an impression. An almost subliminal image, imprinting itself on the viewer's subconscious. Unusually ambitious for a second-year student, especially with the equipment available then. Many surrealist films rely on the same trick—collages and intercutting scenes, samples on top of samples. Shots out of sequence."

"Sounds like that would make it hard to tell a story. At least a coherent one."

"Coherence is not the purpose." The Dean was warming to his topic. "Experimental film doesn't try to *tell* you anything. It uses light and motion and afterimages to *draw* the story from you. What's on the screen is only a prompt. Like a Rorschach test. Our mind sees a shape and tries to give it meaning. It's a reflex, a reaction. In a way, the artist tries to hypnotize the audience. To reach into their minds and implant his vision there." He peered solicitously at Don. "Are you all right? It tends to get a bit stuffy in here."

"I'm fine." Don shook his head, breathing past the nausea that the other man's words had evoked in him. "Like being in a dream, you mean. But dreamed by someone else."

"That's a good way to describe it." Priestley picked up the film canisters, pointed to a door across the room. "You're the first person to be seeing these in quite some time. I'll run the projector for you. Have to—can't risk something happening to the last of our Victor Hudson masterpieces. They have lain in the dark for so long, waiting to be discovered. I'm rather excited by the idea of revealing them to the world."

***

According to the label, the movies were short, each one around twenty minutes or so. Don settled into the dusty dimness of the screening room, waiting for the flickering of the projector beam to settle into a coherent image. He willed himself to relax and focus on the show. Priestley had likened experimental cinema to an inkblot test, the viewer's own mind providing a context to the shapes on the screen. It took attention to detail, perhaps repeated viewings lingering over particular sequences, to absorb the full experience.

But what was he seeing?

Black spots and lines popped and crackled within the frame. A darker circular shadow was irising shut, like a cigarette burn in reverse, eating away at the blank space to reveal an underlying layer. Were these impressions intentional or flaws in the aged celluloid? Don closed his eyes halfway: there was a shape in the center of the screen, or the suggestion of one, loping in a disturbingly lifelike fashion. An animal, like a horse, or a stag, galloping across a blurry background. The burn became a widening tunnel opening up on a chaos of shade and motion, a shifting, phantasmal landscape of overlaid sequences. His brain struggled to discern the imagery that flitted before him, always a beat too quickly for him to fix upon.

Hudson's *Untitled One* was a collage production, snippets of old footage spliced together to create a jerky and distorted, but oddly haunting, story. Silent films, three-strip Technicolor, even bits of what looked like sixties TV ads; somehow he had succeeded in playing them over each other, layer upon layer of picture and movement. The disjointed frames blended into a chaotic procession, circling the dark tunnel at the center of the picture, disappearing into it as if down a gullet. A mouth opened in the flat surface of the screen, sinking further, deeper, extending through the wall and the building behind it, through the fabric of space itself and beyond.

Don's palms slicked with sweat. He could feel the blazing kliegs over the stage, could hear the whisper of the wretched procession in the passage. For a moment, he had the impression of black water lapping his feet. Was this what Priestley had meant by the movie stirring up his subconscious? When he tried to blink the sensations away, afterimages danced on the inside of his eyelids, dots like burnt suns swarming in the mutable beam of the projector.

How had he failed to notice the central figure uncoiling in the middle of the screen, its insect-like body folding around the oscillating imagery, as though preparing to plunge down and feed? He couldn't tell if the entity was standing behind the tunnel or if it was the hole that comprised most of its central mass, wings or misshapen arms flapping to either side of it. An uncomfortable hint of a face sat atop the hole, conveying the image of malevolent hunger.

Inside the opening, or portal, a scene was now unfolding. A solitary man trudged past a series of hand-painted wooden backdrops that coupled together and disengaged before his eyes. The man gazed out with an exaggerated look of amazement, yet he remained oblivious to the scrutiny from above. In a rush of darkness, he was gone, the hole closing, an inter-title card flashing across the screen too quickly for Don to make out the words.

The giant figure hooted without a sound, folded its ungainly anatomy in a dreadful suggestion of a bow. It swept its wings and the man in the inset scene reappeared, pulled open a door, stepping through the background and onto a different stage. Now he stood before a cyclorama painted to resemble a night sky, a black curtain dotted with electric bulbs to simulate stars. Terror, too understated not to be real, seized him. He reached behind him, clearly intending to go back the way he'd come, but the door was no longer there; it had been replaced by a white rectangle sketched onto the curtain. The lights winked out one-by-one, trapping him forever in utter blackness. The man's frightened contortions, his frantic clawing at the painted screen, only served to increase the mirth of the capering shadow above him.

As the last light went out, the screen began to cycle through another seemingly random sequence. A suave man with slicked-back hair lit up a cigarette, smiled knowingly at the camera. A fallow field, its stubble brown and rotting under a pallid winter sun, held a circle of figures with elaborate headdresses or masks moving slowly in a hypnotic dance. Naked bodies lying on a stone floor, silver cords emerging from their open mouths, the camera panning upward, cutting out before it reached the ceiling. Another shot of those same cords trailing off into a black sky from which ashes fell like flakes of leprous skin. Then a cut-to-black, followed by numbers that indicated the end of the reel.

I've seen enough, Don wished he'd cried out, but already he could hear the second film being fed into the projector. He shielded his eyes and peered up at the projection room. The glare of the machine blinded him; all he could see was a faint impression of the operator standing very still next to the shimmering square.

Surely it had to be Thomas Priestley up there, coughing discreetly or chuckling. Don thought he glimpsed a face pressed against the glass, but the features were unrecognizable. Twisted in either cruelty or deep concentration. He sat back down, fighting a nightmarish feeling of oppressiveness, the rapid stutter of the reel repeating inside his head, a vibration absorbed by the thin barrier of his skull. His head felt hot and swollen, as if weighed down by what he was seeing.

Stop this, he thought he'd spoken out loud, but the seat was already swallowing him whole, the darkness leaning in. A pale, frightened face filled the screen, the opening scene of *Experiment Seven* expanding to envelop the room. Don remembered his pen and pad, forced enough stillness on his thoughts and hands to scribble down a few notes. Again, he felt like there was something he'd failed to notice, some clue hidden in the movie, but the buzzing in his head was making it impossible to focus.

Hudson had changed his approach, had rid his work of the extraneous flourishes and frenetic intercutting that had marred his first piece. Compared to the previous film, *Seven* was almost sparse in execution. Ghostly silhouettes—likely spliced footage shot through some sort of transparent curtain—floated across the screen in slow motion. As in *One*, a hole appeared in the curtain, burned away to reveal an unblinking eye, then a second movie played under the surface layer: a fade-in effect that had to have taken the filmmaker hours of practice to pull off so smoothly.

A woman passed through a mirror, and through her own reflection. Then back again. A second woman offered a dazzling canned smile, holding out a bowl and a hand-operated blender. The two superimposed clips, one from a black-and-white movie, the second from a TV ad, played at different speeds, creating a disjointed, hallucinatory effect. Hudson had probably assembled this from strips of discarded film, painstakingly shooting the scene over and over to achieve the right effect. Whatever the technique, it had worked. In the flickering light of the projector, the room was losing its edges, becoming one with the screen, a pocket universe in which up and down were becoming irrelevant. *A space within a space.*

The women were consumed by another black hole unfurling outwards. Don felt the room tilt around him, his vision shrank and juddered with the image emerging from the depths of the screen. A scrolling shot of a stately mansion amid dense trees, framed by a perfect blue sky. Even in that brief glimpse, the disrepair of the place was evident: broken windows, the roof falling in, doors sagging on their hinges, once-immaculate grounds overgrown. The magician from Don's dream was standing on the threshold, one hand outstretched, as if to usher the viewer inside. Past the door, candles burned and dripped, flames dipping as if in a breeze. Robed celebrants knelt on a flagged floor, turned glassy eyes toward the approaching camera. Above their bestial heads, a dark blot hovered like a cloud.

Symbols or numbers flashed between the frames, embedding themselves into Don's mind like nails. Sharp yellow teeth clacked and menaced in protruding snouts. As they descended on him, gnashing and tearing, he felt neither horror nor pain and had no strength left to resist them. White light flared, brightened to an unbearable intensity. A vast and pitiless blaze, charring and curling the edges of the screen, roaring inside his mind, devouring everything in its way.

Chapter 24

"I've never seen anything of the sort," Thomas Priestley said, returning to the table with two pints of dark ale. "Acetate film can melt in the projector, of course, just like sixteen-millimeter celluloid could. You hear about it with old nitrate stock. But complete combustion like that is rare. Practically unheard of."

They sat in a pub near Bournemouth Pier, a broad, shadowy place just starting to fill with people. Don supposed he'd been lucky to make it out of the archive alive, but it was hard for him to think clearly, to comprehend the danger he had been in. His head still throbbed with the pulsing of the projector. Priestley had fed the second reel in and stepped out of the room to take a call. Fortunately, he'd gone no further than the door and had been close enough to smell the smoke when the film went up in flames. The fire was put out quickly, but both the projector and Hudson's *Experiment Seven* were destroyed. Whatever Don had seen on screen, or thought he'd seen, was gone forever.

Not gone, a sly thought intruded. *It's inside you now. In your head. It burned itself off the film to come and live within you.*

Appalled, the Dean had rushed into the small theater to check on his guest. The look on Don's face had evidently disturbed him enough to suggest a drink to calm the nerves. In the gloom of the pub, he seemed embarrassed and distant, his earlier cheerfulness gone. "It must not have been maintained properly," he said, staring into his drink. "The film could have snagged in the gate, or a bulb that short-circuited. Anyway, it's good you weren't operating the bloody thing yourself. There's no one to blame but me."

He hadn't seen much of the second reel, he told Don, and of the first he retained only the vaguest impression. "Bloody builders," he said, holding up his phone with a sheepish expression. "My better half's dealing with them. We're having an extension built, and she's stuck with them today. Phone's been ringing all morning." He sipped his beer, furrowed his brow. "Sorry about that unpleasantness. Can't imagine it's how you envisioned your visit here. But I hope you at least saw what you came here to see."

It sounded too much like a challenge for Don to respond right away. "For your book," Priestley found it necessary to prompt. "It's not a lot of material. Because of Hudson's reputation, no one at the school bothered to locate his older work. Now the last of it is gone. Well, *all but* the last one." He raised his glass but didn't drink from it, only stared into the murky, frothed liquid. "If you don't mind me saying so, perhaps it's for the best."

Don wrapped both hands around his own glass, mostly to stop them from shaking. He didn't trust himself to lift it to his lips without spilling. *At least no one burned you down to the ground*, he thought, almost laughing out loud. *Not yet, anyway*. It was getting harder and harder to ignore the parallel between Last Rite Productions and what had just happened in the projection room. "I wonder what he did to make so many enemies here," he said. "Most of his former associates in the States spoke highly of him."

Thomas Priestley hunched his shoulders as if to make himself smaller. "No one talks about it anymore. Few even remember, if any at all. But it's difficult for secrets to stay buried in a place like this. Academics are the worst gossips and have the memories of elephants. Table manners of elephants, too." He gave Don a weak smile. "That's why one must be very careful on campus. Idle tongues wagging and all that. Reputations bruise easily and take long to recover. Sometimes they don't recover at all."

Don took the hint, lowered his voice. "Do you have the original movies? The ones Hudson sampled for the collage. Any idea what happened to those?"

The Dean shook his head. "Afraid not. For a time, the school kept old stock in what was then the library. Very old film, from the early 1900s. Perhaps older. Castoffs from old cinemas, amateur reels from private collections, from closed museums. Canisters found in moldy boxes that families threw out when cleaning sheds and basements. Silver nitrate, highly combustible, so people wanted to get rid of it." He sighed. "But it was never inventoried or stored properly. Some of it degraded, some was scavenged for class projects. Priceless treasures of early British cinema irretrievably lost. But students also used their own material, so it's hard to say. Hudson could have found those clips anywhere."

He chuckled uneasily, seeming to deliberate about his next sentence. "As a matter of fact, some of the, uh, material young Victor insisted on using was what got him in trouble with the Masters. That, and some, er, unconventional acquaintances he cultivated. Nothing unusual for the sixties, but here on campus more conservative worldviews prevailed."

"What kind of acquaintances?"

The Dean cleared his throat, glanced around. "It was a time of change and upheaval. Of pushing the boundaries of the known. Spiritualism and occultism had made a comeback. Tarot readings, Hindu mysticism, the Beatles traveling to India to study under a guru. Psychedelic drugs everywhere. It wasn't unusual for a bright young lad with an artistic bent to be carried away by the Zeitgeist, especially one who didn't have to worry about money. Beside that, there was a family connection. His grandfather, or great-grandfather, had founded an occult society.

Spirit-tapping, seances, astral projection. The whole lot. It was something of an obsession with our upper classes, going back to Victorian times."

"You seem to know quite a lot about him."

"When you contacted me, I became intrigued." A rueful smile. "These days, transgressiveness tends to come with a political tag. Hudson's vision seems to have been far grander than that. Great questions beget great explorations, and he refused to be constrained by his choice of medium. To fit the mold that class and family expectations tried to force him into."

Priestley took a long swallow of beer as if to fortify himself. "In that, he echoed the sensibilities of the great minds of the Victorian age. Another period in which occultism flourished, when the spiritual and the uncanny became something of a national obsession. Mostly as a pastime for the idle rich, but also as the playing field for the dreamer, the artist. Arthur Conan Doyle belonged to an occult society, as did Yeats, and later Huxley. The mysticism would have appealed to Hudson, an intelligent, sensitive, deeply impressionable young man. He would have fit right in."

"Do you know what this occult society was called?" Don asked, but he already knew the answer. The same cult whose reach had extended across the centuries, across the Atlantic, to cast a pall over his own life. It had resurrected itself as the Order of Astral Enlightenment, keeping to the shadows, gradually accreting wealth and power, all to some unknowable end. "The one Victor's grandfather helped found?"

"The Brotherhood of something or other," Priestley said. "I imagine it was no different from others of its kind. In most cases, these so-called occult societies were little more than gentlemen's clubs. Well-off members would swear oaths, exchange old books, hold ceremonies in dead languages. Odd and pompous, but harmless. You may have heard of the Rosicrucians, or Madame Blavatsky's Theosophical Society. Occasionally, though, some would be involved in something darker.

Nothing supernatural, of course. But a cover for wealthy men who thought themselves above the law to indulge in drunkenness and debauchery. 'Blow off some steam,' as you Yanks would say. The authorities turned a blind eye, and the aristocracy took care of their own. The press would have been warned off. Threatened." The alcohol had returned some of the color to the Dean's cheeks. He drained his glass then walked it over to the bar and traded it for a full one. "Other times, the members would fall prey to charlatans and confidence artists. Being American, you're familiar with the concept. Televangelists and holy rollers, over on your side of the pond."

Don nodded, tried to ignore the gathering crowd in the bar, a wall of eyes behind his back. The story was starting to make sense; Victor Hudson's old connections had sought him out and tried to make him an instrument of some unwholesome design. But things had gone wrong along the way. "Is this why the University got rid of Victor? Because of his involvement with a cult?"

"Not quite." Priestley flinched, either at the word or at the rise in Don's tone. "It's a bit more complicated than that. One of the elder Hudson's contemporaries was a man named Lucien Callas. French, or Belgian, although it's plausible that the name was an invention, along with everything else. Charming, charismatic, persuasive. Well-bred and educated, a sophisticate who had traveled most of the world before he was in his thirties." He paused for effect, his teeth shining wetly in the light. "None of it was true, naturally. Callas was a complete and utter fraud. Nothing to him but tall tales and disappointment. But for a while, right around the Great War and throughout the twenties, he took British high society by storm."

Don fidgeted uncomfortably in his seat. He had a feeling he knew where this was going. "Victor couldn't have known him, then."

"His forebear could, however, and did. It was a challenging time. The old ways were dying out. Science and technology shining a light on the inner workings of the universe. God had retreated into a dark, distant corner, but people still wanted to *believe*. Then the Great War happened." Priestley rubbed his face, looking tired. "Heinous carnage, the worst atrocity in human history. If I were a spiritualist, I'd say it was a massive sacrifice, a burnt offering on the altar of the new world. A turning point. Here in England, so many had lost so much. Rich and poor, villagers and city-dwellers, posh and common—no one was spared. Sons, fathers, husbands, all had been mown down like wheat. Every household in the nation dreaded the knock on the door, the postman with a telegram. People wanted reassurance, a way to communicate with their lost ones, a reason to believe in life after death. Despair and sorrow laid down a fertile breeding ground for opportunists of all stripes, and Lucien Callas was ready."

"Was he one of the Brothers?"

"It's hard to tell whether he was ever initiated into their ranks or not. All I could find were casual mentions in historical registers and reference books. Occult societies were insular, secretive, especially if some of their members were prominent men. A powerful organization like the Brotherhood would have screened any petitioners carefully. Even after they realized who they were dealing with, they would have kept it quiet to avoid public exposure and embarrassment. Callas was a seasoned swindler, and he knew his targets well. But there was a connection. Until everything started to fall apart."

"Fall apart?"

"Rubbing shoulders with the Brethren wasn't enough for Callas," the Dean said. "Certainly not as lucrative as he expected. Even if he were initiated, he could never be a master or a leader due to his lowly upbringing. So, he kept up his side work. He used his connections within the Brotherhood to obtain forged birth certificates and military service records. He staged public psychic readings and peddled his services as an astral consultant. Threw flashy parties at their summer estates and collected donations for the Red Cross, which he would then make disappear. That sort of thing." He laughed and drank more beer. "Disappear. That reminds me. Callas assumed various identities, pretended to be a minor aristocrat, a war hero, even as an American industrialist. You won't believe this, but his favorite act was—"

"Magician." Don's own voice sounded unnatural, distorted. "His favorite act was to pose as a stage magician."

"Exactly." Priestley frowned, deciding not to ask the obvious question. "Anyway, this was a step too far for his betters. It encouraged unwelcome attention. Many among them could never stomach the presence of a common nobody in their midst, but now even his allies balked at Callas's antics. Fraud, deception, lies—these were privileges reserved for the upper crust. But the Brethren were also afraid of Callas. Few among them could match his purported powers, and none delved into the esoteric with such reckless abandon."

"Do you think there was something to it? That Callas had supernatural powers?"

Priestley pondered this for a moment. "Not everything can be explained rationally," he finally said. "According to the records, Callas was a skilled illusionist, and he certainly had great powers of persuasion. There may have been more to it, but that's irrelevant. The Brethren were true believers, and they thought him a danger. Once they turned against him, Callas was done for."

"What did they do to him?"

"He was exposed as a fraud. I couldn't find many details, but it seems to have been an organized harassment campaign. The Brethren had considerable clout with the newspapers, and Callas had made enemies in high places. His fraud schemes unraveled and several of his marks threatened him with court action. England was forever lost to him."

"Where did he go?"

The Dean shrugged. "He disappeared. My own scant research stops there. It was the aftermath of the Great Depression, the rise of authoritarian regimes and persecution, the buildup to the next bloody war. People moved, changed names, made new starts in life. Boarded ships for brighter horizons or vanished without a trace. Callas could have been killed or died of hunger or disease. Then again, he was a resourceful man. I have no trouble imagining him reinventing himself on the Continent, or somewhere in South America. Perhaps running a bogus underground helpline for escaped Nazis in Argentina or Uruguay. Playing both them and the Israelis against each other. He was that sort of creature."

"I still don't follow," Don said. "All that happened years before Victor was born. What's his connection to Lucien Callas?"

"Well, Callas was gone, but the Brotherhood remained active. Their membership was smaller, and they may have operated in secrecy, or at least not fully out in the open. Hudson could have heard about them from his father or grandfather, or a friend of the family. Even if he never took the oath, or whatever the Brethren swore to, he would have been curious." Priestley broke off to greet a group of students who walked past their table, waiting until they had moved out of earshot. "Anyway, that's all I was able to find. Anecdotal evidence and conjecture, and pretty thin at that. But I hope it helps you piece Hudson's story together."

"It does," Don said. He remembered the pint of beer at his elbow, realizing how parched he felt. Flat and bittersweet, but he drank it anyway, watching the faces along the bar. Wondering if even now he was being followed. "You said something else. That it wasn't his extracurricular interests that got Victor expelled. Why did he leave, then?"

"I don't want to give you the impression of some modern-day witch hunt. Victor Hudson was one of the school's most talented students. The younger and more open-minded among the faculty may have even shared his curiosity about mysticism. Most importantly, he came from money. No matter how scandalous his conduct, how unsavory his contacts, they alone would not have been enough to see him thrown out. It was the films that did it."

"What films?"

Priestley let out a long breath. "Earlier on, you asked me about the bits of film Hudson used for his experiments. Where those snippets came from. I'm afraid I wasn't entirely honest with you when I said I didn't know. Some of them were probably discarded used film. Others may have come from the society's private collection. Again, it's all rumor. I never spoke directly to any of the individuals involved. But the faculty seems to have had very...*definitive* ideas about those films."

"About them being used in a student project?"

"About them being allowed to exist at all," the Dean said. "Hudson was convinced that they contained elements of a universal truth. A grand revelation that would shake the world. He saw himself as an acolyte, someone who would continue this esoteric tradition. Usher it into the modern age." He laughed incredulously, but his eyes darted around the pub as if he were afraid of being overheard. "What can I say? The campus drug culture was rather permissive back then. But some of the professors apparently took him up on his offer to watch the forbidden films. Younger ones, who saw themselves as radicals looking for a thrill. Whatever they saw cured them of that curiosity forever. One of them went mad. Another committed suicide shortly thereafter, although it's debatable whether the films had anything to do with that. But the screening caused an uproar among the faculty. Hudson was expelled, and the rest is history."

"What about the Brotherhood?"

"Anyone's guess," Priestley said. "By the time I started teaching here, no one mentioned them. Maybe the society died with the last of its members, or maybe it was subsumed by another similar organization. You'd be surprised at how many of them exist these days. Especially online. It doesn't take much to start a free message board and put up a handful of articles. No physical location needed. Saves on the overhead costs."

Don caught the other man's eyes across the table. "I think they're still around. That they're active again."

"I doubt it." But the Dean leaned closer over the table, almost knocking his empty glass over in the process. "There hasn't been any mention of them in over thirty years. I searched all over the internet. Have you—do you know someone who has been in touch with them?"

"They never disappeared," Don said. "Only moved underground to avoid public scrutiny. Wouldn't you, with that sort of reputation following you around? I think they changed continents. Left the Old World for new opportunities across the water. I believe they established contact with Victor Hudson, and that he continued to spread their teachings."

"That's quite the theory." Thomas Priestley's eyes widened in wary surprise. "You don't think the society had anything to do with Hudson's disappearance, do you?"

"There have been certain...patterns." Don felt uncomfortable sharing his experiences with a stranger, even a friendly-looking one. "But it can't be a coincidence that both men vanished under similar circumstances. After running afoul of the same people. It doesn't add up."

Yet there was an alternative explanation, one that he didn't like to entertain. An explanation that tied together Hudson's missing years and the vanishing of Lucien Callas. One in which young Victor sought out the disgraced magician during his time in Europe. Honed his astral projection techniques until he'd surpassed the old master. Studied manipulation and illusion, learned how to implant hidden messages into his movies. Breadcrumbs for those in the know, or those who were sensitive to them. The thought made Don shudder with revulsion. Whatever Hudson's intentions, his attempts at mass hypnotism were akin to rape.

Except why would a secret society pour millions into Hudson's project while remaining behind the scenes? Producers had egos. They fought to be credited, to announce their presence to the public. Had the Brotherhood decided to come out into the open, use *The Unveiling* as advertising, or a method of spreading their teaching? That made even less sense, after all their effort to be forgotten. Whatever the answer, Don was no closer to it than he had been before his visit to England.

Priestley hesitated, as if reluctant to speak. "I didn't mention this before. But there's another connection. Lucien Callas was an amateur film pioneer. One of the first to incorporate stage magic and vaudeville into motion pictures. It's quite likely that he was the author of the clips Hudson sampled while at the school. The ones you just saw."

Don managed to nod through his shock, the revelation jarring him from his jetlagged fugue. "It's an interesting angle. But I want to keep the focus on Victor's career. Occult societies and long-dead con men may be a step too far for my publisher. It all happened such a long time ago."

If the Dean was disappointed, he did nothing to show it. "Sorry I couldn't be of more help," he said, finishing the dregs of his beer and getting up. "But if you end up using some of it in your book, I would appreciate you *not* mentioning my name. The faculty would not be very happy with me bringing all this up in connection with the school. Not with the budget season coming up."

Outside the pub, he paused, staring past the crowd gathering at the outside tables. "It may not be a bad thing, you know," he said, wistful. "That we'll never know the extent of Hudson's involvement with the occult. The past is the past, and sometimes it doesn't like being stirred up." He laughed, shook his head. "Although it would make quite the story, wouldn't it? A master of the astral, reaching from the other side of the grave. Should you decide to go the fictional route. Just a thought."

Chapter 25

Hello Mr. Ruby,

Apologies for the late response. I only saw your comment on my website yesterday. That page is mostly defunct, and I avoid the comments section whenever possible. I've long reached the end of my tether when it comes to the vileness spouted by keyboard stalkers, cranks, and outright lunatics. As a public personality and an established author yourself, I'm sure you understand.

Alas, the Macabre Marquee Society, America's premium news outlet for outré and iconoclastic cinematography, has grown moribund of late due to scheduling conflicts. I hope to revive the Meta-psychic Motion Pictures Festival in the spring and would be pleased as punch to have you as a panelist. Should you wish to contact me in the meantime, please use this email address or drop me a line on Facebook.

I hope you don't mind me expressing to you how much I admire your work. The hardcover of Being Bellamore graces my coffee table, on the merit of your writing as much as of the great man's paintings, and Ashes Behind is a tour-de-force, later controversy notwithstanding. Victor Hudson was a giant of horror cinema, and I'm delighted and honored to contribute in my own small way to your next masterpiece.

On that note, I have a tape in my possession that might interest you. It's a composite of Hudson's early short films, made while he was a movie student in England. Some time ago I purchased it through Craigslist for the princely sum of $4.95, plus shipping. To my knowledge, it's the last copy in existence. Probably worth a hundred times its purchase price these days. The tape was produced by a Canadian company called Revelation Films. Attached please find a photo of the case.

Sadly, I have no revelations for you concerning that lost gem, The Unveiling. Its status as an object of obsession has reached legendary proportions. Over the years, I have heard sporadic scuttlebutt about a bootleg copy, or one of the original reels, or a compilation of daily rushes from the shoot making the rounds. All of it turned out to be false. There is a collector in Boston, and another somewhere in Tennessee, who are rumored to have fared better than I have. If true, they guard their treasure closely. All my attempts to contact these worthies have come to naught, and my dark connections have likewise remained silent.

Regarding your other line of inquiry, that into the Brotherhood of Lament, I can be so bold as to offer my humble assistance. There was indeed an offshoot of the Brethren here in the savage land of Washington and Lincoln, and they prospered on the West Coast well into the nineties. Attracted some high-profile followers. I have never heard of them financing a movie, and I suspect that whoever told you that was pulling your leg. But Thaddeus D. Headstone, Esq. is loath to dismiss potentially juicy gossip as a hoax, so if this fascinating tidbit is true, I would love to learn more about it.

Would you be open to meeting and comparing notes with me? The Society is a strictly non-profit endeavor, but our repositories of insalubrious information are quite substantial. It may be worth your while. If nothing else, you'll have the opportunity to see the infamous Canadian tape.

If I'm not being too forward, would there be room for an acknowledgement of the Macabre Marquee Society in your masterpiece? It pains me to admit it, but we're in dire need of a shot in the arm.

Below you'll find the Google Maps instructions to the Society's premises, which happen to coincide with the location of my apartment in Red Hook. Or I can drive down to the City of Brotherly Love and meet you for a drink. I would appreciate being given insight into the material you've assembled for your book—or as much of it as you deem fit. As fundamentally reprehensible as I find non-disclosure agreements to be, I would be open to signing one, should you require me to.

Sincerely,

Thaddeus D. Headstone, Esq.
Board President and Chief Executive Ghoul, Macabre Marquee Society

* * *

The email was dated a day ago, while Don was still in Bournemouth. It had taken him a few moments to correlate the content and sender, to remember the comment he'd left on the website. Beyond his most recent memories—constricted spaces, baggage carousels, bright lights and throngs of faceless strangers in enormous halls—stretched a blank, fog-strewn landscape of bewilderment and fear.

He was operating on instinct and caffeine, no longer capable of exerting control over his thoughts. Planes were safe, as were airports, provided that he didn't fall asleep. Maybe being on the move impeded *their* manifestation or made the target harder to locate? But being back on solid ground dispelled that fragile sense of security. He had to stay ahead of the magician and his aberrations. He had to keep moving. The encounters of the past two months left no doubt about that. Neither did the sense of a presence inside his head, a stranger looking out at the world through his own eyes.

Don didn't believe in god, or a soul, but recent events had convinced him of the existence of an afterlife. A dark, cold, awful place between existence and non-existence, inhabited by walking, living nightmares. There was no final repose, no benevolent creator whose love would bridge that terrible gulf. Not even the merciful nullity of oblivion. Only suffering and torment and eternal hunger, for the tormentors and the tormented alike.

Until they crossed over, into the light and warmth and life this side of the astral divide, to feed on those who strayed too close to it. Or until something—someone—let them through.

Yet for everything he'd seen and been through, the impossibility of his experience made it hard to believe. His mind felt like it was about to explode from the contradictions. Fear was the key ingredient in the noxious brew of emotions roiling inside him, followed by disbelief, rage, then a sense of absolute loss. Perhaps what he needed most was psychiatric help. Drugs, some sort of powerful antipsychotic, could still make the apparitions go away. Stop him from seeing things as soon as he closed his eyes, the panicky, vertiginous sensation of leaving his body. Of being *forced* out.

What had he gotten himself into?

Jess would help or would try to help him. At the diner, she'd heard him out, nodding in the right places and not interrupting, but her eyes had told a different story. Disbelief shaded into shock, then outright pity, as the paranoid schizophrenic across the table jabbered about things coming out of the walls to hunt him. Pity, that the man she'd once shared her career and her bed with could have sunk so low, wild-eyed and stinking and deranged. Even guilt: for not having kept in touch, for not encouraging him to seek help, for allowing him to turn into this pitiful demented creature debasing itself in public, plagued by the demons in its mind.

Jess had listened to him, but she had not believed a word. He could hardly blame her; even in the throes of his most depraved past binges, he would have found it impossible to credit any part of his own story. For all that, she'd been the picture of professionalism and support, counting out bills to the irate landlord—almost double what the asshole had asked for, which Don suspected was already higher than the damage warranted—and talking the man out of calling the police. Don dreaded the moment when both her patience and the hereto unbridled generosity of Occultation Press ran out. It would happen sooner rather than later. His phone showed a string of unanswered messages and emails from Jess. *I just want to know you're okay*, the last voicemail said, her recorded voice was oddly hollow and flat. *Call me back as soon as you can. Whatever's happening, we can fix it.* He screened as best he could, telling himself there would be time to make things right with her later.

His trip to Bournemouth had sapped the last of his energy and strength. Not to mention his bank balance. He recognized the signs of an impending crash: the diffused edges of objects, the jerky reactions of his body as his depleted brain struggled to process inputs. If he didn't sleep soon, he would collapse. But stopping wasn't an option. Not with so much left to do.

With the impending breakdown came a gradual resignation, an awful clarity as the horror of his situation became wholly apparent to him. His book project, so close to completion, was dead; all his effort had been for naught. No matter how hard he tried, he couldn't muster the coherence of thought to express himself in complete sentences. The last chapter was not only overdue, but there was no hope of it ever being delivered. He couldn't allow the book to be published, the unimaginable nightmare it contained to be unleashed upon the world. Victor Hudson and his lost movie were best left buried, and with them Don's golden opportunity, what he suspected was his last chance at success.

Gone was also any illusion of saving himself. Of evading the attention of Lucien Callas, or whatever the magician had become, and the *others*. The experimental film he'd seen in Bournemouth was proof of that. The horror was in his head now, its poisonous roots too deep to be removed. Coincidence had not transferred the visions from his dreams onto a film made decades before his birth. He was trapped in a chain of preordained events, and all he could do was watch them unspool around him. Likewise, he entertained no delusions about how it would end, or about his ability to change the course of his fate.

So be it. If he couldn't save himself, he may be able to keep the evil from spreading. From pulling others down with him, like the vortex of a sinking ship. From destroying Jess. The mere thought of her suffering *their* visitations—snatched out of her body, helpless and horrified, or waking up to see an unspeakable not-quite-face hovering over her—was unbearable to Don. All because she'd been there for him in his hour of need.

Sitting in the arrival terminal of Baltimore International Airport, watching the shops close and the lights dim before the approach of night, Don hit reply and began typing.

Dear Mr. Headstone,

No need to apologize. I was out of the country, following up on some promising leads for my book. Which included some of Victor Hudson's early short pictures—the ones that didn't make it onto your Revelation Films tape. I also found out more about the connection between Hudson and the Brotherhood of Lament; I am more than willing to compare notes.

I should note that my interest in Victor Hudson and The Unveiling *is now personal as well as professional. Writing this book, I've had certain experiences that I'm hoping to understand better. Sorry if that sounds weird, but I'm not comfortable putting more in writing. Would be happy to discuss it in person.*

Are you available tomorrow? I realize this may be short notice, but I'm running out of time. Deadlines should be taken seriously, and I'm afraid I've let too many of them fly by. Below is my personal number, in case I'm not reachable by email.

Here's my offer: if you let me watch the tape and tell me what you know about the Brotherhood of Lament, I'll reciprocate and credit you and the Macabre Marquee Society once the book is finished. I'm willing to throw in a dinner at a restaurant of your choice to sweeten the deal.

Regards,

Don Ruby

No sooner had he clicked send than weariness slammed down on his shoulders like a load of bricks. Fear had kept him awake, flooded his system with adrenaline. However, it had been a lethargic wakefulness in which he registered his own actions as if from outside himself, slow and ungainly, like he was wading through water. Now the tide was receding, draining his resistance, his body asserting its demands. Only for a moment, just to rest his eyes. The thought repeated in his head, morphed into an imperative, a weightless drop into the chasm of sleep, the lights in his mind going out one by one.

Don floundered free of the darkness, raised his head from his elbows. The airport terminal hall swam out at him from the gloom. He couldn't have slept for longer than a few minutes. His laptop was still on; the battery saver hadn't kicked in. But the space around him was much darker than he remembered, the shops and concessions empty and shuttered, entire sections of lights turned off. Even the outside illumination appeared muted, a dull glow that failed to progress past the tall panes, only blurring the vista on the other side of the glass. Like moonlight, but more viscous somehow, as if struggling through clouds.

He tried to gather his thoughts, wake up his heavy, unresponsive limbs. Had he been locked in after the terminal closed for the night? That made no sense. Flights were arriving late into the small hours, and someone would have woken him up, asking him to leave. Maybe that was the movement he could see at the far end of the hall, airport staff finishing the last chores before closing. He should get their attention and ask them to let him out. Yet his hand remained stuck to the cafeteria table, and his shout never made it past his lips.

Perhaps that was only his impression, because one of the figures trundling along in the murk slowed down and turned, as if in response to his call. Were they coming closer, or moving further away? The glow through the glass panes made it difficult to tell. He should get up and walk over, see what was happening to the lights. But any movement seemed to only take place in his head; his body remained inert, held down by invisible weights.

Don shuddered as his surroundings came into focus beyond the table. The terminal was derelict, unused for years, gate seats moldering under an accumulation of cobwebs, the departure screens dusty and black. What was left of the tall glass panes was grubby and shattered, the rest scattered across the dirty floor. His laptop was similarly aged, the plastic casing cracked, keys that he'd been typing on moments ago missing. A blurred shape hovered inside the swarm of pixels, a grinning, deformed face that seemed incapable of holding still, its features unraveling and changing.

Slippage. He had done it again, fallen through a crack in the world, into that same gray non-space he'd visited before. Alone and unprotected, but not unnoticed. Because the figures he'd taken for airport staff were heading toward him, the silvery light stripping away the shadows, revealing every awful detail of their anatomies.

Panic jolted him into awareness. Yet each attempt to regain control of his limbs, of his voice, only seemed to push him further adrift from his moorings, floating in the sickly radiance that filled the hall. Below him, close enough to touch, if he only had an arm, he saw his body slumped over the cafeteria table, eyes closed. A thin thread of silver glistened in the air, a fishing line tethering him to the torpid form.

A scream of pure anguish built up inside him, unable to find an outlet. This was no dream, but it wasn't reality either, some unknown state of being into which he had unwittingly cast himself and didn't know how to escape. The hall was threatening to flip over, to hurl him out into the night sky, into the endless dark. He tried to will some order into his disembodied essence, to enforce a sense of gravity and direction. There was nothing he could grab onto to steady himself or arrest his slow but inexorable progress toward the ceiling, away from his sleeping form. Walls would not hold him, nor would the steel beams he was approaching. In this state, he would pass through them unhindered, drifting like an astronaut cut off his line, his body shrinking in the distance, the gulf yawning to embrace him, wide, *infinite.*

Would they be waiting for him in the darkness, those abnormal shapes eager to seize him and drag him into their midst? Or was he already one of their number, his cries melding with the insane mutterings of the damned? Perhaps he should concentrate his attention on the silvery line, his last tangible connection to the world. He had almost succeeded in emptying his thoughts of all interference when the body beneath him shuddered and raised its head.

Horror sent him spinning toward the beams in a rush of desperate, mindless panic. The silver cord flickered, vanished, then caught the light again. Below, his body stood up shakily and gazed round. Its movements were mechanical, uncoordinated, its face an empty death-mask, but only for a moment. Expression and intelligence seeped into it like poison, a dark glee lighting it up from within. There was no mistaking the triumphant look in its eyes. Lucien Callas, the magician, had arrived to conclude the process begun all those weeks ago. To free himself from the lightless place between worlds, where he had rotted until Don had provided a means of egress. Callas, or the disembodied thing that he had been transformed into, bent on complete mental and physical infestation. On destroying whatever was left of Don's sense of self. Now he was smiling up at his victim, still weak, but gaining strength by the moment, establishing control finger by finger, toe by toe.

Even as despair took hold, Don refused to let the intruder sweep him away, to let himself be extinguished, or worse, left at the mercy of the indifferent dark. He had overcome the magician once; he could do it again, could prevent this dreadful reincarnation from taking place. All he had left was his thoughts, and these he cast about the terminal hall, trying to find something to focus them on. Abyss loomed all around him, a relentless vortex pulling him in.

One of the flight information screens guttered to life, letters and numbers running from left to right, lines of scrolling gibberish. He saw Callas hesitate and glance back, distracted, an uncertain look flitting across his new face. Don had to hope that it wasn't just his imagination, that the intrusion was costing the magician just as much effort as his own attempts to keep the intruder out. His mind reached for the screen, summoning the keyboard layout, visualizing the keys depressing, forming a message, letter by painstaking letter.

GET OUT

Now he was certain that the creature had sensed it. Fear and rage twisted the stolen features into a grimace that showed clenched teeth. Plastic rattled and a narrow crack ran down the middle of the screen. Don didn't care. He was inside the sputtering circuitry, spinning, vibrating, fighting the dislocation with every shred of consciousness.

GETOUTGETOUTGETOUT

The screen exploded in a shower of sparks. With a groan and snap of metal, it pulled free of its bracket, levitated for a split second, then shattered on the floor of the hall.

In an instant, Don was hurled back into his body, slammed into it with tremendous force. Suffocating, for it had become a burden, a pile of dead meat that his consciousness labored to animate, to remember the function of its organs, match the position of its limbs. It was repugnant to him, oppressive. It reeked of decay, of the effluvia of its banal functions. A gulp of air filled his mouth, rushed down his throat, into his deflated lungs; his heart thumped a staccato against his chest, steadied, then found its beat.

Don toppled off the chair and onto his knees, retching and coughing, bringing up a thin string of bile. The lights were back on, weary passengers watching him suspiciously, a small crowd gathering around the destroyed screen. An airport security guard was making his way across the hall, heading for Don, speaking into his walkie-talkie.

There was no time for explanations. Don collected his few belongings and struck out across the concourse, head tucked down, looking for the exit signs. No one was following him. The shapeless figure pacing him in the mirrored surfaces was only his reflection. Outside, an Amtrak shuttle was idling in its designated space. He got on, flopped into a seat, and checked his phone for messages.

> *Hi, tomorrow is short notice, but I can make it work. I don't like to part from my tape (no offense, you can't imagine the number of cranks out there), but I'll play it for you on my VCR. You're welcome to any other material that might be useful to you.*

Once Don's hands had stopped shaking, he copied the Google Maps pin into his phone application. The address was a tenement building in Red Hook, next to a tattoo parlor and a venue offering tarot and palm readings. He scrolled past Jess's texts, feeling a wave of guilt wash through him. Better to keep her out of it for now. He would go up to New York and see what knowledge he could arm himself with.

As the bus pulled out of the bay, he logged onto the Amtrak website and booked a ticket to New York. There was an early train that would put him at Penn Station before eight in the morning. If he could stay awake until then. With every moment, every step he took, he felt that his pursuers were getting closer, that he was running out of time.

223

Chapter 26

"You don't hear much about the Order of Astral Enlightenment these days." Thaddeus D. Headstone, also known as Herbert Barnes, chuckled and popped a handful of bar nuts into his mouth. A mouth that seldom remained still. When he wasn't talking, which was rare, his lips moved noiselessly, his jaw making chewing motions even when there was nothing to chew on. Either he was excited about their meeting or quirky beyond belief. With every moment spent in the man's presence, Don was becoming more convinced that the latter was the case. "In fact, they didn't receive much attention even in the seventies and eighties when they were at their most active. They preached an open-door approach, but in reality, they were very selective. Rebranded themselves as purveyors of alternative medicine, physical, and spiritual wellbeing. I'd wager that most of their members remained ignorant of the Order's connection to the Brotherhood of Lament."

Green eyes sparkled at Don over the rims of thick spectacles. "Their teachings and beliefs remain a mystery to this day," Barnes said. "As does their fate. Even scholars of occult movements don't know what happened to the Order. Part of it is due to their secretiveness, the desire to stay under the radar. They didn't engage with the burgeoning occultist movement of the sixties. Their members didn't commit spectacular suicides, like the Peoples Temple or the Shining Path. Nor did they ring doorbells or peddle books and pamphlets in the streets. Another part was due to their ability to quash unpleasant stories, strong-arm the authorities to turn a blind eye when it suited their goals. Although they counted quite a few celebrities among their number, as well as scions of more than one prominent family, there were no exposés, no tabloid journalists creeping through the bushes to snap incriminating photos."

He stuffed his mouth with more nuts, and offered the almost-empty bowl to Don, who declined. "But make no mistake, the Order was a cult, just like its predecessor. Perhaps not homicidal, or clamoring for public attention, but extremely well-connected and funded. Old money from the surviving Brethren over in Europe, new money from robber-baron industrialists and Tinseltown moguls. More like the Freemasons, in that sense, than the Family. Manson's, that is. They preferred to work in silence, spreading their tentacles far and wide."

"The Brotherhood was quite infamous in Britain," Don said, using another feeding to get a word in edgeways. "At least one of their members was. Lucien Callas. His movies led to Hudson's expulsion from film school. In a way, he shaped Hudson's career, although they never met."

Herbert Barnes, who insisted on being called Thad, chuckled again and shook his head. He was a small, rotund man of indefinite age, with an imposing reddish beard and curly hair grown long and unruly to hide a bald spot at the back of his head. An air of manic flamboyance made him look young at times, a boy barely out of his teens, and his enthusiasm was infectious. He'd met Don at Penn Station, insisted on grabbing an early morning drink at a nearby bar, a hole-in-the-wall catering to workers coming off late shifts and the casualties of last night's club revelry.

"You said a mouthful there. I don't think you're even aware of how close you are to the truth. The *real* truth. I see they've fed you the same line of bull that gets repeated in every article about Victor Hudson. That he got in trouble in school. That the movies he sampled were somehow obscene, that they scandalized his teachers. How it ruined him, condemned him to Hollywood and low-budget horror for the rest of his life. Wasted his talent making frivolous trash."

"I take it you're not sold on the idea."

"A man who's been dead for close to a hundred years. Directing Hudson's fate, manipulating the present from beyond the grave." Thad threw his head back and roared with laughter. "Really, and I'm the one with the ghoulish reputation. Callas was a non-entity. A poser who scammed rich, lonely housewives and inbred nobility out of their silverware. Hudson dropped out of school because he wanted to learn from the best, not be constrained by some silly little film course. Life isn't a horror movie. It's both more banal and terrifying than that."

"Do you have any theories on what happened to Callas?"

"Who knows? The man was an embarrassment, and he always had dirt on people. Plenty among the Brethren were happy to see the back of him. Maybe they used the opportunity to get rid of him. You know, *permanently*. What better time to kill someone than during a war? Or maybe he scammed another rich widow, retired to the south of France, and drank himself to death on a beach. Maybe he tricked the Nazis into appointing him head of the Ahnenerbe, tried to out-Himmler Himmler, and ended up dead in an unmarked grave."

A knowing smirk crossed his flushed face. "Point being, we'll never know what happened to Callas. But I'm pretty sure that cock-and-bull story about the movies originated with the elder Hudson. Victor's father. He was an industrialist, and he often visited the States after the war. By that time, his business wasn't doing all that great. Hudson *père* had squandered the family fortune and was heavily in debt. He lapsed on the tuition payments. *That's* the real reason those pretentious old farts kicked his boy out of Bournemouth. Being poor was the only scandal, except it wasn't proper to admit it. Stiff upper lip and all that. They'd rather make up some tall tale of depravity and evil. Or maybe Hudson did it himself after his career took off."

"But I saw the movies," Don said. "Hudson's short work. They're real." *Were real*, he almost corrected himself.

"Oh, I'm sure there's a kernel of truth to it. Victor was talented, after all, and he made his own experimental stuff. He gave the teachers drugs before playing it for them. One of the guys had some sort of breakdown. Never recovered."

"How do you know all this?"

"A few years ago, I met this old Canadian fellow at an indie horror festival. A Hudson fanatic who also saw himself as an occult investigator. He was the one who compiled the tape I'm about to show you. Claimed to have quite a bit of material on Victor and the Brotherhood. Newspaper clippings, posters, old mimeographed flyers from the twenties. Some of them even mentioned Lucien Callas." Thad shrugged, scratched his beard. "He would have been a terrific resource for you, but, sadly, he died sometime after. Allegedly, he'd seen a rough cut of *The Unveiling*, but I didn't really buy that. The dude was getting along in years, starting to get a little not-quite-there, if you get my drift."

"Do you remember his name?"

"Probably wrote it down somewhere. I can look it up." Thad smiled into his drink. "Got to say, I find your angle on the story deeply fascinating. Occult societies, a lost film, two disappearances separated by half a century. Secrecy, conspiracy, mystic rites. I've always thought the Order of Astral Enlightenment to be a formidable beast that no one knew about. A behemoth hiding in plain sight. Sort of like the Freemasons crossed with the Temple of Golden Dawn."

"So, it wasn't all exaggeration," Don said. "They really were influential."

"Oh, yes." Thad gave a satisfied sigh, leaning back on his barstool. "Did you know that the Order owned stakes in most Hollywood studios at one point? Never managed to gain a foothold in one of the majors, of course, but they exerted a lot of pull behind the scenes. They had their own theories about film as a propaganda instrument. Not in a political sense, but in terms of shaping the aesthetic and cultural environment, even the human psyche. Motion pictures as a way to enlarge the consciousness, liberate the astral self. Cinema history would have looked very different today had they succeeded. But they didn't, and their influence waned rapidly, especially after the thing in New Mexico. Twenty years ago, you'd have found plenty of its original members to interview. Today, there are only rumors and secondhand anecdotes, and not a lot of that either."

"What was Victor's role in the Order? Where did he fit in?"

"According to my Canadian source, Hudson was an accomplished master of the astral, or sorcerer. Very respected by the others. His job was to mingle with the local populace, both the grandees and the commoners, and recruit new members to the cause. Which he did with enthusiasm. Threw some of the wildest parties on the block. Like Lucien Callas back in the day, he understood the importance of nurturing donors, attracting disciples and sympathizers with deep pockets. Catering to depraved tastes. But unlike Callas, he never indulged himself. Didn't drink or take drugs, and his own sexual proclivities remain a mystery. Never embezzled so much as a dime. Hudson believed in what he was doing and had a cast-iron reputation for integrity. Even among those who didn't agree with him."

"There were dissenters?"

Thad tried to arrange his jovial features into a cynical expression. "Of course. Every religion worth its salt needs a good schism. A power struggle between its apostates and its true believers. One group left California for New York, then split into two camps. The fanatics moved to New

Mexico, where they lived in a desert compound. Cut off all contact with the external world, locked themselves in to meditate and explore the astral. Some power company surveyors found them several months later. No one knows exactly what happened, but it looked like they'd starved themselves to death."

"Jesus."

"That was the Canadian's version of events," Thad said. "I couldn't find anything to support it. Either because the man was a crackpot, trying to impress me into buying him another drink, or because the Order made the story go away. Depending on what you choose to believe."

He adjusted his glasses, squinting at Don. "The schism happened long before Hudson's arrival in California, and he wasn't in contact with the group in the East. He was too busy working on his movies. After languishing in obscurity during his first couple of years in Hollywood, he had finally built a following. Shown what he was capable of delivering. The grand culmination of the Order's philosophy. It all sounds pretty far-fetched, or at least it did at first. Has any of it come up in your research?"

Don nodded. "*The Unveiling* was financed by the West Coast chapter. I have that on good authority. That's why Victor was able to spend money with such abandon. But it was never finished, as you know, and Victor was the one who pulled the plug on it. That couldn't have gone well with the cult."

"No kidding." Thad let out a long whistle. "But it makes sense. Word is Hudson broke off all relations with the Order in the mid-eighties, which would have been right after the movie fiasco. Apparently, he disagreed with the path they had chosen. He went from messiah to pariah overnight. Couldn't get hired anywhere."

"Did it have to do with money? Was Victor after a bigger cut?"

"Quite the opposite," Thad said. "He was allegedly disgusted by what the Order had become. Felt that the Brethren had betrayed their ideals for wealth and power. He was pragmatic and understood the importance of fundraising. But he wasn't comfortable with some of the elders taking it to an extreme. Abusing the anguished and credulous through what amounted to an elaborate con. Hudson saw himself as a prophet, a benefactor to mankind. His entire career in movies was only a means to an end, a stepping stone to a great spiritual awakening. To an ultimate transformation of the world."

"What kind of transformation?"

"Now that's the million-dollar question." Thad wagged his near-translucent eyebrows in amusement. "The Order had no written philosophy, no sacred book. My contact didn't have a clue. Something about psychic rebirth, a reshaping of corporeal reality through the numinous, the dawning of a new era for humanity. Or some similar claptrap. Whatever suited the Order at any given time would be my guess." He clawed through the empty nut bowl and made a disappointed grimace. "Callas, or whatever his name really was, never bothered writing his ideas down. He preferred to make things up on the fly. His teachings, if you could call them that, were a bizarre medley of ancient myth, Victorian superstition, and Eastern meditation practices, all sprinkled with what at the time was cutting-edge science. Think Theosophical Society crossed with the Egyptian Book of the Dead, explained via atomic physics and magnetic fields. Ritualized to give the whole mess a sheen of respectability in the tradition of the popular pseudoscience of the day. The more obscure and muddled, the better."

The shard of daylight visible through the glass door kept tugging at Don's gaze. Whorls of light and shadow crawled over the faces of the few patrons, playing tricks on his tired eyes. A tall, thin silhouette appeared in a sudden spill of brightness from the men's room, resolved into an old coat rack propped up in the far corner of the bar.

"Was this why he ran afoul of the Brotherhood?" he asked. "Why he was exiled to Europe?"

"Your guess is as good as mine. My Canadian acquaintance said the Brotherhood wasn't so much a society as a loose association. Each adept followed their own path to enlightenment, learned bits and pieces from the others, and tried to pass their knowledge along. There was no dogma in it at all. Callas saw this as a failing. He wanted to coin a new faith, to draw in the growing mass of people disaffected by traditional religion. He was obsessed with challenging leadership, imposing his way on the collective. But he failed. The elders, the high masters, they didn't like the old ways interfered with. If anything, it's surprising that they tolerated Callas's antics for as long as they did."

"Just like Victor Hudson," Don said. "First, they made his movie disappear. Then they did the same to the man who made it."

"You don't think the—" Thad frowned a little, suddenly uncomfortable. "If you don't mind me asking, Mr. Ruby, what is this conversation really about? You seem to be more interested in the cult than in Hudson's horror flicks. I don't see how the Brotherhood could be more than a footnote in your book, and we've been talking about nothing but them for almost an hour."

Don hesitated, but only for a moment. There was no one else to confide in, no time for embarrassment. "I don't know how else to say this," he began, "but I believe that the Order is still active. Some part of it, at least, or a group of former members. Don't know what they're after yet, but I'd guess they're trying to finish what they started with *The Unveiling*."

Thad blinked rapidly behind his glasses. When he spoke, his voice was studiously calm, his features carefully neutral, the default expression for dealing with someone not quite stable. "I won't say that's impossible, but it's not very likely. No one's heard about them for at least two decades. If they were still around, don't you think there'd be something about them online? Nothing can stay hidden in this age. Not for long." He licked his lips nervously. "You don't suppose it could be a prank? Someone trying to string you along to make a buck, or just for the hell of it?"

"I'm open to that possibility, but I intend to find out exactly what's going on."

"Is this for your book? Or are we talking about a different book?"

"That's not it." Don felt he'd come too far to withhold his full confession. "I've had some...let's call them *strange* experiences. Don't want to go into detail. Suffice it to say, I'm being followed. Menaced, threatened, whatever you want to call it. I feel it all started when I started looking into what happened on the set of *The Unveiling*."

"Holy shit."

"I'd rather not say more right now." Don studied the other man's face closely. If Herbert Barnes—Thaddeus D. Headstone—thought he was crazy, then so be it. He'd come too far, seen too much, to care about such things anymore. But the bearded face was agleam with enthusiasm, the eyes bright behind the smudged lenses. "It's really important for me to find out as much as I can, and as soon as possible. You're the only lead to the Brotherhood that I've found so far, and I'd love to see your Hudson tape."

Thad took his glasses off and fidgeted with them again, which Don now recognized to be a stalling tactic. "Right on," he said, wiping them on a corner of his flannel shirt. "That's, uh, that's some story you just told me, Mr. Ruby."

"Don, please. I understand it's not easy to believe me, and I don't expect you to. But I need your help." Don reached into his travel bag, took out Kebbler's notebook and placed it on the bar. "These are notes on *The Unveiling* and Victor Hudson that my...that someone collected before me. A lot of it is unreadable, and much of the rest is downright incomprehensible. Maybe you'll be able to make sense of it, with your background on the Order."

Thad leaned forward until his nose was only inches from the notebook. He glanced from the cracked cover to Don's face and back. A mirthless sort of smile creased his beard, the half-annoyed, half-embarrassed moue of a man suspecting himself to be the butt of a joke. "You're serious about this?" he asked, running a hand through his unruly locks. "You think that the Order is behind what's happening to you. That they want to—what? Silence you? Or make sure you tell their side of the story? Maybe Lucien Callas is reaching out to you from the other side of death."

He started to laugh, stopped when he saw the expression on Don's face. "I mean, it's a lot to take in, Mr.—Don. If I didn't know you're legit, if I hadn't checked out the Occultation Press website, I'd think you're messing with me."

"I'm not," Don said. "Matter of fact, I've never been as serious about anything in my life. Whatever you can infer from those notes would be of tremendous help to me. It may even save my life."

"*Christ.*" His companion's already pallid skin seemed to blanche even more under the ugly bar lights. But Don could tell that the man was hooked. Thad's hand went to the notebook, drew back apprehensively. "You'd really let me take this? Maybe, I don't know, scan or photocopy it?"

Have it, an insidious voice piped up in Don's mind. A way had opened for him out of his predicament; he couldn't believe he hadn't thought of it earlier. *Take Callas's gift. Let it be your burden now. A gift from the other side, taken of your own free will. Let the unexpected guests, the abhorrent ones, come to visit you in the night. Let them fill your ears with their cries.* Thad could take Don's place, lift the nightmare from his shoulders.

With great effort, he overcame the impulse, shook his head. "I wouldn't be comfortable with copies of it circulating around. Just read it. There isn't much, and like I said, a lot of it is probably irrelevant. You can go over it while I'm watching the tape."

"You got yourself a deal." Thad offered a damp, pudgy hand, which Don shook eagerly. "Have to say, this is the most exciting bit of news I've had in years. Maybe ever. You wouldn't mind if I borrowed some material for a presentation at Macabre's next get-together? Only parts that you don't intend to use in your own work, of course. I won't name you as the source, if that's your concern." Not waiting for Don to respond, he picked up the notebook and signaled for the check. "The Society's archive is only a short subway ride away. In my apartment's storage unit, in fact. You can watch the tape in my living room, and I'll read in the bedroom. How long are you planning to stay in New York?"

"As long as I have to." *Also, I have no idea what to do, or where to go after this. You're the last hope I have.* Don felt another stab of guilt at the thought of Jess's unanswered messages, the deadline that he had let slip by without so much as a word of acknowledgement. "I'm due back in Philly on Monday but should have the weekend free. Got a refundable ticket for my train tonight."

"All right." Thad bounced to his feet quickly for a man of his bulk. "The tape is pretty short. Five films, none of them over twenty minutes. It'll probably take me longer than that to read through this." He held up the notebook with a grin. "Maybe you could take a nap in the meantime? You sure look like you could use one."

Chapter 27

There was no denying that the material affected both men profoundly, albeit in different ways. Herbert Barnes practically burst out of his bedroom, glasses askew, the ends of his untucked shirt flapping like tails, with the notebook held aloft like the Ten Commandments. His eternally busy mouth was working, but it took him a moment or two to get out a word.

"Incredible. This could be the most comprehensive document about the Order in existence. There's a whole other book in these notes, one that has nothing to do with Victor Hudson or with horror movies." Jittery with excitement, he seemed ready for another outburst, but checked himself as his guest's condition became apparent. "I suppose you didn't get a chance to rest. Too much coffee?"

Don raised bleary eyes at his host, as if seeing the man for the first time. His back ached from the lumpy sofa on which he had lain for the better part of two hours, drinking cup after cup of coffee from Thad's Keurig. When the tape ended, he had continued to stare out the window, watching the darkness gather outside, mirroring the cloud of hopelessness and despair that was gradually swallowing his thoughts.

"I'm fine," he managed, pulling himself up to a sitting position. "What did you find out?"

Thad leafed through the pages with great care, as if handling a priceless artifact. "Everything we know about the Order is wrong. Well, not wrong, exactly. Just incomplete. We've barely scratched the surface. Their members were far richer than everyone assumed." He jabbed a finger at the open page. "If this is true, their influence was everywhere. Whoever wrote this—I know most of the studios they mention here. *The Unveiling* was supposed to be their move into the mainstream, big time." He clapped the notebook shut, gazed at Don's stricken face with evident unease. "How about you? Get anything useful?"

Unable to find words to express what he was feeling, Don restricted himself to a noncommittal nod of the head. It was a question he'd been trying to answer for the past half-hour or so. Victor Hudson's movies had confirmed his worst fears without offering a solution to his predicament. Five short features in total, compiled by a long-defunct Canadian indie film distributor as part of a series on European surrealism, an attempt to capitalize on the up-and-coming director's popularity. Based on what he'd learned in Bournemouth, Don was almost certain that the movies had been stolen from the school archive, that no copyright had ever been sought or purchased. A limited run of a few hundred tapes would hardly have been noticed by the director or by his legal representatives, or they would have decided that the infringement wasn't worth their time. Prior to the establishment of NAFTA in 1994, there would have been no grounds for an intellectual property lawsuit.

An alternative, and more disturbing, explanation was that the tape was published with Hudson's blessing as a way to spread the Brotherhood's teachings, to seed its message into an unsuspecting world. Whatever the tape's history might be, it didn't matter. What mattered were the eighty-three minutes of video that Don had just sat through that now filled him with cold. Like a shadow had come between him and the sun.

None of the films had a discernible plot or narrative structure. They were strung-together slivers of nightmare. Mostly without dialogue or sound, set against a cosmic backdrop, in which half-suggested forms drifted in the sky or rose from forests, observing their human supplicants from strange camera angles, teaching them how to detach their minds from their bodies. The protagonists would then use this newfound ability to fulfill forbidden desires or enact revenge against their enemies until the narrative structure gave up all pretense of coherence, dissolving into a haphazard sequence of dreamy, weird imagery.

Hudson, to his credit, had accomplished wonders with little to no budget and rudimentary special effects. Secondary edits superimposed images of the actors over themselves or used mirrors to symbolize the loosening of the consciousness from the flesh; in some scenes, the journeyman director had used identically dressed doubles, or twins, to achieve the desired effect. A handful of scenes were accompanied by a soundtrack, an arrhythmic mix of thumping and chanting that evoked the cadence of a language without any perceptible words. The last two features, titled *Ascent* and *New Shores*, consisted of nothing but confusing shots and broken sight lines, Hudson's approximation of an out-of-body experience through a first-person point of view. Yet unlike the first three films, with their obsession with light and space and movement, these last two conveyed panic and terror, an atmosphere of weighty oppression, of being trapped underground or in a gradually narrowing passage. Open skies and starry darkness, meant to symbolize freedom from bodily limits and the transcendence of the spirit, gave way to loss and claustrophobia, hinting at the inability of the wandering consciousness to regain entry into its earthly vessel, at the horror of being observed by one's own flesh, but through the eyes of a stranger.

Much of the footage had been shot in the south of England, as far as Don could work out, the spliced-in segments deliberately made grainy and distorted to blend with the older film. Alienation, possession, a gradual loss of all sense of existence. These reminded Don only too well of his recent experiences, of the dismal realm that had intruded on his reality against his will. Sitting in Thad's small apartment in Red Hook, with garish B-movie posters lining the walls and daylight streaming in, he could feel the gray edges of that other place intruding, waiting to consume him.

Exhaustion and nervous agitation drained Don of resistance. Made it impossible for him to think. The sight of the sofa inspired an indescribable longing for rest. He could put his head down, nap for just a few hours, and wake up refreshed. Or let himself drift into the darkness as a stranger took possession of his mind, his sinews; as he was exiled to that other place, where the damned gibbered and filth rained down from an eternally bleak sky.

His host's cursing snapped him back into the present. Shirt riding up his back, the pudgy man was kneeling over the VCR, stabbing buttons on his home theater system, struggling with something. He retrieved the tape from the slot, inspected it carefully, and slid it back in. The huge screen darkened, then displayed a field of static snow.

"What the hell," Thad said, his voice cracking. He turned on Don in something close to rage. "Did you do this? Did you erase my tape?"

Don shook his head weakly. How could he explain it? Like the reels in the Bournemouth archive, like the snapshots that he'd glimpsed on the internet, the images on the tape no longer needed a physical medium. They had found him, written themselves into his mind; turned him into a living, breathing testament to Victor Hudson's work. A canvas for the message of the Brotherhood of Lament. *A vessel for the master, prepared and anointed, ready to be inhabited.*

Thad had gotten to his feet but seemed reluctant to resort to physical violence. He was breathing hard, and his face was a darker red than his hair and beard. "I've got no idea what's going on here. But it has to stop." He brandished the tape in his hand like a weapon. "Last time I saw a copy of this tape for sale on Amazon, it was worth close to two thousand dollars. Now it's gone. A piece of useless plastic. What the fuck happened?"

"Herbert, I can assure you I had nothing to do with it." Somehow, the other man's anger made Don feel calmer and more focused. "Well, that's not strictly true. I have *everything* to do with it. But I didn't do that to your tape. I would've had to record over it and you can see that's not what happened. I didn't even go near the VCR, or the remote."

"Then who did? There's no one else here."

"I have an idea, but it's difficult to explain. Even if I could explain, you wouldn't believe me. But it has to do with my research, and with Victor Hudson. It's all connected."

"Mr. Ruby, I've had it with the oblique references. I need you to try to explain it in simple terms. Or get out of my home."

"Trust me, you wouldn't have wanted to watch that tape again. Doing so would put you in grave danger. I'm aware that none of this sounds rational or logical, but that doesn't make it any less real. Will you accept that it's in your best interest not to know more?"

"No." But already Thad's rage seemed to be evaporating. Tossing the tape on a stack of dozens of others next to the television set, he slumped into a stained beanbag chair, his head in his hands. He looked so dejected that Don felt guilty for bringing his darkness into the other man's life.

Thaddeus D. Headstone couldn't have been prepared for any of this. In Don's limited experience, fans of horror and the uncanny were usually stolid rationalists who sought art and fandom as a respite from their orderly, regimented everyday lives. The two spheres could coexist, but they couldn't overlap; any hint of encroachment would be soundly rejected, no matter how strong the evidence. Now Thad was facing the unthinkable—an erosion of the strict, defined borders between the real and the fantastic, the harsh intrusion of a stranger, an obsessive maniac, into his carefully curated sanctum.

To his credit, the man didn't crumble or kick Don out of his apartment. He stared at his feet for what seemed like minutes then adjusted his glasses. "I don't suppose you're heading back to Philly today," he said, scarcely above a mutter.

"No. I've missed my train. But there's another one tomorrow morning, around seven."

Thad sighed, flicked through the notebook, held it out to Don. "This is what I wanted to ask you about. These numbers on the last page. Have you noticed them?"

Don peered at the paper with an inward shiver. "Yes," he said. "But I couldn't figure out what they meant. Some kind of code, maybe?"

"Not a code." Thad got up and walked over to his desktop computer. "Coordinates. Without symbols for latitude and longitude." His screensaver—a looping sequence of shots from *Halloween,* a young woman's terrified face interspersed with the empty mask of the killer—faded out as he clicked and tapped to bring up a window. "Read me the one about halfway down the page. The one I circled red."

Don did so, his host typing the number into a basic-looking navigational program. Both men held their breaths as the spinning circle became a blurry square, knitted into a satellite view of hills and forested ravines. Thad zoomed in until a handful of fuzzy blocks took up most of the window, became a farmhouse and outbuildings, a narrow, snaking road leading up to it. Even from orbit, the place looked uninhabited and unkempt, the trail past the farm disappearing into the trees. Don couldn't tell what navigation program Thad was using, decided he didn't want to know.

"This is it." Thad's head dipped myopically toward the monitor. "Doesn't look like a registered address, but I know a forum where I can find that out. If we even want to bother. Chances are it's owned by one of the members of the Order, or their descendants. Or was, at some point. Doesn't look like anyone's paying the upkeep now."

"What are we looking at?"

"In your notes, it's listed as a temple." Thad seemed to have gotten over the loss of his videotape. When he looked up at Don, his eyes were bright with excitement again. "Not that the Order would ever refer to it by that name, of course. They call it a meditation lodge or an enlightenment retreat. A place where the initiated could meet without being noticed. Somewhere isolated, but still close enough to the great centers of power."

"Centers of power?"

"Big cities." Thad waved his hand as if to encompass New York as a whole. "Important cities. The Brethren in Europe believed that crowded urban areas concentrated human energy. Psychic energy. Even their stone, brick, and mortar retained traces of the people who used to inhabit them. Like a giant battery that could be harnessed to elevate the consciousness. To help you free yourself from your prison of flesh." He chuckled and wrote something down on a sticky note. "The real reason was probably far more prosaic. Rich eccentrics in Manhattan are by definition more fleeceable than poor farmers in rural Kansas or Nebraska. Being close to the city also meant being close to one's own accountants and lawyers, if things took a turn. You shouldn't neglect the material world while you're off exploring the astral planes, after all."

His finger traced vague patterns in the air. "Los Angeles may have been the Order's base. But they had lodges—temples—close to almost every metropolis in the nation. This one could have been the New York chapter's base of operations. It's right upstate, in the Rondout Creek valley, north of Kingston. Very secluded, but only a few hours' drive from here."

"Do you think anyone's up there now?"

"Can't tell from this map. But if they are, they don't seem to be eager for visitors."

"Maybe we can look up the owners online," Don said. "See if there's a phone number or an email available. I could ask them if I can come up for a visit."

"You're not really thinking about going there?"

"It's the only way I can find out more." Don set the notebook down, wiped his hand on his trousers before he knew that he was doing it. "Whatever is happening to me feels preordained. Directed, somehow. A summons to this place." He pointed at the screen. "Lucien Callas is alive, Thad. Maybe not *alive* but still *existing* in some form. I don't care how it sounds. It's true. This could be my last chance to get things under control. To banish *them* to where *they* came from. Callas and the presence accompanying him. I don't have a choice."

Thad just stared at him, mouth hanging open, lips still moving. "Mr. Ruby. Don. Can I just say this? You're the weirdest person I've ever met. Coming from me, that really means something. I know a lot of folks who get their kicks from occultism and magical studies. Who read books about Wicca and the Kabbalah, cast spells and burn black candles in their living rooms. Which is cool with me. I'm a live-and-let-live kind of guy. You don't strike me as someone who would be into all that, but you really believe what you just said. I find that remarkable."

"I'm serious. Helping me could put you in very real danger. I'll understand if you won't go any further. You've already done enough. More than I could have asked for."

"Not only will I help you, but I want to go with you." Thad spread his arms in bewilderment. "You're the real deal, man. I don't know if you're crazy, or on drugs, or actually onto something big. Whatever. You've seen into the beyond. Experienced something profound, real or not, and I want to know more about it."

He delved behind the stack of tapes, rummaged through shelves, and opened drawers. "I can bring a camera," he said. "A real camera, not the one on my phone. Shoot some live-action footage like *Ghost Hunters*. Something I can screen at festivals. The Macabre Marquee Society presents the forgotten cult temples of the Adirondacks. Audiences would love it."

"Absolutely not." Don remembered the sightings, the nightly visitations. The entire purpose of investigating the Order was to protect others from danger. He scrambled for a reason that would discourage his host. "I'm going up there without permission. *Trespassing*. If there's anyone at the house, they could be armed. Best case scenario, they'll turn us away and the whole trip will have been for naught. Provided that we can even find the farm in the first place."

"I still want to do it."

"You don't understand. I can't let you go through with it."

"No." For the first time since they met, Thad's mouth was still, his jaw clenched. There was no goofy grin on his face now. "*You* don't understand. This could be it for me, Don. My first and final movie. My legacy, my chance to leave something behind. It doesn't matter what we find up there or don't. When I show it, everyone will see what they want to see. Project their deepest emotions on what's on the screen. That's how reality TV works. People feel fear of what could be lurking inside the house, desire to find out more, or feel relief that there's nothing to be found. The simple act of observing changes that which is observed." He cocked his head to the side. "You never figured it out, did you? Why Victor Hudson's movies appealed to so many. The message they contained, the fundamental truth he wanted to share. Buried in all the occult nonsense."

"I have no idea what you're talking about."

"His films. The ones you just watched." Thad gesticulated impatiently. "To critics, Hudson remained an enigma, if they bothered with him at all. Most dismissed his slasher features as trash. Some appreciated them as camp, a send-up of popular genre tropes. Farces involving buckets of blood. A few even took the movies to be political. Their minds were too small to accommodate grand ideas. Hudson was a master of technique, a virtuoso of style and method, but he was first and foremost a visionary. He had the only gift that really counts. The ability to pick at reality where it was at its thinnest and cautiously peel it away. To sneak the true meaning past your senses, hidden inside a metaphor or a spectacle. A spectacle of nudity and gore, yes, when that was the easiest way. Craft his own reality and share it with the world. That's what it was all about."

"I didn't understand three quarters of what you just said." Don checked the time, felt a huge yawn creep up on him, fatigue crashing down like an avalanche. "But I see you've got your mind made up. I suggest we grab a few hours of shut-eye, then head up to the farm tomorrow morning. As early as possible."

Thaddeus D. Headstone Esquire nodded. "I have a friend with a car we can borrow. You crash on the couch. I think I'm too wired to sleep. What I can do instead is search property records. See if I can't figure out who owns the property."

Already Don's eyes felt weighed down by all the missed sleep. He reckoned he would be safe for a few hours, especially if Thad kept a watchful eye out for an incursion. Wondering how he would explain astral possession to his host, he almost laughed out loud. His credibility as a sane companion was badly eroded as it was; another strange request would hardly make things any worse.

"Sounds like a plan," he said. "One other thing. Keep the lights on while I'm asleep. All of them. Okay?"

"You got it." It was only six o'clock and still light, but Thad reached over and clicked on his desk lamp. "To be honest, I would've done that anyway. Especially after the conversation we've just had. It'll be a while before I turn them off again."

Chapter 28

It took them almost two hours to get out of the city, but once they passed Newburgh, the road opened up; the morning commuters were still asleep in their beds, the rush of night-shift workers and delivery vehicles thinning out. Wet asphalt glistened under the highway lights. Black clouds had dumped a torrential downpour overnight, but the rain had tapered off and the rising sun was doing its best to burn off the cover.

Thad's friend had come through. A fellow insomniac, he picked up his phone at four in the morning and left his car at their disposal, a weathered Datsun with a peeling silver finish. Don drove, refreshed after the first continuous sleep he'd had in days, while Thad dozed in the passenger seat, oblivious to the world, head all the way back and bearded mouth slack, his snores the only sound disturbing the silence.

True to his word and better connected than Don would have imagined, the Chief Executive Ghoul of the Macabre Marquee Society had stayed up the whole night, emailing and perusing illegal search engines, fortified by an inexhaustible supply of black coffee and small orange tablets Don suspected to be Adderall. When Don woke up, he was greeted with a wide, manic grin and a stack of printed pages. The farmhouse they were headed toward was owned by one Caroline Lansing, New York socialite and offspring of old Manhattan money. Her exact involvement with the Order of Astral Enlightenment was unclear, although she had been listed as an occasional donor to their astral travel research program. The house had been the summer home of her grandfather, Caspar Waters, distantly related to the Van Outen's around whom the city had practically been built. After Caroline's untimely demise in the seventies, the Order had come into possession of the estate and used it to hold their enlightenment retreats, long debauched affairs involving fasting and meditation, with hallucinogens handed out like candy.

"Local folks took to complaining and the police got involved," Thad had said, struggling into a rain slicker about a size too small and digging through a tiny and malodorous closet for a pair of hiking boots. "Some of the participants went missing, apparently, or were found naked and wandering the woods. The family got wind of it, decided they'd had it with their name being dragged through the mud, and sicced their lawyers on the Order. There isn't a lot of information on what happened next, but the ceremonies stopped. I imagine the Order decided it wasn't worth the trouble."

"Who owns it now?"

"A company bought it in the eighties. Some developer who wanted to build a hotel. But they went bankrupt a few years later." Thad rubbed his hands, giddy with discovery. "Want to guess what happened just before the bankruptcy?"

Don had a pretty good idea. *The Unveiling* had tanked, dragging the Order's finances down with it. "So, we're good to go," he said.

"Not exactly. I tried to dig into who owns the place now, and it's a mess. Ownership reverted back to the family, but the developer's creditors sued. It's been in limbo ever since, accruing lawyer fees. Neither side thinks the place is worth the hassle, would be my guess. You get that a lot with old property in the middle of nowhere. Back taxes pile up on it until they're more than the land is worth. The tax bill on the farmhouse lapsed, which would mean Greene County takes possession of it, except someone lodged an appeal. If anyone's living there right now, they're not paying utilities, they don't own a vehicle, and they don't have a landline."

"That doesn't sound right."

"Oh, it gets more interesting than that. I found a woman on the Fangoria Forums who claims that she used to go up to the farmhouse. A real woo-woo type. She's not the only one, either. The Order did quite a bit of community outreach back in the day."

"Anyone willing to talk?"

"No. But she did email me about the ceremonies they used to get up to at the lodge. She described some pretty wild stuff.. Sometimes the movie people would fly over from the West Coast, take the red eye to LA and back. Big names. Not that she would name any. But they tended to keep to themselves, steering clear of the decadence. Apparently, all they did was get stoned and watch movies in this big theater. Victor Hudson came out a few times, and that actor he was obsessed with. Kirk Taylor. He was in everything Hudson made for a while."

He must have seen something in Don's face that gave him pause. "Anyway, that's just what she said," he said lamely. "Probably nothing to it."

Making an effort to remain composed, Don nodded for him to continue. "Go on. What did they do up there?"

"She thinks it had to do with rituals," Thad said. "Someone explained it to her once, but she was too high to pay attention. Most of it happened behind closed doors. Strictly by invitation for those who showed potential." He waved down a cab and dictated the address to the driver. "Hudson's inner circle was into some really weird stuff. Like this one time, they gathered everyone in the auditorium and played a blank tape, or a shot of a black screen, with a kind of ambient music in the background. The lady got pretty scared, although she had no idea why. One of the guys in the audience freaked out. Totally lost it, ran out into the woods. Cops found him in a town ten miles away, all scratched up and confused."

"Did you say auditorium?"

"Yeah. Does that sound familiar? Supposedly there was one in a wing of the lodge. Maybe fifty plush seats, cinema-grade projector, the works." Thad stole a cautious glance toward the cab's glass partition, lowering his voice. "Get this. The inner circle wore masks. Animal masks, always the same ones. Made from real animals that had been taxidermized. Badly. The lady said they smelled something awful and were falling apart. Hudson called them their spirit guides to the astral. All they had to do was let their minds open the way. *'Invoke their own reality'* or something along those lines."

"Where is this woman now?"

"I couldn't get her to say. But I wouldn't be surprised if she's still here in the city. Waiting to be summoned up to the lodge once more. Whatever she thinks happened up there, it impacted her deeply. She described it as a religious epiphany."

Before leaving, Don had texted Jess, keeping it short and to the point. *In New York for a few days*, he'd written. *Call you Monday. Got news.* He hoped he would be around to keep the promise. Maybe he could invent an excuse, such as that he'd lost his phone or run out of charge. There was certainly no signal up here in the mountains, and he switched his phone off to preserve what was left of the battery.

In a burst of bravado, he had emailed her the remaining chapters. Unfinished, one of them was no more than an outline, but the bulk of the material was there, fact and speculation about *The Unveiling*. Jess would be able to iron out the wrinkles, fit the pieces into a coherent narrative. It felt like a final act of resistance; the masterpiece that no one would read, the legacy he had destroyed himself over, but that would never see publication.

Or would it? Perhaps his death or disappearance would turn out to be a marketing boon that would drive up sales. Turn him into an urban legend, his fate an uncanny tale that would resonate in the public's subconscious long after his book was forgotten. True crime websites would proliferate and debates would rage on internet forums. Perhaps a few years down the line another writer would pick up the thread to add another chapter to the mystery. Whatever the case, Don Ruby no longer mattered: he had served his purpose, become part of the weft and weave of the story, a symbol greater than the man behind it.

What better way could there be to live forever?

The city passed by. Constellations of bright lights fading into the blossoming pink of dawn. Empty lanes stretched before him, occasional handfuls of houses whisking by, like cardboard cutouts hanging behind a thin curtain of fog. Don steered the car onto a secondary road, then down narrow country lanes, then along old blacktop around which trees huddled like skeletal sentries. Only a few hours away from the hazy Manhattan skyline, the metropolis was but a distant dream, little towns scattered through the undulating countryside, the Catskills humped in the distance, rain-washed and glowering under wintry sunlight. The car's heater labored to wheeze some much-needed warmth into the cabin, finally giving up the ghost just as they passed Paramus. A chill that had little to do with the weather settled into Don's bones..

They stopped at a roadside diner for coffee and greasy food and filled the car up in a combination gas station and general store. Neither man felt compelled to say much. Thad had busied himself with his phone, while Don was wrapped up in his thoughts, anticipating the end of their journey with mounting apprehension. Whatever fate awaited him there would be his own choice. But that was cold comfort and did little to dispel the growing shadow that the Order's retreat cast over his day.

The place had an address, but it didn't register with the satnav, some quirk of the program erased the last few hundred feet of the road, showing nothing but empty hillside. Thad spotted it first, a hint of ruined roof above the trees, and they spent several minutes cruising along slowly, peering into the greenery, looking for an access point. The farmhouse seemed to reveal itself in stages, a large, neglected building seated atop a wooded promontory over a swollen, muddy creek. The remains of outbuildings stuck up like bad teeth. A gravel driveway, steep and composed of tight turns, led up the hillside from the main lane. Don decided not to take chances and parked the car on the flat shoulder. The ground was wet from last night's rain, and more clouds massed on the horizon. Another downpour could turn the poorly maintained gravel trail into a mudslide, dumping the Datsun into the creek and leaving them stranded in the middle of nowhere. They had passed a town a few miles back, but it had looked just as abandoned as the property, and he couldn't recall seeing anything resembling a garage. From this point, they would proceed on foot and hope that anyone who might be living in the farmhouse didn't spot the car parked on the side of the road.

Thad retrieved a clunky digital camera from the back seat, yawned and stretched his legs. "This is it," he said, voice barely above a whisper, reverential. He pointed the camera uphill, angled for a better shot. "Where the Order of Astral Enlightenment held their seances. Where Hollywood executives and Wall Street brokers delved into mysticism and the occult, searching for gateways to higher planes of existence."

He retraced his steps, repeated the same few sentences in a slightly different order. Getting the narration right for his documentary, Don realized. He stared up the uninviting slope, into the trees that perched over the trail, the deepening darkness. The farmhouse was obscured from the bottom of the hill, but he could feel its presence above him, an invisible weight smothering the wet air out of his lungs.

"Follow us as we step into the Order's inner sanctum." Still holding the camera up, Thad was lumbering up the driveway, already breathing hard. "The first men to do so in nearly thirty years. If rumors are to be believed; the lodge was never truly abandoned. Uninhabited, perhaps, at least by human beings. But not empty." He trailed off dramatically, lens aimed at the ceiling of crisscrossed branches weighed down with rain.

Don wanted to tell him to shut up, to put the camera away until they'd had a chance to check the house for occupancy. But he didn't. Part of him hoped an irate redneck would come barreling down the trail, yelling at them to get the hell off his property, and that would be it. They didn't belong here. Even if the lodge was empty, even if nothing stirred the trees, something up in the forest was aware of their trespassing. The hidden scrutiny he'd sensed on the way over was no longer just a feeling. Eyes were upon him, tracking him from a slowly dimming sky, crumbling his resolve with every moment. He pushed the impression from him and hurried after Thad.

It didn't take long for him to spot the wire fence peeking out from a wild tangle of bushes. Fallen over and torn, but still topped by lethal-looking barbs in places. They stepped over it carefully, into wet scrub that snagged Don's trousers and soaked through his shoes. Under the trees, the light cut off abruptly, as if a thick curtain had been drawn over the day. Rotted gateposts bracketed the gravel path, overtaken by foliage and almost indiscernible in the gloom. The gate itself had long ago gone to ruin, crumbling planks protruding from the grass, a single rusted hinge screwed in one of the posts. Twenty or so paces further in, a NO TRESPASSING sign was nailed to a tree and faded almost to illegibility, giving the only evidence that they were on private property.

"A haven in the Catskills woods, far from prying eyes." Thad was trudging through the bushes, narrating between wheezes. Don was suddenly thankful for the relentless chatter, a distraction from the dread that seized him as soon as the farmhouse had come into view. "Left to the Order by a wealthy deceased member—whose name we cannot divulge for threat of a libel suit—this unassuming farmhouse served as a retreat for the acolytes of the New York branch. One can guess at what unhallowed rites took place beneath its roof, imagine the cries and otherworldly sounds that disturbed the silence of these serene woods.

"On the surface, the Order of Astral Enlightenment seems to have sunk into complete obscurity. The reasons for that were never clear, but one of the more persistent rumors involves financial setbacks and a mysterious unreleased horror film. Could a smaller group have gone underground and survived to this day, kindling the light of forbidden knowledge? We're here today to find out the truth."

Through the trunks, a shed or a stable was now visible, three pale gray walls and a moss-grown roof. In a moment, Don's eyes adapted enough for him to see the farmhouse behind it, sagging roof clinging to its last few red tiles, an empty upper floor window sighted through denuded branches. A low inner wall, overgrown with creepers, marked where a garden had once stood. In the spring or summer, or even early fall, when the trees still had leaves, the house and the gravel path would be entirely invisible from the road. Hikers could walk right through the remains of the gate and never realize they were trespassing, unless they tripped over the fence. Thickets and waist-high bushes would discourage anyone from venturing closer to the house itself, yet it was the general atmosphere of the place that posed the more effective deterrent. It had an air of not just neglect, but of things warped, as if that unclean realm were infringing on it somehow, corrupting everything it touched by proximity. No lost hiker or accidental wanderer, no matter how curious, would set foot into these dank and forbidding woods.

Thad lowered the camera, wiped sweat from his face and condensation off his glasses. "Doesn't look like anyone would mind if we went in."

Don wasn't so sure. The gate was decrepit, the chains and padlocks on the shed rust-eaten, the grounds beyond the trees wild and overgrown. But someone, or something, had churned the black loam around the trail, and no birds sang in the branches, no small animals scurried through the tall grass. He knew they weren't alone here, felt that the place was already occupied by an intelligence unlike any he'd encountered before. If the inhabitants of that gray wasteland needed no doors to move through this world, here a door had been opened to them permanently, a beacon to guide them through the long dark.

Thad took a few more shots as Don followed the remains of the wall, straining his ears in the direction of the house, but hearing nothing. Sodden clapboards, black earth, wet, bare trunks; colors muted and runny as if something had fed on the very essence of the place. Even the surviving bushes seemed sickly and pale, like they had never felt the sun. They moved cautiously, aware of every noise announcing their approach. Thad had resumed filming, but he kept the talking down to a minimum, muttering so quietly that Don could no longer make out sentences, only snatches of words.

Past the shed, the bones of a collapsed barn emerged from the vegetation, no more than a heap of boards and beams, an empty doorframe gaping like an open mouth. Thad swallowed hard, stepped deeper into the grass, moving his camera up and down the leaning wall.

"Looks like symbols on the outside," he said in a harsh whisper. "White and red paint. Gone, for the most part, so it's hard to tell what it used to be. An occult incantation. A message to the secret spheres."

He waddled closer to the doorway, aiming the camera into the darkness. A faint whiff of ancient dung and bestial sweat reached Don's nose. If animals had once lived inside, they were long gone; broken pens filled with decaying straw, old stains splattered across the splintered boards. No one had bothered to clean up in a long time.

When Thad made to go inside, Don pulled him back. Without a word, he pointed farther up the path, where wide tire tracks crisscrossed the dirt. They looked fresh, untouched by rain. "Someone's been here," he said, unable to keep the tremor out of his voice. "They could still be here." Thad ducked his head and looked around, suddenly very pale, his eyes wide behind his thick glasses.

Closer to the house, they found overgrown farm machinery, a broken chicken coop, and a mass of rotting wood that had once been stacked into a neat pile. Two stone buildings protruded from the shrubs; their few remaining windows opaque with dust. It had been more than just a summer retreat: the soil had been tilled and planted, animals raised in the barn and pens. The Order had repurposed the place, grown their own food, evidently looking to make the property suitable for long-term occupancy and as self-sufficient as possible.

Dread tightened Don's guts as he reached the end of the driveway and the massive shape of the farmhouse reared up against the sky. Through the ruined roof, through the empty window frames, he could see the edge of the hill that sloped down to the creek, the dark boundary of the woods. Sunlight bathed the other side of the property, but here seemed oddly dimmed, the air cold and clammy against his skin.

Wasting no time, Thad took several shots of the exterior, panned round to capture the abandoned yard and outbuildings. The driveway terminated in a wide circle that went up to the stained front door. Being here no longer seemed like the right idea to Don. Even out in the open, with the sun shining brightly through a scrim of cloud, he felt an unreasoning fear of the presence that had haunted his apartment. The skin on the back of his neck prickled with anticipation. He had fled halfway across the globe to escape the dwellers in the gray waste and was now walking right into their den, offering his throat up for the sacrificial cut.

"Don... Don?" Thad had gone a few paces off to the right but was now crouching behind the woodpile, his camera abandoned in the grass. His voice was suppressed to a terrified whisper, his hand motioning for Don to get down, indicating something on the far side of the driveway. Less than a second later, Don heard it too: noises from the other side of the building, muttered phrases, a car door slamming shut. He flung himself into cover next to Thad, who was breathing heavily, either with panic or excitement.

"Who are they?"

Don crawled forward, peered out cautiously. Saw the rear end of a weathered, mud-spattered SUV parked next to what could only be the house's back entrance, a figure in dirty boots rooting through the back of the vehicle. A dog was barking somewhere in the distance, large by the sound of it. Don's skin crawled at the thought of being discovered or attacked by the animal.

Should they show themselves, attempt an introduction? The new arrivals must have come up some other road; it was possible that they hadn't spotted the Datsun at the bottom of the driveway. Don thought about passing off their presence here as two bumbling New Yorkers getting lost in the woods but quickly discarded the idea. If these were members of the Order, possibly on the lookout for intruders, who knew what they might do to a pair of trespassers? Besides, the unpleasant awareness of that other presence had not diminished with the appearance of the SUV. If anything, it was stronger now, every nerve in Don's body screaming at him to leave.

"What do we do?" Thad was staring at him like a lost child. Perhaps it was just Don's imagination, but the barking sounded closer now. More than one dog now, growling and scratching, probably picking up on the interlopers' scent. Even if they could outrun the animals to the trees, past the wall—an unlikely proposition, given the shape Thad was in—they wouldn't be able to escape. Indecision froze him to the spot, reluctant to so much as blink or take a deep breath.

He listened to the chatter, the sound of doors opening and closing, footsteps crunching on gravel. A gruff voice seemed to curse the dogs into obedience; they whimpered and went silent, a final desperate howl receding down what sounded like an enclosed space. Don grabbed Thad by the elbow and hauled the man upright.

"We'll head back to the gate," he said. "Stay low. Don't let them see you."

He risked another look over the woodpile. Hard to tell with the vehicle blocking most of the view, but he was almost sure he could see boots clomping over the threshold, followed by swishing tails, the men and the dogs going into the house.

"Go now. Go."

They were about to make a break for it when they heard the rumble of approaching engines from the trees. Immediately followed by the snapping of branches and the squishing of tires through soft mud.

Chapter 29

"We have to get out of here."

Don's back and legs were stiff with fatigue and cold. Water had soaked through the thin soles of his shoes, and the sun had disappeared behind an ominous cloud bank, pregnant with the threat of rain. He didn't dare move, didn't dare speak above a whisper for fear of being discovered. His heart was hammering inside his chest, audible from a mile away.

More than twenty minutes had passed since they'd hunkered down behind the wall, narrowly avoiding being seen while listening to the commotion at the front of the house. Twice already, Don had tried to summon the resolve to make a run for the gate and the car parked by the road. But his nerve had given out and his legs refused to move. He could no longer see the people by the front entrance, could no longer hear the dogs. They could be anywhere, roaming the grounds, sniffing for intruders.

Four vehicles had joined the SUV in the driveway. Yet the reunion, if that's what this was, didn't seem to be a happy one. A male voice had spoken in angry, agitated tones, and two of the newcomers had walked away in a huff, coming so close to the wall that Don couldn't believe they hadn't spotted him. The younger of the pair had pointed back the way they'd come, muttering about a car parked by the main road. From the furtive glance he'd cast at the parked cars, Don inferred that he didn't want the rest of the gathering disturbed. The older one, a stout, grizzled man dressed in old-fashioned tweeds, had taken his companion by the arm, not at all gently, and whispered something in his ear. There was no doubt that the two men had seen the Datsun; for whatever reason, they said nothing to the others, and did not appear keen to go looking for potential trespassers.

After a short while, the gathering had moved inside, leaving Don and Thad in their uncertain shelter. A tense silence descended on the woods, broken by the occasional noise coming from the farmhouse. It was their best chance of escape, and any further delays would only increase the odds of being caught. But Don had come too close to turn his back on the mystery. Not now, when the answer seemed so close, a chance to reclaim some semblance of a life, some tattered fragment of sanity.

"What do you think they're doing in there?" Thad had regained some composure. His face was paler than usual, but he kept peering over the wall, glancing back toward his abandoned camera. "Something's going on. Could they be members of the Order?"

"I don't know," Don said. He wanted Thad to leave without him. Things were getting out of hand, and he didn't want to be responsible for another person, especially one who didn't really understand the stakes. Whatever he was about to face inside the house, he would face it alone.

Before he could put any of this into words, a sound reached their hiding place from the house, silencing them both, making them forget the discomfort and cold.

"What was that?" Thad was no longer bothering to whisper. His stricken gaze blundered past Don, across the overgrown yard, toward the ruined roof. "What the *fuck* was that?"

Don realized he was holding onto the wall for support. The noise was deep, rhythmic, and he felt it with his body more than with his ears. It took his frozen brain a moment to realize that it was coming from human throats: a chant, low and sonorous, a wordless vocalization picked up and reshaped by the old walls of the building, carried up into the darkening sky. A single voice dominated, high and strong and masculine, rising and falling in long, steady cadences. It seemed to be leading the rest in prayer, although Don could not discern what divinity was being entreated, what power called upon. Folk dances or throat singing came to mind, but neither seemed to quite fit the sound emanating from the dilapidated farmhouse, gathering in the middle of him with a queasy lurch.

Light flickered behind the remaining windows, a sickly radiance illuminating the blackened walls from within. Gone almost as quickly as it appeared, like a beacon or a sign of something lurking beyond the thin scrim of sky. Which had changed in some indefinable way, the sun going out as if snuffed by an invisible hand, the atmosphere taking on a bleached dimness akin to dusk. Don's first thought was that clouds had closed overhead, but when he raised his eyes not a wisp was in sight. The sun was high up, but shone dully, like a lamp seen through a smoky film. Like an invisible veil had gathered between it and the world.

"The unveiling," Don said, surprising himself. "It's begun."

But Thad was no longer listening. He had scrambled over to his camera and was filming the building, the sky, and the wild, unkempt grounds. Don wanted to warn him, but a sudden surge of despair left him speechless and overwhelmed. All he wanted was for this to be over, to curl up in a secret corner somewhere, or right here on the wet grass, and wait for whatever fate awaited. To close his eyes and let the nightmare take him.

Except he knew there would be no end to his torments, no salvation. The presence that dwelled in this place, or had been called down to it, was aware of him. It had come to seek him out, drawn by the prayer that was sounding more distorted and distant by the moment. As if the farmhouse and its physical occupants were traveling away from him and fading from reality. Other voices were intruding upon the chant, voices incoherent and wailing, the cries of the damned pouring out of their desolate prison, heralding some ineffable arrival.

"I've got to get all of this," Thad said. His mouth was open, his face shiny with sweat, coppery beard glistening. "What's inside. What's happening out here. People have to see this. They have to know."

"No." Don placed a hand on the other man's shoulder, but couldn't find the strength to grab on, and it was shrugged off. "If you get closer, you'll be seen. Not by those inside, but by what's coming. If it touches you, you will regret it. You'll wish you were never born." The words felt strange on his tongue, as if another language had invaded his brain, pushing out the familiar.

"They won't see me." Thad pointed to the side of the building, where a four-post shed framed the rusted bones of an old tractor. "I'll go around the side. Try to take a shot through one of the windows, see what's going on." He was talking too fast, and his eyes were bright, like he was psyching himself up for the effort. "Maybe I can see *them*. The ones making this noise. There's still plenty of light." He gestured loosely with the camera. "We'll never get this opportunity again."

"You don't know what we're dealing with here. It's dangerous."

"I'll meet you at the front of the house. Then we can get the hell out of here."

"What about the dogs?" Don said, but Thad was already off, humping awkwardly through the long grass, trying to keep the camera on the farmhouse. He paused at the shed, crouched lower, and half-crawled to an open window, then rose slowly and pointed the camera inside. Turned and gave Don a thumbs-up sign; his face wore the stunned expression of having witnessed something he couldn't quite reconcile with reality. Then he moved along the wall of the farmhouse, stopping at every opening to film the interior.

At the last window before the corner, he jerked back, like a man scalded. Don waved him back, but whatever was taking place behind the glass had captured all of Thad's attention. Holding the camera at chest height, keeping the lens trained on the pane, he rounded the corner and disappeared from sight.

Don got up and looked around for a weapon. Found nothing but a few loose, damp bricks. The voices from the damned place sounded closer now, both desperate and agitated, as if the inhabitants were sensing a way out. A dull film seemed to gather over his senses: the wall, the house, the grass, all felt less substantial, the noises muffled. The forest was like a greasy reflection of a real place floating on the surface of a scummed pond. What light still made it down from the sky was dirty and gray and made his eyes hurt. Maybe this was for the better. Maybe not being able to see clearly was beneficial here. Anything to keep him from perceiving the faces of the multitude he suddenly sensed close to him; their lament vibrating the air, their touch like cold slivers passing through his skin.

He went past the parked vehicles, one eye out for the dogs he'd heard earlier. Surely, the animals could feel the change coming over the house and the trees just as well as he could; yet he saw no trace of them, either in the yard or through the open door. Perhaps they'd shown better sense than their masters and taken off into the woods. His foot was on the bottom stair when a glance down almost made him stumble. A huge muzzle emerged from between the rotten boards of the porch, then retreated below, followed by a scuffling noise.

Overcoming an instinct to run, Don bent down and saw the dogs huddled under the porch, pressed back as far as they could against the side of the house, terrified out of their wits. Eyes rolled back to white and teeth gleaming in the gloom. There were four of them, a large and shaggy breed, trying to make themselves invisible, not daring to bark. The look in their eyes was so human in its dejection that Don forgot his own terror for a moment, felt only pity and a shared helplessness. For a moment, he wanted to crawl in with them and let his thoughts dissolve to instinctive terror.

The nearest of the dogs whimpered, shied away farther into the shadows. It wasn't looking at Don, but at something past him, on the far side of the grounds.

Turning, Don followed the animal's gaze across the muddy field, to where the forest began. Only the trees were no longer there, replaced by a vast stretch of gray water. An ocean from a fever-dream of desolation, spreading all the way to the skyline, its filthy waves churned by an intangible wind. A solitary figure rose from that dreary emptiness, a dark smudge standing on some forsaken shore, tall but stooped in sorrow, or anguish, its rags flapping in the breeze. Even before Don beheld the bearded face, he knew that he was looking at Kirk Taylor, condemned to forever walk that dismal strand, to seek the end of the seething ocean and never find it.

Further across the sea, battered by a gale that seemed to affect only its immediate surrounds, a boat struggled against the waves that roiled around its prow, its white square of sail furling and unfurling like a broken wing. Victor Hudson, trapped in an eternal voyage, exhausted and terrified, desperately watching a coast that never got any closer. Here, at last, Lucien Callas had gotten his movie made: a vignette of abiding torment, its meaning, if there ever had been one, long lost even to its creator. High overhead, cresting into the pitiless sky, a dark mass heaved, composed of thousands of individual shapes. Legions of the lost, entire nations, released from their lightless abode, their shrieks filling the distance between the worlds.

With a heavy, sinking feeling, Don turned his back to the scene and went up the creaking steps and into the house.

***

Mildewed furniture lay pushed up against damp-rotted walls. The big room past the foyer was empty, its surfaces filmed with grit and dust. On a dining table the size of a barn door, dried flowers wilted in a porcelain vase. No one had used the room in years, maybe decades, except as a thoroughfare: dozens of muddy footprints stained the ratty rugs and the cracked hardwood floor, leading to a passage into a blackened, lightless kitchen and beyond.

Don made his way deeper into the farmhouse slowly, listening for the chanting prayer or approaching footsteps. The narrow, claustrophobic corridors evoked an unpleasant memory of the tunnels from his dreams, with tall arched ceilings and bare brick walls, lighter squares where framed pictures had once hung. The singing sounded further away than when he'd first heard it outside, as if the walls absorbed the voices.

Doorways lined the hallway, opened onto stripped, empty rooms containing rotted mattresses, some with the added luxury of a crude wooden chair and desk. Many of the spaces had once been large chambers, partitioned into smaller rooms by sheetrock walls. *Smaller cells.* In some of them Don saw bunk beds with rusty frames, in others the disturbing sight of iron manacles hanging from bare masonry. The very thought of what could have been summoned and imprisoned here made Don's head swim with terror. Around the chains, the wall and floor bore thousands of scuff marks, as if razor-sharp claws had struggled against the restraints, as if pointed teeth had broken upon the iron, or tried to gnaw long, mottled limbs free.

An air of misery and suffering permeated every inch of the great house. Walking these floors was like stepping under a heavy black cloud, being cut off from light and warmth forever. Don could imagine Victor Hudson presiding over retreats here, starving his followers and feeding them drugs, hypnotizing them into a dream-state from which they would embark on voyages into the unknown. A voyage from which many would never return. Regret and self-disgust left Don no room for fear; this was the last stop of his own journey, along which he'd rejected sanity, turned his back on the realm of reason and light. Defeat filled his mouth with bitterness. There was no leaving this place. Even if the presence beneath this sagging roof allowed him to depart; there was no path for him to return to anything that resembled normalcy. Only one way to go, and that was deeper inside.

With every step it became more obvious that the mystical experiments conducted here had all come to naught. Whatever elevated spheres of existence the astral travelers had once traversed, they could not escape the poverty and decay of the house. Here and there, ghostly reminders of better times surfaced from the beggarly gloom, rosewood cabinets filled with nothing but cobwebs, fine carpets gone frayed and faded, gilded picture frames holding cracked, dusty glass. This was what Lucian Callas's grand design had been reduced to, what the Brotherhood's esoteric philosophy had yielded... A place as lifeless and barren as the gray wasteland into which they had once ventured searching for secrets, a grim monument to their ultimate downfall. These very rooms, from which they had dreamed of dominions beyond the stars, now sinking into filth and mold, forgotten by all except a dedicated and possibly unbalanced few who still clung to the old ways. Who had again gathered here to chant prayers into the void, vainly seeking to free themselves from their earthbound forms. Don was so overwhelmed by numb despair that he could no longer feel horror or even trepidation at the thought.

Voices accompanied him past the ramshackle chambers, past the interminable rows of open doors. A man cried out that he was lost, implored another unseen someone to turn around and look at him. A woman, her voice cracked and harsh as if she'd been screaming, muttered to herself that this was only an illusion, that she would find her way back, that everything would be all right. Another disembodied whisper urged Don to stay inside, to not go into the field until the darkness had passed from the sky. Other, more menacing noises blended with the entreaties: the labored, eager breathing of a thing whose head was too heavy for its neck, the click of sharp talons on a stone floor, the rattle and scrape of chains against rough walls.

Some implausible distance into the farmhouse, broken double doors led into a huge, windowless hall. Trembling with exhaustion, Don peered through the doorway in confusion at the scene before him. A stained white sheet had been stretched across one wall as a makeshift screen. The only light in the room came from a film projector playing a reel upon it in utter silence. Incoherent smudges of shadow and light that moved in patterns that suggested a purpose.

Chanting figures formed an uneven circle before the screen, hands joined, masks perched on their heads. Even in the flickering light, it was evident that the masks were old, their edges shabby and frayed. Some were missing an ear, or a clump of threadbare fur, while others had rotted away around the muzzles and snouts, showing sharp teeth like old ivory.

Something was moving along the walls and across the high ceiling. Don raised his eyes upward. The boundaries of the hall were alive, crawling and distending with barely glimpsed forms. Patchy, skull-like heads, bony torsos, emaciated arms with long fingers; behind the roiling masonry, the damned surged back and forth, a wave of agitated motion breaking across the house, ebbing, then gathering new strength. If he focused, he could hear a light scratching, as if plaster and solid stone had become an elastic membrane at which the unwelcome visitors pawed and raked, drawn by the lilting prayer, frenzied by the promise of an end to their suffering.

His arms wrapped around himself. All reason drained out of him, Don slid down the wall and closed his eyes. Pressed his hands to his ears. None of it stopped the sights from coming, the frantic imprecations of their inhuman voices. Victor Hudson had been deceived and had deceived others in turn. This astral realm was no vision of paradise, no escape from the existential horror of human existence. His exalted visions were mere projections, illusions fed to the Brotherhood by what dwelled in that dreadful void. The reality of it was an appalling half-existence; it was loss and desolation, a profound alienation from everything the mind recognized as sane and real. Those who were unfortunate enough to become trapped in it were irreparably changed, shadows with no way back to the world they'd left behind. Driven insane by the endless roving through lightless passages, by their own awful condition, by the bleak ocean and cold, filth-hued sky, that vista like the end of all hope.

Lucien Callas had seen his dreams come to fruition and lived to regret it. Was this his dream for all mankind, the destruction of the world in which he was shunned and ridiculed, that had rejected his prophetic vision, offered nothing but scorn in return? Don's mind shrieked at the notion of such monumental hatred, such diabolical desire to foist one's will upon the earth. It was this desire that had kept Callas going throughout his long imprisonment in the astral, preserved at least some traits of the magician's personality: his ego and his conviction in his superiority over the rest of the human race, his yearning to avenge himself on his detractors. Victor Hudson had been his last acolyte, but Hudson had turned his back on the Brotherhood, perverted their message, and had paid the ultimate price for it.

A scream brought Don out of the paralyzed chaos his thoughts had descended into. One of the celebrants, a man lifting a badger's head up to the ceiling, must have sensed the forms swarming overhead and was nearly undone by the sight. His body was rigid with terror, and he seemed to be yanking his hands out of those of his neighbors, attempting to break the circle. A sharp command from the tweed-clad man, who wore the mask of a wolf or jackal, and the terrified badger seemed to settle back in. Or at least resign himself to his fate. But the circle wavered, more beasts glancing at one another in apparent panic, a tremor passing through the linked bodies.

The projection on the screen was gaining consistency, coalescing into the black-and-white interior of a room like an unfinished film set: a fuzzy outline of tables and chairs, the long-curved line of a counter. A smudge of shadow at its center became a man, dapper and poised, dressed in a sharp three-piece suit.

The movement in the room intensified, the voyagers from the astral sensing the lapse in concentration below. Hands tipped with black, broken nails reached through the separating medium; fleshless faces pressed up against it, the naked hunger in them both heartbreaking and hideous. Still the circle held, the revelers finding their strength, resuming the invocation, albeit in feeble and quavering voices. The floor at their feet, Don now noticed, was covered in symbols, chalked or painted on the floorboards, that reminded him of the ideogram he'd found carved into his own front door what seemed like a lifetime ago. A ward to keep him protected, he now realized, to bar the nightmare from finding its way in.

Kirk Taylor had done it and had tried to warn him. Sacrificed his life, and more, for a complete stranger. Don couldn't understand why, and he was running out of time to look for an answer. Maybe there wasn't one to be found here, where the barrier between the spheres ran thinnest. Maybe all he could do was retreat and go into hiding. Wait for whatever horrors nightfall would bring, or for Lucien Callas to drive him out of his own body, into that gray and hopeless place beyond the veil. As if his thoughts had been heard, he saw the handsome face on the screen twist its lips in a cruel smile, its eyes turning black, caves filled with oily water.

When the first flash of illumination appeared on the other side of the hall, Don dismissed it as a figment, a reflection of the projector's beam in a mirrored surface. It vanished just as quickly, but then repeated itself, a small rectangle of daylight intruding into the darkness of what looked like a storage closet, revealing heaped boxes and the shapes of furniture stacked under dusty sheets. A thin blade of light folded into itself, danced along the bare stone floor of the hall.

In an instant, Don understood what it was and wanted to shout out a warning, but his throat had shrunk to a pinhole. The chanting figures were oblivious, the figures on the ceiling suddenly still and silent like predators scanning for prey. All he could do was watch in horror as Thad entered the hall, camera up and filming, either unaware of the eager movement in the shadows, or too focused on his task to notice anything other than the masked celebrants in the circle. His boots rubbed out the signs on the floor, blotting them with mud.

A petite woman wearing the mask of a ferret noticed him first and screamed, her scream lost in the hurricane of frantic howls that blasted down from the ceiling as the damned fell upon the living souls below.

Don retained enough presence of mind to stagger backwards, away from the doorway and the pandemonium that broke out around the masked cultists and their hapless intruder. But not before the sight of the carnage seared itself into his mind. Misshapen skulls with long jaws clacking, pointed teeth rending, bony limbs scrabbling down the walls or dropping from the teeming vault amid a cacophony of high, hungry screeches. Amazingly, Thad's hands remained on the camera, holding it in place even as an impossibly long talon, or finger reduced to sharp bone, sheared off a chunk of flesh and skull, as a thing composed of ropy muscle and dry sinew and knobs of fleshless spine hauled him to the ground. The man's face bore a look of stunned surprise, as though his brain had not yet caught up with the violations perpetrated upon his body. Mottled, leathery throats gurgled greedily as his assailants found arteries in the neck and arm and thighs, as desiccated lips fastened on them to feed.

For an instant, Don thought their eyes had met across the room, that he could see the horror and agony inside, and a terrible understanding. Then he registered the glassiness of shock and could only hope that death had spared Thad the worst. Within moments, the writhing bodies had covered the cameraman whole. Don could barely feel his legs as he backed into the corridor, his vision swimming with tears.

But still he saw.

A woman screamed and tried to dash for the door. Broken, the circle scattered, the stout man in tweeds vainly trying to reassert control, to keep the revelers together. In a rout, some tried for the back door, or surged toward Don, or simply stood frozen in place; shocked by what had descended in their midst, by the mass of limbs twitching and glutting itself on the remains of the intruder with the camera. At first, the dark shapes held back, as if uncertain about attacking the cultists. Then the badger made a surprised noise, pulled off his mask to touch his cheek. A hand had struck out, almost timidly, fur and skin parting under a nail as sharp as a razorblade. Blood glistened on the badger's hand, reflected in his wide, unbelieving eyes.

Perhaps the attack had emboldened the astral visitors, or perhaps the delay had been nothing but a taunt. Other hands reached out, ghastly mouths opened. A raptor cried out and fell, gouts of red staining his tailored trousers; the ferret shook off her heels and raced for the window, ripping off her mask, thick red hair tumbling down her back. The ring of shapes surged closer, and the woman's wet hands slapped the floor, her eyes wide in a bloody, flayed mask.

Time began to flow again. Don's terror broke, or his mind had somehow become inured to it, allowing survival instincts to kick in. Moving as fast as his numb legs would allow, he ran for the dim light of where he remembered the entrance to be, scraping his hands and elbows on the corners. Anguished shrieks followed him, and grunts of savage bloodlust, the splat of bloody meat on stone, the scrape of heavy furniture as some of the revelers tried to barricade themselves in the storage room. There would be no survivors behind him, and the longer he tarried in the farmhouse, the lesser his chance of leaving alive.

Daylight exploded around him, filling his eyes with stinging needles. From an unseen door, a figure stumbled out, its head the torn and gory mask of a hound, its open throat gushing blood. Don ran past the shed, past the fallen barn, focusing on staying upright, on keeping on his feet. If he fell down now, if he allowed the bestial squeals and what produced them to catch up, he would be lost.

Gradually, the noises of butcher and quarry dwindled in the distance. The patter of his feet on the ground reached his ears, the rustle of grass underfoot, his own heavy breathing. Between two blinks of an eye, the unnatural pall had lifted from the day. The thin sun warmed his face and wind whispered through the trees. Don slowed down, turned to glance back in the direction of the farmhouse. Already he was questioning the reality of what he'd witnessed inside. Any moment, Herbert Barnes, who insisted on being called Thad, would come running down the trail with camera in hand, sweating and excited to show Don what he'd filmed at the house.

A lone scream floated on the wind, shattering Don's illusion and sending him racing downhill, slipping in mud and dead leaves.

Fortunately, the car was still where they'd left it. Don pawed the door open with palsied hands, experienced a flash of abject panic until he remembered the key in his soiled jacket pocket. Squeezed his eyes shut until they hurt. Scenes of the butchery played behind his closed lids like a film reel. There would be no compassion shown to the Order, no way of controlling what they had summoned; only hunger and fury, savagery that didn't differentiate between ally and foe. He had to believe that would be the end of it, that the curse Kebbler had placed upon him was now put to rest. If he didn't believe that, then he might as well get out of the car and walk back uphill to meet his fate.

When he felt capable of moving, when he realized that Thad wouldn't be coming, when a nameless fear started to settle in again, he turned the engine on, put the car in gear, and pulled into the road. Executed a clumsy four-point turn and headed back the way he'd come here, not thinking about the drive ahead, not thinking about anything. Content for the time being to just watch the landscape go by, bare trees and blue sky and dirty, swollen water. Pushing to the very back of his mind the reeling horrors: strong, skeletal hands grabbing and tearing, shards of teeth ripping, unspeakable mouths sucking marrow out of steaming bones, twisted bodies feasting on those who had gathered to command them, or show them obeisance. Those would remain with him as long as he lived, would always lead him back to the abandoned farm and what stalked the silent rooms up there, unseen.

When he checked the mirror, he saw only the hill and the woods, the road winding round the curve of the land. But the absence of pursuers didn't make him feel any less watched. From a place somewhere beyond the lowering sky.

Chapter 30

Smudged light and the distant awareness of a murmuring crowd pulled Don up from a black abyss of sleep.

He stared at a brightly lit ceiling, at the shadows passing by him, trying to remember where he was. Saw his own reflection, murkiness beckoning behind it, a concrete tunnel studded with sodium lights.

A hand was shaking him by the shoulder, none too gently. The driver was leaning over him, broad face emanating apprehension and disgust. He was on a bus, the six o'clock service from the Port Authority to the Filbert Street Greyhound Terminal. Consciousness trickled back, and with it the recollections of what had happened in New York. Don struggled up, grabbed his backpack, watched all the while by the wary driver. He knew he looked a sight, and a quick glance in the glass confirmed his worst suspicions. Unshaven and ring-eyed, he hadn't eaten in a few days and couldn't remember when he'd last showered. Mud-spattered his jacket and jeans; clamps of yellow clay caked his ruined shoes. To the driver, he probably looked like a junkie, or a transient, or someone dangerously close to becoming one. Just another piece of human flotsam buffeted by the indifferent waves of fortune. Or maybe a drug dealer, strung-out and armed, flying under the radar for a nighttime delivery. The truth, of course, was incomparably worse than that. He smiled to himself, saw the driver glance at the muddy backpack, then look away, suddenly wanting no part in whatever was happening.

Don walked down the bus aisle, prompting another unwanted memory, and out into the frosty night.

Of the drive from the farmhouse to New York, he retained only fragments: rolling hills under leaden clouds, winding country lanes that took him nowhere. Several times he'd had to stop and backtrack, the unpaved roads narrowing or disappearing altogether, washed out by flooding waters. As if the very earth, whose stability he could no longer take for granted, conspired to hedge him in, under open skies, to wait for the hungry night.

Eventually he'd hit upon the freeway, drifting behind trucks and afternoon traffic, following the tide back to the suburbs, then into the city. His mind was blanked by exhaustion and shock; even the simplest feats of navigation were beyond him now. He'd left the car in an empty lot in Brooklyn. Remembering Thad's friend's name and address was an impossible task, as was attempting to explain the events that had transpired earlier. There would be questions later, when the police got involved, and Don would probably be brought in and questioned about Thad's disappearance. But all that lay a long way into the future.

His entire thought process had narrowed down to a single thought, repeating with the force of an obsession: destroy the book. Destroy his work. Burn all the printed excerpts and notes, delete all computer files. Smash the hard drive to pieces, if that's what it took. He would call Jess and his publisher, tell them to erase all copies of the chapters he'd sent them. Threaten or sue them if they refused, although he had no idea how he'd come up with the money. He'd think of something.

Because whatever he'd stirred up fed on attention. It needed human eyes to fix it in the world, like a solution fixing the image on film. Art was its conduit into the human mind, the bright ember of imagination which made it real. Lucien Callas had conjured this dark companion out of old photographs and silver-nitrate reels; Victor Hudson had tried to subjugate it to his talent, unaware that he'd already fallen under its thrall. The passage of years had weakened and starved it, imprisoned it in obscurity. But it could wait, for it existed beyond time. Until another medium came along to lead it back into the limelight.

Don thought of the first artist, a primitive human who had discovered the dark companion in the depths of a cave, or a pit in the forest, or among stones on some inhospitable hillside. Who had knelt before it in worship, coaxed it into material form through clay and flint and coarse pigments. Served it with his hands and eyes, feeling a space open up behind his eyes, pervaded by strange images. Had he too killed to appease it, crushed the skull of an unsuspecting tribesman, or snatched a babe from its mother's arms? The companion wouldn't be content with mere abstractions; it demanded fresh blood and meat, reveled in the screams of the slain, the ferocity of the killer. Once awakened, it would never be sated, seeking to spread itself like a virus, to reach and infect more minds. The ritual of death and dormancy repeating across the millennia.

From the station, Don took a cab to his hotel. Lassitude had muddied his head again, stretched the night lights of the city into filaments threading through the blackness, the car windows flickering like old film. When he sensed the motion stop, he peeled off bills and hurried into the comforting brightness of the lobby. He could think of nothing else but the room and his desk, of getting a hold of his wandering thoughts, imposing some sort of control.

The receptionist regarded him with a blank stare. For a cold moment, Don was sure that his reservation had been canceled: J. C. Latham had given up on waiting and trying to reach him, decided to cancel the contract. Then the man's face softened into a frugal smile.

"Welcome back, Mr. Ruby." A key was placed in Don's hand, a heavy brass tag with a velvet red tassel attached to it. "Your room is ready. If you'll hold on a moment, sir, I believe there's a message for you."

Don realized that his mouth was hanging open. He closed it and watched the receptionist search under his desk. "Message?"

"From your associates." The man's face was professionally closed off. He passed a cream envelope across the counter. "This is all we have under your room number and name. But I can check with the day clerk and let you know if I find anything else."

Don thanked him and made his way slowly up the stairs to his floor. At the room door, he paused, key in hand, listening for sounds inside. None came, but he no longer felt safe here; there was a sense of occupancy, of anticipation on the other side of the wall.

Opening the door slowly, careful to not set foot inside, he reached in and groped for the light switch.

The room it illuminated looked identical to the one he'd left behind. His bed and a few clothes neatly made and folded, his laptop on the desk, alongside a stack of paper, the faint smell of cleaner in the air. He walked in, letting the door close behind him, and sat down on the bed, turning the envelope in his hands. No reason for it, but he didn't want to open it, felt almost an aversion for the rough stock and the heavy paper inside.

He plugged his phone in to charge, went into the bathroom and stared into the mirror. It was the face he'd known all his life, but now it seemed subtly different, something unfamiliar about the long, saturnine features, an elusive change around the eyes. Discarding his soiled clothes, he stepped into the shower and turned the hot water on full blast, letting it draw the last of the shivers from his tired muscles. He left the door open, reluctant to allow the mirror to fog over, afraid of what he might see when he wiped his hand across the glass.

Once cleaned up, he went through his papers and notes, stacked them on his laptop, and placed Kebbler's notebook on top. Stuffed the whole lot inside his travel backpack and pulled the zipper shut. There were several ways to get rid of it for good: burn it, or toss it into the river, let the water efface all traces of his book, swallow it as it had swallowed countless dark secrets over the years. He wasn't sure if this would spell the end of it but he was ready to try.

Before all this, he had to call Jess. Figure out a way to break the news to her, to convey the urgency he felt without giving her cause to doubt his sanity. Even if she did think him crazy, even if she never spoke to him again, she would be safe. He was less enthusiastic about contacting Occultation Press, but he would have to cross that bridge when he got to it.

The envelope. Don held it up gingerly, opened the flap as if expecting it to explode in his hands. Read the typed message once, then again, the embossed letters bouncing off the surface of his mind, failing to reveal a meaning.

We did it! Occultation Press cordially invites you to a book launch party for Volume One of the Forgotten Frontiersmen of Fright, *Don Ruby's scintillating return to the art of film criticism. Saunter down Scream Avenue with the works of macabre maestro Victor Hudson, get your copy signed by the elusive author, and hear him read his favorite passages.*

Stunned, Don reached for his phone, checked the date and time on the invitation against what was displayed on the screen. Tonight. The party was scheduled for tonight, a couple hours away from now. It had to be a mistake. The book was nowhere near finished, and now never would be. Had Jess misled the publisher into believing otherwise?

He had to concentrate, had to get rid of the material, yet he couldn't think clearly; his intentions, once simple and direct, now seemed jumbled, uncertain. Maybe he'd missed a message exchange during his trip to New York. But his eyes were no longer up to the task, or his phone had malfunctioned. When he unlocked the screen, broken shapes and colors scrolled under his thumb, each like the piece of a message, but bereft of coherence.

In the bathroom, he ran the faucet, splashed cold water on his face. Watched his reflection again, searching for some hint that would give it away. It looked and felt as unreal as a mask, eyes burning, lips stretched in a smile. The more he watched it, the more alien it seemed to him, like it belonged to someone else.

As he stared, the smile in the mirror grew wider, the mouth opening as if to speak.

Don's mind reeled as he felt his own facial muscles move in response, his throat vibrate with emerging words. The room shrank down around the mirror, and he was falling into it, dwindling. Any moment now he would hear the impostor's voice emanating from his own mouth. When that happened, he would go insane. Trapped in the reflection, cast out into the astral to join the tormented, to send unheard laments into the void.

Pounding. The pounding reached him through a gathering fog of blankness. Someone was knocking on the door, hammering with all their strength.

He went over and opened it, hefting his backpack as if to weigh himself down, to harbor himself in normality.

Jess was standing in the corridor, holding her phone. Her hair and clothes glistened wetly. Don could hear the rain drumming on the windows, impatient fingers on glass. She opened her mouth, shook her head, as if too overwhelmed to berate him.

"I was this close to calling the cops," she said. "Getting someone to break down the door. I texted you four times, but you weren't responding." A smile flashed through her pallor and was immediately extinguished. "You better hurry up and get ready. I've got a taxi waiting for us outside. Can't be late to your own party. It's almost started."

Chapter 31

Hustling him down the stairs, into the pouring rain, Jess made an effort to bring him up to speed. "Latham just about shit a brick," she said, bundling Don into the waiting car. "They've been trying to get through to you for days. I told him you had a family emergency." She jumped in behind the driver, slammed the door shut. "You scared the hell out of me too, for the record. I thought you'd done something to yourself. You didn't sound all that stable last time I saw you. Thankfully your publisher likes your book so much he's willing to put up with the less savory facets of your personality."

"Jess," Don said. "There is *no* book."

"Oh, shush. Everything's going to be just fine. You're the man of the hour. Enjoy it while it lasts."

"It's gone." Or it would be, as soon as the party was over, as soon as he got back to the hotel. The book launch was a sham, in spite of whatever story Jess had spun up. He stared at his hands, still gripping the straps of the backpack. There had to be a way to explain it all to J. C. Latham, work out a repayment plan for the advance he'd spent. But an insidious doubt wormed past his conviction. Why was it so difficult for him to follow what was happening? "My book. The manuscript. You can't read it. You shouldn't."

"It's a little late for second thoughts, don't you think?" A disposable cup of coffee was thrust into Don's hands, the warmth like a furnace through the Styrofoam. A bar of shadow covered Jess's face, but he could feel her annoyed stare. "Here. Drink this. They're expecting you. It's your big night, so you better sober up."

Don sipped the hot coffee and did his best not to think. The car wound down indistinguishable streets, headlights groping into the dark, brightly lit intersections flying by. Up front, the driver was a shapeless hulk, hunched forward, his face invisible in the mirror.

Jess smiled at him, squeezed his knee. Another black bar erased her face. Don drank more coffee, tried to remember what he'd wanted to say. It had seemed important at the time, but he no longer knew why. His head was swaddled in warm cotton, the missed sleep making his body heavy, a lead weight pulling him deeper into the seat.

Impressions slipped through the rain-spattered windows, vague and unimportant. Light slid off wet brick and pavement, shattered into neon rainbows. Wipers moved in a hypnotic rhythm, trailing tiny diamonds in their wake. There was something he wanted to tell Jess. Something important. A life-or-death sort of situation. He would tell her soon. If only he could open his mouth, break the silence inside the car.

They went under an overpass, graffiti-painted to look like a flower bower. The driver drove slowly, cautiously, stopping at every sign, giving way to oncoming traffic. One of his hands was misshapen; he was wearing gloves, or at least *a glove* on the hand visible to Don. This struck Don as unusual. For a while he tried to figure it out, then decided against bringing this up with Jess, who had retreated as far from him as the space in the back seat would allow and was fiddling with her phone, her screen flashing.

Rundown streets went by, sooty walls and chain-linked lots clothed in shadows. Undefined shapes sailed under the lamps and were quickly absorbed by the dark. Don couldn't remember the last time he'd seen another car. They were gliding along an infinite stretch of dark road, the lights like islands in an ocean of night.

The cabbie hadn't turned his meter on. This bothered Don to no end. He looked over at Jess but couldn't make his mouth work. Turned away from him, she was gazing out the window, her face a vague pale oval in the glass. *We have to stop. We have to go back. It's dangerous.* None of the words made it past his lips. His head swam wildly, but his body was welded to the seat, replaced by stone. The car was a fixed point around which the universe rotated without a sound, slow, swooping circles that filled him with sick vertigo.

Jess reached over and plucked the coffee cup from his inert hand, seconds before it tipped over.

"Better not get any on the seats," the driver said without turning. Don thought he recognized the gruff voice but couldn't remember where from. Remembering anything was beyond his ability. He watched the window roll down, felt a blast of wet, cold air, saw Jess toss the cup out of the car, the liquid arcing before it hit the pavement. Jess's face betrayed nothing as she picked up Don's hand, let it drop like a lead weight.

"He's fine," she said. "Everything will be fine."

"Sometimes they piss themselves." The cabbie half-turned, the scrolling light falling on a gauze-covered ear. It wasn't a glove on his right hand, Don realized, but another clumsy wrapping of bandages, stained with iodine and dried blood. In the shifting light, his jowly face was tired and afraid. Ugly red gashes marred his cheek, just starting to scab over. There were more stains on his collar, the lapels of his tweed coat. "We ought to keep him awake," he said, uncertain. "They insisted on this. Don't let him fall asleep."

"It's just a muscle relaxant." Don heard Jess move. Her face appeared out of the murk, looming over him. There was anxiety in her expression, but neither guilt nor pity. "He'll stay awake for as long as we want him to. We're almost there anyway."

The car had picked up speed slightly, passing lighted bodegas, glassed-in bus stops full of passengers huddled from the rain. A police cruiser parked at the curb strobed a message into the dark. Don clawed frantically at the door handle, beat his fists against the windows, screamed himself hoarse. Or rather his mind did these things; his body remained slumped where it sat, incapable of producing more than a weak gagging noise.

Moments later, or hours, the car pulled onto a dark street, halted, backed into a driveway. Don was beyond horror. If he pulled back deep enough into himself, he thought, nothing would touch him, even as he sensed the presence of that which soon would. Doors opened; hands seized him under the arms, dragged him out unceremoniously. His legs dropped to the pavement, sending a distant shock up his buttocks and spine.

"Wouldn't kill you to give me a hand, you know," the driver said between grunts, addressing someone whose feet crunched down the driveway. His odor, tobacco mixed with old sweat, took Don back to the farmhouse, the circle chanting within. The stocky man with the wolf's mask, dressed in tweeds. "Bled me half to death earlier. Took my ear off. I'm barely holding myself up."

"The path to enlightenment is strewn with peril, Brother." A tall, thin man with a shock of dark hair entered Don's field of vision, wearing a sardonic grin. "You shouldn't begrudge the martyrs their fill. Heaven knows they've waited long enough."

Don felt his legs grasped behind the knees as the two men half-dragged, half-carried him through a door. Walls and ceiling replaced the starless night sky. He was dropped into a sagging padded chair as his captors panted and coughed with the effort.

"It's too soon," the older man in tweeds said, wiping sweat from his brow. The cuts on his face were bleeding now, and fresh red was staining the gauze over his ear. "We're not the right ones for this. Maybe no one is. There aren't any of the Elders left to guide us."

"Don't tell me you're losing your nerve," his companion said, moving behind Don. Rubber wheels creaked across the wood floor as something was rolled into position behind him. "This has been years in the making. *Decades*. Some of the Brethren spent their whole lives working toward it. Some of them *gave* their lives for it to happen. We can't turn back now, so close to the revelation."

"You don't need to remind me." The driver held up his bandaged hand, pointed to his missing ear. Blood seeped through the wrappings; the wounds had probably reopened by the labor of hauling Don out of the car. "I was there. I was the only one to make it out of the temple alive." He chuckled, and blood trickled from the cuts on his face. "Minus a few choice parts, of course."

"All the more reason to succeed." Cables snaked across the floorboards, followed by a clicking noise. The thin man reappeared, laid a gentle hand on the driver's shoulder. "Otherwise, your sacrifice was in vain. We have no idea why the Master has chosen him. But there is no doubt about it. Don't you see? That's how he escaped the temple untouched."

"Such a tragedy." Tears welled in the burly man's eyes. "Why summon us there? So many gone and in the worst ways imaginable. You didn't—you can't imagine what it was like."

"It isn't ours to question the Master's will. You should have learned that by now." The younger man's tone was suddenly cold, heartless. Just as abruptly as he'd placed his hand on the wounded one's shoulder, he drew it back. "His perspective is one of centuries, where we live in minutes. He exists beyond time, waiting, preparing us for a higher existence. Now his wait is over."

"If only you saw those things, Brother. If only you felt their wrath. Whatever hell they come from; it doesn't look like a higher existence to me."

"This isn't about us, Fuller," the younger man said. "It's about the Master, and the potential he's recognized." He spun on his companion with sudden ferocity, forcing him to take an involuntary step back. "I don't remember you complaining when you were raised from the gutter. When you transcended to bear witness to miracles. There are consequences for those who turn their back on the truth."

Chastised, or cowed into silence, the burly man busied himself with drawing dusty curtains over the windows. The room they were in was bare, an exposed bulb hanging from the ceiling. Rows of chairs were lined up along the walls as if waiting for an unseen audience. On the wall facing Don, a white bedsheet had been pinned flat, the corners held in place by masking tape. A movie screen. Don's mind felt like it had shrunk inside his skull, a pebble rolling down a long tunnel. A weak, mewling moan rose from him, a mechanical sound that his body was making independently of his brain.

The dark-haired man heard it. He leaned over Don, placed a finger on the side of his neck, then his wrist, feeling for a pulse. Perhaps it was the projector starting up at the back of the room, but to Don his eyes seemed to light up with pale fire.

"Mister Ruby. What a pleasure you have been to work with." He leaned over Don, reached behind the backrest. "My name is Latham, and the dour gentleman over there is my associate, Fuller. The lovely Miss Danvers, I trust, requires no introduction." For a moment, Don thought that Latham was about to shake his hand, but the editor-publisher merely tightened the restraints on Don's wrists, squatted down to check the ones on his ankles. Don hadn't felt the zip ties close around his limbs. His entire body had been numbed by a huge shot of the drug. Only his mind remained untouched, a frightened animal bloodying itself against the confines of its cage.

"I'm sure this is all confusing to you," Latham said, "and more than a little frightening. But there's nothing to be afraid of. You have been chosen for a great honor. A glory that many would kill for or sacrifice themselves readily."

"His meddling got the rest of the Brethren killed." This came from Fuller, who remained turned away, as if unwilling to look Don in the face. "He and that other one. The nosy one with the beard. They were the ones who broke the circle. Who brought the disaster upon us."

Latham shook his head, shooting an irate glance at his companion. "We've been over this. There are no coincidences, and there never were. *In blood shall their eyes be opened*. It's all the doing of the Master, through whose astral journey our own existence is elevated."

"I didn't see any elevation earlier." Fuller's stubbly cheeks were blazing, his cuts a darker red against the flush. He waved his maimed hand like a bloody trophy. "What I saw was awful. People I know were torn apart. Men and women who gave their all to the Brotherhood, bled and drained like pigs. It didn't feel like enlightenment to me. It felt like slaughter."

As they argued, Don sought Jess across the bare room, found her leaning on the wall near the doorway, arms crossed on her chest. There was no way she could be in league with these fanatics, conspiring against him from the start. *Not Jess*. Don felt like he'd missed the plot entirely, becoming utterly lost in his own story.

Latham caught the direction of his gaze and clapped his hands. "Betrayal. A twist at the very end. Certainly, you should have seen that coming, or the writer inside you should have. We had nothing to do with it, as a matter of fact. Miss Danvers was entirely your own contribution, one we couldn't foresee but appreciated. Without her, the whole scheme would have fallen apart weeks ago."

"You did this to me," Jess said, her voice flat and hollow. She walked over to Don, set his backpack by his bound feet. "You sent me your manuscript, you piece of shit. You made me look. Poisoned me. Before I knew it, I saw him everywhere." Disgust and rage twisted her features; for a moment, Don thought she would spit in his face. "I saw Callas. In my dreams, at first... But I knew he had no intention of staying put. Once he was in my head, all I could think of was getting him out. If I did what they wanted—what *he* wanted—maybe I'd be left alone."

"We have a long reach," Latham said, nodding. "You know that only too well, Don. There is no place in heaven or earth where we can't find you. You'd be well advised to remember that."

A beam danced in the middle of the screen, revealing fretful shapes. Images appeared as though from a negative, flipped back and forth, a hypnotic animation in the blankness.

"I didn't ask for any of this," Jess said. "I thought I was done with you years ago. Until you decided to insert yourself back into my life. Then again, you never knew how to do anything else but take, did you? The world and everything in it serves no other purpose but to cater to the whims of Don Ruby. The misunderstood genius, the flawed golden boy. Look how far that's gotten you."

"Betrayal," Latham repeated. He was pacing the room, hands laced behind his back. "It hurts. The Brethren have dealt with it in the past. We came close to it, once, only to see our hopes for a rebirth dashed to pieces. This was before my time, but Brother Fuller can attest."

"Brother Victor was one of our own." Fuller didn't seem eager to explain anything. "Our greatest hope."

"A talent who could see beyond the veil." Latham passed out of sight, racked a reel into the projector. "Who could translate the dream into the heads of others. Send a spark and let it catch in the imagination. Fan it to life. He gazed into the ineffable but didn't have the guts to go through with it. The world broken and reborn, his work was instrumental in the great awakening. But he destroyed his own masterpiece."

His voice was almost drowned out by the whir of the projector. "Oh, he paid for it. A terrible price. I told you the Brotherhood has a long reach, and we were far more powerful all those years ago. But the damage was done, the spark extinguished. Until you came along. Another great talent. A fearful symmetry through which the Master's design is revealed."

Until I started writing the book. This single thought was worse than the awful anticipation of what was about to happen. Don struggled with the dead muscles of his jaw, with a tongue that seemed to weigh a hundred pounds, that cleaved to the dry bottom of his mouth.

"Wasn't me," he mumbled, every syllable an exertion, the voice nothing like his own. Was that an after-effect of the drug, or the first stirring of an alien presence in his head, assuming control? "Someone else. A notebook."

He couldn't see Latham, but his words drew a harried look from Fuller. "Another part of the master's plan," Latham said, a touch too quickly, as if reassuring both himself and the man in tweeds. "We did our best with that third-rate hack, but all that achieved was the pilfering of the Brotherhood's archives. Offered the opportunity of a lifetime, he was blinded by material gain, as small minds are apt to do. Rest assured, it was the Master's invisible hand that precipitated your meeting, that guided the fool's razor in the end."

His companion seemed unconvinced, although he said nothing. As surreptitiously as he could, Don tested the bonds holding him to the chair. If his tongue had loosened enough to speak, could the same be happening with his muscles? Trembling with the strain, he wriggled his right hand, then the left, until the plastic chafed against his skin. Was it wishful thinking, or did the ties feel loose with plenty of give? The chair itself was heavy but loosely put together, wobbling when he tested it. For all their posturing, these were no seasoned kidnappers, but bookish zealots, anticipating a doped-up, pliant captive. Whatever drug they'd given him; he was almost sure they had gotten the dose wrong.

The news didn't give him much hope. The ties were strong, the chair beneath him seemingly bolted to the floor. Even without the poison circulating through his system, even on his best day, he was hardly the Incredible Hulk. But for the first time since getting into this predicament, Don allowed himself a glimmer of hope.

Which was extinguished the very next moment as the opening scene of the movie jumped up on the screen. A dimly lit bar shot in black and white, two men, both visibly drunk, leaning over a table in the corner. Don pushed himself back against the chair. A third man, or the silhouette of one, somehow unobserved by the duo, was standing between them, bending down to whisper in their ears.

"No," Don said. "Please no."

"His chosen one," Latham's voice droned above him. "Once the Master found you, he would accept no substitute. You have received His message by studying the work of His foremost disciple. The apostate Hudson. Now you have become the Master's word. Soon to be made flesh. His greatest work. A holy vessel into which he shall be born again."

Don's body was no longer a prison, but a crumbling berth, his anchor to it growing weaker. Foreign, traitorous, it seemed to be trying to expel him, to make room for the intruder. His mind was losing ground, collapsing into a rotten pit. A voice spoke out of the pit, slick with corruption, insinuating itself in every crevice of his being. Not a single voice, but a barrage of them, insulting, threatening, offering promises.

Occultation, they said. *Absence of light. By passing through the lacuna, by being stripped of the self, the essence is consecrated. Prepared for occupancy by a higher presence. What have you left to cling to? No name, no personality; a life littered with mistakes and regret. Embrace the jubilation. Don't fight it. The Master has traveled so far, seen so much. Close your eyes and let him in. Let go.*

He must have obliged, for Latham's hands were on his face, dry and leathery fingers hooked painfully into the corners of his eyes. "Please keep them open. Watch the screen. If you won't comply, we have devices we can use on your lids. Neither I nor Fuller are trained in using them. But we will, if we have to."

In the movie, the writer sat in his old apartment, naked to the waist and dressed only in boxers, empty bottles collecting under the table, a half-full one within arm's reach. He was typing furiously on his laptop, his face a mask of exaggerated concentration. The camera moved over his shoulder, showing a dead screen like a black eye in the middle of the scene, a hole sucking the air out of the room.

A second, identical form, transparent and weightless, floated in the air above its earthly counterpart, tethered by a scarcely visible silver cord. Black limbs appeared seemingly out of nowhere, grappled with Don's astral double, ripped it apart. A thin, shadowy body descended down the cord, hand over hand; a face that was all eyes and gaping maw, sidled up to the writer, who remained oblivious of it. Words in a dead language spilled from its lipless mouth.

On screen, the writer reached for the bottle, took a long pull, then resumed his furious typing.

In the room, Don pleaded and thrashed but could not avert his gaze.

A cut to a new scene showed the writer driving up an empty road into the hills, a dark shadow in the seat beside him, flickering in the sun. They pulled up to a crumbling mansion, where the door was opened by an older woman. At the sight of the shadowy figure, her face flashed terror, then drooped to weary resignation. The scene's final frame saw the woman standing on the edge of a cliff, limned by the sunset.

More shots followed, out of sequence, the movie speeding up or Don's sense of time disappearing. Maskfall's performance in the club in Fishtown, where the writer's appearance cast a huge and cartoonishly malformed shadow over the stage, driving the art director insane with fear. The image of a plane crossing a sky like black glass, faded to the writer sitting in a projection room, long arms clawing toward him, the scene dissolving in flames. A frontal shot of Lucien Callas laughing into the camera, his glamor slipping to reveal a ruined face plastered over with strands of lank hair, a pile of bones swaddled in dirty rags and held together by papery skin and a fierce will to live. The ruler of a domain of defilement and despair, transformed by suffering, sensing the moment of rebirth.

Don saw the thing step off the screen and shambled toward him, eyes triumphant, chin wet with idiotic glee. It flickered and shifted as it came forward, one moment Callas the handsome charlatan in a finely made suit; the next a crawling, drooling inhabitant of the astral sphere. The screen blazed with unbearable light, the room disappearing around it, losing solidity.

Panic overcame his drugged torpor. Insanity did not seem like the worst possible option until he realized it would not mean escape. His body convulsed against his restraints. Pain lanced through his wrists and ankles, but it was distant, inconsequential. His mind surged with savage loathing, a beast's urge to chew its own leg off to break free from the approaching nightmare.

Suddenly, inexplicably, one of his arms was free. He looked down. The plastic had sawed into the skin and flesh of his wrist, down to the tendon; dark blood dripped down his hand, slicking it enough to slip through the zip tie. Too much blood. Don didn't care. There had been a way to resist Callas before, that time on the plane, and more recently at the airport. He wasn't helpless, or something out there would not allow him to be. His shredded hand reached across his body, ignoring the pain, and started to pick at the other restraint.

Out by the window, or where he remembered the window to be, Fuller was a negative image, a slim curl of charred film, twisting in the hurricane of images and sensations that blasted from the screen. Latham's discarnate voice boomed from the walls, thundered up through the floor. It *was* the floor and walls; it was the only thing Don could hold on to, his last link to who he was. Lucien Callas was closer now, the sound of his laughter like the scream of the earth shattering, like the stars dying out in a black and empty sky. Yet Don sensed something else beyond the magician, a cold and remote visitant as infinite as the universe. The dark companion, the god of images and illusions, to whom the Brethren and the Order had pledged their worship. Whose divine spark they had sought to capture in silver nitrate and celluloid, use it to open doors to exalted realms. They were beneath its notice, too trivial to so much as rate its contempt. But now he felt it awaken, turn its steady, inscrutable regard upon the world, upon a dark house on a lonely street where memories and dreams poured out of the projector, where a breach had opened between the spheres, the crack thundering across creation.

Because gods died when they were forgotten. When that spark went out in the hearts and minds of their followers. Seizing on this thought as a last defiance, Don let go of his physical self, flung his mute plea out into the night.

The darkness out here was boundless, unbroken by even a speck of light. Yet even here there were shades and layers, and the deepest of them were shifting, an entity raising itself from the cosmic abyss, opening a vast and baleful eye. He glimpsed almost nothing of it, drew his psychic gaze away after the merest glimpse, and the life-negating indifference of its scrutiny all but obliterated him. He could feel its alien thoughts rip through his disembodied essence like barbed hooks, taking him apart, putting him back together, over and over. Then he was drawn back—with such force and speed that he didn't have time to be afraid—into the slumped slab of meat tied to the chair, while the projector clicked on.

He rocked the chair until it crashed over, howled as his ankles were twisted underneath him. His palms slipped in his own blood as he dragged himself backward, pulling the chair like an anchor. But it worked: the bonds around his ankles, never properly secured to begin with, had loosened further. Kicking off one shoe, he worked a foot free, started to work on the other.

Fuller came at him out of the light, bellowing, both arms flung out in rage. Only to be flung up by an invisible hand, arching, falling, falling not down, but into the screen, a dark scratch on the painful brightness, then not even that.

A man was screaming—Latham, although the name seemed remote to Don, something he'd overheard—and backing away from a heap of burning plastic, pictures and faces billowing from it like smoke. Screaming as he was sucked up into nothingness, dragged by half-seen, thin-limbed things that scurried like spiders. On fire, the projector rolled up against the wall, fell over and crashed to the floor, sizzling and popping. Incredibly, it was still rolling, throwing a confusion of fractured images on the ceiling.

Don saw himself up there, bleeding out on a bare floor, struggling to stand up. Saw Lucien Callas's face, wrenched by horror, flesh falling from it, becoming something else; that same face reflected in his own pupils, perspective changing, turning his irises into twin tunnels. Black water rushed through them, a tide tugging him out, past the stars, into the unknown.

Chapter 32

He came to in the early hours of the morning, stiff and shivering, and struggled to get up to his feet. The projector lay next to the bloodied remains of the chair, the plastic melted solid, a small, blackened circle on the floorboards marking where it had burned. Of his tormentors, of Latham and Fuller, there wasn't so much as a trace. If he looked closely, he could just about see a discolored blotch on the plaster of the wall, a dusting of cinders on the sheet across the room. A yellowish stain had seeped into the floor, about halfway between the projector and the makeshift screen.

A memory niggled at him, but he left it alone. His mind was a blank slate upon which he was in no hurry to leave impressions.

Outside the world seemed flat, dimensionless, a bleached imprint on a film left exposed to the sun. Don Ruby walked down once-familiar streets, navigating through muscle memory, unwilling to follow the images swarming his head to their original source. An impalpable feeling of permeability, of the edges of the world turning soft and rotten, dogged him with every step. Every reflection he caught in a window or puddle, every dirty bus stop scrawled with obscenities. He understood why. *He* was that soft spot now, a breathing, traveling weakness in reality, belonging both to this place of pink dawns and dirty brick and early morning traffic—and that other one—where a gray ocean laved a bleak shore of sand and ashes, the cries of the lost carried on a miasmic wind.

The spark was inside him now, a million splinters lodged inside the raw wound of his consciousness. It had broken through and become trapped there, either by accident or by design. Perhaps Victor Hudson had wanted it that way; a single keeper of the dream, at once possessed by it and in control of it, a conduit between the seen and the unseen.

Street names, subway stops, fragments of overheard conversations. Secret associations nested inside the everyday, an intricate diagram mapping the hidden layers of the world. Currents pulled him in the right direction with no conscious input from his brain. Tastes and smells, sounds of the waking conurbation. Plumes of fragrant heat from the open door of a pastry shop. Steam rising from sidewalks. A woman lit a cigarette outside a hair salon, watching him with hard and suspicious mascara-ringed eyes. A homeless man sat on a bus shelter bench, singing a snippet of a tune, repeating it over and over. All this he saw, all this he took into the growing pit inside of him. His own self was a flicker beneath the skin, the electric thrumming of nerves, the slosh and gurgle of bodily fluids inside secret hollows.

The dream wanted more. This was its world now or would be soon enough. It chafed against obscurity, wanted to be let out, to inhabit millions. To bring people together, infect their collective subconscious, rebuild them in its image.

But it couldn't do this alone. It was lost and confused, constrained. Like any other deity, it needed a messiah. Don wasn't sure if he wanted to play the part yet, or if he would be allowed a choice when the time came. A story couldn't die, no more than it could be contained: where one ended, a hundred others began, and from those birthed another hundred. But he would be prepared, and he would do his best to usher it into being.

At the entrance to his old apartment building, he paused, inhaling the musty smells, the air from unclean filters, the excretions of leaky pipes. He took the steps slowly, running his fingers along the wall. Feeling the hiss and boom of that faraway ocean on the other side.

His unit was the way he'd left it. The window was open and rain had come in, soaking the mildewy carpet. But his backpack was by his desk, the laptop propped up on a pile of old manuscripts. Kebbler's notebook lay next to it, open on the last page.

When he sat down and moved the cursor, he saw the mouth of the passage, the dripping bricks. He tried to catch his own reflection in the screen, but it evaded him, a sly, quick thing dissolving with the image of the tunnel, replacing it with the white glare of a blank page. The sight didn't frighten him, nor did his own condition fill him with revulsion. There would be plenty to occupy him in the days to come. For the first time in a long while, perhaps ever, Don Ruby knew what he wanted to say.

He took a deep breath, flipped the notebook closed, and laid his fingers on the keys.

ABOUT THE AUTHOR

Damir is the author of the story collection *Collapse Years*, the novels *Blood Ground*, *Kill Zone*, and *Always Beside You*, and short stories featured in multiple horror/speculative fiction magazines and anthologies. An auditor by trade and traveler by heart, he does his best writing thirty-plus thousand feet in the air and in the terminals of far-flung airports. He lives in Virginia with his wife and a dynamic duo of cats. When not writing fiction, he reviews horror movies, discusses books, and shares unsolicited opinions on just about everything on his blog, Darker Realities.

www.ingramcontent.com/pod-product-compliance
Lightning Source LLC
Chambersburg PA
CBHW020126310726
48970CB00006B/1749